"We'll Be
We've No Reason to Wait."

She forced herself to speak. But it was as if her heart were squeezed in an iron grip. . . . She gasped. "Richard, no! Listen to me. I can't marry you."

He knew that she spoke, but his hunger deafened him. His pulse pounded in his temples. He held her tightly, forced her head back, and fastened his lips on hers.

Need, hunger, so long repressed, swept through him. Even as he told himself, too late, that he must free her, his grip tightened and his body covered hers. . . . Leaping to her feet, she fled, and he went after her, meaning only to apologize and soothe her. But when he had cornered her against the veranda railing, the regret and shame died in him, fire flooded his veins, and he threw her down on the creaking chaise. . . .

Books by Daoma Winston

The Adventuress
Gallows Way
House of Mirror Images
The Mayeroni Myth
Mills of the Gods

Published by POCKET BOOKS

MILLS OF THE GODS

Daoma Winston

PUBLISHED BY POCKET BOOKS NEW YORK

Distributed in Canada by PaperJacks Ltd., a Licensee
of the trademarks of Simon & Schuster, a division of
Gulf +Western Corporation.

**POCKET BOOKS, a Simon & Schuster division of
GULF & WESTERN CORPORATION**
1230 Avenue of the Americas, New York, N.Y. 10020
In Canada distributed by PaperJacks Ltd.,
330 Steelcase Road, Markham, Ontario.

Published by arrangement with Simon and Schuster
Library of Congress Catalog Card Number: 78-25837

ISBN: 0-671-81601-2

First Pocket Books printing September, 1980

10 9 8 7 6 5 4 3 2 1

Printed in Canada

Acknowledgments and thanks for the answering of many questions, and for assistance in gathering background material for this novel, to

Mrs. Florence C. Brigham, Curator, The Fall River Historical Society, Fall River, Massachusetts, and her staff

Mrs. Eileen Stafiej, Reference Librarian, The Fall River Public Library

Mrs. Maureen Harnett, Audio-Visual Section, The Fall River Public Library

For
Evelyn Winston Freedenberg,
the book lover

Chapter 1

A QUICK OCTOBER WIND SPUN OFF THE CHANNEL and sent thin white fingers of mist and coveys of oak and locust leaves whispering down the streets of Rye.

For centuries the town had been among the great ports of southeastern England. Once Norsemen had used the broad creeks that flowed inland as highways for looting and rape. Later the French had swarmed ashore with sabers and muskets and flaming torches. For a time pirates and then smugglers had roistered in its taverns and swaggered on its cobblestoned footpaths. Then, as one of the Five Ports Confederation, Rye supplied ships and men for the fleets of the King's Navy. But, slowly, under the assault of thrusting tides, its harbor and estuaries silted up. The sea retreated. Rye's days of glory ended. It became a fishing village and market town, a place where day trippers down from London munched fish and chips as they wandered the crooked streets.

It was this debasement that made Vicki Davelle sigh as she peered through the curtains at her window into the lane below. For all its fishing smacks in the River Rother, and salt flats, and pottery kilns, and artists' exhibitions, the town, in the year 1901, had little that commended itself to her.

The quarter boys of St. Mary's Parish Church struck fifteen minutes to the hour of three. It would be a long while before her cousin arrived. She turned from the window to stand before the cheval glass in the corner.

Frowning, she regarded her reflection. A jagged crack split the glass from corner to corner. She was

1

accustomed to the odd image it presented of two separate bodies, the one above the waist rounded and full and blurred, the one below scrawny and misshapen and sharp. But now the distortion displeased her.

She lit the lamp, looked again, decided she wouldn't do. Her amber-colored hair was wrapped in tight braids around her head. Her shirtwaist hung like a bag from her shoulders. She looked like the young daughter of an impoverished parson, a child who had been nowhere and seen nothing. It was all too true. She *was* the daughter of an impoverished parson. She *had* been nowhere and seen nothing. But she didn't intend to be trapped in this small house forever, and she mustn't look this way when her American cousin arrived.

Why it was important to her she didn't know. Yet ever since she had heard of his impending visit she had felt that he must meet the reality of her, her spirit and soul, and see beneath the shell of unsuitable garments and cracked boots.

Another glance at her distorted reflection decided her. She pulled out the large horn pins that held her bound hair. Seizing a brush, she worked it through the tight braids until they separated into a mass of thick gleaming curls. She fashioned a wide white ribbon from the remnant of an unmendable bedsheet, and tied her curls back from her face in a large bow. Gamin dimples flickered at the corners of her mouth. Her dark blue eyes sparkled. She would hear about this from Mrs. McVey, that was certain. But it was a beginning.

Hurrying now, Vicki went into the box room used only for storage. She pulled a small dusty chest from beneath the trundle bed. When she opened it, the scent of lavender rose in a sweet cloud. She drew out one of her mother's gowns. Mrs. McVey would have something to say about that, too, no doubt.

Back in her own room, Vicki undressed. The ribbons on her camisole were frayed and faded, the lace on her petticoats worn. One day she would wear nothing except the finest of silks next to her skin, and

2

have yards of white and blond Brussels lace on her intimate apparel. For now, though, what she had on must do since she had no other.

When she turned to the cheval glass she didn't notice the crack nor her distorted image. The gown her mother had worn fit as if cut to Vicki's own size. It was some seventeen years out of fashion, but still becoming, and the heavy blue rep was of good quality. The bodice was snug over the high round curve of her breasts and tight at her narrow waist. The skirt hung neatly over the smooth line of her hips, belling out into a fullness that swayed when she moved.

The quarter boys struck fifteen minutes past the hour. She bent to blow out the lamp, turning her face from the stink of its smoking wick. Only the downstairs rooms had illuminating gas, for money had been in the same short supply ten years ago as it was now. The high collar of the gown brushed her chin. She undid three of the button loops and smoothed the flaps down. They rose up like two awkward wings when she took her hand away, but the narrow wedge of white flesh against the gown was just right. From the chiffonier she took a small heart-shaped brooch, and pinned it at the bottom of the wedge. Satisfied that she had done for herself what she could, she turned from the glass and went downstairs.

Mrs. McVey appeared in the kitchen doorway. She stared, dark eyes aglint with disapproval. "Victoria! Your hair . . . your mother's gown . . ."

"I want to be at my best," Vicki said.

"Your best indeed! A parson's daughter should have some sense of the proprieties."

"There's not much time," Vicki answered, and escaped into the parlor.

It was a dim room, smelling of lemon oil, which she herself had vigorously applied to the splintered wooden tables, and smelling, too, of Brussels sprouts, which had been dinner the day before. The settle cushions were worn to their meager stuffing. The antimacassars on the horsehair-covered chairs were noticeably darned. The aspidistras were stunted.

3

The only color in the room came from the two bright chrysanthemums Vicki had earlier brought in, hoping to beautify the place. But she saw that there was no way she could hide its air of discouragement and decay.

She had no idea of what she had accomplished by her small efforts before the cracked cheval glass. She didn't know that her own beauty brought a glow to the simple room. She had turned seventeen only that same month, and had been too sheltered to have learned vanity. And if, by chance, there had been a touch of it in her, Mrs. McVey's sharp tongue would soon have scraped it off.

Now Vicki gazed at the sepia-toned picture of her mother, who had died in the first hours after Vicki's birth. Her mother had been lovely, with soft hair piled high, and tiny curls artfully arranged over her ears. Her eyes were large, and a smile trembled on her lips. Had she lived, Vicki was certain, her mother would have understood her, for it was her mother's spirit that Vicki herself possessed. It was hard to believe that Maude Jensen had fallen so deeply in love with Alban Davelle that she had fled south with him when he had his call to Rye, and left all her family behind. But it had happened that way, according to Mrs. McVey, who years before told Vicki about it, clearly disapproving of the whole affair. Vicki's mother had loved intensely, had turned her back on home and family, and escaped to what she knew to be her heart's desire and dream. She had dared to live as she wanted. The same need burned within Vicki herself. She awaited only the opportunity.

Mrs. McVey often told her that she was the cause of her mother's death, and that she'd come into the world half drowned in her mother's life's blood, so that the original sin in which every human being is born was compounded by that second sin.

Early in her childhood, Vicki had asked, "But what sin are you talking about?" There had been no reply. Mrs. McVey, first the midwife who saw her into this

4

world, later nanny, and finally housekeeper, had never appreciated being questioned.

Alban Davelle said nothing to her remarks. He was a good man, Vicki considered. But he was weak. He was bullied by his parishioners, and by Mrs. McVey. He used platitudes as if they were a linked armor to shield him. "The meek will inherit the earth, Vicki." She saw only that the meek inherited all the unpleasant chores. "A soft answer turneth away wrath," he insisted. Vicki saw that a soft answer led to louder demands. "Let he who is without sin cast the first stone," he adjured her. She saw that many stones were cast, and few that threw them were without sin.

He had pleading eyes that seemed always to weep dry tears, and gray hair shrinking at the temples, and a cowlick that instead of being endearing was only absurd. It was strange that his very weakness had a peculiar force. It had hardened Vicki. She wore the mask of complaisance, but inside she was all iron.

In this moment, as she looked wistfully at her mother's smiling visage, Vicki heard the long slow whistle of the steam train that came down from London. She went to the window, even though her cousin had written a week before that he would be coming by carriage.

She craned her neck, and could see, beyond the narrow curve of Mermaid Lane, an angle of the street known as The Mint. The early October dusk had fallen now. Horsedrawn conveyances of every sort rolled past, and a scattering of bicycles skimmed between the pony carts and drays and phaetons crowding every inch of the way. Behind them, regal on high tires, with polished lamps gleaming, there followed one of the new motor cars.

Loneliness is a fertile ground for the growth of imagination, and Vicki had ample acreage in which to cultivate it. She was prone to quick fantasies that seemed almost real to her. Now she supposed herself wrapped in nets and veils, tucked into the shining vehicle, with her face lifted to the Channel wind.

The quarter boys struck thirty minutes past the hour. The motor car had disappeared. She pressed her nose to the mullioned glass, praying that nothing had changed her cousin's plans. His first message had arrived just two days after a madman-assassin's bullet had struck down the American President, McKinley.

Hearing that news, Alban Davelle had declared, "Richard Cavendish won't travel in such times. If the President dies, and he probably will, what will happen?"

Soon William McKinley succumbed and Theodore Roosevelt took the oath of office on that same day. No further word came from the state of Massachusetts in America.

To anxious Vicki, it seemed that a change in the person who occupied the White House in far-off Washington, D.C., had no more dangerous effects on America than did the change in the royal personage who occupied Buckingham Palace in London on the affairs of Great Britain.

In the past August, Queen Victoria, for whom this young Victoria had been named, died after sixty-four years on the throne. Now Edward VII, long known as Bertie, was king, though his formal investiture was delayed because of his illness.

Vicki had seen no great calamities afflict the nation, and therefore, in spite of her father's dire prognostications, had known no reason why her cousin should delay the journey he had planned. Still, she had been relieved when word came that he was in Lancashire and would come by carriage for a few hours' visit in Rye.

She imagined him to be large, loud-voiced. He would have a beef-flushed face, a bristly blond mustache.

And now, as she watched, a huge carriage drawn by fine sorrels swung into Mermaid Lane and came to a precipitate halt under the flickering street lamps.

Anticipation flashed through her. This must be Richard Cavendish! None but strangers to Rye would

6

attempt to bring a carriage of that size up Mermaid Lane. The only way to approach, except on foot, would be to go all the way down The Mint, swing back along Mermaid Street, drive through Mermaid Passage past the Inn, leave the carriage in the coach yard there, and walk down the lane to the parsonage.

She thought of rushing out to give the driver directions, but the carriage door swung open, and a man stepped out. Instead of going to greet him, she rushed into the kitchen, crying, "He's here! Papa! Mrs. McVey! He's coming!" She eyed the preparations. The tea kettle simmered on the hob. The freshly washed cozy was ready to cover the pot. Mrs. McVey's grudgingly made scones and new-filled jam jars were shielded by starched napkins.

"We're prepared," Mrs. McVey said dourly. She was a woman of forty-nine, full-faced, and round of arm and hip, her curves suggesting a tenderness she didn't have.

Alban Davelle rose. He eyed Vicki reproachfully, taking in the gown, the exposed flesh at her throat, the brooch at her breast, the amber curls that hung midway down her back.

But there was the knock at the door. Vicki dodged around Mrs. McVey's bulk, ducked under her father's arm, and flung back the door.

The early dusk had turned to early dark. The small front garden was astir with moving shadows. Within them a man waited. He was tall, over six feet in height, and so wide of shoulder that he filled the stoop and dwarfed the garden and blocked even the narrowest view of the sky. He was hatless, and his dark hair was smoothed straight across his high forehead, and curled low on his collar. His eyes were dark, too, long and narrow under flaring black brows. His face was sculpted lean, the skin tight across the bones of his cheeks and jaw. She guessed him to be twenty-eight years old.

For the space of a breath that seemed to stop time, with only the two of them alone in an emptied world, they stared at each other. Though the quarter boys struck out fifteen minutes to the hour, she didn't hear. Though her father and Mrs. McVey moved in the hall behind her, she didn't notice. This was most certainly not the stout and mustachioed cousin she had envisioned earlier. Even as that thought widened her welcoming smile, his eyes swept her up and down in a look that told her why she had primped and prettied before the cheval glass. He saw her not as a child, but as a woman, the woman she had been trying to become.

Then the hard line of his mouth softened. "Im Richard Cavendish," he said. "And you, you must be Victoria, although I had somehow thought . . ."

"I'm usually called Vicki," she answered. "And you somehow thought me a little girl, I suppose." Her eyes shone beneath the fringe of her thick, curling lowered lashes.

"Vicki," he repeated. "I'll remember."

She moved aside and gestured to the hallway. While her father and Mrs. McVey greeted him, she hurried in to light the gas jets in the parlor, to kindle the fire on the hearth. A pool of flickering golden light thrust the shadows into the farthest corners. The dank chill of the room retreated before slow spreading warmth.

"Yes, it was a long journey," Richard Cavendish was saying, as she rose to her feet, the blue rep swaying around her. "And I must return home within a few days. Though I have my brother John, and a good superintendent, too, overseeing the mill for me in my absence, I don't like to leave it for an extended period of time. Still, the trip was worth it." Speaking, he glanced at Vicki. But he thought, with a part of his mind, of Rosamund Dean, the girl he had been taking around before he left his Fall River home. She was handsome, as black-haired and black-eyed as himself, and the same age, too. Until this moment Richard had thought to marry her. But he knew now that she would never be his bride, wear his ring, share his bed and life. At twenty-eight, he felt that he had been a bachelor far too long, but in the past he had had other goals to occupy his attention, a fact for which he was presently grateful.

"Tell me of the family," Alban Davelle said, waving his guest to a chair. "I so rarely hear from your relations in the Midlands. How are your grandparents, Richard?" And to Vicki, "Richard's grandfather and mine were brothers."

"I'm sorry to say that they've both passed on. It was some thirteen years ago. My father followed them three years after. He was Edward, you recall, their only son."

Alban shook his head sadly. "Edward, too." He nodded at Vicki. "Edward's the one that was born in mid-Atlantic when his parents emigrated in 1846." Then, to Richard: "And your mother? I've heard of her, of course, though we've never met."

"She's well." He looked at Vicki. "Her name is Matilda."

"Yes. My father has spoken of her." Vicki was obscurely glad to have learned that she and Richard were very distant cousins. But she considered that enough time had been devoted to his family. "Tell us why you came to England," she suggested.

"To see what advances there have been in the milling of cloth."

"You've no desire to return home to live?" Alban asked.

Richard smiled faintly. "America's my home. Every day I'm thankful that my grandparents had the good sense and courage to make their lives there, as my father gave thanks before me. Can you imagine it, I wonder?" He looked at Vicki as he went on. "My grandfather worked at a loom, just as he had done in Manchester. At age twelve my father took his place in the mill, first as a sweeper, then as a carder, and finally as a weaver. Born here, he'd have been a weaver all his life. And it's likely that if I'd been, I'd have done the same. But by the time my father died nine years ago, he owned Cavendish and Sons, with two hundred looms, and a weaver to every five of them, and a bobbin boy to every twelve or so. We ran a full twelve-hour shift, and had a payroll of around one hundred. In the past nine years, I've built from there. And what I have is only the beginning."

Mrs. McVey tugged Vicki's skirt. "We'll get out the tea." In the kitchen, her hands busy with the scones and jam pots, she went on sharply, "You stared in a most unseemly manner. Richard Cavendish is a mere man, and not a god to revere." And when Vicki didn't answer, "I don't believe I like him, anyway. He's too American, very forward."

"You don't know him. There's hardly been more than a 'how do you do' between you."

"I don't need more than that to make up my mind."

". . . a man has a chance to better himself," Richard was saying, when Vicki returned to the parlor. "The Cavendishes have proven that. And why else would a man work his heart out, except to better his condition? Of course my father and I had very different ideas. He was much more cautious than I am, and set his sights lower. But it was he who laid the foundations."

It had been a bitter struggle. Richard had for years considered himself full grown, with a hunger for power that required increasing sustenance. He had imagined Cavendish and Sons as rebuilt to a block square, and five floors high, with a second building beside the first. He had known he could establish a rival to Fall River's great mills, to Troy and Pacific. But Edward had had no such visions and would take none of the necessary risks. He had ruled the business as autocratically as those two English kings for whom his sons had been named. After his death, Richard had been free to act, except for his mother's carping, which didn't stop him. Cavendish and Sons was now a block square and five stories high, but he dreamed of seeing it larger still.

Vicki saw that he was already clearly prosperous. In Fall River, Massachusetts, there would be no small parsimonies. His heavy gold watch, swinging by the chain across his waistcoat, showed that. The fabric of his suit, the silken elegance of his broadcloth shirt, bespoke the successful entrepreneur. In Rye, the Davells lived on the fine line of penury, where every farthing counted. Alban's parishioners weren't the fashionable folk of the town. They were the fishermen, the hop pickers, the net makers and menders, and they had only little to give to their parson.

Now Mrs. McVey rose, refilled the men's cups. Her face was stiff as she murmured, "You think only of worldly goods, Mr. Cavendish."

He laughed. "Worldly goods indeed. And what's wrong with them?"

"Nothing's wrong with them," Vicki said. "Except not having them."

Richard smiled at her. "Vicki is a true member of my family." He went on to Alban. "It's something you should think on. The opportunities for you, for your daughter, are boundless in America."

"We have what we need here," the parson answered.

"What you *need*." The ironic tone underlined the word. "Is that enough? Consider what you could build in Fall River." Richard spoke easily, his voice deep, yet there was the suggestion of a tension in him, a coiled spring that could snap, something closed in and constrained, that might be unexpectedly unleashed.

Alban shrugged. "It's fine for you, Cousin Richard. But I'm bound to my country by ties of blood and the past. This is my home. I've been in Rye since I was first called from Lancashire. My work is where I'm needed." He didn't say what had been on his mind for some time—that his health was failing, that any great change was beyond him now and forever.

Vicki herself saw only half a life before her. Days giving Sunday School lessons, overseeing sewing meetings, distributing charity. At best, finally, there'd be a job as governess, in which she would teach someone else's children what she had scarcely learned herself. She had always dreamed of escaping, and now, suddenly, Richard Cavendish told her it was possible. She

11

said in a low passionate voice, "I'd go, and gladly. There's nothing in Rye for me."

Mrs. McVey's sniff of disapproval was loud, and Alban Davelle's hurt look said without words, "Always a rebel, my Victoria."

"You see," Richard said, smiling. "It's as I commented before. Vicki plainly takes after the Cavendishes."

She didn't argue with him, but she knew she resembled her mother, who had gone out to seek life and love.

Richard deliberately turned his head to stare at her, his face suddenly remote, and in that instant he swore to himself that he would have her.

"All I need is a chance," she went on. "I should love to see America, to see your Fall River."

Her father asked, "Vicki, would you really go so far away and leave me?"

"Of course, Papa. Sometimes children must leave their parents behind them. And my mother did the same, didn't she?"

"That was different," he told her. And then: "I'd never allow it, Vicki. Your future is here with me."

She cast an exasperated look at Richard, and saw him smile faintly, but she said, "Oh, Papa, that's just what I thought you'd say."

Mrs. McVey intervened with a tart, "Victoria!"

But Vicki went on, "You're just afraid of any great change. But people who live by fear have nothing, and end as nothing."

Again Mrs. McVey intervened. "Say what you will, Mr. Cavendish, you'll not convince me that America is aught but a savage place. And Fall River, from what I've heard, is no better than the rest of it."

Vicki flung her head back impatiently. "Mrs. McVey believes that the Indians still rule in Massachusetts, Cousin Richard. But never mind. Tell me about Fall River. Is it a nice village?"

"It's more city than village," Richard answered, "and Indians did once live there, but no longer do."

But Mrs. McVey was an avid reader of London's

crime weeklies, with a well-developed taste for gore. She said, "I didn't refer to such savages as Indians."

Vicki saw the swift change in Richard's face. His hands, resting on his thighs, curled into fists. But he said evenly, "You speak of the murders, Mrs. McVey."

"Murders?" Vicki asked. "What murders?"

"A horrible crime," Mrs. McVey told her. "You're too young to remember. It was nine years ago in Fall River. A woman killed her father and stepmother, using an ax." There was obvious enjoyment in the older woman's tone.

"The Borden case," Richard said. "I ought to have known you'd have heard of it. The journalists came from all over the country, and wrote of nothing else for a long time. Patricide has always seized men's imaginations. But Miss Borden was acquitted. That she was accused at all, a woman of an old family, raised the hue and cry and shocked us, of course."

"It was the ax, the blows and the blood," Mrs. McVey said softly. "That's why the millworkers poured out of the factories, leaving their looms for the hot August streets, and stood before the house, staring, until the police took that woman away."

A chill touched Vicki. She saw the crowds, silent and watching. She saw a door open, a woman appear.

"It's over and done with. We're glad to forget it," Richard said.

"And what happened to *her?*" Mrs. McVey demanded.

"She lives with her sister in a house not far from me," Richard answered. He turned to Vicki and firmly changed the subject. "You asked about Fall River. As I started to tell you, it's a small city, with a population of some one hundred thousand. The English settlers came first, men from Lancashire. Since then we've received some Portuguese, some Irish, some French-Canadians, too. Of course we've had our ups and downs. Just as any mill town would. As when the price of raw cotton rises . . . It's the same in Manchester. But, in this country, I confess, I see

13

something that troubles me. Your government doesn't leave business to men of business. But meddles, passing laws, and always with ill effect. Now take the Factory Act of 1890 that regulates working hours. I consider that ridiculous." He shrugged. "Not that we don't have demands for similar measures at home. There's been agitation for shorter work days since my father was at his loom. But we know what's best for the workers, as our government never could."

"I have little knowledge of business," Alban said, "however, I wonder . . . what of your unions?"

"I'll not be told by anyone how much I pay my workers," Richard answered. "Nor how long they'll work. *I* own the mill. And no one else."

Vicki murmured an apology, rose and hurried into the kitchen. Richard Cavendish, it seemed, could only speak of industrial conditions. She wanted to hear about America, about Fall River. She felt that she would trade her soul for a few more bits of information out of which she could fashion her dreams. Fall River . . . even the name was enchanting.

Following her, Mrs. McVey muttered, "Now that's a nice way to behave! Dashing out while Mr. Cavendish is in midsentence."

"I'll go into the garden for a minute," Vicki said, refusing to take up argument. Whatever she had hoped when she gazed at her reflection in the cheval glass was come to nothing. Richard Cavendish sat with her father and sipped sweetened tea, and talked only of his looms. Her joyful expectations had faded before the onset of a cruel reality. Her cousin's visit meant nothing to her after all.

She snatched a knitted shawl from the hook on the back of the kitchen door, and hurried outside to the side path and into the front garden.

Light from the window gleamed faintly in the shadows. She leaned against the mossy brick wall, her hands clenched into the fullness of her skirt. The two remaining chrysanthemums glowed in the ribbons of light that fell on them from the window.

Tears welled in her eyes. She tried to blink them

14

away, for the door opened, and Richard came down the front steps.

He held up a cigar, grinned. "Your Mrs. McVey wouldn't approve of my smoking in the parlor, I'm sure."

"She approves of little," Vicki answered. She moved away slowly, her eyes again brimming with tears. He followed, and when she stopped in the back garden, he stopped, too.

He took the end of her shawl and dabbed at the tears on her cheeks. Around them were the mingled scents of the herb borders, where marjoram and mint and rosemary had begun to wilt. He said quietly, "It's not so bad as all that, Vicki. I don't object to having my smoke outside. My mother feels the same about cigars."

"Who cares about your cigars!" Vicki cried. "I'm thinking that I'll never be free. I'll spend my days going to Evensong at church, taking part in Matins, walking along The Mint on Sunday afternoons. All for want of something better to do. The highpoint of my years will be a chance to peer at Mr. Henry James when he bicycles away from Lamb House on West Street to do his shopping, or an invitation to sit for a portrait by Mary Stormont whenever I have the time, which will be always, and then, without ever having lived, I shall wither and grow old and die."

"You give up your hopes too soon," Richard said quietly.

"It'll be just as I tell you. Unless I can make it different. There's no one to help me."

"Shall we wait and see?" Richard asked. And before she could answer, "I think you're going to enjoy Fall River."

"If I ever view it."

"You will."

She laughed suddenly. "You sound so certain, Cousin Richard."

"I am," he replied.

She looked into his face, then said in a surprised voice, "Why, I think I am, too."

15

The carriage waited beneath the street lamp at the foor of the lane. The horses snorted and stamped impatiently. Somewhere in the distance a dog yelped, and running footsteps receded in fading echoes.

It was close to midnight, and much later than Richard had intended to stay. He had found taking his leave more difficult than he had expected. At last, though, he made his farewells to Mrs. McVey, who had gone to the kitchen to wash the tea things, and to Alban Davelle, who departed to immerse himself in his papers.

Only Richard and Vicki remained. He stood looking down at her. The night mists had blown away, and a thin crescent moon hung overhead. He had already said his goodbyes to her, but he lingered. There was a sudden discomfort in him, a stirring of the loins and a deep belly heat, which under other circumstances could be the most intense of joys, but was presently only an embarrassment. He had always considered himself settled and controlled by the dreams which had driven him since he was hardly more than a boy and able to observe his parents' timidities in the face of the vast horizons before them. But now, though it was beyond reason and belief that such a thing had happened to him, his single-minded vision of the future was transformed. Within it was Vicki Davelle. He knew that he must have her.

He said quietly, "I wish there were more time."

"Yes," she breathed. "Oh, yes, Cousin Richard. So do I."

He took both her hands and held them in a possessive grip. He felt the quick current that came from the touch of her flesh against his. He stared at her long and hard and hungrily, impressing her image in his mind so that he could take something more with him than the too-brief touch of her fingertips. It wasn't enough. He put his hands on her shoulders, drew her close so there was no space between them, and she felt the touch of his body against hers. He bent his head, and pressed a long hot kiss against the softness of her mouth, while she resisted his strength. When he

16

let her go, he said slowly, "Were I to apologize to you, it would be a lie. All I can say is, I'll make more time."

She felt a pulse flutter in her throat, and a sudden weakness in her knees. She drew a deep shaky breath against the constriction of her heart. She had known ever since she first heard that he was coming to Rye that it would have some special meaning to her. Now, again, he held her hands tightly captive, and looked down at her from his overwhelming height, while her lips stung from his kiss. It was as if he were drawing her into himself, so that she had no will of her own. He asked, "Would you come, Vicki? Suppose it were possible. Would you be willing to leave all you know, and come to me?"

"I would, Cousin Richard," she whispered.

"Then promise to remember me."

She freed her captive hands from his, moved a single fearful step backward without knowing why, without knowing what it was she feared. And then, with a soft, "Of course I'll remember you, Cousin Richard," she hurried into the safety of the house.

Chapter 2

THE CHRISTMAS WREATH LAY ON THE WINDOW SILL, the holly leaves curled, silvery gray, the once red bow faded. When Vicki had taken it down from the door on New Year's Day a week before, it had already begun to wilt. But she hadn't been able to convince herself to throw it away. It had been delivered by a whistling boy on the eve of the holiday, nestled in

17

golden paper, from a London florist, and the card within had said, "From your Cavendish cousin." She supposed that Richard had ordered it before embarking on the ship that took him home. It was all she had left of the too-brief October visit.

You'll see Fall River, Richard had told her.

Promise to remember me, he had said.

Though she recalled too well the brief moment when she had feared him, had felt herself almost engulfed and overwhelmed and had fled indoors atremble, she had prepared for the escape he had promised her. She moved the small chest from under the trundle bed into her own room. With infinite care she drew from it her mother's clothes, deciding what she herself could wear, what must be altered, what could be redesigned.

One afternoon Mrs. McVey had come in search of her, and found her sewing at a wine-colored China silk. The older woman had opposed Vicki's using her mother's long-unworn garments, saying it would hurt Alban Davelle to see his daughter dressed thus and be reminded of the wife he had lost. She ridiculed Vicki's obvious hope that she would be invited to Fall River, insisting that the girl would never hear from her Cousin Richard Cavendish again. She tartly insisted that the parson would never permit Vicki to make the journey, even in the unlikely event that an invitation was forthcoming.

Vicki's lips had set in a stubborn line. There was no use supposing. Her father *must* agree. Cousin Richard *must* ask her to come.

So, still remembering the fear that had bloomed in her at Richard's touch, she had gone on doggedly preparing herself until she had done all she could do. Meanwhile she eagerly scoured the London *Times,* always a day late, for whatever news she might possibly glean about Fall River, in Massachusetts. She never found mention of its name. But from London first, and then from New York, she read that the United States and Great Britain had between them signed the Hay-Pauncefote Treaty, which gave the United States the right to build a canal across the Isthmus of Panama.

The next month she read that wireless telegraphy had become a reality when Mr. G. Marconi developed an apparatus that made it possible for him to hear a signal sent without wire across the Atlantic Ocean from Wales to St. Johns, Newfoundland.

The weeks, then months, had passed. The church bells rang out the year 1901, and rang in the year 1902. Time blunted both her fear and hope, and drove her to more practical matters.

Now she looked at the Christmas wreath with its grayish holly leaves. She would consign it to the trashcan when she went downstairs. With a sigh she hitched her chair closer to the window. She needed all she could get of the cold winter light. The infant's gown she held was as small as a man's handkerchief, and difficult to work on, but she wanted it to be perfect. It was of coarse fabric, and would have no satin ribbons nor gathered lace, so its seams must be the finest she could do. It, along with the three others already completed, would be wrapped in thick paper and stored in the parsonage cupboard until Mrs. McVey doled it out to whatever parishioner needed it. The baby who finally wore it would have been conceived by a couple too poor to afford even swaddling clothes, would grow up stunted by a bad diet—if it was fortunate enough to survive its first year—and would be in want until the day it lay in its pauper's coffin after a too-early death.

For an instant Vicki's arms were full of a small squirming warmth, and she felt against her breast a heartbeat as quick and insistent as a bird's.

Then she bent her head and took a slow careful stitch. The needle pricked her finger. Instantly a drop of blood spread on the white of the gown. With her thumb in her mouth, she ran down the stairs to the kitchen.

As she held the gown under cold water, Mrs. McVey said, "It happened because you don't think what you do."

Vicki didn't reply. She watched the stain fade. She spread the small garment on the table to dry.

"And when will you braid up your hair?" Mrs. Mc-Vey demanded. "You're your father's daughter. You have a responsibility."

"I prefer it this way," Vicki said coolly.

Back in her room, in the chair by the window, she clasped her fingers into the fullness of her skirt to still their trembling. In spite of Mrs. McVey's nagging, Vicki wouldn't braid her hair. It meant giving up, and she'd never do that.

If only she had the fare . . . she didn't even know what it was . . . but surely there was a shipping agent in Rye where she could enquire. Her eyes fell upon the withered Christmas wreath. She tasted bitterness as she carried it downstairs.

From the lane outside she heard the mailman's whistle, but this time she didn't go racing to meet him, to wait impatiently through his pleasant, "Good morning, miss," and then to be disappointed. This time she continued on to the kitchen, where Mrs. McVey was rolling out dough for a gooseberry cobbler. The older woman made no comment when Vicki threw the wreath away, but Vicki saw the flash of satisfaction in her eyes.

An icy wind whipped down the High Street. Vicki pulled her shawl closely around her. It took time to find the shipping agent in a shed near the railway station. He blinked at her, said, "I don't know, miss. We ship parcels, not people," when she made her request. At her downcast look, he went on, "But I could write and find out. Stop in again in a week or ten days."

She was no longer downcast. She went so briskly up the road that she nearly missed the sign in the tobacconist's shop. *Help Wanted,* it said. And she wanted she didn't know yet how many pounds. She hesitated. She had never had a job, nor even applied for one. What could she do? How would she ask? She went on to the corner, then turned to retrace her footsteps, imagining that she had earned the money she needed . . .

She climbed from the train into the surging crowds

of Charing Cross, and stayed at a nearby hotel overnight. In a gray dawn she embarked on the boat train for Liverpool, to find her way into the milling confusion of the docks, and . . .

But she didn't have ship's passage. She looked at the tobacconist's sign, drew a deep breath, and went in. It was a tiny place crammed to overflowing with packets of cigarettes. cans of tobacco, with pipes and cleaners and holders. There were newspapers and journals piled in high stacks, and even small bags of sweets. She breathed cautiously of the varied aromas, and smiled at the tiny man who peered at her from behind a high counter.

Within moments, she was on the street again. She would work three half-days a week. She would save every penny of her pay, yet it would be a long while before she had enough saved to think of the trip ahead. Still, she was elated as she hurried through the chill dusk. She had made a beginning.

It was two weeks later. Neither Mrs. McVey's oft-repeated objections, nor her father's reproaches, had stopped Vicki. She had learned the stock quickly, enjoyed her job and remained determined to continue at it.

Now, as she took off her shawl, Mrs. McVey peered from the kitchen. "Oh, you're back, are you?"

Vicki nodded, went to help with preparations for tea.

Alban Davelle walked with slow, dragging footsteps down the hallway, hardly hearing the homey sounds from the kitchen. The pain in his chest had worsened in the past few months. It came oftener, lingered longer, cutting his breath when he wheeled his bicycle around the town, spreading deep when he walked the lanes. But at the sight of the flimsy envelope he now held crumpled in his hands it nearly felled him.

The letter was not unexpected. His knowledge of men had warned Alban that he would hear from his Cavendish cousin.

In the kitchen he nodded at Vicki, at Mrs. McVey. He sank into a chair, unwrapped the thick muffler from his throat, but remained huddled in his worn outdoor wrappings. His pale eyes seemed to weep dry tears. Silently he regarded Vicki. He dreaded to be alone in his old age. He had seen too much of it. But there was Vicki to consider. He knew what his Maude would say now if she lived. She had said it when she left her parents to go with him. "What shall she do, Alban? Shall she give up her young life for old ones? And when that's over, shall she spend her nights alone and weeping?

His hand shook when he smoothed the crumpled letter, saying, "It's from Richard Cavendish, Vicki."

She said nothing while fear and joy warred within her. Joy won, and Alban saw the cautious hope burgeon in her eyes.

He was unimpressed by the worldly goods the Cavendishes had to offer her. But she must have someone. She mustn't be alone. With a quick gesture, he opened the envelope and read what was written in the letter within, his certainty confirmed before he studied the words by the bank draft he found folded inside.

He breathed easily now. The pain was gone. He knew it would return. He nodded. "It's what you hoped for, Vicki. The Cavendishes have asked you to visit them."

"For how long?" Mrs. McVey demanded.

"They don't specify." He offered the letter to Vicki. "Read for yourself, if you like."

Almost she was afraid to read lest her father had misunderstood. But as she scanned the words she saw that he had read correctly. Richard had written to say that his mother, Matilda, would like Vicki to come for a stay. A bank draft for passage at the beginning of February was enclosed. By good fortune he had learned through a friend that a woman named Mrs. Elise Parker, and her brother, Mr. Leslie Winton, were making the crossing on the same ship. His friend had obliged him by asking that they be Vicki's chaperons. Cousin Alban was assured that Mrs. Parker and Mr. Winton were of the highest reliability. They were coming to Fall River to assume ownership of a first-class private shool for boys, and were also re-lated to his friend. Cousin Alban was asked to inform Richard if he was agreeable to Richard's proposal.

Vicki looked at her father, waited in breathless expectation.

Mrs. McVey said, "I never heard of such a thing." She rose in a rustle of angry skirts to peek into the stove. The odor of burned sugar and boiling apples filled the air. Flushed, she turned back. "You told him when he was here that you'd not allow Vicki to go so far from you."

"Did I?" Alban asked absently. "I don't recall it."

"Papa?" Vicki whispered.

He gazed at her solemnly. "Do you want to go?"

"Of course she wants to," Mrs. McVey cut in. "It's all she's thought of since Richard Cavendish was here. She doesn't care what her responsibility is."

"Please," Alban said. And then, "Vicki?"

There was an instant's hesitation while she thought of Richard, and wondered what she really wanted. Then the yearning for escape overwhelmed all else. She murmured, "If you'd only allow it, Papa."

"Then I do," Alban told her. "I shall."

With a cry of joy, she threw herself into his arms.

Mrs. McVey hid a small smile. She had done her duty and made her protest. But after all these years she saw how she could have her own way at last. She was as good as mistress of the parsonage, though she didn't have the name. She wanted the name, too. Now she saw the opportunity which she had supposed would never come. She thrust a proprietary finger into the crusty soil of the aspidistra and hurried to get the watering can.

A chill February breeze blew through the station as a door opened and then slammed shut. Clear, cold sunlight lay in wide ribbons across the dusty floor. A potbellied stove glowed red but gave off little heat.

23

Vicki clasped her reticule tightly. She wore the wine silk, and over it, a hip-length coat of heavy gray wool. A thick gray shawl covered her amber curls, and thick woolen mittens encased her hands.

She had spent her minuscule earnings on minuscule purchases. Rice powder, with which she had cautiously dusted her face that morning. Lavender scent, which she had also applied.

She looked sideways at Mrs. Parker, wishing that she herself had so charming a hat to wear, and then, quickly, she looked at Mr. Winton. She had met the couple only moments before, and had spoken no more than a few words to them.

"Cousin Richard will meet you on your arrival in Fall River. Please do write to me as soon as you can," her father was saying.

Cousin Richard. She had dwelt on that name for so long, but now, suddenly, her mind went blank with fear. She could no longer remember his features, recall the sound of his voice. She fought terror down. Her new life was ahead of her. And there would be Cousin Matilda to meet, and Cousin John. And there would be a new city to explore.

"Vicki," her father said.

"You mustn't worry," Elise Parker told him. "We'll see that your daughter is safely delivered to her relations."

She was a woman of thirty-five, widowed several years before. Though of middle height, she seemed taller, her full figure held ramrod straight by disciplining corsets. She wore her dark auburn hair in a thick roll that swooped off her face into a high chignon. A large hat, wide-brimmed and decorated with glistening make-believe cherries, was tilted over her forehead. Her voice was crisp and cool, her diction as clear as would be expected in the schoolteacher she had been. The ruffle of lace at her throat relieved the black of her gown and coat. Now she glanced at her brother, murmured, "Leslie?"

"Be assured, Parson Davelle," Leslie Winton said, "we'll have a good voyage together. And we'll remind your daughter to write to you just before we make our goodbyes."

"Thank you," Alban Davelle answered, a forced smile on his bluish lips. He could do no more for Vicki except to kiss her farewell one last time, and return home to Rye where Mrs. McVey awaited him. This way, regardless of the hurt to him, Vicki would have a chance at happiness.

The whistle blew. Great clouds of white steam rose up from beneath the train. Red lanterns swung in quick arcs while the warning calls went out, and compartment doors slammed along the platform.

"We must board now," Leslie Winton said.

Alban's arms enfolded Vicki. She felt smothered by them. She pressed a quick kiss on his cheek. "Goodbye, Papa." With that she hurried onto the train.

After making their farewells, Elise Parker and Leslie Winton followed her.

There were only three vacant seats left. Vicki took the single one near the door, leaving two together across the aisle for Elise and Leslie.

When she looked out, she saw that her father stood alone, a hand lifted. A pang touched her. He seemed a stranger. An old man, frail, bewildered by the bustle around him. Until then, she had thought only of herself. Now she wondered how he would fare alone. She almost rose to go to him. She had time and life ahead of her. What of him? Then a cloud of steam billowed. The train jolted. The wheels rattled. The carriage lunged on its tracks. When the window cleared, he was gone, but she looked back until she saw nothing but three black gulls wheeling against the gray velvet sky.

She sank down, her heart pounding. He would be all right. He had wanted her to go. This was the beginning. She couldn't imagine what lay before her but she embraced it with all her rising hope.

Leslie Winton asked, "Are you comfortable there, Vicki?"

"I'm fine. Just so happy that I don't know what to say."

"It's only the beginning," he answered, as if echoing her earlier thought.

Leslie Winton. She spoke his name soundlessly. It had a pleasant ring to it. He was thirty years old, tall and lean, with blond hair that curled on his high crisp collar, and a thick curly blond beard. His eyes were a soft warm brown, and even in repose his lips seemed to quiver with a barely controlled smile.

"I hope the accommodations on board will be comfortable," Elise was saying.

Leslie packed a pipe with fragrant tobacco. When he had lit it, he grinned at her. "My dear girl, you've nothing to fear. At least you know who'll be sharing your nights. I must say you'll be fortunate." He ignored the small sound of protest his sister made. "I shall probably be sleeping with some old gent who snores in his mustaches."

"And I hope the weather is all right." Elise sighed deeply and confided to Vicki, "I'm not the best sailor in the world, I fear."

"I don't know how I shall be," Vicki told her. "But whatever happens, it'll be worth it."

"Which means," Leslie said, "that you'll prove to have an iron constitution."

"And if she doesn't, she'll pretend to." Elise smiled. "Which will do just as well."

"If you try that attitude yourself," Leslie answered, "you might find that it would help you, too."

But Leslie's suggested remedy against seasickness proved ineffective for Elise. She tried gallantly, but by the third day of the voyage she could no longer even try.

Vicki hardly managed to hide her jubilation. By then, all she wanted was to be alone with Leslie.

Chapter 3

IT BEGAN LATE IN THE AFTERNOON OF THE FIRST day of the trip. They had climbed the gangplank under the bright pennants as strangers, and watched while the tugs busily nudged the big ship into the Channel. Later Vicki and Elise had gone to their cabin to unpack, while Leslie went to his. Soon they met to visit the public lounges among the other passengers bent on similar explorations. They had stood in the sharp cold February wind that scudded across the main deck, and paced off the promenade twice. By the time they sat in reclining chairs, tucked into woolen blankets, and sipped the hot bouillon that the steward had brought them, they were no longer strangers.

The sky overhead was thick and gray. The sea moved in slow undulations, its surface laced with small whitecaps.

Vicki, between Elise and Leslie, felt cradled in luxury. Her mind ranged ahead to Fall River. Richard would meet her. How sharply she recalled his lean height, dark eyes and hair . . . how intensely she remembered his touch, his kiss. A weakness born of recollected fear swept her. She had subdued that fear because Richard represented escape. But now her gaze slid sideways to study Leslie. How handsome he was. And how familiar in his Englishness.

Nearby a stout man grumbled loudly, "Sherman's Act has got to go. They'll use it against Morgan now, but we'll be next."

The man beside him murmured a reply.

"It's what comes of Roosevelt's being in," the stout man went on, disgustedly flinging his cigar into the wind.

"Politics." Leslie grinned, seeing the direction of Vicki's glance. "A complicated affair in America."

Elise set aside her bouillon cup, and shivered within her blankets. She eyed Vicki speculatively. It was, she decided, a pity that the girl's so evident beauty was almost obscured by her lack of style. Elise was already bored. The prospect of the seven-day trip stretched endlessly ahead. She thought it might be diverting to see what she could do for Vicki. She turned to Leslie. "If you'll excuse us, I'd like Vicki to come to the cabin with me."

"What for? You've nothing to do there now."

Elise rose, struggling free of her blankets. "You'll see later what we do."

"Be careful," he said, smiling, as Vicki, too, rose. "I see by my sister's face that she's plotting something. And she has a way of drawing one into situations before one realizes what she's about."

Elise's eyes sharpened. She wondered if he were obliquely referring to what she had done for him. But she hadn't entrapped him, and he couldn't think she had. On the contrary, she had flung him a lifeline when he most needed one. It was for him that she had uprooted herself from her pleasant London life, investing her inheritance in the Fall River school that Rosamund Dean had told her about. And Elise had been glad to do it. She loved Leslie. She didn't expect gratitude from him, but she also did not like suspecting that he felt coerced, when what she had done had been for his own good.

Within his blond beard, his mouth slanted in a slow teasing smile, the smile that always made him so irresistible to women. He was saying, "But I should tell you, Vicki, that my sister's plans are always to the good. So lend yourself to her schemes with a free heart."

Elise let out her breath in a long sigh. "Never you

mind, Leslie. Have your pipe. We'll return soon." She drew Vicki down the narrow flight of steps that led to the cabin deck, clinging hard to the rail, for now there was a noticeable roll to the ship.

Within the confines of the cabin, she explained what she had in mind. Delight bloomed in Vicki as Elise searched through her trunk. Vicki had realized as soon as she saw Elise that her own efforts to prepare herself for the voyage had been to little avail. That knowledge was confirmed on the boat train. Her few gowns were nice enough, but unlike the styles worn by the other ladies. She had known she would be uncomfortable, but that nothing could be done.

Elise proved something could. The transformation took less than an hour. Vicki's hair waved smoothly off her brow; the amber curls glistened in a soft high chignon. The hat that Elise gave her was a mass of silken flowers in cornflower blue. The skirt was a shimmering blue as well, deeply ruffled and tantalizingly full. By the time Vicki had tightened the waistband, Eise had found a top the same shade of blue with a darker ruching at the throat and cuffs.

It was while Vicki stared wonderingly at herself in the glass that Elise put both hands to her head, and sank down on the edge of the lower bunk, moaning that she didn't feel well.

Vicki was untroubled by the increasingly erratic movement of the ship. She even found the lift and fall exciting. Still, she felt quick sympathy for Elise's plight, and said, "Perhaps you'd better rest."

Elise agreed, but suggested that Vicki go to dine with Leslie, promising that she would find another outfit for Vicki the following day. She moaned softly as Vicki left the cabin.

The wind was cold, steady, a thick moving wall that thrust her along the open gangway and whispered in the crisp taffeta of her skirts. The sound was sweet music to her, as sweet as that she heard from the distance. She paused to adjust the tiny hat as she stepped into the warmth of the lounge.

Leslie was talking with a group of men. He gave

her a long steady look over the heads of the people that passed between them. A searching, narrow-eyed look that left her somehow hesitant. But, as she moved toward him, he interrupted his conversation and left his companions. He crossed the space between them, and reached for her hands, clasping them tightly. He stared into her upraised face. At last he said hoarsely, "My God, Vicki, I didn't realize how beautiful you are until this moment."

Her heart gave a lurch within her. A burning ripple spread through her. She said breathlessly, "This was Elise's surprise."

"There was a moment when I actually didn't know you. I couldn't believe it was you, even when you smiled at me."

He still clasped her hands. She didn't want him to release her. She felt a wordless exchange in the touch of his flesh on hers. But the lounge was crowded. People passed back and forth, greeting each other with first-night camaraderie. She became aware of sideways glances that measured her and Leslie. She tried to draw away. He said, "Let's go outside."

"The wind's strong. Didn't you notice when you came in?" she asked. And then, quickly, "And Elise isn't feeling well. I thought I'd bring her something to nibble on."

"Already?" He laughed. "I expected she'd wait a day or two."

"I doubt she can help herself."

"Take her whatever you like," he said, drawing Vicki with him. "But do it later."

They stood shoulder to shoulder at the rail, he with an arm around her waist, holding her close to him. They had known each other only a day, yet she felt that she had been with him forever.

He said, "I thought you were a child until just a little while ago."

"I'm not a child," she answered soberly. "I'm seventeen and a half, nearly. And I haven't been a child for a very long time. Although my father has refused to admit that."

"Still, it must be difficult for you to leave him, to go to a strange new place."

"It's what I want more than life itself, I think." She drew a deep breath of the salty air. She had begun to wonder even then if what she wanted most in life had changed.

A steward passed, playing the first call for dinner on his chimes. Leslie held her arm when they went down to the dining room.

It was an enormous place lit by chandeliers that were like pyramids of pink-shaded bulbs. There were many large round tables which held places for eight, but Leslie insisted that they be served at a small table alone, from which they laughed together at the number of vacant seats across the room.

They had a meal of fresh salmon and boiled potatoes, beef steak with tiny green peas, a trifle of many layers and flavors for dessert. The champagne Leslie ordered made Vicki pleasantly giddy.

Afterwards she brought crushed ice and salted crackers to Elise, but the older woman only moaned and turned her face away.

Vicki undressed in the dark and climbed into her bunk, snuggling against the soft sheets, but she didn't fall asleep. She lay there, hearing the wind, the creak of the ship, but she imagined Leslie's face as he had walked toward her . . . the glow in his eyes, the faint narrowing of his lips within his blond beard . . .

The next morning Elise rose and dressed, pale with determination. But she was on her feet hardly more than two hours when the wind rose, the ship's motion worsened. A sheen of sweat spread on her brow. A pallor spread beneath her fair skin. She apologized to Leslie and Vicki, and retreated indoors.

It was as if fate decreed that Vicki should be alone with Leslie. Elise, once collapsed in her bunk with her face turned to the bulkhead, remained there. Vicki brought her ice, bouillon, and dry toast. Vicki bathed her face and combed her hair, and did it willingly. But the rest of the time was Vicki's own. She spent it all with Leslie.

31

They wandered the decks, rocking as the ship rose and dropped with the gathering and sinking of giant waves. Windblown and breathless, they sat side by side in deck chairs. They joined in games of backgammon and cards and chess. But when these were finished, he drew her away from the advances of the other passengers, so that she spoke only a few words to them on the whole voyage. The two of them dined in the glow of the chandeliers, leaning together at their small table, he faintly smiling over the flower centerpiece, her eyes like brilliant stars. She wore the blue gown that had been her mother's, with the heart-shaped brooch beneath the deep plunge of the neckline, and she saw how his glance lingered on the high white rise of her breasts.

Later they walked the promenade deck in the dark, avoiding the clusters of people who stood at the railing. He held her close, and a strange vibration, a hot-and-cold shivering trembled through her at his touch. She felt it penetrate the silken sheath of her skin and go deep into the marrow of her bones. She felt it echo hard and quick in the pulse of her heart. She quivered against him.

At those times his desire for her was so intense that he could hardly speak to her, hardly even think his private thoughts. He told himself that a madness was about to possess him. Elise had everything, and he had nothing. What he felt for Vicki could not change the reality. He had been a school master since the age of twenty-three. It was seven years since he had begun the chores which had become so onerous. To be headmaster, brother of the school's owner, was a different situation entirely. It meant escape from the classroom, from long hours of drudgery at books. And there was the other thing. East Grinstead was best forgotten, but Elise had given up all she had to make a new life possible for him. He couldn't jeopardize it.

One night he and Vicki walked together. The clouds broke. A silver moon shone on them, paling the lantern shine, and burning in her hair.

The bosun's mate passed them by, his peaked hat

tipped low on his forehead. He turned back to look at them, a slanted smile on his lips, before he went on.

Leslie was relieved when the man disappeared into the shadows, but Vicki hadn't even noticed him. She looked up at Leslie, yearning in her eyes, and said, "I wish this voyage would never end. I wish it could go on, just as it is right now. I would be content with that forever."

He grinned. "You only think so. You'd be surprised how soon you'd tire of the confines of this narrow world. After a bit, the meals take on a sameness. The faces around you become excessively familiar, too. The motion, the sounds . . . all turn wearing beyond belief."

She shook her head from side to side.

He held her by the elbow. His fingers tightened. His voice was thick as he said, "We must go down now, Vicki."

She murmured agreement, but there was a quickening in her blood, a bittersweet hunger to prolong the moment. She took three unwilling steps, then paused in the deepest of shadows formed by an angle of bulkhead and gangway. Without speaking, she waited.

He touched her cheek gently, his fingers molding curve and line and silken skin, then moving on to lay feather strokes along her mouth. She leaned against him, and he pulled her closer, enfolding her tightly in his arms, so that she could feel the fastenings of his coat bruising her breasts, and the heat of his body enwrap her. She pressed her face into the curve of his neck and felt the quick drum of his pulses against her brow. When his lips finally claimed hers in a long breathless kiss, she knew that she had wanted that kiss all her life, and would never stop wanting it.

The bosun's mate passed by again, and stared at them from beneath his cap, swinging his lantern so that circles of light danced along the deck. Once more Vicki didn't notice him. But Leslie did. Embarrassed, he released her quickly, saying, "Go down now, Vicki. I'll have a last pipeful before I turn in."

She tiptoed into the cabin, undressed in the dark, and climbed into her bunk. Hugging the pillow in her arms, she thought of Leslie, the heat of his mouth on hers, the softness of his beard against her cheek. When she finally slept, she dreamed of him.

It was a calm morning at last.

Elise decided that she would rise and dress and breakfast in the dining salon. When, some time later, she entered there with Leslie and Vicki, there was some confusion about the table to which the steward led them. It was suitable for two. A larger one had to be found. Elise realized that Leslie and Vicki had taken all their meals alone together. She had envisioned them surrounded by elderly ladies and gentlemen who observed all, and not in constant tête-à-tête. Soon she saw the starshine of Vicki's gaze when it touched Leslie, and the way he bent his head to her.

Elise frowned. Pink gathered on her pale cheeks. She breathed deeply, her large bosom rising over the table edge, her firm chin rising, too. She quietly asked Vicki to run down to the cabin for an extra shawl. The moment the younger girl had gone, Elise said, "It won't do, Leslie. You must stop it. I hope it hasn't already gone too far."

"Stop it? Gone too far?" He parried her attack with false bewilderment. "What's all that supposed to mean, my dear?"

"*You* know," she said in a level voice. "I won't have it. Wasn't the once enough? Do you have to do the same thing twice?"

He flushed, said defensively, "I don't know what you're talking about. Has your seasickness addled your brain?"

"It must have done for me to have supposed I could trust Vicki Davelle with you."

"You owe me an explanation for such remarks."

"I speak of the seduction of a girl nearly young enough to be your student, even your daughter."

"I've done no such thing," he cried.

Elise studied him briefly. Then: "Your denial must refer to Vicki. I hope you're not lying to me, Leslie. She's under the protection of the Cavendish family. If

34

there's trouble, not only they, but Rosamund, too, will turn against us. And remember that Fall River is a very small city. We could lose everything."

"You accuse me without reason."

"I hope so. I also hope that you don't have such a short memory that you've already forgotten why you had to leave East Grinstead, and why you could never find another teaching position in England."

"I thought we weren't going to mention that," he said coldly.

"I'd no intention of it. But you force me to. You impregnated that child, Leslie. Do you intend to risk the same catastrophe with Vicki Davelle?"

"Of course not! What kind of a mind do you have? I find her amusing, and you know what an ocean voyage is."

"It won't do," Elise retorted. "I've invested everything in making a new life possible for you! I'll not allow you to throw that away."

He smiled warmly into her eyes. "You worry for nothing, my dear."

She could say no more because Vicki returned to the table then, handed her the green shawl. Although it was excessively warm in the salon, Elise put it around her shoulders. She sat in silence and discomfort through the rest of the meal.

By afternoon, the weather had worsened again. Elise had to retire once more to her bunk. She lay retching into a basin, but her imagination trailed along behind Vicki and Leslie as they leaned against the wind in a stroll around the tilting deck.

Elise no longer viewed Vicki as a child. She saw the girl as a nubile and beautiful woman, and Leslie, no matter what he said, couldn't be trusted with her. Elise didn't propose that whispers about him circulate through Fall River while they began an enterprise in which reputation was more important than anything else. She also didn't propose to be left alone to deal with the school, to manage the settling into a new life with no one to help her. Leslie must keep his head, no matter what.

35

Before she fell into a fitful sleep she promised herself that she would speak to him again, and she would make him listen to her, too.

Vicki threw her head back, allowed the wind to stroke her face and wished that time could swing back in its course. Just six days before, her thoughts had gone racing ahead, hurrying her past the ocean voyage and into her new life. Now she would be willing to have no more new life than the one she had discovered on the ship. She and Leslie . . . the two of them . . . his arm at her waist, as it was in this moment.

For an instant she imagined that this was their wedding trip. They had been married in London just before the sailing. She wore a narrow gold band on her finger, and below in the cabin they shared, she had pressed three small pink roses from her bridal bouquet. In Fall River they would live together in a suite of rooms at the school . . .

"Such deep thoughts," Leslie said softly.

She didn't answer him. She could think of nothing to say. Her small daydreams gave her nothing to cling to. She knew that once they reached Fall River, Leslie and Elise would go one way. She would go another. She asked herself if she would ever see them again—if she would ever see *Leslie* again. A sharp pain arrowed through her. She had always hoped for love. But she had never imagined that it could come so quickly as joy mixed with anguish. A nod, a smile, a cool exchange had become the feeling which possessed her now. Having found it, she couldn't suppose giving it up and surviving the loss.

"What is it?" he demanded. "You're not suddenly frightened, are you? There's no need to be. Believe me, all your expectations will be answered."

"My expectations," she repeated softly. "Why, Leslie, I hardly remember what they were. I began this trip scarcely more than a child, although I didn't think so then, and I had a child's dream of escape to freedom and adventure." It was true. She could hardly remember the conversation which had fixed her mind so firmly on Fall River. She had wanted escape from Rye. But for what?

Leslie laughed. "And do you think you're suddenly aged? And become wise?"

Without willing it, she found that her fingers had clasped his, drawn them to her mouth. She kissed them. Then, still holding them to her lips, she spoke around them, her breath warming his skin. "I haven't aged. And I'm probably not so wise. But I *have* grown up."

It was only the shadow of Elise, standing tall in his mind, that kept him from sweeping Vicki into his arms. What had begun as a small flirtation, undertaken out of the habit of his adulthood, had developed into a genuine hunger. A need he had known many times before, and one that had already brought him near disgrace, and into Elise's hands. He knew her possessive nature. She would allow him nothing that might draw him a single step out of her world. Her marriage hadn't been happy. Though she had never admitted it, Leslie knew she had been relieved to gain her freedom, while meticulous in the forms of widowhood. She clung to him now, as she had when they were younger, with a doting love that had always smothered him. And it was she who held the purse strings.

Vicki said, "You know what's happened, Leslie." Her voice trembled. Her eyes met his beseechingly. "I've fallen in love with you. And now . . . now I can't bear to think of not seeing you again."

He stroked his beard, smiled. "My dear girl, you will see me. Rosamund Dean is a friend of the Cavendishes, and neighbor, too, I understand. Through her we'll certainly have introductions to your relations. And then there'll have been our connection with you, too."

But he hadn't said what she had wanted to hear. She had given her heart away, yet he carefully avoided any response to her declaration. She knew she mustn't speak of it again. Yet she heard herself saying, "You've given me no real answer, Leslie."

For his future's sake he fought down the rising hunger, even then considering those small stratagems that had stood him well in the past. He and Vicki could meet. He'd find a way. She could slip off to join him for late at night strolls. If one had the will . . . He stopped the planning with an effort. Fall River was a strange place to him. Elise would be alert to any absence of his.

He said, "But what can I tell you, dear Vicki? I'm sure you believe now that you love me. Wait until tomorrow. Until next week. Then I promise you that you'll look at me and wonder." He laughed softly. "You'll ask yourself what you saw in such an old man." He thought that he had put it well, but there was no answering smile on her face, and no concession of doubt either.

"I'll always feel the same," she told him. "I wish this ship would never reach land. I won't want to see America. Not any more. I don't care about the future. Except as it has you in it for me."

"It will." The words were forced from him by his own desire. Which he even then knew to be a temporary thing. He had been through this many times, while this was her first. He hesitated for only a moment, then pulled her tightly against him.

The ship heaved and strained, its empty decks shining with wind-driven spray that became icy pellets on Vicki's cheeks. She felt nothing but the warm safety of his arms as his lips sealed hers in an unspoken promise.

She was happier than she had ever been in her life. All her seventeen years seemed as nothing to this single moment. She vowed to herself that she would never give him up.

Chapter 4

FALL RIVER, UNTIL 1862, WAS A DIVIDED CITY, WITH part of it in Rhode Island and part in Massachusetts. Then the Massachusetts state line was moved two miles south, and the town was unified.

It began in 1659, the first sites bought from the Pocasset Indians, Massasoit, Wamsutta and Weetamoe, for twenty coats, eight pairs of shoes, six pairs of stockings, one iron pot, two kettles, one dozen hoes, one dozen hatchets and two yards of good broadcloth. It was called the Freeman's Purchase, and later, Freetown. The second group of sites was known as the Pocasset Purchase, and was taken by force of arms from the Indians and conveyed to willing settlers by the Plymouth government for a consideration of eleven hundred pounds, British sterling, in 1679. Together they were named Fallriver, then Troy, and finally in 1834, Fall River, from the Indian word *quequechan,* which meant "falling water," and referred to the Quequechan River that flowed from the Watuppa ponds through the city and into Mount Hope Bay.

Now, in 1902, it was sometimes popularly called Spindle City, after its major industry. There were approximately ninety textile mills in operation, with eighty-three thousand looms and three million spindles, employing thirty-two thousand hands and producing fifteen hundred miles of cloth every day, in addition to yarns and threads.

It was a bustling and growing place, with two electric companies, two telegraph companies, and an electric suburban railroad as well as the electric trolleys that had replaced the old horse-drawn cars. It had a public library and a poor farm. It had a parks commission, a merchants' association, and a police patrol-wagon system.

The city rose on ledges cut from the rocky side of a steep hill that hung above Mount Hope Bay and the Taunton River that emptied into it. Below, at water's edge there were docks and coal yards, with long gleaming tracks winding to huge warehouses and lofts, and mills of native granite. Above them, leaning against each other, were shops and saloons and markets and banks. Rising higher were rows of houses, with paint-blistered front porches and rotting clapboards. Over those reared great houses of stone, their surrounding acreage dotted with the tall crowns of trees, and the oval copper domes and slender reaching spires of many churches.

At five o'clock of a cold winter morning, with a foot of February snow frozen solid in the streets, the *Plymouth,* a luxurious white-painted sidewheeler of the Fall River Line, blew its shrill warning whistle and snugged into its berth at the foot of Ferry Street.

Two carriages were tied up side by side just within the circle of light that cut the predawn shadows. Their horses stamped in the cold, blowing great wreaths of steam around their heads. Their drivers stamped, too, and smoked hand-rolled cigarettes, leaning together to complain of the hour and the cold.

"A damn bad thing to be pulled out of bed so long before sunup," Harry Beamis said. "Lucky for us the *Plymouth*'s on time, else we'd freeze in our wrappings."

"Yes," Mitch Ryan agreed. He raised a booted foot to the rusty iron horsetrough nearby, rested his weight on it. "And for three English, too!" He spat disgustedly, as if the word *English* left a bitter taste on his tongue.

Harry Beamis knew that indeed it had. He had heard Irish Mike's feelings on that subject many times. He had a small spot of sympathy for Mike, knowing his life, or so Harry thought, and certain how he himself would feel had he to face Boston's "No Irish need apply" signs as Mitch Ryan had. Here, fifty miles from Boston, it was much easier. Still, there was a certain sourness to be faced down. He grinned at Mitch, saying, "Three English or not, there's been plenty of preparation."

Momentarily Mike's face was stony. He thought of what had just happened in England. The Irish had asked for a separate Parliament in Dublin and supported the Boers in South Africa. For that, Lord Roseberry had declared himself, and the Liberal Party, opposed to home rule. It was another English blow against Irish freedom.

But now Mike forced a grin. "I've heard of *your* preparations from what Miss Rosamund has said behind me, not thinking this Irishman can hear and understand. She says that the old lady and John, and King Richard, too, have been in a fine lather." Mitch enjoyed referring to the Cavendish family in those familiar terms. It brought the high and mighty down to his level.

"She's a parson's daughter, and out of a small town."

"Then she'll fit in fine in your fancy house," Mitch muttered, pulling hard on his cigarette so that its glowing end brightened to show his square pink face and ginger-lashed blue eyes. "And as for those other two English," he went on, "we'll see how they do among your Yankees."

The two men grinned at each other, and, as the gangplank went down, stamped their cigarettes under heel.

When the warning whistle shrilled, and the ship jolted into its berth, Vicki gave the cabin a quick searching glance to make sure that she had already repacked those few necessities she had taken out the night before. But the comfortable sleeping quarters were no more than an indistinct blur to her, and she hardly remembered the elaborate meal she and Elise and Leslie had shared soon after embarking.

41

The clearest memory she had of her arrival in New York was of when she had stood at the rail, Leslie beside her, and gazed at the Statue of Liberty looming ahead, and thought that her destiny in this new land was linked to Leslie. Her life was beginning with him at her side.

The formalities were completed on the ship. When the three of them had disembarked, they had had to hurry to Pier 14, on the North River, to make the evening five o'clock departure of the *Plymouth*. Vicki had only a faint impression of New York City. There was a thin snow sifting down. Everywhere she had looked were signs of construction. Scaffoldings reached upward, high over the sidewalks. Ladders had leaned against tall brick walls. Red lanterns marked ditches at the curbs and in the roadways. At every corner there were groups of men in tattered overcoats huddling over pushcarts. Some were piled high with flowers spilling over in colorful profusion. Others steamed with hotpots containing a variety of foods, she had supposed. There were men tending braziers of roasting chestnuts, and others swinging strings of beads beefore uncaring eyes of hurrying passersby.

Elise had muttered disconsolately of restaurants she had heard about. Sherry's, Delmonico's, the Palm Court at the Plaza, mourning the lack of time which made it impossible to visit them. But Leslie had laughed and promised, "We'll all three be back in New York one day to try them."

Elise had given him a sharp sideways look and said nothing, and Vicki had known for certain then that her friendship with Elise would end when they landed in Fall River.

That moment was now at hand. There was a shout in the corridor. Elise gave her cherrry-trimmed hat a small adjustment, and said, "We're ready, I think."

But Vicki felt compelled to ask, "Do you really mean for me to keep the things you gave me, Elise?"

"Of course," Elise retorted. "They are gifts. I hope you enjoy them." But her voice was cold. She

42

had given. She would not withdraw. Yet she wouldn't allow Vicki to make too much of that. She opened the door, stepped out.

Vicki followed her to where Leslie was waiting on the upper deck.

It was still very dark, but the faint twinkling lights of the city hung above them as if suspended in the cold air beneath the fading stars.

Vicki was swept along in the current of the surging passengers and onto the crowded dock. All was confusion here. Men shouted in words she barely understood. Heavily loaded carts rattled by behind straining horses. Wagons of every description lined up wheel to wheel to await the longshoremen. Doors slammed, dogs barked, and steam hissed in a smoky white cloud from beneath standing freight cars.

The crowd tightened into a knot to squeeze through an iron gate, then plunged outward, light a rope unraveled, into a thinning mass byond the gas lights high overhead.

Just at the edge of the shadows, well back from the hurry and scurry, Richard Cavendish stood waiting. He had had no single doubt in his mind in the four months since he had last seen Vicki, and at his first glimpse of her now, his certainty was confirmed. He wanted her more than ever, more than he supposed was possible for a man of his temperament.

At the same time that Vicki saw Richard, Leslie said, "Elise, look. There's Rosamund waiting for us."

The two groups moved toward each other.

Leslie grinned at Vicki. "The end of the voyage. But the beginning for you."

She didn't answer. She couldn't. They would separate now, but surely he would come for her. He loved her. Every glance, touch, kiss had told her so.

Then Richard was there, smiling at her, while his dark glance swept her in open and delighted approval. "Vicki. Welcome at last." His voice was rough, very deep; the dark of his hair, his eyes, sharp next to Leslie's golden look.

She sensed again the tension in Richard, the suggestion of implacable power held in restraint, and knew a familiar fear. Her gaze moved to touch Leslie. It would be all right.

Richard introduced his brother John. The younger Cavendish was slender. His longish hair was the color of wet sand, and his eyes were a bright hazel. He stood slightly off balance, with his weight on his right leg, favoring the left, which had been crippled at birth and was encased from toe to knee in a heavy corrective boot. There was something youthful in his face that made him seem less than his twenty-three years.

He grinned at Vicki when she cried, "I'm glad to meet you, John." And grinned more widely when she said to Richard, "You were right. I shall see Fall River after all."

"Rosamund," Elise was saying. "How good to see you. And," she added dryly, "to stand on firm land at last. What a voyage it was! I don't know how I survived it."

"A pity it was so difficult," Rosamund said. "But you must forget it now." She hugged Elise before she turned to raise her cheek for Leslie's kiss. But even as she spoke, she was staring at Vicki.

Rosamund was small, with dark hair drawn back into a severe chignon, and deep dark eyes. Her skin was fair, her nose just faintly crooked. She was twenty-eight, but there was nothing old-maidish about her. She wore an austere riding habit of black, with a tightly fitted jacket, and a full skirt that came to the tops of her shiny black boots. Her hat was a simple derby, with a black velvet band and a shimmering veil gathered into its curled brim. When she had embraced Leslie, she stepped back and continued to regard Vicki with open interest. Meanwhile she introduced Leslie and Elise to Richard, then to John. Her high breathless voice came to a stop while the four exchanged greetings, and then she went on, "This, of course, is your young cousin, Vicki, who has come to stay with you."

"Vicki Davelle," Richard said. And to Vicki, "I hope you didn't suffer on the crossing."

"I found it pleasant," she answered, and fought to keep her eyes from Leslie as she went on, "Leslie, that is, Mr. Winton, and Elise, were very good to me." Vicki smiled at Rosamund, but felt no warmth for her. "I thank you for arranging for me to travel with them."

Richard thought that there was a particular note in Vicki's voice when she spoke Leslie Winton's name. He wondered what it meant. He had already dismissed the man as soft, and without force, and had no further interest in him.

While the others were speaking, John had limped away, giving no explanation. Now he returned to say that he had arranged for both sets of luggage to be delivered to the two carriages, while Rosamund explained to Elise that the parties had come separately, since Rosamund was certain Elise and Leslie would want to go directly to the school.

Leading the way outside, John fell into step with Vicki. "It's not the best time to arrive, I fear," he said. "But the light's just beginning to come up now. The ship's schedule is adjusted to the tides instead of to the traveler's convenience."

"As long as I'm here," she answered. But her eyes went to where Leslie walked between Rosamund and Elise.

He had given Vicki the address of the school, and she had written down for him the Cavendish address. She began to wonder even then, before they had parted, when she would see him again.

The sky was streaked with the first fingers of pale light. The stars had faded. An icy wind blew along the waterfront, raising drifting clouds of powdered snow.

They stopped between the two carriages, shook hands around, and exchanged goodbyes.

Harry Beamis winked at Mitch Ryan, and Mitch carefully spat between his boots, then opened the door for Elise.

Richard drew Vicki away. She turned back to smile, to wave, to call out tremulously, "Thank you, Elise.

Thank you for everything, Leslie." Then, with one foot on the carriage step, she retreated. She pulled away from Richard and hurried a few steps toward Elise and Leslie. "We'll be together soon, won't we?"

"Of course we will." Rosamund's high breathless laugh was indulgent. "I'll attend to it myself, I promise you."

Richard's fingers closed once again around Vicki's elbow. They were tight, bruising, and it would have meant an open struggle to free herself if she had followed her instinct. She allowed him to hold her, to draw her back to the carriage, where Harry Beamis gave her a twinkling look. "Ready now, miss?"

Richard handed her up before she could reply. As she settled herself next to John, Richard took his place beside her, saying, "I hope Rosamund's cousins *did* look after you properly."

"I've arrived safely, haven't I?"

"It looks as if you have," he answered, smiling.

She turned to look through the half-curtained window. The riding lights of Rosamund's carriage disappeared as she watched. "I'll never forget how nice they were to me."

Richard believed less in tact than directness. He said, "They? Don't you mean Mr. Winton?"

She heard a faint bitter amusement in Richard's voice, saw that his hands were curled into fists on his thighs.

She had a swift recollection of the last time she had seen him. They'd stood alone on the stoop of the house, a slim moon overhead. He'd held her hands and kissed her deeply, and said, "Remember me," and she had promised that she would and fled indoors, enwrapped in a chill of fear she'd never forgotten. Now she understood that in the moment of her promise she had led him to believe more than she had intended.

It was because of that that Richard had sent for her. More than anything she wished she could be candid with him. But she didn't reply. Color rose slowly along the slender column of her throat, spread into her cheeks. She told herself that it was no concern of Richard Cavendish's. Yet she wanted to explain her feelings, tell him what had happened on the voyage. Fear alone held her tongue. Suppose she spoke of the love she had found? What would Richard do? It was conceivable to her that he might decide she must be sent home just as she had arrived. He could possibly conclude that he must separate her immediately from Leslie. So she dare admit to nothing. She and Leslie had made no plans yet, had exchanged no promises. She must bide her time for now.

She fixed her eyes on the scene beyond the window. The carriage riding lights twinkled at her through early dawn. The sun had not yet risen but the road was awash with a pale blue haze. Oil smoke drifted above some of the street lamps, yet from a block ahead there was the steady greenish haze of gas. The footways were crowded with hurrying women and men wrapped against the cold. Bells chimed for early Mass, and small clots of people surged through open doors of churches. The big granite buildings were beginning to spill light from high, wide windows. The horses danced skittishly as an electric trolley passed by, loudly clanging its bell, then danced again as one factory whistle, then another, shrilled through the gathering noise of carts and wagons and slamming gates.

Richard said, "A shipboard crossing is odd. One is thrown together with people and affected by them, but once one reaches land, the friendship that seemed so strong turns out to be of no consequence."

He sounded indulgent, but she saw that his hands were still fists.

"That must often happen," she agreed, her tone light. But she knew that nothing he said would convince her to feel otherwise than she felt. She would go where love took her.

John stirred, coughed behind his hand, but when she looked at him, he said nothing.

She studied the houses they passed. Each one seemed so very large that she was surprised until she realized that they were actually for two or three families, with separate entrances and porches.

The carriage made a sharp skidding turn, and Richard leaned against her, his shoulder pressing hard into hers for a long moment before he shifted his weight away. In that instant she felt a quick surge of alarm, a familiar one. She had been entrapped, imprisoned, a small, helpless beast at bay before a predator. Now again she remembered the last time she had seen him. She had fled into the house in the midst of their farewells, driven by that very same feeling.

He said now, "We're very nearly there. You'll meet my mother, and have something hot to drink, and perhaps you'd like to go to bed for a while."

"Oh, no," she laughed. "I shan't be able to do that. I'm too excited. I want to see everything that I can."

Again John stirred, but this time he offered to take Vicki for a drive, if Richard planned to go into the office.

Vicki said she would like that, thinking that she would enjoy getting to know John.

Richard agreed, said he would send Harry back with the carrriage after being dropped off at the mill.

Ahead there was a steep incline. The horses' hoofs slipped and skidded on icy cobblestones. The carriage rocked on sliding wheels.

"We're going into Highland Avenue," Richard told her.

A turn, then another. The carriage slowed, crunching through hard-packed mounds of crusty snow. The horses labored up a steep slope. Below, there were the tall smokestacks of the mills, their square bell towers, the narrow twisting roads where the sun was just beginning to shine on glass and steel and dirty snow. All the workaday bustle was there. Here, above, was a magical stillness. The roadway was white with snow, rutted by few wheel tracks. Overhead there were old arching trees, draped with icicles that glistened like strings of diamonds dropped from the skies. Empty walkways passed fine large homes, each one

48

set apart on spacious grounds, each in its own way reminding Vicki of some great manor house.

At last the carriage skidded to a stop, then angled into a narrow driveway.

"We've arrived," Richard said.

Vicki stared wide-eyed at the Cavendish house. It was set back from the street in the midst of a long sloping lawn that was blanketed in white, broken only by tiny footprints left by scampering squirrels. On either side of it the grounds stretched away for a huge full block, so that only the tall chimneys of its nearest neighbor were visible over a grove of hemlock trees.

The house was of granite, and two full stories high, with well-spaced large windows. Large chimneys smoked at either end of the center building. An ivy-grown porte cochere was at one side, and at the other, there was a long low room with a steep slanting roof. Beyond the house, at the end of the drive, there stood a small replica of the main building. It was a big carriage house, of two floors, with curtained windows on its upper level.

"Imposing . . ." Vicki breathed. "I'd no idea . . . you'd never suggested . . ."

John said proudly, "Richard designed it himself." He climbed down slowly, as Harry opened the door for him.

Richard got out, helped Vicki off the high step.

She thanked him. Then: "And thank you for sending for me, Cousin Richard."

His dark brows arrowed up. His mouth slanted in a grin. "Cousin Richard? I shan't settle for that formality."

"Richard, then."

"Better." He drew her toward the front door along a path of irregular flagstones that were filmed by a thin sheet of ice.

As she moved with him, her foot slipped, and she swayed against him. He lifted her easily into his arms, ignoring her gasp of protest, and carried her to the steps, and then up them, to the door.

Matilda Cavendish, watching from the curtained window, frowned.

A small, very thin girl, somewhat younger than Vicki herself, opened the door, smiling sleepily.

Richard set Vick down. The carpet beneath her feet was soft, thick. It was of various shades of dark blue with a center of shades of red in an Oriental design. The foyer had wallpaper that repeated muted tones of the dark blue, and a long narrow table of well-polished mahogany. The round wheel of the chandelier was hung with bell-shaped shades of red silk dangling a twisted fringe, and within them there glowed small incandescent bulbs.

As Vicki allowed Richard to help her off with her outer clothing, Matilda Cavendish opened the door of the drawing room. To the maid she said, "Bring us our chocolate in here, Nettie. And see to Miss Davelle's unpacking as soon as Harry brings in her things." With that attended to, she turned to Vicki and Richard. "Cousin Victoria, I'm glad you've arrived."

"And I'm happy to be here," Vicki answered. As she dropped a curtsey, she caught a quick gleam of dislike in Matilda's jet eyes, and wondered at it.

John went ahead, leading her into the drawing room. It, too, was large, but comfortable and subdued. There were a pair of China vases on the white mantel, and a large log fire burned in the grate, giving off the scent of pine. The walls were papered in an embossed linen-like finish, the pattern green flowers with sweet peas. The floor covering was silky, and without design, but a dark green, so that it was almost like a perfectly tended lawn. The furniture was all fine old mahogany that had been in Matilda's family for several generations. Two occasional chairs were covered in pink and red petit point, and the sofa was of the same deep red plush. On a marble-topped table there were small, gold-framed pictures of John and Richard, and beside them, a Rogers group, cast plaster showing a wedding party, the smiling minister, the happy groom and his shy bride, with a frisky dog as onlooker. Nearby there stood a tall cloisonné vase.

All was precisely as Matilda had wanted it. She had dismissed Richard's suggestions and suited her own taste. She had a deep dislike for ostentation. She distrusted it as wasteful, even uncouth.

She was tall, with black hair worn parted in the middle and wrapped around her head in tight braids. She was fifty-five and not a person of sentiment, but loved her sons devotedly. Even so, since her husband's death she had chafed at Richard's domination of the mill and the house. She had learned, though, that it was useless to oppose him. He would listen politely, and then with cool deliberation do exactly as he pleased.

The expansion of the mill had been one of his projects. The building of this house, which was far too large and ornate to satisfy Matilda's conservative tastes, was another. A third stood before her now.

Matilda had no more approved of the invitation to Vicki than she had of his other two undertakings. She had had no interest in her husband's distant relations. Richard's bland insistence had created an uneasiness in her. In the instant of seeing Vicki for the first time, Matilda's disapproval had become an active dislike. The girl was young, and much too beautiful, flauntingly so. And she had nothing to offer Richard.

One single question had burned in Matilda's mind in the months since Richard's return from England. It was answered now. Before he had departed, he had seen a good deal of Rosamund Dean. Since his return, he had not. To Matilda, Rosamund was eminently suitable to be Richard's wife.

But Matilda was careful not to mention her name while she poured the hot chocolate Nettie had brought on a silver tray, and passed thin butter cookies, and asked Vicki about the trip and her father, and made the unimportant conversation she was accustomed to make with strangers.

When Vicki refused a second cup of chocolate, a

51

last cookie, Richard rose. "I'll show you to your room before I leave for the mill."

Matilda pursed her lips, but remained silent. She had decided to visit Rosamund that very afternoon.

Vicki followed Richard, glad to be released from the weight of Matilda's presence. It had been a difficult three-quarters of an hour, and though Matilda had said nothing that Vicki could give as example, she had felt as if she were trying to converse with Mrs. McVey. There was the same sense of disapproving judgment.

The thought of Mrs. McVey reminded her that she must immediately write to her father. She mentioned that to Richard, and he said he would send off a cable. "I'll stop when I'm down street, so he'll know of your arrival more quickly, and you can write to him in fuller detail yourself."

She thanked him. Then: "Did you say 'down street'? Is that an American expression?"

"A Fall River expression. It means downtown. Where the shops and businesses are. Literally, down off the hill."

"Oh." She smiled. "Like the High Street at home."

"You'll learn American in no time." He grinned, and opened a white-painted door for her.

Startled, she paused on the threshold. The contrast between this place and the tiny lantern-lit room she had left in Rye was overwhelming. Here a large shallow bowl of stained glass, that she later learned came from Tiffany's, shaded an electric light bulb that spilled soft and glowing color on living quarters fit for a princess. The four-poster bed had a canopy of royal blue velvet that matched the velvet drapes of the three wide windows. Beneath those drapes, cream-colored lace fell in soft ruffled curtains to the deep pile of floor covering that was of the same royal blue, but with an intricate flower pattern in cream wool. There was a dressing table in one corner, a cheval glass in another. She recalled the jagged crack across the one she had left at home, and noted that this one was smooth and unmarred, and the reflection she caught of herself as she turned from it, was in no way divided.

"I hope you like it," Richard was saying. "I hope you'll be happy here, and I mean to see that you are."

"It's lovely," she breathed.

He took her by the shoulders, turned her around to face him. He drew her close. Hands cupping her cheeks, he tipped her head back and pressed his lips on hers.

For an instant she was dissolved into a thin coursing weakness. She didn't struggle. She couldn't move, so she was still in his arms. But when his mouth touched hers, she thought of Leslie. If only it was he who held her. If only it had been he who had brought her to this room. She twisted her head to one side, said sharply, "Let me go at once, Cousin Richard."

"Cousin Richard again?" His brows angled up.

"Let me go, Richard," she said, stressing his name.

But he held her, said, "I've waited a long time for you, and it seems much longer. I won't rush you, believe me. But some day you'll belong to me, Vicki. And some day you'll want to."

"Cousin Richard . . ." she began. Then: "Richard . . ." But she didn't know what to say, how to explain. Once again she thought of Leslie.

There were footsteps, the sound of humming on the stairs. Nettie appeared on the landing with a feather duster tucked under her arm.

Richard was momentarily distracted, and Vicki brought her arms up between them, thrust her small hands at his chest, and dodged into the room. As she threw the bolt home, she heard him swear under his breath.

She waited, her breath coming fast. After a moment she heard his footsteps retreating, and then Nettie's humming again.

Listening, Vicki scrubbed furiously at her lips, and then, turning to look at the room, she cried, "I'm here! I'm here!" She pulled off her hat and flung it aside, and swooped about in a wild and joyful dance.

Chapter 5

RICHARD TOLD HIMSELF THAT THE FAULT WAS HIS own. He'd had no right to suppose that her imagination had followed him through the months of being apart. His hunger had driven him to the behavior of an untried boy. As Harry drove him down street, Richard made up his mind that it wouldn't happen again. He'd be patient and court her as was her due.

He asked Harry to stop at the Postal Union office, and went in to send the cable to Alban Davelle. From there, Harry drove him to the mill.

He forgot his disappointment when he went outside. The new mill, the monument to his accomplishment of the past few years, never failed to please him, and to further his determination to put into effect his plans for the future as soon as possible. He thought in terms of a second plant beside this one, his object being the addition of new looms, but ones so made that there would be no enlargement of the work force.

He crossed the dim loading area, climbed the wooden steps. At the landing he paused to look down. Three men were busily employed at stacking raw cotton baled in burlap. After a moment, he went on.

He was so accustomed to the rhythmic slam of the shuttles as they hit the loom frames and flew back that he hardly noticed it, just as he hardly heard the whirring, buzzing, clanking that vibrated through the enormous room. Overhead there were pulleys, wheels, straps, ropes, gears and wheels. Each made its own sound, shifting the warm moist air necessary in a mill, not for the workers who breathed it, but to keep the spinning threads from breaking. Pale light caught the drifting dust motes, and made them gleam as they danced before the high floor-to-ceiling windows. The walls of the place were thick and bare. Heavy columns were carefully aligned to support the weight of the machinery on the floor above.

The word went along the rows as he approached, and though he couldn't hear the whispered murmurs, he knew the workers were saying, "King Richard is coming. Here comes the king." They had begun that years before, in derision. Then he had been his father's errand boy, though his father had always called him the strong right arm that made the difference between success and failure. In truth, his father had made the decisions, and with no advice asked or listened to. Though Richard didn't see it, he had become the same. Now when the whispered "King Richard" went up, it was in wry acknowledgment.

He went into the area he used as his office. It was beneath a window, and he had only the building wall on one side. There a framed set of a Charles Dana Gibson girl panel, cut from an issue of *Harper's Weekly,* brightened the drab stone. Richard had hung the panel himself, for the girl reminded him strongly of Vicki. Along the same wall there were rows of wooden file cabinets.

The other three sides of the area were separated from the rest of the loft by partitions in which glass windows were set, so that, when the door was closed, the ever-present noise was muted, though not shut away completely.

Richard's desk was large, scarred by the cigars his father had smoked over it for many years. Richard used it now without examining his reasons for doing so. A second desk, close by, was just as scarred.

Richard closed the door behind him, and nodded at the man who sat at the smaller desk. "Good morning, Ezra."

Ezra Saunders shoved aside the ledger over which he had been working, peered at Richard through small steel-rimmed spectacles. "Did Miss Davelle arrive as expected?"

"She did. And I turned her over to my mother and John. They'll keep her busy the rest of the day."

Ezra nodded, returned to his ledger.

Richard removed his coat, hung it on an old clothes-tree and sat at his desk.

"Price of coal went up again," Ezra mumbled.

"But we need it, don't we?" Richard said dryly.

"Cotton, too," Ezra muttered to the ledger.

"Something else we need," Richard answered. He picked up a copy of the previous day's *Fall River Daily Globe,* but only pretended to read it. He had already seen in "Globe Gossip" the item that said, *The Cavendish family of Highland Avenue anticipates the arrival of a houseguest, Miss Victoria Davelle of Rye, Sussex, England, for a protracted visit.*

Ezra's hairless head was speckled with brown spots. The back of his neck was cross-hatched with the fine wrinkles of age. He had been a fixture at the mill from its earliest days, a crony as well as employee of Richard's father. Along with the mill, Richard had inherited him, a relic of the past that refused to be put aside. He was somewhere between sixty-five and seventy years old, never more specific than that. He was a childless widower, and lived alone in a tenement, where he spent his Sundays making small wooden puppets for the neighborhood children. In his thirties he had served in Georgia with a Massachusetts regiment, the only time he had been out of Fall River. He had grown up with the textile industry, and had fought every change Richard had made with a resentment that bordered on terror. Richard had long wanted to be rid of him, but the man was too old to find other employment, and though he might have something put by, it wouldn't be much. Besides, he had worked all his life. What would he do with his time when he knew only the mill?

"There's hiring at Pacific," Ezra said.

"How many?" Richard asked. That Pacific was hiring surprised him, since most were not. Only two weeks before, the Sagamore Mills had proposed a wage cut, offering to allow the weavers to measure the finished cloth once a month to prove that production, and thus profit margins, had fallen. The weavers had refused, discussed a strike, then voted to postpone such action. Richard believed, however, that it would happen soon.

Ezra was saying, "I don't know how many they're taking on. I'm trying to find out."

"Bobbin boy!" The shout came clearly through the partitions. It was the signal that a bobbin was empty and the operator needed a full one. The cry went up so frequently during working hours that Ezra and Richard were as accustomed to it as they were to the noise of the flying shuttles, the rattle of pulleys and gears.

"Probably they'll be taking on more girls," Ezra added.

Richard nodded. Girls worked for less, and though many of them would need training, it wouldn't take long, and they could do most of the jobs as well as men could. In his own mill Richard had women working as carders, pickers, winders and inspectors. New England farm girls had been the mainstay of the industry in the old days of Lowell and Waltham, for instance, but that was no longer true in 1902.

"Oh, yes," Ezra said after a moment. "Mr. Albert Cosgrove was here earlier. On Board of Trade business, I think."

"Did he say what?"

"Something to do with the Textile Council." Open dislike tinged Ezra's voice. He and Richard shared this one thing in common. He disliked the Textile Council with the old-timer's suspicion of any type of union organization. Richard's feeling was more personal. He owned the mill. He'd have no one dictate hours, wages or working conditions to him. The Fall River Textile Council coordinated the activities of the locals, which were organized along the old English pattern of crafts, and dealt with the manufacturers for the union locals. On Richard's return from his trip abroad the previous October, he learned that the International Union of Textile Workers, which had never had much success, had consolidated with the American Federation of Labor to form the United Textile Workers of America, greatly improving its bargaining position. Richard had considered reactivating the Cavendish Company Union, formed in his father's time, but then decided against it, believing that the era of company unions was past. He knew that the Fall River Manufacturers' Board of Trade had kept a weather eye on union activity for years, and did so now in the person of Albert Cosgrove. Richard decided to see him as soon as it could be arranged.

Ezra suddenly swung back from his ledger again. "We need a loomfixer. I don't think Carter's going to hang on much longer, the way he's coughing and spitting."

Carter, too, had been inherited by Richard. He was not quite as old as Ezra, a magician with the many recalcitrant parts of the looms. He was probably the most important man in the mill when it came to keeping production up. He had been coughing for years. His hacking was as much a part of the noise of the loft as the slamming shuttles.

Richard waited. He knew that Ezra was leading up to something, backing into a suggestion he had, in hopes of getting Richard's agreement. Ezra, during Richard's absence abroad, had been acting superintendent, although John had dutifully reported to the plant every day. John had no interest in Cavendish and Sons, and was content to allow Richard to run the business as he saw fit. Unless Richard specifically asked him to, John wouldn't appear at the mill for months on end. On Richard's return, Ezra had backed into a suggestion in just the same way he was doing now. Then it had concerned John, and Ezra had finally come out with the stern hope that Richard would see to it that his younger brother took a more active part in the concern. Richard had laughed then, said, "Why burden him with what he doesn't want?"

But Ezra had something else on his mind now. Two

days before he had been walking in South Park. He'd seen a twelve-year-old boy standing alone, wistful eyes fixed on a crowd of young ice skaters. He'd stopped to talk with the boy, met his father soon after, and ended up by inviting them back to his tenement room for supper. The man's name was Gus Markeson. The twelve-year-old was Jamie. Ezra was taken with both. To Richard he said, "I know a mechanic, very experienced with looms. He's looking for work."

"And what about Carter?"

"They could work together," Ezra said, and added, "For as long as Carter can go on."

"Suppose you bring him in, this mechanic of yours, tomorrow."

It was thus that Richard came to see Gus Markeson for the first time.

There was snow early that day. It came down in thick swirling clouds for two hours before it stopped. Gus Markeson's white hair was crusted with it under the roll of the knitted cap he wore, and his outermost sweater of dark blue was whitened at the broad shoulders and sleeves by it. The small cap on the head of the boy he led in with him was frosted with it, too.

Ezra introduced the man, then departed on unstated business.

Richard waved man and boy to the straight-backed chairs near his desk. Gus Markeson sat down, took off his cap and dropped it to the floor beside him. He unbuttoned his sweater, and Richard saw dark green suspenders against a patched blue work shirt. When the older man smiled at his son, the boy, too, removed his cap, unbuttoned his sweater. In the warm moist air of the room, the flakes became large wet drops that sparkled in the light.

"My boy Jamie," Gus said. "He'll be in school tomorrow, if I can manage it."

"Hello, Jamie," Richard said.

The boy smiled shyly, his alert eyes fixed on Richard's face. Richard went on to the father, "Ezra tells me that you're a mechanic and loomfixer."

Gus nodded. He was a man of fifty-two, with white

hair, a long yellow-white mustache that drooped around the corners of his mouth and expressionless yellow eyes. His nose had been broken and healed unset. There was purple scar tissue under both his eyes.

"Worked at it long?" Richard asked.

"All my life. I started as a helper when I was Jamie's age. And never quit, but went up as I learned."

"And where have you worked?"

"New Jersey. At first. Then I had a spell out West doing other things." He paused, but didn't explain. It was politic that he leave to silence some of his past.

He had been thirty-four years old in 1886 when the Knights of Labor had three-quarters of a million members and was at the peak of its power, and he saw it break apart under the strain of competing internal forces. He watched the rise of the American Federation of Labor, that began as a cigar-makers union and was organized by crafts.

He had been at Homestead in 1892 when the Pinkertons were called in, and he took part in the fight when seven steel workers were killed along with three Pinkerton guards.

Now he was tired, and looking for a place to rest. All he had was Jamie, whom Gus called his son, although the boy had been an abandoned infant squalling under the stoop of a boarding house, where Gus first found him.

Now he said, "I came East to be a loomfixer again."

"I know Pacific is hiring," Richard said. "Did you try there?"

"Yes. And they'll have me." Gus didn't explain that he suspected the larger mills like Pacific employed spotters to pick out known union men.

Jamie sat so still that he seemed to hold his breath. His dark eyes were fixed on Richard's face. They were round with hope, aglow with admiration. Each time the shuttles banged, his small shoulders twitched.

Years before a boy his age would have worked in the mill as Richard's father had, and Gus, too. But now state law forbade the employment of children so young in mills and factories, and though they could work elsewhere, in shops, for instance, it couldn't be during school hours unless they attended night school. Richard would not have hired such children himself, but opposed the law that banned it.

Finally Richard asked Gus, "If Pacific will have you, then what are you doing here?"

"I like a smaller place."

"We're not all that small," Richard answered. And with a grin: "If you're on, we'd keep you busy."

"I like being busy."

Richard didn't know what it was, but something held him back. He eyed Gus doubtfully. He said, "You understand you'd be working with another man. Carter. He's been with us for years."

"Mr. Saunders told me. I don't mind that." Gus gathered himself as if to get to his feet, but Jamie slipped from his chair, and went to lean against his father, seeming to hold him in his place.

With his eyes on the boy, Richard said, "You can start tomorrow. We'll try you for a few weeks and see how it goes." He thought of the old agreement, very common in previous years, called a yellow dog contract. His father had left the forms in his desk. They remained there. Richard never asked a man to sign his name to a promise not to join a union if hired, which was what a yellow dog contract was. A man, Richard considered, could sign anything. That was no way to prevent unions.

"Anything else?" Gus asked. He was waiting for the question, and was prepared to be truthful. He had been a founder-member of the National Loom-fixers Union since it was organized two years before. Now it had some fifteen hundred members. But he was no longer one of them. He thought now that only one union for skilled and unskilled workers, as the Knights of Labor had been, could present a united face to the owners of production centers. But he was battle-scarred and weary. All he wanted was work, a place for him and Jamie.

"I'll see you tomorrow," Richard said, as Gus got up. Jamie didn't speak, but it looked as if a candle had begun to shine behind his eyes. He turned to look back at Richard before he followed Gus out.

Watching, Richard decided that the big man would probably work out, but if not, nothing would be lost. He could be let go if Richard found a reason for it. Richard turned to look at the drawing of the Gibson girl who looked so much like Vicki.

"What did you think?" Ezra asked from the doorway.

"I took him on. If it works out, I'll keep him. You'd better explain to Carter."

"I have," Ezra answered. "He's not happy, at least that's what he told me. But between us, I think he's relieved." Ezra himself was very relieved. Now that Gus had a job it would be easy to persuade him to stay on with Jamie in the Bogle Hill tenement with him.

As Ezra settled at his desk, Richard looked through the windows at the looms. He knew that among the men who worked for him there were those who belonged to unions of the four most important crafts in the business. The Slashers, Carders, Weavers, and Spinners were each organized now. He felt no animosity for those who paid their dues, but he respected old Carter, the loomfixer, who had refused to join the Loomfixers' Association because of an old-fashioned and tough individualism. Now Richard rose, took a few restless paces back and forth.

He paused at the window. The sky was a dull gray. An icicle that hung from the roof was thickening and lengthening. The yard below, where carts and horses moved, was churned with snow and dung and mud. He looked at the grandfather clock in the corner. It was just barely nine.

He went to the desk, settled down to work over his production figures. The next time he looked at the clock it was nine-thirty. He sighed, wishing that what seemed to him an endless day were already over.

At noon, he rose quickly. He always took his midday meal at home, but he had never before been so anxious for it.

Harry had the carriage at the gate, and it didn't take longer than usual to reach Highland Avenue, but it seemed to Richard that every cart in the city dawdled along the way in front of his fast-stepping horses.

Nettie met him at the door, took his coat and told him, when he asked, that only his mother was waiting for him, that John and Vicki had gone out.

Richard hoped that he hid his disappointment when he suggested she bring in the soup.

His mother sat at the foot of the big table. She smiled and said, "Did you tell Nettie to start serving?"

"Yes." He seated himself, unfolded the linen napkin and put it on his lap. He took a sip of water, wishing now that he had forgone the meal. He could have sent out for a sandwich and coffee, and stayed at his desk, which would have done him just as well.

His mother asked, "Is anything new at the mill?" It was a question she asked every day, as she had asked it before of his father. Richard had never realized until that moment how much it irritated him. But he managed a civil "Nothing much."

Nettie brought in a steaming tureen of pea soup with bits of ham floating in it. After she had filled the serving bowls, she offered warmed brown bread to Matilda, then to Richard.

When she had gone, Matilda said, "I hope it will go nicely tonight."

"Tonight?" Richard asked blankly.

Matilda stared at him. "You *are* distracted today, aren't you? Surely you remember that we're having a small dinner party for Victoria this evening?"

"Oh, yes," he said, and grinned. "I don't know how it slipped my mind." He paused, then asked the question he had been wanting to ask ever since he came into the room. "And where is Vicki now?"

"John took her out in the sleigh." Matilda's voice held faint disapproval. "It appears that Victoria will be his new vocation."

"You don't object, do you?"

"No." But she sounded doubtful. "You know, Richard, we've never discussed how long you intend Victoria to visit with us."

"It didn't occur to me."

"Surely she's given you some idea . . ."

"We haven't spoken of it. I see no reason to." Richard's glance was level, forbidding. "Is there a purpose to your having raised the question?"

"No." But again Matilda sounded doubtful.

He ignored that. "Who'll be here this evening?"

"Rosamund, of course."

"Of course."

"And Mrs. Parker. With her brother."

Richard said nothing. He had supposed that Elise and Leslie would be asked to the Cavendish house at least this once.

"And Albert and Eustacia Cosgrove."

He raised his brows. "I *did* want to see Albert. But aren't they rather old for Vicki?" They were middle-aged. Albert had five mill corporation directorships, as well as his work for the Manufacturers' Association, for income. His wife was a gossip who had no peer, in Richard's opinion.

"For Vicki?" Matilda was saying. "I hadn't thought of it. I dined at the Cosgroves' ten days ago. You'll recall that you were invited and begged off. Which is why I felt obliged to have them so soon."

"They'll do, I suppose," Richard answered.

When he finished his soup, Nettie removed the plates, brought thick sandwiches of hot roast beef with horseradish, boiled potatoes and a slaw of wilted red and white cabbage. After she poured the coffee, she left the dining room.

Matilda gave Richard a careful smile. He waited patiently, already certain of what was to come.

"I've wondered," she said, "if you and Rosamund have had some falling out."

"I suspected that might come up about now." Then: "No, we've had no falling out. I'm not interested in her."

"I hardly see why not. She's most suitable."

"And there's money in the family," Richard added. "Which we no longer need."

"What an extraordinary remark," Matilda retorted. "Everyone needs money. But it's rude to speak of it. I should have thought you knew better than that."

"And I should have thought you'd be accustomed to my manner of plain speaking. Why beat around the bush? You'll always want more money to hoard. I'll always want more to spend as I please."

"But we're speaking of Rosamund's suitability," Matilda answered.

"Which I admit to, but which doesn't matter," Richard told her.

The trip to England had changed him, whether for good or ill he didn't know, nor did he care. He was certain, however, that the change was forever. In the four months since his return, he had managed for the most part to avoid seeing Rosamund alone. But three times he had been trapped by circumstance. Once he had taken her driving, at his mother's instigation. Another time he had escorted her to a dinner party, again something his mother had arranged. The third time he had met her by chance on North Main Street and allowed her, out of politeness, to serve him tea at her home. He had noted the quick warm looks she sent him, the way her hand lingered on his when she passed him the teacup. He had made up his mind to avoid her from then on.

"How peculiar," Matilda said. "I do wonder what made you change. You seemed interested in her for a while, you know. And she . . . indeed, I don't doubt that she would accept you."

"Forget it," he answered. He was determined to allow his mother no notion of what he planned. Given any hint of what he wanted, she would do what she could to frustrate him. It was in her nature to count on what she considered a good marriage for him.

She realized it wouldn't do to press him further. She changed the subject by asking if Richard would need Harry that afternoon. When Richard said that he

wouldn't, she suggested that she drop him at the mil
and have Harry take her shopping down street, and
return to collect Richard at six o'clock.

He nodded agreement. Within a year or two, he
would order a motor car, perhaps a Locomobile, perhaps a Haynes. He was only waiting to see what the
new models would be like. Meanwhile he decided that
he must have another conveyance to use himself so
that the carriage would be available always for Vicki's
use. And for his mother's, too, he told himself as an
afterthought. He would ask John to stop in at Wm.
Anderson on Bank Street to see what sort of one-horse,
two-passenger wheeler was being offered.

At six that evening, Harry was waiting. The hill
was icy again. There was the hint of more snow to
come in the air. The bare limbs of the trees glistened
in the pale lights of the street.

The drawing room was empty when he arrived.
He heard sounds from the dining room, went to look.
Mrs. Beamis was examining the table settings. He
withdrew as she nodded at him, her thoughts on her
sixteen-year-old daughter, Nettie. Mrs. Beamis moved
salad forks and dessert spoons. She told herself that
the girl wouldn't keep her mind on her work. She was
all eyes for Mitch Ryan, who, in Mrs. Beamis' opinion, wasn't good husband material, though he did have
a nice laugh and dimples. Mrs. Beamis headed for the
kitchen, calling ahead softly, "Nettie? Nettie, I need
to speak to you."

Upstairs, in his bathroom, Richard shaved with the
straight-edged razor he kept on the shelf over the
marble sink top. It was a chore he disliked, and he
cursed when he nicked his chin, but he had a heavy
dark beard that required twice-daily attention if he
were to appear presentable. When he had changed,
he went down to the drawing room again.

Vicki sat near the fire. She wore a simple blue skirt
and a white shirtwaist. Its collar had a tiny frill. The
heart-shaped brooch he remembered having seen before was pinned to it. The firelight gleamed in her
shining amber hair, and in the deep blue of the wary

66

eyes she raised to him. It seemed hardly possible, but she was more beautiful than ever.

She had been in the house only a day and a half, yet everything was changed. The emptiness he had always noticed before was banished. The air which had once been so still now hummed with expectation.

This was the first time he had seen her alone since he had foolishly allowed his feelings to overwhelm him. Given time she would see, as he had from the first, that they had been made for each other and belonged together. Yet he wanted to wipe from her mind all memory of those few too-revealing moments, to set her at ease with him so that she would permit to grow what he was certain must follow.

He said, smiling, "We can be friends, can't we, Vicki?"

"Of course, Cousin Richard." She smiled back at him, relieved. She had begun to think he would stand over her, silent and staring, forever. His tone was easy, his voice kind. Still, she felt the constraint of memory . . . His mouth on hers . . . his hands on her shoulders . . . his hoarse whisper, "I've waited a long time . . . one day you'll belong to me."

"Cousin Richard?" he demanded.

"Richard," she said.

He poured a small glass of sherry for her, one for himself. When he brought it to her, she thanked him. When he asked how she had spent the day, she told him about the sleigh ride with John. They had gone a long way on Highland Avenue, then returned home and changed to the carriage. Then they had driven down Plymouth Street into Second Street. There, John had stopped before a house and said, "This is where the Borden murders happened," and with a grin, "Fall River's claim to fame." She had shuddered. The place looked so ordinary. The house was plain, a barn behind it. Once, she supposed, it had been a good street, fashionable even, but now it looked gone to seed. She was glad when they drove off. But no more than half an hour later, John turned the carriage into a narrow, tree-lined road called French Street, though she didn't know why. There he stopped again. "And this is where Liz Borden lives now." Vicki had looked at the house known as Maplecroft and shuddered once more, and turned away, murmuring, "It's morbid, I think, to come here." But John had laughed. "I promised to show you the sights. And this is one of them. But there are others, so we'll go on." She had enjoyed being with him. Though he was the elder, she felt as if he were a younger brother. She had already begun to understand why he was so quiet when there were others about him, why when he sat in a chair he carefully thrust his bad leg well back and out of sight. The knowledge made her feel close to him. But now, all the while she was telling Richard about what she had seen, her delight at the snow, the jingling sleigh bells, the comfort of the carriage later, her ears were cocked for the sound of horses' hoofs in the driveway outside.

Her thoughts leaped ahead, trying to imagine the moment when she would at last see Leslie again. In spite of the excitement she had felt in exploring her room, hanging away her clothes, in spite of her special pleasure in John's company, the day and a half since she had said goodbye to Leslie seemed years to her. The need for him blunted her perceptions. All the fevered hope for the future that she had burned with in Rye was concentrated now on him. When she had written to her father she had barely managed to include a description of Matilda, John, of the house, because Leslie had been so much in her thoughts that she wanted to write only of him.

Outside there was the rattle of a carriage, the crunch of frozen snow. Quick footsteps hurried down the hall at the knock on the door.

Richard said, "That's probably the Cosgroves. They always arrive a bit early and leave a bit late."

Vicki smoothed her skirt nervously. First the Cosgroves. Then, surely, Leslie and Elise . . .

Matilda ushered the small plump couple into the room, and made the introductions. They looked more like brother and sister than man and wife. Both were pink-cheeked and wore spectacles, but Albert Cosgrove had a single lock of brown hair combed forward over his bald head, and wore thick brown handlebar mustaches, while Eustacia Cosgrove had an enormous pompadour consisting of rolled and plaited and puffed-out switches.

"And you're the English visitor," Eustacia beamed. "I've heard so much about you from Matilda, and from Rosamund, too. You must tell me all about your country, Miss Davelle. I'm a Yankee, that is, of English stock, too. And so is my husband. Although we've never been to England, we should like to go some day. But first things first. And there's always Newport."

"Oh, yes," Vicki said politely with not even a faint idea of what Eustacia was talking about.

"And you'll go there, I'm sure," Eustacia went on, "to Newport, I mean." She sank into a chair, her well-corseted figure breaking into two balanced sections, the great curve of her bosom offsetting the great curve of her buttocks. "Though I'll confess that the very best people don't always behave in the very best way."

"My dear," Albert Cosgrove murmured, his voice pained.

It was, Vicki was to learn during that evening, a frequent comment of his.

Eustacia ignored it. "I was in New York last week. Shopping. And stopped at Henry Maillard's for luncheon, on Broadway at Twenty-fourth Street, you know. They had delightful confectioneries, but some of the ladies there were not quite . . ." She gave Matilda a meaningful look. "Painted, you see."

"My dear," Albert repeated.

She was diverted by John, who came silently into the room, and took a seat, immediately hiding his booted foot.

Richard took advantage of the opportunity to draw Albert Cosgrove aside. "You came in to see me this morning?"

Albert's face grew glum. "I did. About the State Federation of Labor. You know they met in Holyoke last October. Come next October they meet again in Brockton. Very active, these agitators, Richard. They have our streetcar men, coal teamsters and station agents, as well as textile workers. I don't like it."

"We'll deal with them, if we have to," Richard said.

"And there's talk of forming a Massachusetts Federation of Labor."

"It'll take time," Richard answered, shrugging.

"Old Judge Edwards was right in 1836 when he said trade unionism is a criminal conspiracy, John Whittier notwithstanding."

Richard grinned. "We've come a way since then, Albert."

It was then that Rosamund arrived with Elise and Leslie.

Vicki waited in still expectation while the newcomers were made welcome and introduced to the Cosgroves. Then, Elise gave her a friendly smile, asked how she was, while Leslie nodded at her, and accepting a glass of sherry from Richard, leaned against the mantel and engaged Richard in conversation.

It seemed as if she were invisible to Leslie after that single nod. When the group went into the candle-lit dining room, Leslie was seated at the far end of the long table near Rosamund, who was on Richard's right. Vicki was bracketed between Mr. Cosgrove and John.

She tried to catch Leslie's eye over the tall crystal candelabra, but he seemed not to notice.

Rosamund led the conversation, speaking of the school Elise had purchased, drawing her and Leslie into describing it.

"Fifty boys," Elise sighed, "are a handful. Particularly such boys, you know. They've had no discipline. I can't think that American parents realize what they're doing. Why, at home, it would never be allowed. Still, we'll see to it, won't we, Leslie?"

"We will indeed." He smiled at his sister, stroked

his beard. "But it may take some time and some doing." To the company at large, he explained, "We'll be assuming our authority gradually, you see. Moving in, so to speak, by bits and pieces. Our full responsibility will only begin at June's end. And then, of course, we shall see daylight."

"You'll be building, I suppose?" Albert asked. "If you plan to expand, that is."

"Not for some time, I fear," Elise answered. "We'll maintain what we have, and see to some improvements. Perhaps, in another few years, if all goes well, we'll add another house. Then we'll be able to board eighty boys."

"Things *will* go well," Rosamund said in her high sweet voice.

Vicki allowed the conversation to drift past her. She sat fighting her disappointment by telling herself that Leslie couldn't speak to her in the presence of so many strangers. Perhaps later, after the men had had their cigars, there would be an opportunity, or he would make one.

But the evening went by, and she had still not spoken to him. When Rosamund rose to say good night, the others rose with her.

Matilda said they must all get together soon again, and when Elise agreed, Rosamund promised to arrange it. Leslie suggested that Matilda and Vicki, as well as the Cosgroves, visit the school one day, and Matilda said she would see to it.

So Vicki went up to bed happy after all. Soon, she thought, they would drive out to the school. She would find a means of speaking to Leslie. She would make him remember their moments together on the ship crossing, if he had forgotten them. She would give both of them more moments to remember if he had not.

At dawn, while snow drifted slowly against the window, she fell asleep and dreamed of holding him in her arms.

Mitch tucked his chin into his collar and swore. The wind off the Taunton River was icy and promised more snow before morning. The few dollars he had won from Harry at cards wasn't nearly enough. Nettie had been busy serving the company in the big house, so he hadn't even had a chance to tip a a wink at her.

From behind him, he could hear faint snatches of conversation. Elise had been enthusiastic about the Cavendishes and their home. About Richard. Rosamund had agreed, but with restraint. Tall blond-bearded Leslie, whom Mitch had loathed on sight, was saying, "Vicki is fortunate to have found such a home."

The English, Mitch told himself. They always land on their feet. He raised his whip and lashed the horses, his narrow mouth turning down. The carriage jolted, and Rosamund cried from within that he must take it more slowly.

They, riding inside, were in no hurry, Mitch thought. It was always that way. What did they care if he froze his ass off?

It was the same in Galway, where he'd been born. His mother, God rest her soul, had carried him in her arms, and carried nothing else with her, when she came to Boston with his Uncle Shamus. Mitch, with his mother's thin milk, had taken in hate for the English. It had grown through each of his twenty-four years. He blamed the English for every one of the many beatings his Uncle Shamus had given him, for it was the English who had hunted down Mitch's own father and killed him by hanging, and left Mitch at the mercy of Shamus. And it was the English, too, who had made Shamus a twisted and bitter man, who lived only for guns to ship to men like himself in Galway.

Mitch lashed at the horses again. Money for guns. That was what Shamus understood. One day he would provide it, Mitch promised himself. Then the two of them would drink together, and sing the old songs, and Shamus would smile at him again.

Chapter 6

IT WAS A FULL MONTH BEFORE VICKI SAW LESLIE
again. In that time, no mention was made of a visit to
the school, and she felt uncomfortable about suggesting it herself.

Her time had been well occupied. Richard had
brought home four bolts of fabric, one a bengaline,
another a silk; two were of summer-weight cambric.
Matilda had had her own dressmaker in, and Vicki
had stood through innumerable fittings. Now the large
walk-in closet in her room was crowded with gowns,
with the matching cashmere shawls Richard had insisted that she buy, with a beaver-trimmed coat and
matching muff that he had had made for her in Boston, guessing perfectly her size and what style would
please her.

There had been only a few outings. Once she had
gone iceskating on Watuppa Pond, while John
watched from the bank. Another time, Richard and
John had taken her driving in South Park, where they
had flung walnuts to the squirrels and breadcrumbs
to the birds.

Always she hungered to see Leslie, but the days
passed, and when they finally met again it was
at Rosamund's house.

Matilda informed Vicki only that morning of the
engagement, saying, "It's to introduce Elise and Leslie
to some of Rosamund's friends. There'll be quite a
large number of people, and a musicale after supper.
We'll leave here at six-thirty. You will be ready, won't
you?"

Vicki promised that she would be, although Matilda plainly didn't listen to her answer. The barely veiled admonition to be punctual was Matilda's way of covertly expressing her disapproval. Increasingly she directed these small comments at Vicki, reminding the younger girl more and more of Mrs. McVey.

This time Vicki wasn't troubled by Matilda's words. She rushed upstairs, planning what she would wear. Surely Leslie would find a moment for her that night.

She looked lovely in a new gown of blue bengaline with a matching cashmere shawl draped from her bare shoulders, and a matching bow in her piled-high curls. But as the evening progressed she was increasingly convinced that how she looked didn't matter. Never mind that Richard smiled his approval. Never mind that Rosamund's eyes had narrowed with jealousy, and Elise had been cool. Vicki was introduced to dozens of people and didn't remember their names. She nibbled at a lavish meal and hardly knew what she ate. Afterwards she listened to the music and didn't know what she heard.

Elise was constantly at Leslie's elbow. She greeted Vicki, the rest of the family, clinging to his arm. He said, "Good evening, Mrs. Cavendish. How are you, Vicki?" Then he turned to Richard and John.

How are you, Vicki? Those were the only words he spoke to her. A brisk shake of her hand was the only time he touched her. Slowly she sank into a numb despair.

How was she to see him, talk to him? John sighed beside her. She decided then. She would ask him to drive her to the school. He was always eager to do whatever she wanted. He had taught her the use of American money so thoroughly that she was already able to calculate in it without trouble. He had shown her how to mount a horse, and was beginning to give her riding lessons. No matter what wish she expressed, he saw to its fulfillment in a way that touched her. Yes. She would ask John and see what he said.

She determined on that at the moment that Richard loomed over her, holding a crystal cup of punch for her. From across the room, she saw Leslie's glance touch her and linger. She smiled at Richard through her lashes, dimpled her cheeks. "Thank you," she murmured, with another quick look at Leslie. He was still watching intently. She asked Richard, "Do you know all these people?"

"I do," he answered.

"Rosamund is very sweet," Vicki said.

Richard didn't answer that, and a moment later Matilda came to ask him to speak to an acquaintance of hers.

John said, "I wish it were time to go home." He wouldn't have been there at all but for Vicki. He found such affairs tedious. He saw her look at Leslie before she answered, "So do I, John."

At last the evening came to an end. Harry drove them the two blocks home. The front lights were on at the house, glistening on the snow sheets blown across the sloping lawn by the March wind.

Matilda frowned. "I wonder what Nettie's thinking of." She allowed Harry to help her from the carriage and hurried inside.

Nettie stood in the foyer, wringing her hands, while Mrs. Beamis lingered in the kitchen doorway. "Oh, Mrs. Cavendish, a cable's come. We didn't know what to do."

Richard took it from her, saw that it was addressed to Vicki. "For you," he said. Then: "Shall I?"

She shook her head, took it from him. She was barely able to open it. Her fingers trembled. She felt a pulse beat behind her eyes. It was less than two months since she had left home. What could have happened? The words leaped up at her and then faded before a sudden blur of tears.

"What is it?" Richard asked.

Matilda stood waiting, a frown cutting her forehead with deepening lines.

John took the flimsy from Vicki, read it quickly and took her hand in his and held it as hard as he could. Then he looked at Richard, saying, "Alban Davelle is dead."

75

Chapter 7

Two weeks later the letter from Mrs. McVey arrived. She wrote to say that Vicki's father had fallen ill only ten days after her departure. He had been adamant that she not be told. He lingered on, bedridden but not in pain, and spoke often of his satisfaction that Vicki would have the opportunity in America that she wouldn't have had at home, and that she was with her relations, and wouldn't be left alone. He died early one morning, having a nap, after two cups of strong tea. The house lease expired with his going, Mrs. McVey continued, and she would have to empty it. She would sell, with Vicki's permission, its contents and send Vicki a bank draft for the proceeds. She had already packed and sent by ship those items she believed Vicki would want, which included her father's Bible, the picture of Vicki's mother, and some bric-a-brac of no great value. On her own blasted hopes, Mrs. McVey had no comment to make.

By then, Vicki was able to read these words calmly. She had wept until she could weep no more. She had accepted the burden of self-reproach for having left her father to die alone but thinking of her. When she had so eagerly embraced the chance Richard had offered her, she hadn't realized that she was closing a door behind her that could never again be opened. She saw that clearly now.

Richard and John had been kind to her in her bereavement, seeking to distract her, offering her continual reassurance. Mrs. Beamis and Nettie had tried to tempt her into eating. Harry had taken her on long quiet drives along the river. But there was a growing discomfort in Vicki. While Matilda pretended to sympathy, she stopped treating Vicki as a guest and began to ignore her.

There was, as Vicki saw it, nothing to look forward to and nothing to hope for. Leslie was the center of her thoughts, but she hadn't heard from him.

It was Rosamund, finally, who brought them together.

One Friday afternoon Vicki sat in the morning room. The sun warmed her through tall glass windows, its brilliance burning along the walls. She could almost believe that it was summer. Yet the snow had only just begun to melt, and the wind remained cold, for spring was slow in coming.

Outside there was a long loud cry. "Pond lilies! Pond lilies for sale! Buy your pond lilies now!"

She leaned to look. At the foot of the sloping lawn, a horse and wagon had drawn up. Great basins filled with water held a profusion of thick-petaled plants. As she watched, Harry hurried down the driveway.

She returned her attention to the embroidery hoop on her lap, but didn't work at it. Owen Wister's *The Virginian,* a new novel bought for her by Richard, was on the table close by, but she hadn't begun to read it. She heard John's limping step beyond the door, and looked up expectantly. He would distract her from the dismal emptiness of her thoughts.

He wore his outdoor clothing, and carried hers. "Dress," he told her, grinning. "Rosamund's waiting. We're going for a drive."

"Rosamund?" Vicki asked, surprise in her voice. Rosamund had always been civil to her, but nothing more. It had taken Vicki only a short time to realize that Rosamund considered her a rival for Richard's interest. Vicki wished there were some way she could demonstrate to the other girl that she didn't care for Richard, but didn't know how to do it.

She put on her coat, then threw her shawl over her hair. In the hall, Matilda eyed her up and down, and

77

said coldly, "Ladies, in Fall River, wear hats, and not shawls, when they go out. The Irish domestics wear shawls and the Portugee wear red scarves."

It was another expression of Matilda's feeling about the Irish and the Portuguese, but also about herself, Vicki knew. She made no attempt at reply.

But John told his mother, "Never mind. We're just going for a ride."

Rosamund smiled as he helped Vicki to the seat. "It's a nice day for an outing," she told Vicki. And, leaning to the driver, "Mitch, stop first at Mrs. Wood's grocery."

He flicked the reins. It was all one to him. He didn't care where they went. The carriage rolled from under the porte cochere into the driveway and turned into Highland Avenue. Soon it swung into Rock Street, the horses slipping on the steep hill.

After several familiar blocks and a few more turns, Vicki, watching the route, was suddenly lost. This was a part of town she didn't recognize. There were several small clapboard houses with three-step stoops and no front yards. There was a livery stable, which emitted the pungent odor of horse droppings. Close by were several shops, windows dingy and paint weathered.

Mitch stopped before one and helped Rosamund down. She asked, "Vicki, would you want to come in with me? Perhaps you've not been in such an establishment before."

Vicki followed her inside. Rosamund ordered potatoes, many pounds of chopped meat, porridge by what seemed the bushel. To Vicki it appeared food enough for a small army. She forgot her wonder at that when she looked around. The shop reminded her of the tobacconist's where she had briefly worked in Rye. It was a vast conglomeration of goods and odors, of shelves and stacks and counters. But its owner was not the small elderly man who had hired her. Here the owner was a woman, plump and pink-cheeked, with wispy white hair and worried blue eyes. Recalling her father's pained disapproval when she had taken the job, Vicki winced. He had wanted only the best for her always.

"Thank you, Mrs. Wood," Rosamund was saying. "You'll put it on the bill, won't you?"

The elderly woman nodded, and Mitch carried the packaged goods out.

Vicki trailed after, looking back to smile at the shopkeeper, but she had already gone behind a flowered curtain.

John tucked Vicki into the heavy Scottish wool rug as they drove away.

Soon the traffic of carts and wagons and buggies thinned; the rows of houses disappeared. They were on the open road, driving between still snowy fields bordered by stone fences, past occasional farms.

Until Vicki saw the sign, she had no idea of their destination. Then, smiling, she said, "The school, Rosamund! Are we visiting Elise and Leslie?"

"We are." Rosamund said crisply. "Elise suggested that you and John might enjoy it." In fact, it had been Rosamund's own suggestion. And there had been a purpose behind it. Elise, Rosamund knew, would have been less than enthusiastic unless provided with a good reason to cultivate the Cavendishes. Rosamund had provided it.

They drove past two stone buildings, ivy-covered from ground to roof, with brown doors and matching window trim. They stopped before a small ivy-covered cottage. Elise waited on the stoop to greet them.

She smiled warmly, then bent her auburn head to press her cheek to Vicki's. "We were so sorry about your father. We'd have come to you, but were certain that your family would take good care of you, and felt we mustn't intrude."

Vicki murmured acknowledgment, but her eyes searched the stoop, the windows. Where was Leslie?

Elise led the way inside, took their coats, saying, "It must have been a shock for you, Vicki."

"We mustn't dwell on it," Rosamund said.

"Of course," Elise agreed. Then: "We have an unexpected guest today. A gentleman from Boston, who's thinking of enrolling his son."

Rosamund moved from the tiny foyer into the parlor, as if she and not Elise were mistress of the place. The others followed her.

Leslie was leaning an elbow on the mantel, saying, ". . . and not so far that it would be inconvenient . . ." He broke off the sentence. "Ah, Rosamund, John." He looked at Vicki for a long moment, then came to her and took her hands. "My dear, what pity it had to happen."

Vicki, so intensely aware of his touch, hardly noticed the presence of the man who had already risen to his feet.

But Leslie turned from her as Elise said, "Rosamund, may I present Mr. Davis Peabody, of Boston?"

The two exchanged greetings, then Elise completed the introductions, and rang for tea.

John took a chair in the corner as always, and Rosamund sat on the settle beside Davis Peabody.

He was a man of forty, with dark hair gone gray at the temples and a small dark mustache. He said, "I hope I'm not intruding. It was a spur of the moment decision on my part to visit today. I was in Fall River on business and it seemed sensible to come now."

"Of course you're not," Elise told him. "We'll have tea, and then we'll show you about the school. My friends are here for that purpose, too."

Rosamund asked, "How old is your son, Mr. Peabody?"

"He's ten. And a handful," Davis Peabody grinned. As he went on, his grin disappeared. "I've been a widower for three years. He greatly misses his mother."

"Then it would be good for him to be among boys his own age," Rosamund said.

Vicki sat on a brown velvet love seat with Leslie beside her. While the others continued their conversation, he asked, "Do you have any plans?"

As she shook her head, she noted that Rosamund looked at her sharply, and Elise became very still.

John said, "She'll remain with us, of course."

But Vicki murmured to Leslie, "I'm not sure what I'll do." When he didn't reply, she looked around the parlor. It was a neat room, not luxurious but comfortable. It had a white marble mantel, gray rep drapes, a plain gray carpet on the floor. She could easily imagine herself living here with Leslie.

Later, after tea and cakes, Elise and Leslie took them on a tour. They left the headmaster's cottage and went to the adjacent buildings. Both had common rooms on the first floor, with deep chairs and stools and tables. Both had well-polished floors and gray-papered walls. From every direction there came the sounds of their young residents, laughing, arguing, shouting.

For an instant Vicki imagined herself wearing a plain blue dress, white collared and cuffed, a shawl at her shoulders, smiling down at an eager young face.

Then Elise said, "Mr. Peabody, you must see the boys' quarters," and he nodded agreement.

She led the way, the others following. They saw several rooms, he murmuring appreciatively.

Downstairs again, Elise asked, "Would you like to see the grounds?" and Vicki reminded herself that Elise was mistress here, and likely to be forever.

Leslie smiled. "Our grounds are what you see as you drive up.'"

Rosamund cut in, "The real problem is that there's no athletic field." She turned to John. "The fault is mine. I hadn't thought about the importance of that."

"Yes." Davis Peabody was thoughtful. "I suppose it *is* important. But there's room enough for a game of ball." He slipped his watch from his waistcoat and looked at the time. "Ah, it's later than I had imagined. I must start for Boston." He made his farewells, and went out, accompanied by Leslie.

Rosamund took Elise by one arm, John by the other, and drew them with her. "Let's show off your fascinating kitchens, Elise. Those, at least, I chose wisely."

Vicki hung back. She heard the sound of a door

closing, and deliberately dropped her reticule. She had just retrieved it when Leslie joined her.

"I'm glad to see you," she said. "I'd begun to think it would never happen."

He glanced down the hall. The others were beyond the closed kitchen door. He could hear Elise speaking. He said, "We can't talk now, Vicki. I do the grocery shopping for the school at Mrs. Wood's on Thursday, where Rosamund stopped today. Can you meet me there next week, at three o'clock?"

"Oh, yes," she breathed. "I can. I will."

The rest of the visit passed for her in a blur of happiness. She began, even as she pretended to listen to the others' conversation, to count the hours until the following week.

The sun had warmed. The ice had thawed, and the snow had begun to melt. Fast-moving streams awash with sodden paper and brown leaves overflowed the gutters. The sky was a sharp blue, smudged here and there by wisps of smoke from the mills' towering stacks.

Vicki slipped from the house and walked quickly down Highland Avenue, taking the same route that Mitch Ryan had driven the previous Friday. She went astray only once, and knew it by midblock. Turning back, she found her way again. It had seemed a ten-minute distance in the carriage. It took twenty-five minutes on foot, by the watch she wore pinned to her bosom.

Hurrying, she tried not to think ahead. Yet an unwilling dream enveloped her. She saw Leslie waiting. She pictured him offering her a small box with hope in his face. She imagined the gold ring . . .

She was flushed, starry-eyed, when she reached the grocery store. Leslie was not on the street waiting for her. She tried the shop's door, found it locked. Bewildered, she pushed and tugged. It didn't open. No one came. As she turned away she saw the small note thrust into the window crowded with dusty cans. *Shop closed due to illness,* it read.

She looked indecisively up and down the road. Had Leslie already been here, and not found her, and gone? She looked at her watch. It was moments only past three o'clock. He would have waited. He couldn't have arrived yet. He must have been somehow delayed. A carriage turned the corner, sending an icy spray over the footpath. Eagerly she watched it approach. It slowed as it neared her, then rolled by and disappeared into an alley. A pony cart pulled up, and a woman stepped out. She tried the shop door, frowned. "Oh, dear, what now?"

"There's a note," Vicki said. "Illness."

The woman shook her head. "Mr. Wood, I'm afraid. What a shame! He's been ailing for so long. I should suppose he's gone to the hospital. His heart, you know. Ah, well . . ." Murmuring still, the woman retreated to the pony cart and drove away.

Vicki remembered the worried look of the lady she took to be Mrs. Wood. A sadness touched Vicki. Illness, sorrow, death . . . these were all a part of life. She remembered her father's goodbye kiss, and an ache grew inside her. He had died alone. She lived alone. If only Leslie would come . . .

It was as if the thought made him materialize at that moment. A buggy rolled up. Leslie called, "Vicki!"

She ran to him. "Oh, I'm so glad you're here."

He drew her to the seat beside him. "When I found the shop closed I went elsewhere, and it took me longer than I expected." He jerked his head toward the back of the buggy which was loaded with baskets and sacks and jugs.

She clasped his hand tightly. "The wait doesn't matter, now you've come."

"We'll ride a little," he told her. "I don't have much time. Elise will be expecting me back soon."

"You speak like a schoolboy," Vicki said. "A boy fearful of punishment if he's tardy returning home to his mother."

Leslie frowned, didn't reply. In truth, what she described was almost what he felt. Though he couldn't admit it to her. Were he late, Elise would tap her toe, eye him steadily and ask where he had been, what he had done, whom he had seen. She was become like a many-armed octopus, her tentacles weaving themselves into every crevice of his life. Yet he saw no remedy. He banished his discontent. There was no reason to spoil these few moments with Vicki by dwelling on what couldn't be changed.

But when he had driven into a lane that came to an end on a bluff high above the river, Vicki said softly, "Leslie, do you remember how it was on the ship?"

"Of course I do. I'll never forget it."

"And . . . and is it over now?" In love, she told herself, there could be no pride. There was only this anxious hunger that she seemed to have known forever.

He took her into his arms, the embrace gentle and all-encompassing. He kissed her long and deeply, his beard silken on her cheeks. She yielded herself to him, to the touch of his tongue on hers, to the urgency of his hands at her breasts. A magic spell was broken when he put her from him, sighing.

"What, Leslie? Tell me," she asked softly.

He only looked deep into her eyes, as if seeking an answer there to a question he hadn't asked.

"Leslie," she whispered. "Please . . . please . . ."

"No," he said. "No. It's not over. I would give anything . . . all this time, I've thought of you . . . wished . . ."

She leaned against him, looked into his face. "I don't understand. You know that I love you. That you're all I want in this world. I care for nothing and no one, only you. You tell me that you care for me, and then put me aside, sighing."

"I can't help that, Vicki."

"But you can," she insisted.

"You're young," he answered. "In a little while you'll find someone else."

"No, Leslie. I promise it."

"You must."

The sun seemed less warm now. A chill ached in her fingertips. She folded them together in her lap. But she kept her eyes fixed on his face. "Then what Richard once told me is true. A shipboard romance, or friendship, is nothing once one comes to land."

"Richard?" Leslie demanded. "Why did he say that? What did you tell him?"

"I told him nothing," she retorted. "He seemed to have guessed something, and spoke to me of it."

"What more did he say?" It concerned Leslie that Richard Cavendish should know of Vicki's feelings. The man was important and rich. Elise already counted on the playing field that Rosamund was certain Richard, through John, could be persuaded to give the school. Nothing must turn him against Leslie, against Elise.

"What does it matter what Richard said?" Vicki asked. "He has nothing to do with us."

"But he does. You're his relation, and live in his house. He mustn't be misled concerning us."

"Misled." She said it flatly. "You mean he mustn't think we care for each other."

Leslie nodded. "Vicki, I have nothing to offer you. We must forget what we feel for each other." He moved from her side, so that they were no longer touching. He stared straight ahead. "From now on we shall be the dearest of friends."

"And nothing more?"

"Nothing," he said.

"I can't give you up," she cried. "I won't. We must find a way, Leslie."

"There is none. I am on a salary, which Elise pays me. I can look forward to no more than that for years to come."

"Then we'll do without. We'll manage somehow." She clung to him now, half in laughter and half in tears. "I've had so little in my life, I shall hardly know the difference. And if I matter to you . . ."

"It's impossible." Once again he drew away from her. "I must return now."

She couldn't speak. The effort to hold back her

tears used all her strength. In the river below, a tug hooted. A mourning dove cooed from a nearby tree. Both seemed to mock her. She could only nod dully as he turned the buggy back to town.

He drove her to Rock Street, and stopped there. "Do you know your way from here? It would be best if I didn't . . ."

In a choked voice, she murmured, "I know the way."

"I'm sorry, Vicki. It isn't what I want."

She climbed down from the buggy, hurried to turn the corner. She didn't look back, but she knew when he went on by the clip-clop of the horse's hoofs.

Leslie didn't want her. All his excuses and explanations meant nothing. He didn't want her. He didn't love her. He had pretended at romance when it was convenient, and now that it wasn't, he was determined to pretend nothing had happened between them. He didn't want her. The ache of hurt, of love lost, became anger. She would show him! She would make him sorry. She would make him wish that he'd never turned his back on her.

Dry-eyed, flushed, she walked through the melting snow, and up the driveway to the big house of stone that Richard had built. Leslie had said he had nothing to offer her. Now she realized how much Richard had. For the first time since her arrival it sank in upon her mind that she had been given comfort and luxury and wealth beyond measure when she was brought to live in the Cavendish home. She would show Leslie that she had no need of him.

Nettie, eyes bright in her thin face, opened the door, and beamed. "Oh, there you are. We began to wonder, Mother and me. And Harry said you'd gone for a walk, he thought."

"The snow's melting," Vicki said, as she handed Nettie her hat and coat and muff. "Spring's on the way."

"It is indeed. Harry's just brought in a crocus to show us." Nettie started down the hall, then swung back. "There's a letter for you on the table."

Vicki saw it on the silver salver and took it up, reading Mrs. McVey's crabbed hand.

She opened the envelope when she reached her room. The note within was brief, saying only that the contents of the house had been sold, a draft for fifty pounds was enclosed. Mrs. McVey hoped Victoria was well and happy.

Vicki carefully put the letter and draft into her dressing table, and then sank into a chair. She saw her reflection in the cheval glass, and the past, the present and the future all rose up to overwhelm her. She buried her face in her hands and wept.

Chapter 8

IT WAS THE MONTH FOR THE HANGING OF MAY BASkets, a custom probably descended from old English celebrations of spring. In Fall River the women occupied themselves with making fudge and bonbons and sweet cakes. They wrapped small portons of each in colored tissue paper and, along with jams, jellies and perhaps flowers, stuffed them into baskets decorated with brightly colored ribbons. The baskets were then delivered to the homes of friends, left hanging on the door knobs to be discovered as a surprise.

Vicki had made toffee, Mrs. Beamis ginger cakes, Matilda a mixture of exotic roasted nuts. They had bagged the confections, working together in the kitchen, and then Harry had gone off to deposit them according to Matilda's instructions, on the first day of May.

In the weeks following, dozens of baskets had appeared at the Cavendish house, and Matilda had seen to it that a large number of them were delivered to Elise and Leslie at the school.

It was a custom Elise didn't understand, but she understood perfectly that Rosamund Dean had her own reasons for the entertainment she had arranged with Matilda's connivance. Still, Elise felt obliged to be part of it. She weighed her concern that Leslie might behave in a foolhardy manner against the very real possibility that Richard might be persuaded to invest in the athletic field for the school. Torn between the fear of the one and the desire for the other, she had equivocated until it was too late to refuse Matilda and Rosamund. Both women were intent on throwing Leslie together with Vicki, hoping to divert Richard. Elise promised herself that she could manage Leslie. She also asked Davis Peabody down from Boston to be her guest at Rosamund's.

Thus it was that she and Leslie and Davis appeared at the ball Rosamund had given in Vicki's honor "to introduce Vicki," Matilda Cavendish had said, "to Fall River Society."

The ballroom was filled with vast arrangements of flowers. Four crystal chandeliers cast a shimmering light over the company. The Germania ensemble, dressed in formal black and white, played Vienna waltzes. The ladies were gowned with suitable elegance, their hair dressed high, their shoulders powdered. The men were dapper in long coats and narrow black trousers, satin cummerbunds and gleaming dancing pumps.

Elise smoothed her white gloves over her wrists and watched as Vicki danced with Albert Cosgrove. Their conversation seemed animated, but it was interrupted too soon for Elise's taste. Leslie approached the couple and smiled at Mr. Cosgrove, who openly sighed, relinquishing Vicki with disappointment, before retiring to the refreshment table where Rosamund stood talking to Richard. She wore a gown unlike any Elise had seen on her before. It was a peach satin with a bodice of pale lace, cut wide and deep so that the whiteness of her perfumed flesh was clearly discernible. The full skirt was banded by peach ribbons, and these tightly encircled the narrow span of her waist. In her hair she wore a peach-colored feather, which, as she moved closer to Richard, brushed against his chin.

Elise, even from a distance, saw that he shifted back from it. Rosamund, Elise decided, would have little success with her campaign, but hoped still that her own goal might be accomplished this evening.

She turned to Davis. "Shall we have another punch?"

His eyes on Rosamund, he said he would like to.

Leslie, holding Vicki in his arms, said softly, "You're lovely this evening."

Vicki looked up into his deep brown eyes. It was weeks since she had last seen him, since she had fought her tears, and raged in anger, and cried herself to sleep for need of him.

With his arms around her, those moments seemed only a bad dream. She could have hoped for nothing more than to see his tall figure across the ballroom, see his gentle smile, have him walk toward her.

She thanked him for the compliment, managing to keep her voice light, but unable to keep the joy from her eyes.

"Rosamund's good to have arranged this for you," Leslie went on. His glance slid sideways. He understood the intentions behind the affair, and they promised of fruition. Rosamund still stood with Richard, laughing, and Richard himself appeared amused. His mood augured well for Elise's plans, too, Leslie decided. But he knew he must be careful to walk the fine line between courtesy and excessive interest. Elise would be watching him with hawk's eyes.

When the music ended, he led Vicki to the refreshment table, where Albert Cosgrove immediately poured her a cup of champagne punch. She smiled her thanks, concealing her disappointment as Leslie walked away. They would dance again together. He would hold her in his arms once more.

"Coal miners demanding an eight-hour day," Albert was saying. "A twenty percent wage increase and union representation . . . And President Roosevelt insists that the owners come to Washington to discuss it! Arbitrate it! It won't work. The answer must be, 'No, and be damned to you!' "

Vicki smiled, nodded, but didn't know what he was talking about.

Close by, Rosamund looked earnestly into Richard's face. "My dear, I'm sorry that you weren't available to visit the school when Vicki and John did. You'd have been so interested. We must arrange a special trip just for you."

"Perhaps," he said.

"It's a beautiful place, Richard. And properly handled, as it will be by Elise and Leslie, it'll be a success as well. There's only one problem." She sighed. "The matter of the athletic field. You'll agree with me, I'm certain, that the school must have one for boys of that age to work out their energies."

She turned to Davis Peabody, who had just approached her. "Oh, Mr. Peabody, good evening. Do you know Mr. Richard Cavendish?"

The two men shook hands, exchanged greetings, and Rosamund went on, "Mr. Peabody is considering the school for his son."

"I've decided on it," Davis Peabody told her. "My boy will enroll at the beginning of the fall session in September."

"How nice," she said. "Then we'll expect to see more of you." She turned back to Richard, "Now as for the field . . ."

But he was hardly listening. Vicki, he saw, stood with Albert Cosgrove, one small toe tapping gently as the music began again.

Richard made a brief apology to Rosamund, nodded at Davis, and turned away. Rosamund put a hand on his arm, "We'll speak of it later, won't we?"

"Of course." He angled through the crowd to Vicki and Albert, the man speaking quickly, Vicki nodding.

"My turn, Albert," Richard said, and Vicki gave him a quick grateful smile, as he took her into his arms and whirled her away. He went on, "You seemed greatly in need of rescue just then."

"It was something about anthracite coal miners," she told him. "And Albert was growing quite red in the face. I confess that I didn't understand."

"The strike," Richard said; then grimly, "And if it goes on much longer we'll feel it here in Fall River." Then he grinned. "But if I explain I'll only confuse you more. So never mind. Tell me how you're enjoying your ball."

"It's lovely," she said. But even as she spoke, her eyes went past the breadth of his shoulders to where Leslie was dancing now with Elise. A pang touched her. Leslie and Elise, brother and sister, and gazing into each other's faces with an interest that seemed to close out the people who swung through the waltz around them.

Vicki tossed her head, looked through her lashes at Richard. "I'll always be confused if nothing is explained."

"Then I'll do it one day, but not now." He was aware of the quick glance she had given Leslie, and knew that he himself had only half of her attention. He was willing to outwait her infatuation, but the silken smoothness of her shoulder under his fingertips, the dimple at the corner of her mouth, made him impatient.

She was saying, "One day, Richard, I should like to visit your mill. You go there every day, and disappear into another world. I'd enjoy seeing the place."

"But why?" he asked.

"If I were to see it, I might understand the fascination it holds for you."

"It's noisy, damp, and mostly unpleasant," he laughed. "Ask John, if you don't believe me."

"I do believe you. But I'd like to see it anyway."

"It wouldn't be much of an outing, but I'll take you, if you agree to balance that experience with other outings as well."

With her eyes on Leslie, she answered, "I should like that, Richard."

There was a pause in the music, and she stepped back, but he drew her into his arms again. For the rest of the evening, except for those few dances claimed by others, whose names she never remembered, Richard managed to keep her with him.

In spite of Davis Peabody's assiduous attentions, Rosamund's face grew as white as the lace of her bodice. Matilda's eyes narrowed in held-back rage.

But Vicki was a brilliant jewel sparkling among bits of glass. Always, always, she was aware of Leslie. If he didn't want her, Richard did. That thought was in her mind with every smile she gave Richard, with every laugh, with every clasp of her hands. It was that thought which obliterated all memory of the fear Richard had once evoked in her. Leslie might not want her, but Richard did.

It was still in her mind the next day when, at breakfast, Richard suggested that if she remained interested in the mill, he would take her there that morning.

Matilda said quickly, "But why? The mill has no charms that I know of for Vicki. And I thought," she improvised, "to have her accompany me to Mrs. Cosgrove's for tea."

"That's not much of an entertainment," Richard answered, while John grinned.

"Nor is the mill," Matilda retorted.

"But I'd like to go," Vicki protested. "Only last night I asked Richard about it."

"I see," Matilda murmured. "Oh, indeed, I see."

"Now these," Richard said, "are the inspectors."

Vicki and he were now virtually at the end of the tour of the mill. She looked at the long wooden tables set under the unshaded light bulbs. At each end of each one of the four there were single large bolts. A girl unrolled the woven fabric and leaned over it, searching for flaws. She used magnifying glasses rimmed in brass that opened into two lenses. Her shoulders were bent, her head strained. As she finished with a section, the girl at the other end carefully wound the fabric onto a new bolt. It was slow careful work. When flaws were found, the fabric was tagged. Some were amenable to repair; others were sold as seconds to jobbers who produced cheap goods.

"Tedious labor," Vicki murmured to Richard, seeing the girls' red-rimmed squinting eyes.

"But necessary." He smiled, led her into the main loft, where the sweepers were busy clearing the floor of accumulating fibers, an essential job performed through most of the shift, since the fibers were an additional fire hazard in a building that already had many of them.

The shuttles slammed, and Vicki winced. The pulleys and wheels and straps hummed and clanked overhead. Dust motes floated in the air, which was heavy with heat and the odor of sizing. Bobbin boys hurried back and forth.

When the noon whistle went off, the men and women at the looms simply opened sacks and remained before their work, eating with one eye always on the loom, while Gus Markeson shambled back and forth, watching for trouble before it came.

Richard called him over, introduced him to Vicki.

The big yellow-eyed man looked her up and down, while Richard said, "Gus here is a master loomfixer. Maybe the most important man in the place. If he can't repair a loom, then it can't be done." His earlier doubts about Gus had long been replaced by confidence. The man had proved all he said himself to be.

"It hasn't happened yet," Gus answered. "So far it's been easy."

"Everything seems so complicated," Vicki offered.

"Machines seem that way until you take them

93

apart," Gus told her. "But if a man made it, I always say, a man can fix it, too."

Richard restrained a grin. Even surly Gus Markeson was responsive to Vicki's smile.

He led her to his office, remembering too late the Charles Dana Gibson drawings on the wall. But she didn't seem to notice them. She sat in his chair, surveyed the place, then said, "So here is where you spend so much time."

"I begin to feel I spend too much time here."

"But you think it necessary."

"I used to."

She dropped her eyes from his, knowing why he no longer thought so. It was in his voice, his look. *She* had made him begin to question what he had never questioned before. She decided uneasily that it was time to leave, although it had been pleasant to be with him until now.

But Ezra Saunders came in. When Richard made the introductions, Ezra said, smiling timidly, "Oh, yes, I've heard of you." He sat at his small desk, mumbled, "The coal strike is a bad business. We can buy now, but prices are already going up. And they'll go higher."

Richard laughed. "We'll speak of it later, Ezra."

She made that an excuse to rise. "It's been an interesting tour. I'd no idea what the mill was like. So big, so noisy, and so full of life. From the outside it seems dead, Richard. Like a huge granite mausoleum."

"Noisy enough," Richard agreed. "Which is something one becomes accustomed to. And, though it's big, it's not nearly as big as it will be one day. But you're right that there's life here, and it's no monument for the dead."

Ezra chuckled. "I think of it as an ant hill."

Outside Richard led her to the surrey they had come in. It was a neat conveyance, shiny black, with a fringed top folded back to honor the fine May day. John had found it and brought it home more than a month ago, but Vicki had never ridden in it before.

"We'll stop for lunch," Richard told her.

"But do you have so much time to waste with me?" she asked.

"It's hardly a waste," he told her.

Mason's was a simple and sedate place in which many ladies of the city gathered after shopping or between errands for the Fruit and Flower Mission, one of their most popular charitable activities. The menu was limited, but the silver was good, the linen impeccable.

It didn't surprise Richard to see Rosamund there. Nor did it embarrass him. He had no interest in what she thought, nor in her feelings. They exchanged greetings, and he refused Rosamund's suggestion that they join her. "You're on your dessert now," he said, seizing the excuse, before leading Vicki to a back table.

Vicki was well aware of Rosamund's cool measuring gaze. It never faltered until Rosamund finally departed. When the door closed behind her, Vicki sighed in relief. But it was only then that she realized that she hadn't thought of Leslie in hours. Not since breakfast had her mind turned to him. It was, she realized, because of Richard. When he wanted, he could be diverting.

He laughed softly now. "You mustn't mind Rosamund."

"I don't." And it was true. Surely Rosamund would mention this meeting to Elise, to Leslie. Surely she wouldn't forget that Richard had been the man escorting Vicki. Leslie would know.

But it was to Matilda that Rosamund went when she left the tearoom. Her face grim under her toque, she said, "Matilda, I was startled beyond belief to see Richard, and with him, Victoria, in Mason's a little while ago."

"He took her first to see the mill," Matilda answered. Then: "I'd best not interfere, Rosamund. You know what Richard is."

"I had hoped . . ."

"As I had, my dear."

Rosamund was silent for a moment, then rose. "I suppose we must wait and see."

Chapter 9

THAT DAY RICHARD WORKED LATE. HE HAD SPREAD on his desk the plans for expansion he had been toying with for some time. He went over them now, making small alterations.

Ezra watched from over the top of his ledgers and framed silent imprecations in his mind. Later that evening he sat in his room with Gus Markeson and Jamie. He pulled half a pie wrapped in brown paper from his pocket and looked at it critically. "I hope I haven't smashed it," he said, passing it to Jamie.

The boy grinned, peeled the wrapper away and expertly caught the crumbs on his fingertips. "It tastes good, Mr. Saunders. Thank you."

"He gets little enough pie in his life," Gus laughed, "to be too particular about it."

"I suppose," Ezra agreed. He yawned and stretched, glad of the companionship. Seeing Richard at work on the plans reminded Ezra that an ax hung over his head. He felt its sharp edge come closer daily. He and Richard did not share memories of the old days. They were a generation apart, and never to grow closer.

"Changes," Gus Markeson said softly, as if he had read Ezra's mind.

But Gus was thinking of himself. Here he sat in the company of a twelve-year-old boy and an old man, content to have left the battles behind. He lowered his yellow eyes to study the broken knuckles of his right hand. Who'd have thought it would ever come to that?

Much later that night, Mitch and Harry finished their game and set the cards aside.

Mitch had won two dollars, hardly worth the walk over, if that had been what he came for. He slid a look at Nettie, who had just brought a pot of coffee and a deep-dish apple pie from the big house. Her cheeks were bright; her dark hair wind-tousled.

He thanked her when she served him, but eyed the closed door to the bedroom. Mrs. Beamis had taken herself off half an hour ago, but Harry seemed wide awake and prepared to stay that way.

Mitch drank his coffee and ate his pie, wishing that Harry would disappear. A mourning dove cooed in the eaves. A warm breeze fluttered the window curtain. There was no moon, and it was just right for a hug and a kiss in the hemlock grove. But how was he to persuade Nettie outside when Harry sat like a lump on a log?

Nettie took away his empty cup and plate, and he patted her hand, but he said, "What happened here today, Harry?"

Harry shrugged.

"When I brought Rosamund this afternoon, she was spitting mad. I thought she'd explode before I got her to the house."

"I saw that," Nettie said, "when I let her in to talk to Mrs. Cavendish."

"And what then?"

"She left in a little while.'"

"Didn't you hear?" Mitch grinned. "I'd have thought you'd know what he said in the kitchen."

Harry struggled to his feet, yawned loudly. "Bedtime for you, Nettie. And for me, too."

Mitch took the hint. He rose quickly, said thanks for the cards and the refreshment, and left. As he crossed the dark grounds to Highland Avenue he looked up at the big stone house. One day he'd own a manor himself, but not here. Not where the Irish were hated and held back from being what they could be. Not here, but in Galway, green Galway, and Shamus would knock at the door, and be asked in for meat and drink, and together they would laugh about the old days.

Chapter 10

"LOVELY," EUSTACIA COSGROVE SAID. SHE RAISED HER hand to straighten her flower-bedecked hat. Her round bosom heaved another sigh as she repeated, "Yes. Lovely. That's all one can say."

Matilda set the silver tea pot on its tray and looked up to follow the direction of Eustacia's gaze.

It was a hot bright day at the end of July. The sun hung like molten gold in a blue sky. The air was soft, still. A breathless hush hung over the garden. Birds sang in the hemlock grove; blue jays chattered in the elms. Close by the house yellowjackets were busy at the trellis roses.

But Eustacia had spoken only of Vicki. She sat just beyond the window, a white towel thrown around her shoulders. As she drew the brush through her hair thick loose waves and curls burned reddish golden against the blue of her gown.

She *was* lovely, Matilda thought grudgingly. Her chiseled profile gave her face a patrician perfection. Matilda would admit that much, yet wish that she had never seen Vicki.

It had been a frequent thought in the past two

months. Most particularly because Matilda knew herself to be in the wrong. It was a feeling she didn't find tolerable, yet it couldn't be gainsaid. It wasn't Vicki who pursued Richard, but the other way around. Vicki avoided him when she could. It was with John that she went to Island Park to hear the band play or saw the matinees at the Academy of Music.

Eustacia was saying, "I hear that Rosamund sees a good deal of Mr. Davis Peabody these days."

Matilda made a noncommittal sound, but thought that Rosamund was proving to be wise. Richard had set his mind on Vicki, and Matilda had no doubt that he would eventually have his way. That was why she hid her feelings for Vicki. It would never do to have a daughter-in-law who disliked and feared her. So she had begun to spend more time with Vicki. She had interested her in learning crewel work and petit point, and taken her shopping on North Main Street. In the process Matilda had found the girl sweet, endearing and an interesting companion.

Now Eustacia asked, "And how does Richard feel about Mr. Peabody?"

"I imagine he feels nothing," Matilda answered. She poured more tea for Eustacia and passed the cookie plate, and suddenly wished that Eustacia would go home.

But Eustacia remained. She wondered aloud if Elise Parker would succeed with the boys' school. She mentioned that the Misses Borden were seen often down street doing their shopping.

Matilda heaved a sigh of relief when Eustacia finally departed.

The candlelight flickered like small brilliant jewels in Vicki's newly washed hair, and glowed on the curve of her cheeks.

Watching as she turned to speak to John, Richard clenched his hands beneath the table. It was all he could do to keep himself from reaching out to touch her.

After Nettie removed what remained of the parsnips, carrots, potatoes, beets, cabbage and corned beef that had comprised the boiled dinner, and replaced the enormous platter with servings of raspberry pudding, he said, "I've been thinking of looking at some houses in Newport. And I've heard of a villa for sale that I might be interested in." He paused. Then: "Will you drive over with me tomorrow, Vicki?"

But Vicki looked at Matilda. "You're going to Boston tomorrow, aren't you?"

"I am," Matilda answered. "And I fear I can't change my plans now." She understood that Richard had chosen that day for the outing because she wouldn't be available, and she had no intention of interfering with him.

"And you, John?" Vicki asked.

"I'm sorry. I can't join you either."

She turned to Richard. "Perhaps we should wait for another day."

"Tomorrow's most convenient. So, if you'll agree . . ."

"I'll have Mrs. Beamis fix a hamper," Matilda said.

There seemed nothing to do but accept, so Vicki smiled. "I'd like to go with you, Richard."

They left soon after the morning six o'clock mill whistles shrilled, assuming that the twenty-mile trip would take close to four hours. The same journey could be done in ninety minutes, Richard told Vicki, if they boarded the Old Colony Street Railway trolley at City Hall.

But, he said, he wanted her to have a closer look at the countryside, and they would find the surrey convenient when they went house-viewing in Newport.

At Tiverton, while they waited for the ferry to arrive, he helped her from the surrey and left her for a little while on the bank of the Sakonnet River. When he returned his arms were full of the blue cornflowers that grew wild along the slope. Smiling, he offered them to her, and when she took them, he said, "They're pale beside the color of your eyes."

She turned away, her face half-hidden by the huge

brim of her straw hat, and answered, "They're lovely, Richard. Thank you."

The ferry hooted and slammed into its slip. He led the horse and surrey aboard. As they crossed to Portsmouth they stood at the rail, and watched the construction gangs working on the new Stone Bridge being built to improve the trolley service between Fall River and Newport. From there they drove south along Aquidneck Island, through high rolling meadows beyond which they caught glimpses of Narragansett Bay on their right and the Sakonnet River on their left.

As the sun rose higher, he offered to raise the surrey top to shade her. But she said, "Oh, no, I like having the wind on my face."

He pushed back his round white straw hat, and a dark lock of his hair fell across his forehead. "I like it, too." And he added, "And being here, like this, with you."

She didn't know what to say, so she only smiled. They rode on in a companionable silence.

The island had been bought in 1638 by William Coddington for forty fathoms of wampum, which equaled about two hundred English shillings. The wampum, made by the Narragansett Indians, came from the purple portion of the quahog clam shell.

A few months after the purchase thirteen Boston families established Pocassett, the first town on Aquidneck. A year later six of these moved southwest to establish Newport, a town of rich farmlands and easy access to the Atlantic Ocean. From then on it profited by infusions of new blood. First there were the Quakers from England, then both Christians and Sephardic Jews from Portugal. Newport became the captial of the state of Rhode Island on May 4, 1776, when the General Assembly declared its independence from Great Britain some two months before the rest of the colonies.

By the end of the nineteenth century it had become the haunt of the Astors, the Vanderbilts, and the Oelrichs, who hired such architects as Richard Morris Hunt, Horace Trumbauer and Stanford White to design for them the mansions, palaces and chateaux that they called their summer cottages.

Now as Vicki and Richard drove into the street called Broadway, they found themselves surrounded by fancy equipages of all descriptions, and two motor cars were angled into hitching rails for which they had no need.

Richard handed Vicki down, then paused to look at those shining vehicles.

She suddenly remembered leaning from the window to look for his arrival in Rye, and seeing the gleaming hood and high wheels pass along The Mint, and imagining that she rode in it, wrapped in veils. It seemed years since, yet it was only nine months ago.

They spent only a little time in the real estate office. Richard knew his own mind. He read four descriptions, accepted four keys, refused the services of the agent, and they were back in the surrey again.

Soon they rode out Bellevue Avenue. Both sides were lined with large marble and stone establishments centered in elaborate gardens and shielded by high walls and iron gates.

They turned off into a tree-shaded lane and saw the golden glint of the sea ahead of them.

Richard tethered the horse to a post in front of a big white house. He looked at it for a few moments, then turned away. "First let me show you Cliff Walk."

She followed him across the daisy-starred meadow, through the broken gate of a wooden fence that sagged under the weight of wild climbing roses. A dirt-and-stone path ran along the coast, close by the sea in some places, high above tumbled rock cliffs in others. From there the houses of stone and marble gleamed through the trees.

As they walked, the sea breeze caught the ribbons of her hat and flung them forward over her face. Laughing, he plucked them away, held them before he let them go. Just as he did, the same wind blew under her skirts and filled them, so that they

102

puffed up around her, rippling and swaying, leaving her slender legs revealed for a single flashing moment. She fought her skirts down, but it was as if the wind had inflated her spirit. She was light-headed with sun and wind and a joyful mood.

She was sorry when they left Cliff Walk behind and returned to the house.

But Richard shook his head. "We'll go on to the next one on the list."

"Don't you want to see what it's like inside?"

"No need. It's not what I have in mind."

He felt the same about the next two houses, though one of them had interested Vicki, it's white widow's walk capping its third-floor dormer windows having caught her attention.

By then it was late afternoon. They returned to Bellevue Avenue and stopped for coffee and petits fours in a small stone house, and when they had finished, they drove to the last address he had chosen to view.

It, too, was just off Bellevue Avenue. It, too, had a view of the sea, and a widow's walk. It was of white clapboard, with a deep veranda that ran around three sides of the first floor.

"We'll go in," he said, unlocking the door.

They made a slow tour of the fourteen rooms, the huge kitchen, the grounds at the back. Then Richard said, "Yes. This is the place I want."

Vicki laughed. "But can you really make a decision so quickly?"

"Of course. I always know precisely what I want. I have only to see it." A faint smile touched his lips. It had been the same with her when she first opened the door of the house in Rye. And she didn't realize that seeing her here, her slender form climbing the stairs before him to stand on the widow's walk at his side, had made any uncertainty impossible. This was the house for her summers from now on. It was to this place that he would return from the city, and she would be waiting, smiling as she was just then. He said, "We'll go in to Broadway and tell the real estate agent now. And after that we'll return to have our supper on the veranda by twilight."

Within little more than half an hour he had made the arrangements for the purchase of the house he decided to name Cavendish Cove. He promised to return in two weeks with the plans to electrify the place, with outlines for some other smaller alterations he would consider. At that time, he told the startled real estate agent, he would be prepared to sign the transfer papers. Meanwhile he handed the agent a check for ten thousand dollars as a deposit.

It was so quick and easily done that Vicki was astonished. The joy that had brimmed in her all through the afternoon rose to euphoria in the face of Richard's matter-of-fact manner. "I still can't believe it," she said, laughing. "We've hardly been here six hours, and you own a new house. And such a beautiful one."

"Not beautiful yet," he told her, as he handed her from the surrey. "But it will be by the time we move in next summer. I shall expect you to have a hand in the redecoration."

"Whatever I can do," she promised. But the words echoed in her mind. *Next summer.* By then, would Leslie have learned how much he needed her? The question itself made her realize that only now had she thought of him through the whole of the day. It seemed so long since she had seen him. And today, with Richard always at her side, she hadn't even whispered his name in her mind.

Richard took down the food hamper. He carried it to the veranda and set it on a table. When she offered to serve, he said, "No, Vicki, just sit in that chaise, if you dare, of course, and enjoy the view of the sea. I'm going to look for some candles. We'll need them soon, and I think I saw some in the kitchen when we were here before."

But she got to her feet as soon as he left her. She went into the garden and plucked five pink roses from a bush at the edge of the walk and brought them back to the veranda. She arranged them as a centerpiece on the table and then unpacked the food. Mrs. Beamis had prepared cold chicken and potato salad. There was peach pie, and cookies, too.

Richard brought a single white taper with him, and a saucer. "You've readied the meal." He wished she had waited. He'd have liked to watch her lay out the food. But no matter. They'd picnic again like this many times. He set the light on the table, opened the tall jug of wine and filled the two glasses.

"We'll toast your new house," Vicki said. "To Cavendish Cove. May you always be happy here." She sipped the wine then, not knowing that she would one day remember those words and wonder at them.

"May you be happy here as well," Richard answered.

"It's kind of you," she told him.

"Kind?" There was a hoarse note in his voice. His eyes were suddenly dark and fathomless. "Kind, Vicki?"

"That you include me in your plans."

He moved to the chaise, settled beside her. "Vicki, you *are* my plans. Surely you know that."

She bent her head over her hands and slowly drew off her long white kid gloves. Cousin Matilda had insisted on taking her to Higgins and Frazier only that week, and bought these gloves, and another pair like them for everyday, because the new elbow-length sleeves exposed so much of the lower arm. But even as she had told Vicki that, Vicki had realized that Matilda no longer sounded like a disapproving Mrs. McVey. Now Vicki folded her white gloves neatly and put them on the black-beaded chatelaine bag that Matilda had also bought for her.

Richard was saying, "You don't answer me, Vicki. You don't look at me."

She said gently, "You've been so good to me. You, and John, and your mother, too. I'm more grateful than I know how to tell you. But you must understand that I . . . I . . ."

Richard put his hands on her shoulders, said swiftly, "No, I don't want to hear anything now. Forget what I said. Just remember that I love you, and have from the first."

"Please let go of me," she whispered. Her heart was hammering inside her chest now. She felt quick hot prickles in her skin. The old familiar fear was suddenly upon her. She felt that he was absorbing her, sapping her will, that he would soon so devour her that nothing would remain of her essential self. She remembered fleeing from him in Rye. She recalled thrusting her hands against his chest and slipping away to close the bedroom door in his face. She moved to rise, but he held her tightly.

The breeze was hot, scented. The twilight sky had darkened and faded into the sea. Fireflies suddenly sparkled on the boughs of the nearby elms.

He was aware of these, yet out of touch with them, so that he felt as if he existed in a different place and time.

Now her voice was urgent. "Let me go, Richard."

But he couldn't release her, though he saw and understood the fear in her eyes. He couldn't let her go. It didn't occur to him. She belonged to him, and he would have her. He said thickly, "We'll be married. We've no reason to wait."

She shook her head, unable to speak her refusal aloud.

"We'll be married," he repeated. "I'll give you all you want, my love. I'll make you happy, I promise."

Now she forced herself to speak. But it was as if her throat were squeezed in an iron grip, and she had to drive the words out, each taking more breath than she had. She gasped, "Richard, no. Listen to me. Try to understand. I can't marry you."

He knew that she spoke, but his hunger deafened him. His pulses pounded in his temples. He held her tightly, forced her head back, and fastened his lips on hers.

Need, hunger, so long repressed, swept him. Even as he told himself, too late, that he must free her, his grip tightened, and his body covered hers and he felt the trembling of round breasts and raised locked thighs. She pitched and thrashed beneath him, and broke away. Leaping to her feet, she fled, and he went after her, meaning only to apologize and soothe her. But when he had cornered her against the veranda railing, the regret and shame died in him, and the fire flooded his veins, and he threw her down on the creaking chaise, and took her brutally and quickly.

His shoulders blocked out the sky. The weight of him held her. His sweat burned on her tear-wet cheeks. There was a pain that left her breathless. Then it was gone, and her heart faltered within her. She felt a slow and giddy spinning, a surging. Without knowing it, her arms tightened around him; her body lifted to his, with his. She had forgotten whose arms held her, whose thighs grasped hers. Then he whispered, "My love, my love," and she remembered. Her faltering heart became a stone within her chest. The slow and giddy spinning ceased abruptly. Leslie, she whispered silently. Limp as cold death now, she endured until Richard moved away from her. When he reached out to cover her breasts, to try to straighten her disordered gown, she cringed from his touch.

"I'm sorry," he said quietly. "I didn't intend for it to be this way. I never meant to hurt you or frighten you. But I love you. I've waited as long as I could."

"You love me," she said bitterly. "You call that animal wallowing love? I loathe you, Richard Cavendish. I shall loathe you as long as I live."

Those were the last words she said to him.

When he locked up the house, and settled her in the surrey, he apologized again. But she pretended not to hear him.

"We'll be married," he told her, as they drove away from Cavendish Cove. "I've been thinking of it since you stepped down off the *Plymouth*. It's not as if I've taken you lightly and mean to forget it when we reach home."

She gave him a look of intense disgust. He became silent, telling himself that she was hurt, angry, and that she had the right to be. A man was only a man, though she didn't know that yet. But he loved her, and he would prove it, and time would cure her wounded feelings. She would understand how he had come to the end of his control. Already her own body, judging by her response, knew what had happened. She *would* understand. He had only to wait a little longer.

She stared at the riding lights that bobbed before them, her tear-blurred vision fixed on them as if she dare not look away. The bouquet of cornflowers he had picked for her that morning lay on the seat. Slowly, without thinking, she plucked at it. One by one she took up the flowers. One by one she flung them away into the night.

When, at last, they reached Fall River only a single light burned in the hallway. She hurried to her room, determined to see no one, to be seen by no one.

That night she relived the whole of the day in Newport. The real estate office on Broadway, the ride along Bellevue Avenue, the stroll on Cliff Walk.

The candlelight flickering on the veranda. The taste of the wine, and her own voice saying, "To Cavendish Cove, Richard. May you be happy here."

Her shoulders were bruised where his fingers had bitten deep into the softness of her flesh. She remembered how he had held her, his body's weight pressing her down into a breathless darkness. Her lips stung from the hardness of his mouth on hers. She remembered how he had kissed her. Deep within, she was torn, still faintly bleeding. She remembered the gross invasion, the quick fading pain, the trembling within her. And Leslie . . . if only he had held her thus. If only it had been his limbs entwining hers, his hands at her breasts. But it had been Richard. She hated him, and she hated herself for what she had felt while they writhed together on the chaise.

When morning came, she knew what she must do.

She watched from the window until Richard drove away from the house, and John mounted up and went for his usual morning ride. She listened until she heard

Nettie murmuring with Matilda in the room at the end of the corridor. When she looked into the hallway, it was empty. She caught up her wicker basket. It held only what she had brought with her, and her mother's picture, which had arrived along with a few odds and ends that Mrs. McVey had shipped to her months before. In her reticule she had what remained of the money Mrs. McVey had sent her for the sale of the things in the Rye house.

Quietly, cautiously, she went down the stairs. There was a clatter of dishes from the kitchen, but no other sound.

She carefully closed the door behind her and stepped into the steamy morning air.

It was as she had whispered to her mother's smiling picture the night before. She must go where love led her. First she must find a place to stay. She had the bit of money to go on, but it wouldn't last, so she must find work to support herself. She would never see Richard Cavendish again.

She hurried to Rock Street and went quickly down the hill, as the mill steam whistles tore holes in the fabric of stillness. Somewhere on her walks she had seen several houses with small "room for rent" signs in their front windows. She hoped she could find them again.

It was late afternoon. She was tired, having spent hours in fruitless search. She had stopped for tea and a roll, and then pushed on. Now she heard the clang of the trolley a block away on Bedford and turned into Seventh Street.

At once she saw the house she was looking for. It was three stories high, its white paint weathered to gray, the glass of its window panes age-speckled and streaked. The two stone steps which led to its sagging front porch were cracked. Its front door had split across and was held together with a single board of raw wood. Once it might have been pleasant enough, but time and lack of care had joined to become an undammable current, and the house had sunk in it.

She eyed it uneasily, then looked again at the fly-spotted sign that was propped against a splintered railing. For an instant she imagined the house on Highland Avenue, then the place called Cavendish Cove in Newport. But, with her lips tightening, she climbed the steps and knocked at the door.

It swung open. A tiny woman tipped an iron-gray head to stare at her.

Vicki said she had seen the sign, was enquiring about the room.

"Irish?" the elderly woman demanded.

"No. I'm from England," Vicki answered.

The woman grunted. "Where do you work? Are you on steady?"

"I'm looking for a job now," Vicki told her. "If you'll show me the room . . ."

"Show me your money first," the old woman cackled.

"How do I know I'll want your room unless I see it?"

"Maybe you will. Maybe you won't," the old woman answered. "But you'll never know if I don't see the color of your money."

"How much is it?"

"Two dollars the room, and fifty cents extra daily for breakfast and supper."

"And if I decide I won't have the room?"

"Then out you go, and with your money of course." At Vicki's doubtful look, the old woman went on, "You don't have to come in, if you don't want to. You're a cautious girl, and it makes me wonder why."

Vicki took the money from her reticule, waved it in the old woman's face. "I have it, you see."

"All right, my girl. Come have yourself a look." The woman reached a clawed hand for the bills, but Vicki tucked them away.

Chuckling, the old woman led the way up a shaky staircase. When she reached the second floor, she pointed at a door. "In there, and make up your mind fast. I've no time to fiddle with silly girls. I've supper to get for my boarders tonight, and for you, too, if you want it."

Vicki went in. The room was tiny. A single be-grimed uncurtained widow hung over a slant of roof where moldy leaves had gathered. There was a narrow iron cot, a single thin cover, a table on which a big white bowl and pitcher stood, and near the bed, a chamber pot.

"Well?" the old woman demanded from the hall.

"It'll do for a week at least," Vicki said. She put the money into the old woman's hand.

"Supper at seven," the woman told her. "And mind you're on time. Be late and you'll get leftovers, and I can promise that won't be much."

When she had stamped her way down the steps, Vicki closed the door. The place was barely tolerable. But so much of the day was already gone, and the money Mrs. McVey sent her wouldn't last for long. Vicki knew she must save it for an emergency. She must quickly find a way to support herself.

She put the wicker basket on the cot, smoothed her hair and readjusted her hat, and immediately set out.

It was a long hot three hours. She spent it trudging the streets, looking for shops where she could ask for work. She had served in the tobacconist place and felt she could do the same again. But wherever she asked, she was told there was nothing, and that she would do better at the mills.

She ignored those suggestions. She didn't want to go near *any* mill. She wondered if Richard yet knew what she had done, and what John had said when he realized she was gone. For all her more recent kindness, Matilda had probably heaved a sigh of re-lief when she found Vicki's bedroom empty.

She returned to the boarding house in time for supper, and then wished she hadn't.

The six men at the table stared at her in silence. Hard male eyes lingered too long, grins touching hard male mouths. Vicki thought of Richard, and felt her throat close.

The old woman chuckled, "We've a nice addition

to our little family, haven't we?" And, "This is Miss Victoria Davelle, or so she says. But she hasn't told me what she's doing here."

Vicki knew she had told the old woman that she was looking for work, and wondered why she didn't say so. At last Vicki herself explained to the listening men.

"What kind of job do you do?" one demanded.

"And you're English by the sound of you," another put in.

Vicki looked at the plate of greasy mutton chunks, the soggy boiled cabbage. A vast uneasiness arose in her. The move from the Cavendish house would be much less simple than she had thought. She stiffened her spine, and told herself that somehow she would manage.

Later, when she awakened from a sleep of exhaustion, she wondered.

There was a sound at the door, a rattle of the latch. Wood scraped hard against the loose bolt. She scrambled from the bed, planted herself in front of the door, and said loudly, "You go away, whoever you are!"

She heard a drunken laugh, a scuffle. A heavy weight thumped the panel.

"If you don't leave me alone, I'll scream and rouse the house."

"What for?" a slurred voice cried. "Why would you want to do that? We're only after a bit of fun, and we can pay. We'll hand you the cash the minute you let us in."

Vicki cast frightened eyes around the shadowed room. There was no heavy chest with which she could barricade the door. There was no weapon handy to use in defense. The door shook and shuddered under the thrust of a shoulder.

She drew a sharp breath as her eyes fell on the slops jar she had used earlier. In a swift motion, she caught it up, then unbolted the door and threw it wide open. Before the shadowy figures could move, she flung the slops jar. It hit one man full in the face, spilling its contents far and wide, and then smashed into the wall, exploding into a shower of odorous splinters.

The house came instantly alive with shouts and cries. The old woman appeared in a tattered wraparound. She peered over the light of a smoking lantern.

"What's going on?" she demanded. "What do you think you're doing, waking up decent folk in the middle of the night?"

"Decent folk?" Vicki demanded. "If you run a bawdy house you ought to say so to strangers."

"A bawdy house? And what makes you think you can fling chamber pots about my hall, I'd like to know?"

"Just keep these people away from my door," Vicki said sharply. "I'll be gone in the morning. And you may be sure I won't come back."

Chapter 11

IT WAS NETTIE WHO HAD FIRST REALIZED WHAT HAD happened. Early in the morning, she had listened at the closed bedroom door, and then had gone on to her chores, assuming that Vicki still slept. Later Nettie had listened again, even knocked softly. At noon, when Matilda returned from her overnight visit to Boston, she asked for Vicki, and was told that the girl hadn't yet come down. Matilda looked surprised and said, "You'd better see if she's unwell, Nettie."

So Nettie had gone into the room, opened the drapes. She knew at once that Vicki was gone, for the picture of Maude Jensen no longer stood on the mantel. It took Nettie only moments to examine the armoire and the chiffonier. All the new clothing remained. Vicki had taken only what she arrived with.

Now, some three weeks later, Mrs. Beamis asked as she had before, "You are sure she took only what she brought? You're not making it up?"

"Of course I'm sure. I helped her unpack, so I remember."

"And tried everything on she left behind, I'll bet," Harry said in his deep voice, "hoping Mr. Richard would turn the lot over to you." Harry grinned. "Which he won't. He'll keep clothes and room as is, for her shrine."

"Harry," Mrs. Beamis said warningly.

"Oh, Ma, you know he went to the mill an hour ago."

She ignored that. "I wish I knew what happened to the girl."

"So do all of them," Harry told her.

Nettie stared at him. "Whatever makes you think so? I've not heard a single one even say her name. I'm the only one that cares."

"A lot you know about it," Harry answered.

Mrs. Beamis sighed. "It's no business of ours." And, as the dining room bell rang, "There's Mr. John, Nettie. See to him."

The girl went on the run, returning to ask for bacon and eggs and coffee. When the meal was ready, she brought it in to him.

He thanked her absently, his eyes on the empty chair that had once been Vicki's. It was three weeks and three days since that noontime when he had returned from a long ride and found his mother bewildered, Nettie red-faced and anxious and Mrs. Beamis in the full tide of apprehension.

"We've just realized it," his mother said, a surprising pallor in her face. "She didn't come down so I sent Nettie to see if she was all right."

"But she's gone," Nettie cried. "We don't know where. And she took only her old clothes, and her mother's picture, and . . ." It poured out of Nettie while Mrs. Beamis made shushing sounds as background.

"Send Harry for my brother," John had said, and gone up to the room to see for himself. There had been nothing to see, however, and he had stood there, his leg aching, until he heard Richard's voice below, and Mrs. Beamis and Nettie repeating their counterpoints of information. He heard his mother say, "Richard, I assure you . . ." and stop, and add painfully, "I know nothing of this."

And Richard had replied, "I know."

He had left the others still speaking among themselves, and gone into the morning room. He didn't look up when John joined him. He leaned his head against the chair back and stared at the wall, and John thought Richard looked more tired than he had ever seen him. There were fine new lines around his eyes, and his lips were set as if molded in iron.

John had asked softly, "What happened at Newport? Did you know Vicki was going to leave?"

Richard didn't answer, but his face changed color. He turned a slow awful red. It was as if his flesh had suffered multiple wounds, the blood rising up to mottle his cheeks and forehead, while his mouth turned white. And then, as John stared at him, the color had receded, leaving the pallor of illness.

Finally he said, "I ought to have guessed it."

"But what happened?" John had demanded.

Richard didn't explain. Not then. Not ever.

Soon after, John had mounted his horse and combed the neighborhood, riding through the alleys and lanes, going down street, finally, into the busier areas. No one knew when Vicki had left the house, but surely it had been some time after dawn. She'd had hours in which to disappear.

He went on, aimlessly looking for her until twilight. The next morning he started out again. She'd have searched for lodgings, he told himself. She would find a room by looking for signs in the windows of houses, or notices in shops, or perhaps in the columns of the *Daily Globe* or *Herald*. He bought a paper on North Main Street, and found just such an advertisement as might have interested her. He rode to that address. The landlord shook his head. "No, the room's not taken. There are too many to let hereabouts."

John decided to look further in that neighborhood. He pulled up after a block when he saw the small crooked sign tipped against the porch railing.

It hadn't been a place he would have wanted for Vicki. It was ugly, and he suspected, not even safe. He guessed that only from its appearance. He had been certain of it as soon as the door was opened. But he greeted the old woman who stared up at him, asked if a Miss Davelle had rented a room.

From behind the old woman, there was a subdued laugh.

John drew a bill from his waistcoat pocket. He rolled it neatly between his fingers as her clawed hand reached eagerly for it. "Do you know her?" he asked.

From behind the old woman there was another laugh. Then: "I'll warrant she does. The girl threw a chamber pot at her boys, who only wanted a bit of fun last night. And out she went this morning, nose in the air, and skirts swinging."

"Out where?" John had asked the woman.

She narrowed her gaze to the money in his fingers. "I don't know any more."

"Did she go by carriage?"

"On foot."

"Alone?"

The old woman simpered. "More's the pity. But yes, all alone."

"Which way?"

She jerked her head toward the intersection, then plucked the dollar from his hand. "Lost me a good roomer because of her. You ought to pay for that, too!"

John had laughed and turned away.

At home that evening he told Richard what he had

learned, then said, "Maybe we ought to call in the Pinkertons from Boston."

Richard frowned. "We can't hunt her down as if she were a common criminal."

"We can't do nothing, either," John protested. Richard hadn't answered him.

Now three weeks later John pushed his uneaten breakfast aside. He limped to the stable, had Harry saddle his horse. The August sun burned his face as he went into Highland Avenue.

Ezra Saunders looked sideways at John. The boy had no use for the mill. Ezra had no use for him. Ezra considered that a man needn't love what he did, nor consider it a pleasure. A man worked to eat, and there was the pleasure, not the labor that paid for the food.

Gus Markeson shambled past the glass window, his yellow eyes flicking toward Ezra in acknowledgment. The loomfixer didn't appear to be moving quickly, but he'd get there before poor coughing Carter. Ezra bent his head back over his ledgers, ignoring the conversation between Richard and John.

Richard knew the old man heard, and didn't care. He stared at John, frowning, but suddenly full of a quick hope. "You had news of Vicki."

John shook his head.

The hope drained away, leaving a bitter taste in Richard's mouth, a burning in his eyes. "I see."

"We must do something."

"We'll wait." It was hard to say, to find patience when there was so little of it in him. He had driven her away by his own act. He had to suffer for it.

"I've gone everywhere I could think of, Richard."

"So have I," Richard answered.

"You?"

"Of course. Did you imagine I haven't searched for her?" Hours spent in fruitless riding through the town, in neighborhoods he'd never seen before. His eyes ached with squinting. His heart hung like a stone in his chest. He felt as if there was only emptiness

117

where before there had been life. But, always, he had told himself that he would have her back.

He had completed the plans for the wiring of Cavendish Cove for electrical power. He had sketched out the alterations and given the plans to a carpenter. He had ridden to Newport on the Old Colony trolley and paid the balance on the place. All the while he told himself that he would have her back. She would stand with him on the widow's walk, and the wind would blow her hair from her lifted face.

Now he asked heavily, "Do you think I don't care?"

"I know you do," John answered.

"Then allow me to do what I think best."

"Just wait?"

Richard nodded.

"I won't give up," John told him.

Richard gave him a sober look. "Neither will I."

It was the same day. Matilda stood near the trellis roses. There were garden shears in her pocket and garden gloves on her hands. But the basket at her feet was empty. She watched the yellowjackets dart over the pollen at the center of the red petals, and wondered where Vicki was, and how she fared.

A horse clip-clopped up the driveway. Sighing, she saw Rosamund alight from the carriage, murmur to her driver, and then start toward her.

Matilda was in no frame of mind to receive guests, but Rosamund was here, and had seen her. There was nothing to be done.

"I've come for only a moment, Matilda," Rosamund said. "I did so want to know how you are."

"Well," Matilda answered dryly. She led the younger woman to a stone bench beyond the rose trellis. "Shall we sit down?"

"I wondered if there were news of Vicki. It seems so odd. Richard must be beside himself."

"We've heard nothing," Matilda said.

"And you're worried, too, I know. Still, in a way, you must also be relieved."

Matilda fixed her eyes on the tall crowns of the

maples. Here and there a red leaf hung among the green. It would be autumn soon.

Rosamund went on, "And the worst is, I suppose, not knowing. But of course she had her reasons."

"Perhaps," Matilda said.

"Such an odd way to behave. I always did wonder about her, Matilda."

Matilda's black eyes swept Rosamund up and down. She said softly, "There's nothing odd about Vicki. And you never wondered about her either. You were only jealous."

"Indeed?" Rosamund's voice was tart. "And what about you, Matilda?"

"I want Richard to be happy. I was wrong. I wish she'd come back so I could tell her so."

Vicki was at home in the small room. It was clean and neat. Light curtains at the dormer window, a potted plant on the sill and an old patchwork quilt on the bed gave it a cared-for look even though the paint was peeling.

From the open window a hot morning breeze brought the scent of ripening peaches mingled with the stench of coal smoke.

Vicki smiled as she pinned her hair up before the looking glass. She smoothed her skirt over her hips, and slipped on a long white apron, its ruffled hem starched. There was a stir downstairs, and in only a few moments, Mrs. Wood would open the shop door, and the first customers of the day, usually women returning from early Mass, would stop in for milk and day-old rolls.

Vicki turned to straighten the quilt on the bed, thinking of the lucky chance that had brought her here.

She had left the old woman behind, five and a half dollars poorer, but somewhat wiser, and much more cautious. She had wandered the streets for the better part of a day before turning into a familiar road. There she had seen the grocery store at which Rosamund had once stopped, the place where Vicki had met Leslie later on. Vicki had frozen then, caught in such compelling pain that she couldn't move.

Leslie. She must forget him now, as she must forget the Cavendishes and everyone left behind on Highland Avenue. She must ignore her loneliness, stop wondering how John fared, if Richard looked for her, what Matilda had said when she learned Vicki was gone.

Leslie. She had begun a new life, which had in it no place for him. But still she imagined him holding out his arms to her.

A two-wheeled bicycle rolled by. A child's ball bounced at her feet. A dog frisked at her ankles. These combined to break the fantasy.

She went to the shop, pretending to study its window while she fought her tears. When her vision cleared, she saw the hand-written sign. *Help Wanted*.

It was as if Good Providence had seen her in her need. That was what her father would have called it. Hearing the distant echo of his voice, she walked inside.

A bell tinkled. Mrs. Wood hurried from behind the flowered curtain. She was small, round, pink of cheek.

Vicki introduced herself, spoke about the job.

Mrs. Wood asked no questions, but instead, murmured, "My husband's ill. It's his heart. He needs much attention." She cast an anxious glance at the doorway, and a wry smile touched her lips. "So do my customers. Which is why I must have help." She looked down at the wicker basket at Vicki's feet. "You have no place to stay?"

"I was looking for a room when I saw your sign, and decided to stop here first."

"If it suits you you can stay here," Mrs. Wood smiled. "There's a room upstairs." She tipped her head to listen. Then: "My husband. I'll be back."

Vicki looked around the shop. Barrels of onions and potatoes stood in a corner. Bins of oranges and peaches were against the wall. There was an ice chest with milk and eggs and cheeses. Racks of bread and rolls leaned against each other. A counter scale stood near the cash drawer.

It was somehow familiar to Vicki though the goods were different. Here there was the odor of food rather than tobacco. Just then the bell tinkled. The door opened.

A woman stepped in. "Oh, dear, where's Mrs. Wood? I need my milk."

"I'll get it for you," Vicki had smiled. She made her first sale then, carefully counting the change she received, and putting it near the cash drawer.

So Vicki had started to work immediately. It was only after she blew out the lamp and fell into bed, having passed a long busy day, that she suddenly realized that she was in the one place where, more than any other, she was most likely to meet either Elise or Leslie or Rosamund.

She stared into the dark. Any one of them could walk in tomorrow or the next day with a list of needs for the school. Why hadn't she thought of it before? Some time or other they'd see her, and they'd no doubt tell Richard.

And what if they did? she asked herself. She had no reason to hide. She had determined that she must live independently, and she was doing just that. Slowly her alarm faded. She leaned against the pillows. She need explain nothing to Elise or Leslie. She need say nothing to Rosamund. She could work and live where she pleased.

Finally she closed her eyes, drifted into tired sleep. But Richard invaded her unwilling dreams. She felt his fingers close on her jaw, tilting her face up. His burning eyes were fixed on hers. He whispered hoarsely, "I want you, Vicki."

Now, three weeks later, still remembering the dream, she hurried downstairs. She put her head between the curtains and smiled at Mr. Wood. He lay propped on a thick bolster, his mouth blue-lipped. "Good morning," he whispered, breathless as always.

Mrs. Wood stirred a thin gruel, offered her husband a spoonful, but spoke to Vicki. "It's a lovely day."

"It is," Vicki agreed. Then: "I'll open up."

Soon, and not a moment too soon, the shop was ready for business. The window was washed, the counters scrubbed. Newspapers and bags were lined up for wrapping. The scale was polished; the cash drawer unlocked.

The door bell tinkled repeatedly. While Vicki weighed cheese and produce, toted up bills, the day passed.

That evening after supper, Mrs. Wood said, "You've hardly been out of the shop for an hour since you came, Vicki. Wouldn't you like to visit a friend this evening?"

Vicki shook her head. But she thought of John. How pleasant those days spent with him had been. The tinkle of the sleigh bells as they rode past St. Patrick's Cemetery at the bend in Highland Avenue. His quiet voice as he told her to look quickly to see the faint glint of the lights of Providence across the river and some twenty miles away.

"My church has a youth group," Mrs. Wood was saying. "They meet in a little while. Perhaps you'd like to see what it's like."

Again Vicki shook her head.

The next morning Mitch Ryan came in. He masked his surprise, said with a crooked grin, "I never expected to find you here, Miss Vicki."

She had known that sometime either Elise or Leslie or Rosamund would see her. Mitch Ryan was as good as Rosamund, for within the hour, he'd no doubt tell her that he'd seen Miss Victoria Davelle, working in a food shop. And Rosamund would go to Richard, or to Matilda. Either way, Vicki would have to face Richard once more.

But Mitch, looking her up and down, had other ideas. He owed nothing to Rosamund, or to the Cavendishes. He said, with a meaningful look in his blue eyes, "You must be lonesome, now you've left your friends behind."

"It's no concern of yours," Vicki answered.

"No need to take that tone." She was, after all, only

a shop girl now, he told himself, an English snip who needed to learn her place.

"Was there something you wanted to buy?" she asked.

"Ah, well," he smiled. "I can't blame you. Why look at a lowly groom when you can set your sights higher? Though how you plan to do that from here, I don't know." He grinned, went on, "Here's what Miss Rosamund wants for the school. We'll be going out later. Want to come?"

"No," she retorted. She took the list, turned away. Rosamund's script was hard to read. Working quickly, she began to pull down canned goods from the shelves. Tomatoes, beans. Flour by the sack. When the order was made up, she gave Mitch the bill. He put his mark on it, thanked her, and then said, "Miss Rosamund says that Mrs. Parker will settle the account. They'll shop closer to the school from now on."

Vicki nodded, careful to hide her relief.

Mitch said, "But I'll see you again, Miss Vicki," as he went out.

There had been a heavy emphasis in his voice. She told herself that she had imagined it. But that night her room seemed too hot. She moved restlessly from the window to the bed and back again. She took up her mother's picture, then put it down. Finally she decided to go out. She tiptoed down the stairs, left through the side door. The street was empty, quiet. A pale light shone in the middle of the next block, and there were voices, so she went that way.

The pale light spilled from beyond the swinging doors of a saloon. She hurried past it with catcalls and shrill whistles trailing her from inside. By the time she had reached the far corner, she was frightened.

She didn't want to pass before the saloon again, but wasn't certain that she could find her way home without retracing her footsteps. She hadn't explored the neighborhood and didn't know it. And it was too late to be out alone. At last, squaring her shoulders, she crossed to the far side of the street and turned back. Again, at midblock, there were catcalls and whistles.

But this time the saloon doors swung back. A short dark-haired man grinned at her. A taller one loomed behind him.

She took small quick steps, hurrying on. But suddenly there was a man on each side of her. Then there were two men before her, and two more behind. They grinned drunkenly when she said, "Let me pass by, if you please," and they mocked her in voices that were very nearly familiar.

"Let me pass," she said again, and one of the men retorted, "You've no pisspot for protection now, have you?"

She knew why the voices had been almost familiar. She had never had a good look at these men, but she had heard them before. She had heard them at her door, in the old woman's house.

A carriage rolled near, slowed, and picked up speed again. A trolley bell clanged blocks away. A cloud passed over the narrow crescent of the moon.

One of the surrounding men put a large calloused hand on her arm, cried, "Come on, lady. Have a drink with us, and we'll forgive you."

She tried to free herself, but couldn't. She took a step forward, but the circle around her tightened so that she had to stop.

From beyond the rim of pale light there came a loud laugh. Mitch Ryan pushed his way through. He drew her close to him, faced the men around them, his ginger head down and his jaw out, plainly ready to brawl.

Then the saloon keeper appeared at the swinging doors, looked over them, and shouted, "Drinks inside on the house, boys!"

Vicki felt her heart beat through a long moment of pulsing silence, then with a shout of laughter the circle broke. The men trooped into the saloon.

"Thank you, Mitch," Vicki whispered dryly. "I don't know what I'd have done if you hadn't come by."

He grinned at her. He didn't tell her that he'd been following her since she left the shop. The minute he'd seen what was coming, he'd known what he would do.

"I'll walk you back," he said. "This isn't the place for a lady to be walking about after dark."

She was grateful for his company until they reached the shop, but when she thanked him again, prepared to go in, he said, "Ask me to visit for a little while."

"I can't do that."

"You can't? Why not? Or is it because you've no need for me now?" He pulled her close. "But I don't see anybody else around.'"

She thrust him away and went indoors.

He swore under his breath. But he was relieved that her unfriendliness made him feel good about what he already knew he was going to do.

Later that night, he put down his cards when Harry said, "I guess that does it for me."

Mitch was glad that Harry had called the time, but he didn't tell Harry so. There were some things a brother didn't have to know.

He made his farewells, and clumped down the driveway. When he reached the road he angled back on stealthy feet. Nettie was waiting for him in the hemlock grove.

Mitch waited until John reached the end of the driveway. He had thought it through for the past three days, considering the best for himself. He could have gone to the mill and spoken to Richard, but for reasons he didn't examine too closely he preferred not to deal with the older Cavendish brother. He could have told Rosamund, but he was certain she wouldn't thank him for the information. So he had settled on John.

When he called out, John stopped.

"A few words with you?" Mitch asked.

John climbed down, held the reins in one hand, patted the horse with the other, while Mitch explained, and ended triumphantly, "So that's where she is. I knew you'd want to know."

John's expression was unreadable. He asked, "Have you spoken to Miss Dean as well?"

"I thought I'd leave that to you." Mitch waited. Then: "And if you don't want me to say anything, my lips are sealed."

John gave him a level look. "I don't care what you do." He pulled out a five-dollar bill. "Take this for your trouble."

Mitch eyed it, held mute by disappointment. He couldn't believe his planning had come to this. He'd been thinking of hundreds, and ended with nothing. He considered demanding more, then decided that John might mention that to Rosamund. Mitch grumbled his thanks, and went away.

John pulled himself into the saddle. He wasn't surprised at what Mitch had told him. He had supposed that Vicki must be somewhere close by. But he was possessed of an anxious eagerness to see her. He rode directly to the food shop. He tied his horse to a hitching post and stood outside, peering past the window that Vicki had washed earlier that morning. He could smell the oranges and apples on display, and the smokiness of cut ham. There was a constant bustle within, as men and women passed him by. By the dim light he saw the glow of Vicki's hair. He saw the flash of her smile when she handed over a newspaper-wrapped parcel.

Finally he went to the mill. When he told Richard, his brother smiled bleakly. "She has spirit, hasn't she, John?"

"What're you going to do?" John asked.

"Let me have time to think."

"You can't let her stay in such surroundings."

"You know that I don't want to." Richard took a deep breath. "But I'm not sure there's anything I can do."

It was on the tip of John's tongue to ask what had happened. But instead he asked, "What about Mother? What about everyone else?"

"They'll have to be told where Vicki is," Richard said.

After John left, Richard sat for a long time, hardly aware of the noise around him. The slam of the shuttles, the cries of "Bobbin boy!" all seemed far away. By his own intemperate action he had blighted his hopes. He supposed that time alone might mend the damage he had done.

But he had to see Vicki. He could no longer wander in the emptiness her going had left behind.

Late in the afternoon he went to the food shop.

Vicki turned pale when she saw him. Her hands, roughened by strong soap, went still on the counter top. Since the night when Mitch had rescued her from the street thugs she had been expecting this. As the days passed, her expectation dulled. But even so, when she saw his wide shoulders in the doorway, a cold blanket of shock enveloped her. In her mind there was the single flickering taper on the veranda at Cavendish Cove. She felt his sweat on her hot cheeks, and his body against hers. She had prepared for this moment, planning small speeches that would dismiss him. As she raised her eyes to look at him, she forgot them all, and gasped, "Richard!"

"I wanted to see you," he said.

"Mitch told you?"

"He told John."

"I ought to have known," she said bitterly.

"And what if you had? Would you have run away again, Vicki?"

"No," she said. "There's no reason for that." Then: "What do you want?"

He wanted everything. To see her smile. To hold her in his arms. He said only, "Just to be certain you're all right."

"I am," she answered. But her voice shook. Her eyes refused to meet his. It was as if she were that divided woman she had once seen in the cheval glass. A part of her wanted to rage and scream at him. Another part of her insisted that she pretend nothing had happened, that she would only shame herself by remembering the day in Newport.

He was saying, "You needn't have slipped away a:
you did. We were all very concerned for you."

"Would you have allowed me to go otherwise?"

His lips turned in a narrow smile. "I'd have arguec
with you. But I couldn't have stopped you."

"It seemed best this way," she said finally.

A small boy trotted in, asked for a loaf of bread
She turned to serve him, and the smile Richard hac
wanted to see was on her lips. When she turned back
to Richard, it was gone.

The tinkle of the doorbell seemed loud when the
boy departed. There was the tick of a clock from
somewhere, the murmur of soft voices from beyonc
the curtained doorway.

He said. "I'm sorry, you know . . . Sorry for what
happened."

She shook her head, unable to speak for the surge
of anger that blocked her throat.

"I'd give anything if I could turn time back."

"I don't want to speak of it," she said quickly. "It
doesn't matter."

"It does matter. But it's done. And for all that I
bitterly regret it, I can't change that." He looked into
her eyes. "Vicki, I'd like to think that we could be
friends, though."

"Friends," she cried. "Friends! Even now you don't
know what you've done to me."

"But I do," he answered. "And if there were a way
to undo it, then I would." It was as far as he could
go in humbling himself. He said stiffly, "In any event,
I still feel responsible for you."

"You needn't."

He went on as if she hadn't spoken, "If you should
need anything, please let me know. Let John or my
mother know."

"Thank you," she said, and turned away.

She didn't watch while he went outside. She stood
frozen until she heard the surrey roll off, then with a
sigh of relief, she caught up a rag and began to scrub
the counter.

That evening Rosamund said, "But how extraordinary, Matilda. What on earth will people say when they learn that a relation of yours is working in a grocery store?"

"I don't care what they say," Matilda answered. "But I hope she'll decide to come back where she belongs."

"I quite agree," Rosamund answered, but when she reached home she broke two cut-glass decanters, and then sat down to write Davis Peabody to suggest he stop for tea the next time he came down from Boston.

Chapter 12

JOHN VISITED VICKI TWICE IN THE WEEKS THAT FOL-lowed. He limped in, waited quietly until she wasn't occupied with a customer, then presented her with a box of Lowney's chocolates. After a few minutes of conversation, he left. The next time he came he brought her a copy of Mary Johnston's *To Have and to Hold* from Adams Book Store. She ate the bonbons and read the book, but she refused both of his tenta-tive suggestions that she go to the house, if only for tea.

Gradually the memory of the last time she had seen Richard began to blur, and as that happened she al-lowed herself to believe she was rid of him, and would never see him again.

It was mid-September, with the maple leaves turn-ing scarlet and gold on the hill, and the nights lengthening and growing cool, when she realized that there was a consequence beyond what she had ex-pected from her trip to Cavendish Cove in Newport with Richard.

She rose into a dark morning very tired, but that

was as usual. She was washing her face when suddenly a wave of sickness overcame her. She leaned over the white porcelain basin, retching. Sweat spilled from her forehead and down her cheeks. The floor heaved beneath her feet. She trembled violently, and in the looking glass, she saw her muddy color.

She breathed in deep hard breaths. Slowly the spell passed over. She swallowed the sour taste in her throat, and finished dressing and went down to the shop.

Mrs. Wood frowned with worry when Vicki refused breakfast. The porridge was unthinkable; the coffee brought dampness to her upper lip.

"I've some Red Blood Makers that I got from the Apothecary Corrigan," Mrs. Wood said. "Will you take it?"

Vicki answered, "I really do feel better. I don't think I need any medicine now."

She went through the day without further incident, and Mrs. Wood looked relieved. But the next morning, Vicki had no sooner arisen when she was seized with nausea again. She barely made it to the basin before green bile spewed from her throat, and her body shook with chill and then with waves of burning heat.

When she could think, she knew that she couldn't dismiss these morning convulsions as transient stomach upsets. A suspicion was upon her. She remembered those of her father's parishioners who had whispered together over the problems of women. She recalled Mrs. McVey's blunt remarks.

She refused to believe it. All the while she moved through her usual chores, she adamantly refused to accept it. But the knowledge was there, a lump in her heart. Her smile of greeting began to falter. Her thanks when she made change became forced. She waited, but nothing happened to disprove her fear. By the end of the month she was certain. And at last, unwillingly, she admitted to herself that she was pregnant with Richard Cavendish's child.

It was insupportable that an infant could have

been conceived in those moments of anguish. She had to do something, she told herself. She would not have Richard's baby. The words echoed in her mind through every moment of every day that passed. Her breasts grew rounder, and more tender. Her body was preparing itself against her own will and beyond her own control.

Mrs. Wood watched her, pale eyes concerned. One day, after feeding her husband, she came into the shop, and stood close by Vicki, and whispered kindly, "Vicki, dear, you're in trouble, aren't you?"

Color flamed in the girl's cheeks as she nodded.

"But it's not the end of the world, child. We must think what to do."

"It's the end of the world for me," Vicki said. "I won't have it! I mean to get rid of it as fast as I can."

"You don't mean that," Mrs. Wood said, eyes round with horror. "It would be wicked, Vicki. Whatever you've done, however you feel, you needn't stoop to that. Perhaps he . . . the man . . ." Mrs. Wood's voice faltered, then steadied as she went on, "Perhaps he'll marry you. I could talk to him, Vicki." The small woman, usually so bent and weary, was suddenly straight and abrim with energy. "I could make him see his sin," she said firmly.

"He . . . the man . . ." Vicki laughed bitterly. "You don't know."

"And you've your cousins to turn to. You're in no way helpless."

But Vicki folded her lips tightly, shook her head. She didn't want to think of it, speak of it. There was only one thing for her to do.

"If you love the man," the older woman whispered, "then why can't you marry him, have the child?"

"Love him?" Vicki burst out. "I despise him. I'll not tell him what's happened, nor ask for his help."

"He has the right to know," Mrs. Wood told her.

"Never." Vicki turned away. Her hands became small fists at her sides. "I'll destroy the child, and every reminder of his touch. Oh, I'll have nothing in me of his to curdle my soul!"

"You can't stop what's begun," Mrs. Wood said.

"I will," Vicki told her.

Mrs. Wood barely moved her lips, asking, "But what will you do?"

"There are women who can prevent a child from coming," Vicki answered. "I'll find one to help me."

"It's dangerous," the older woman protested. "Don't you know the risk you take with your own life? And don't you see the evil in it?"

"I'll take the risks," Vicki retorted. "And whatever happens will happen." Then, with a laugh, "Don't speak of evil to me. The thing inside me comes from evil, and it's going to be destroyed."

But, for all her determination, Vicki found herself to be helpless. She knew no one who could give her the information she needed. She knew nowhere to seek it. She marked time, waiting, but she didn't know what she waited for.

One evening, as she and Mrs. Wood were closing the shop, John came in. He gave her his usual diffident smile, then asked her to go for a drive with him.

While Mrs. Wood nudged her meaningfully, Vicki refused. She felt as if she were choking, all her feelings rising up to overcome her. She left him quickly so that he wouldn't see her tears.

He stared at the doorway through which she had fled, then asked Mrs. Wood, "What's the matter?"

Mrs. Wood wanted to tell him, but she feared what Vicki might do. Finally she said, "Vicki's not feeling well."

"I see that. But what is it?"

Mrs. Wood answered firmly, "You must ask her yourself."

But John knew that would be useless. The same night he told Richard about his visit to the shop.

Richard listened, said nothing. But soon after, he left the house.

He stood at the side door of the grocery, his mouth grim, a muscle jumping in his cheek. If Vicki were ill, then she must allow him to care for her. It didn't matter what had happened. She must see a doctor, be

132

made well. She couldn't stay alone here, nor work at this back-breaking job. He knocked at the door, listened as her slow footsteps approached, remembering how lightly she had always walked.

"Who is it?" she asked.

He answered, "Let me in, Vicki. I must see you."

She stared at the door in appalled silence.

"Don't turn me away now, Vicki."

"Oh, why can't you leave me alone?" she said.

"Open the door," he answered. "Or I'll break it down. I want to see you, and I mean to."

She flung the door back and cried, "All right. Look at me then."

The hall was in shadow, a single gas jet flickering. But he saw the whiteness of her face, the dark places beneath her eyes.

"You're ill. I want to help you," he said softly.

"Help me, did you say? You've done all to me that you can do. Just leave me alone and let me help myself. That's all I ask from you; that's all I want of you."

He knew with instant clarity what had happened. He understood her bitterness and pain. He had brought her to this. Now he must mend it. He kept his arms at his sides, though he wanted to hold her. He kept his voice even, saying, "You're expecting my child."

She gasped and went paler still, though that hadn't seemed possible. "No, no," she cried. "Oh, no, you're quite mistaken."

"But you are, Vicki."

Her answer came as a harsh whisper, words trembling on her lips. "Very well. Yes, I am. But I don't mean to have it. So you needn't worry for me."

"You don't mean to have it!" His dark eyes narrowed. "Then what do you intend?"

"You know," she retorted.

"But there's no need," he said. "I love you, and want only to care for you. Now you have no choice."

"I do have," she answered coldly. She looked down

at her trembling hands, and spoke to them. "I'll find a way."

"I won't let you destroy what we've made between us. I won't allow you to risk your life."

"It's not your decision to make," she told him. "I'll do as I please with my body. I'll take whatever risk I choose."

"And die of it?" Richard asked quietly. "Or live to regret it for as long as you live?"

"I won't listen to you," she said.

His anger was a living force. It leaped between them like lightning. But he answered only, "Consider further, and you'll change your mind," and then he went away.

"Two pounds, Mrs. Taylor," Vicki said tiredly. She passed the bag of potatoes over the counter, accepted some change.

She didn't hear Mrs. Taylor say goodbye. A lethargy had wrapped her since she had seen Richard three days before. She had thought of moving away, but how could she with so little strength? How could she hide if he were determined to find her? Now she could hardly remember what she had told him. But the expression on his face was burned into her mind. He had looked like a man flayed when he left her.

The doorbell gave its usual ping. A warm wind swept the shop, billowing in the doorway curtain. From the darkening sky, there was a grumble of distant thunder, and the clip-clop of horses' hoofs in the road.

Vicki looked up.

Richard stood there, John beside him. Without speaking they moved toward her. Richard tall and straight, his shoulders blocking out the gray light, John smaller, slight, limping.

She wanted to turn and flee. She was suddenly frightened. But she held her ground.

They faced her across the counter. From the back room, she heard Mrs. Wood saying cheerfully, "Now there, dear, clean sheets and fresh pillows are such a comfort, aren't they?"

When silence fell again, Richard said, "I want you to come with us."

"No, Richard."

"But you will. I've told you that I'm sorry for what happened. I can't do more than that. Now I shall take care of you, as I want to and must."

"No," she said again.

"Then let me tell you how it's going to be," he answered. "You'll come with us whether you want to or not. The arrangements are made. We'll discuss it no longer."

She backed away from him, but it was too late. He was around the counter, on one side of her, John was at the other. There was a hand at her right elbow, another at her left.

"John?" she asked softly.

"It's for your own sake, Vicki."

She opened her mouth to cry out, but no sounds came.

Mrs. Wood poked her head from behind the curtain. She gave Richard and John quick startled looks. "What's this, Vicki?" she asked.

"You know my cousins," Vicki said hoarsely.

"We've come to take her home," John said. "We're concerned about her health." He gave Vicki a faint smile. "She's a brave girl, and always wanted to be independent, but we can't allow her to make herself ill."

Mrs. Wood smiled. She was relieved that Vicki had someone to take care of her. It had been a burden on the older woman's heart, not knowing what would happen, knowing only that she herself could do nothing for the girl.

"We'll get your things, Vicki," John said.

The three of them climbed to the room above. Within moments, Vicki had packed. The last thing she put into the wicker basket was her mother's picture. But she didn't look into the well-loved face, and think of her heart's desire. Leslie was become a distant dream to her now. She hadn't seen him since she left the Cavendish house. She supposed she might never see him again.

As he helped her into the carriage, John said, "Don't worry, Vicki. All will be well."

She knew that he was blameless in this. She doubted that he even knew the truth. It was all Richard's doing, and John simply followed after to see to her well-being.

Richard. She stole a quick look at his face. It was set, as if carved in stone. His jaw was hard, his mouth tight. He didn't say a word to ease her mind. He didn't care how she felt. He would have his own way. That was all that mattered to him. Bitterness rose up to nearly drown her. Love was what she had wanted. And it would be denied her. Leslie was a longing that had never been fulfilled. Because Richard Cavendish was determined to have his own way. She closed her eyes against the burning tears that flooded them. She wouldn't let him see her weep. No matter what happened. He'd never see her weep.

The carriage jolted over the Plymouth Street bridge. She looked out at the black oily water of the Quequechan River. Once it had cut through the city, dropping in a series of falls to the river. Now it mostly ran underground in huge pipes and surfaced only in a few places. Not long before she had read of a body found drifting near here at dawn. She shuddered and turned her head away.

Soon the carriage rocked to a stop before a small house. It was set back from the street in a neatly kept garden. Roses burned in the sunlight of late September. Overhead there was still the rumble of distant thunder.

"It's all arranged," John said encouragingly.

She folded her hands in her lap, but didn't move otherwise. "What's all arranged?" she asked finally.

Richard looked at her now. She saw in his eyes the light of mockery. "I thought that you understood. Our marriage ceremony will be performed here in a few minutes, with John as our witness. It will be proper, and legal, and binding. And whether you like it or not, you'll be my wife." He paused for the space of a breath, then added, "And our child will be born in wedlock."

Her first thought was that John knew. The heat of a blush burned her cheeks. But she said to Richard, "The child is what matters to you."

"Think what you want," he retorted. He got down, offered his hand.

She had no choice. The child was within her body and growing with every instant that passed, however resentfully she sheltered it. There was no way to erase what had happened. She must somehow teach herself to live with it. She must learn to look to the future.

It was with that thought in mind that she allowed Richard to hand her down from the carriage, loathing the touch of his fingers on her arm. She walked with him up the path to the house, feeling as if she had left her body and soul behind, and that those major parts of herself stood off at a distance, to watch in dazed bewilderment, at what followed thereafter.

Like most young girls, she had dreamed of her wedding. She would wear white, a trailing of lace that hung to her shoulders and was fixed to her head with a tiara of orange blossoms. Her gown would be white, too, and gathered below the breast, falling softly to matching satin slippers. She would carry a bouquet of lilies of the valley, and a Bible covered in white doeskin. And since meeting Leslie, she had been able to picture the groom as tall with golden hair and a gentle smile.

The reality was nothing like what she had dreamed. From the distance to which those major parts of herself had retreated, she watched a wooden-hearted puppet stand beside Richard. Its shirtwaist was blue with a limp fichu. Its darker blue skirt was wrinkled. Its broad-brimmed straw hat had a single wide ribbon that fell to its rigid shoulders. And the man beside it was dark of eye, dark of hair, with no smile on his face.

Pastor Farley was small, bald, and abrim with good

will. He rubbed plump hands together, saying, "Now then, Mr. Cavendish, are we ready?"

"We're ready," Richard answered.

For an instant Vicki seemed to see her father before her . . . his defiant cowlick and sad eyes suddenly alight with joy in the wedding rites. An ache of hunger rose in her. Oh, to turn back the hands of the clock . . . to be a child again, listening to his sermons . . .

The familiar ceremony was a blur of words which she hardly heard. Those parts of her that stood aside noted that John's hands were clenched, that a muscle twitched in Richard's lean cheek. They saw a slant of fading sunlight pierce the shadows of the room to wrap a pot of geraniums in gold. They heard the rustle of a turning page.

Richard took a cold hand in his. They watched as he placed a slim gold band on its finger.

"I now pronounce you man and wife," Pastor Farley said joyfully. "Mr. Cavendish, you may kiss your beautiful bride."

Richard tilted her face up. Their eyes met. His lips brushed her cheek as she turned her head away.

It was done, she thought. There was no way she could make it undone. But she'd render him sorry for it, she told herself.

Later, driving away, she said the words aloud, "You'll be sorry, Richard. One day you'll regret this. I'll make certain of that."

He didn't answer her. It was as if he hadn't heard. He took from his pocket a small box, handed it to her. "Open it, Vicki." When she didn't, he himself removed the blue lid.

A large square diamond encircled by tiny sapphires gleamed at her blindingly like a second sun. She stared at it, said nothing.

Richard placed it on her hand. "It's the ring with which we sealed our secret engagement on an evening last July."

Her eyes flashed to his face. She saw hunger there, and hope. He could pretend, but she could not.

"There was no engagement," she said.

Again it was as if he hadn't heard. "If the ring

doesn't suit you, or needs adjustment, we can take it to Gifford's."

"It doesn't matter," she told him, her eyes on John's back. From where he sat in the driver's seat, he could surely hear. But that didn't matter either. She said, "What happened on an evening last July was no engagement. Why act as if it was?"

Richard was silent for a moment. When he spoke, his voice was gentle. "This is the beginning, Vicki. *This is.* You can make the future what you will."

Bitterness curled her lip, burned from her eyes. It roughened her voice as she demanded, "You expect me to pretend I'm a willing partner in this farce?"

"I'm asking you to accept that you are Vicki Cavendish now, and my wife, and to go on from there. I say it for your own welfare, and that of the child you'll have."

Hating him, she didn't answer.

He went on, "A few years ago you'd have had an arranged marriage. You know that as well as I do. How is this so different from that?"

"A few years ago isn't now. And I'd never have married without love. It's you that's made it different."

He turned from her to look from the carriage window.

Soon they reached the driveway.

She braced herself to enter the house she had left with a vow never to return.

A gown lay spread on the canopied bed. It was silk, with blond ruffles at its high neck and on the cuffs of its long full sleeves. A matching peignoir lay beside it, and on the Turkey carpet below, there were white silken slippers embroidered with silver threads.

Richard had no doubt bought them for her, Vicki thought, just as he had bought the narrow gold wedding circlet and the diamond ring that sparkled on her finger. She had no idea how he had accomplished everything in the past three days, yet somehow he had managed it. She couldn't imagine what he had told his mother, Mrs. Beamis, the others. He wasn't given to explanations. But they had all been prepared to receive her.

Nettie had bobbed a curtsey, smiled broadly. "Welcome home, Miss Vicki. And good luck."

"A happy day," Mrs. Beamis had cried, and touched a red finger to the corner of her eye. "Oh, I'm so glad to have you back where you belong!"

The surprise had been Matilda, waiting in the morning room, with a decanter of sherry at the ready, and plates of small sandwiches, and a huge bouquet of forced chrysanthemums, which reminded Vicki of those she had tended so carefully in the small garden in Rye.

When Vicki, followed by Richard and John, had entered the room, Matilda held out her hands, saying, "All my best wishes are for your future, child."

Vicki had searched her eyes for anger, seen nothing but welcome, and found herself speechless. Her silence was covered by John, who described the wedding ceremony, and by Richard, who poured sherry for the four of them, and then lifted his glass to say, "To my bride."

Later there had been a dinner, with champagne, and flowers on the table, and a cake of eight layers made of white sugar. A tiny silver bell had decorated the top, and Richard had presented it to her while John and Matilda smiled.

She accepted the bell, her face stiff, hating him for mocking her, but powerless to prevent it. How it galled her to be part of the charade in which they were engaged. She'd rather have flung the bell in his face and torn the wedding ring from her hand. But she knew that however satisfying such acts might be, they would also be useless.

The evening had dragged on, with Richard passing champagne to her until she was quite dizzy with it. The sight of the gown on the bed, the look of the room which she had never seen before, but where she had heard Richard pace through the nights, had driven the wine giddiness away.

Now there was a sound at the door.

She turned quickly as Richard came in. "You must be pleased with yourself," she said.

"It was a good dinner, I think."

"Delightful," she agreed. "Your mother and Mrs. Beamis went to a great deal of trouble, and with so little time in which to do so much."

"They're fond of you."

"Mrs. Beamis is, I suppose. As for your mother, I can't imagine what you've done to change her so."

He grinned suddenly. "You may believe what you like, of course. But my mother's feelings changed of her own accord. Why, I'm not certain myself. But I know she was concerned when you . . . when you left us. I know she's glad you've returned."

"But I am not glad," Vicki said.

He ignored that. "I hope you'll find this room comfortable. If there's anything you need, please tell me."

"Thank you, but what does it matter?"

He said coolly, "You may enjoy it here, or hate it. That will be entirely up to you."

"It's as simple as that, is it? You've arranged the life of your subject, King Richard. You've decreed, and she must obey."

His face was suddenly suffused with color. King Richard. That was what the girls in the mill called him behind his back. He had laughed at it, but he couldn't laugh when Vicki flung the taunt at him. He said harshly, "Obey was part of the vows you took this afternoon."

"Those oaths were nothing to me," she returned. "You forced me to marry you, but you can't make me love you."

"Then don't," he said. "But you'll still have certain duties to perform. The same as any wife."

"You'll make certain that I don't shirk them, won't you?"

He gave her a long level look, but didn't answer.

It wasn't necessary. She understood.

She lay curled at the edge of the big bed, as distant

from him, he knew, as he would allow her to be. She was still, but he was certain that she didn't sleep.

He remembered the first time he had taken her into his arms, unable to rein the tides of his hunger. She had fought him then, but only briefly. Yet before she had become that lifeless doll beneath him, he had known and savored her body's unwilling response. Tonight she had been that lifeless doll again, and there had been no instant even when her body acknowledged his. She was passive to his hands, his lips, passive when he entered her with such care that he felt he must burst with it or weep with it.

Now, emptied but still in hunger for her, he wondered how many dawns they would face together, sleepless but unspeaking, warmed by each other's bodies, yet remaining in a chill.

Chapter 13

"COME IN," EUSTACIA COSGROVE SAID. BUT SHE didn't move aside, so that Richard was left standing on the threshold while she continued, "And how is your dear wife? She looked wonderfully well at the Academy last evening. And wasn't the Boston Symphony good?"

A cold wind ruffled Richard's hair, and billowed in his coat, and on the breath of it, it seemed, Albert Cosgrove whispered from behind her bulk a pained, "My dear."

"She's lovely indeed," Eustacia went on, unperturbed, but stepping aside, and closing the door hung with its Christmas wreath. "Women in her condition always are, aren't they? But you must be careful. The roads are icy these days . . ."

"My dear," Albert said once more.

Richard smiled at Eustacia, untroubled that she might count on her fingers, and wait with bated breath for Vicki to be brought to confinement. Vicki was five months pregnant now, but still slim, and the voluminous gowns she wore covered the thickening at her waist. The child would be born early, but Vicki would suffer no embarrassment. He would see to it himself.

He stripped off his gloves, allowed Albert to take his hat and outdoor coat. It wasn't necessary to respond to Eustacia, for while she still spoke, Albert led the way down the mistletoe-decked corridor to his library.

There Richard found some nine other men. The room was blue with cigar smoke. There were decanters of port on the table, and platters of fruitcake.

Richard greeted the others, took a velvet chair near the fireplace and allowed the warmth to enwrap him.

Albert looked at the ormolu clock on the mantel. "There should be more of us. But, as it's still the holiday season though Christmas is past, perhaps they've been delayed. Shall we wait, or go on with the meeting?"

There was a chorus of "Go on. Or we'll be here all night."

Albert was pleased. He wanted to proceed. He had before him a few members of the Fall River Manufacturers' Association, an offshoot of the Board of Trade. They were either private owners, or represented owner corporations, of textile mills in Fall River. They met as the occasion required to consider matters of common interest, to deal as a unit with union demands, to suggest legislation to the State Senate and House of Representatives or to organize against proposed laws antithetical to them.

Albert said, "I have a copy of the report of the State House Committee on relations between employer and employee to be filed the first week of January."

"Is it favorable?" one member asked.

"Favorable enough, I'd say."

"On, on," another man urged.

Listening, Richard stifled a yawn. He'd sooner be at home, watching as Vicki bent her head beneath the light and worked at her needlepoint.

"First there's the section on child labor. No children under fourteen work in factories. In all other occupations they may not work in school hours unless they attend night classes."

"When the law's enforced," was one comment.

"Which is rarely," was another.

"It's in the report," Albert retorted. "And it sounds good." He continued, "On the subject of firing and blacklisting . . . it's illegal to intimidate a worker for union activity."

"Notwithstanding," Richard said, "I'll have in my plant only those I choose to."

There was a grumble of agreement.

Albert nodded, paused to light a Cremo. Then: "And on compensation. The maximum for the death of a man on the job is two thousand dollars."

"Too much," one member said.

"Not enough," countered another. "What of the families?"

"It should be determined by the owner," Richard put in, "and every case judged on its merits." The statement reflected his feeling, but his coming fatherhood had made him more aware of the men who worked for him, of their families, and needs. He found himself often asking Gus Markeson how his Jamie fared.

"Should be," Albert was saying, "but isn't, Richard. This report states the situation under present law." He smiled faintly. "I think you'll agree it's a satisfactory report, if you consider that it'll lead to no further legislation."

There was a single yelp of laughter, amid small grunts of satisfaction.

"Nothing on the eight-hour day," someone said.

"If it's brought up, it'll be ignored," Albert said. He went on to discuss other business.

Richard no longer paid attention. He pulled his watch from his waistcoat pocket, flipped the gold lid. It was nearly nine-thirty. Vicki would be in bed by the time he returned. She would pretend to be asleep. He would count her slow breaths, and feel the warmth of her across the space between them, but he wouldn't touch her. Not that night. Instead he would wait for dawn, and wonder how long it would go on. There were hours, even days, when he would almost believe she had forgotten. When they were with others her ways were beyond reproach. Then, suddenly, when they were alone, her eyes would flash hate, and her sharp tongue rake him. It became harder for him to control his temper.

"Richard . . ."

He heard his name, brought his attention to Albert. "You spoke to me?"

"I was asking if your plans for expansion go on?"

Richard nodded. "We'll break ground as soon as the earth thaws after the first of the year."

"You've heard the talk among the operatives that they'll have no more automation?"

Richard shrugged. "It's possible that I'll have eight looms to a man."

"You'll hear about it," Albert predicted.

"Perhaps."

"You're a brave man, Richard Cavendish," one of the other men said, "to be expanding now when the profit margin is falling."

"I hope that my margin will rise," Richard answered.

He made his farewells quickly, and left before the others. He managed to avoid Eustacia in the corridor.

It was cold outside, dark. The horse's breath steamed in the air. He was glad to reach home. After taking off his outer garments, he looked into the drawing room. The fire was put out; it was empty.

Silently he made his way up the stairs. His bedroom was dark. He leaned beneath the velvet canopy of the four-poster. The quilted robe of satin that he had given Vicki for Christmas lay folded at the foot of the bed. He had still to see her wear it. She lay sleeping on her side, her arms curled around her, her hair a shining fan partly on her pillow, partly on his. He watched her for a long moment, then bent and kissed her cheek before he turned away.

That same night Gus Markeson and Jamie were in the Central Bowling Alleys. It was a long smoky room, dim except for the unshaded bulbs that hung over the bowling alleys and the middle of the pool tables. There was a constant hum of chatter, punctuated by the crash of the bowling balls, the yelps of glee or rage, and the sharp crack of accurately wielded billiard cues. In one corner there was a wooden table with a coffee urn, a huge bowl of pretzels, and pitchers of beer.

Gus and Jamie had a few games of pool. Then Jamie went to sit with Ezra Saunders, who had come in during the play. It was a chance meeting, but Ezra was grateful for it. He enjoyed every moment with Jamie.

But, after a little while, the boy asked, "Is something the matter, Mr. Saunders? You're very quiet."

"I guess I've gotten a bit tired," Ezra answered. "As old men do."

"But you're not old," Jamie protested.

"I'm bald, but I'm not a newborn babe."

Jamie dismissed the joke with the wave of a hand. "No, you're not old." His gaze slid to the billiard table where Gus was playing now with a group of men from the Cavendish mill. Ezra *was* bald, and had large brown spots on the back of his neck, but he had a contagious and breathy laugh and a twinkle in his eye. Gus hardly ever laughed and when he did there was a wrongness in it. Even his occasional smile was not right. It seemed to Jamie that his father was the oldest man in the world, and that it had nothing to do with age.

Gus glanced at Jamie and Ezra before leaning over the table to take his shot. The boy and the old man always found subjects to talk about. But Jamie was a funny kid, and liked grown-up conversation. Gus himself much preferred the ease of listening.

He did that now as he took his turn. The men around the table had just come from Textile Hall, and were still thinking union business.

George Thompson, a weaver, small, slight and black-haired, was saying, "Nobody likes to give a dollar for the initiation fee, and then fifty cents a month for dues. And you can't blame them, not when they don't see what they'll get back."

146

"They won't see that until trouble comes. Like a wage cut," Rex Taylor answered. He was a weaver, too. A middle-aged man with a beer belly that hung over his belt.

There was a murmur of assent. Then George went on, "Five cents a head a month for the national union doesn't seem much but it doesn't leave us a lot to work with. I'd like to see that cut by half."

"The national treasury needs it," Rex objected. "And we'll have our share when it's necessary."

Gus stood back while George angled his cue for a shot. The conversation went on, but Gus looked at Jamie and Ezra, and wondered what they were talking about. He went to the wooden table, bought a dish of pretzels for Jamie and a beer for himself and joined them.

At the other end of the long dim room, Mitch Ryan checked the clock on the wall and decided it was time to go. He wrapped his muffler tight around his neck when he stepped into the cold wind and started up the hill. The road was empty. A narrow moon hung in the sky. He wished he could visit Boston. It was so close, but seemed so far away. If he had money in his pockets, that would make the difference. He could face his Uncle Shamus then, and the door wouldn't slam against him. He imagined it. He, his arms loaded with presents, being welcomed in. Strong tea, a warm fire. Later some beers in the corner saloon, with Shamus introducing him around.

He left all that behind when he reached Highland Avenue, and turned into the dark driveway.

He went quickly, silently, to stand looking up at the windows of the carriage house. No light gleamed behind the curtains. No shadows passed behind the glass. He waited through the space of a few breaths. Nothing. He flicked a pebble at a corner window, and heard its faint rattle as it hit. A curtain was jerked aside, then dropped into place.

He grinned and went to the door. Within moments Nettie was there, her eyes shining at him. "I can only stay a minute," she told him.

He put his arms around her. "We'll go into the stables where it's warm."

147

Chapter 14

THE ROOM WAS STILL NOW, AND DARK.

All through the day while she labored, intent on the task before her, she had been aware of voices and footsteps, and the brilliant April sun that scorched her eyes.

Finally her body was torn asunder by a pain so vast that it burned away all memory of the pain she had had before and left her sinking into sweet-smelling waves of chloroform.

She was suddenly aware of an indignant mewing, and Dr. Stilton's soft chuckle, and she knew her striving was over. The baby that she had unwillingly sheltered was born. She was at last emptied of her burden. Bruised from its own struggle, it still signaled its freedom into life. She dozed, listening to the swift movements around her.

Then Dr. Stilton said, "Mrs. Cavendish . . ."

"Mrs. Cavendish." She was become "Mrs. Cavendish" to him again. But all through the long hours before, he had called her "Vicki," saying, "There's my brave girl. Only a little bit harder. You're almost done, Vicki. Now. Once more."

"You have a son," he told her. "A beautiful boy, Mrs. Cavendish." He leaned closer to put into her limp arms a tiny blue-wrapped bundle.

Mistily she remembered sewing tiny clothes for pauper infants, imagining the small bodies against her breast. This was real. There was a warmth, a softness. Of their own accord her limp arms enclosed the infant protectively. Where she had felt only emptiness before there was sudden joy. She felt herself lifted on a vast wave of exultation. She rode its crest without thought. This was hers. He had come from her body. She had carried him within her flesh, had held him under her heart. He was hers, and of herself.

Then Dr. Stilton said, "Your husband will be happy. I'll go and tell him now."

The mite stirred in her arms. She looked down at him . . . a tangle of curly black hair, minute lines that would soon be dark arching brows . . . Her exultation became pain. She was gripped by it as if a tight fist had suddenly clenched around her. Her husband. Richard.

She turned her face from the infant. The joy drained away. She was emptied, chilled. And into the cold void crept the memory of how the baby had been conceived. It spread dark wings through her.

Dr. Stilton whispered to her, but she shook her head, not listening. When he took the infant from her arms, she didn't look at him. She heard his voice, heard Nettie's answer, knew there were footsteps and rustlings, knew when the big chandelier was turned off and a small lamp lighted nearby. She allowed her linens to be changed, rolling obediently when hands touched her. She allowed a fresh gown, all silk and soft lace, to be slipped over her head, and her hair to be brushed. She was aware of all the preparations, but she didn't open her eyes, nor speak. At last there was silence. Grateful for it, she lay still.

She had been married for seven months. By all accounts she was still a bride. She felt more like a slave who acquiesced in her own enslavement. Yet she had never, not for an instant, been treated that way. Richard had forced her into a marriage that she didn't want, but he refused to acknowledge her feelings. He treated her as if she had gone willingly into his arms and willingly into the life he had made for her. It was as if he believed that by the force of his own desire he could make her feel what she didn't feel.

Her pregnancy had been an easy one, the morning

sickness ending very soon after she returned to the house. She had carried well, hardly showing even until a few weeks before. He had himself planned the nursery, consulting with Matilda when Vicki showed no interest. When he saw that she did no sewing of small gowns, he ordered elaborate layettes. He had had telephones installed in the mill office and house, so as to be reached quickly were she to need him. He was always courteous and considerate. Even in the height of his passion, she sensed that he was careful of her. And lately, he had not touched her, so that she had no longer feared the moment when he came to bed with her.

He was generous to a fault. In October, when he had learned from John that she was to have her eighteenth birthday, he bought her a heavy jade necklace. At Christmas, he gave her an ermine-trimmed cloak and a satin nightgown as well. In March he had brought home bolts of fabrics to be used for the summer wardrobe he insisted she order.

He took her often to the Academy of Music for performances by touring actors, for Sunday afternoon drives, for walks in South Park. There were whole days when it seemed to her that they were an ordinary young couple becoming accustomed to each other in a new marriage. Then something would happen. He'd touch her, give her a sidelong glance. Suddenly all her resentment, rage, would rise again. She would remember, and think of how it might have been. She would dream once more of Leslie.

If Richard guessed her feelings then, he didn't show it. He seemed content as things were. He planned for the baby, saw to the redecorating of the Newport house, prepared for the ground-breaking for the new plant.

John was quiet as always, and ready on the instant to do her bidding, while Matilda continued friendly, as if she had never harbored harsh thoughts of Vicki.

Now there were footsteps in the hall. Vicki lay still. Richard was coming.

It had been a long and grueling wait for him. John

had telephoned the mill the moment Vicki had begun to count the time between pains. Richard had come home at once. He and John stayed together in the morning room, noting each tick of the clock for the past twelve hours, while Matilda came and went, offering occasional encouragement to them. Still, they had listened with raised heads to the unearthly silence that seemed to pour ominously down the steps. Sometimes there were footsteps, and they exchanged glances. But when no call came, they sank back, shrugging uneasily.

Twice in these hours Dr. Stilton had come and then departed, saying, "All's well. I'll return later." Now he had been with Vicki since ten o'clock, and it was near midnight.

Richard's dark hair was tousled, falling in waves on his forehead. His cravat was undone. He wore his jacket open, and beneath it his shirt was damp with the sweat of fear. What if something went wrong and the path of nature took a crooked turn for Vicki? What if his decision to keep her here at home would prove to endanger her?

"Why don't we hear her?" he said now.

John held up his hand, and Richard went still, his face suddenly drawn. Women died in childbirth; even young girls, healthy and strong and beautiful girls, suffered mysterious complications sometimes. He couldn't imagine living without Vicki. Ever since he had seen her on the stoop of the house in Rye, she had been the center of his world. He felt that his very breath depended on her. Nothing mattered to him except her. So he waited, fearful and uncertain, learning such feelings for the first time.

From afar there was the sound of a door closing. Then there were slow footsteps on the stairs.

Richard got up quickly, his tall body rigid, braced as if for a blow.

John sank back in his chair, as if hiding within its large sheltering arms.

Dr. Stilton appeared in the doorway, beaming. He felt the delivery of a child, in any circumstance, to be a miracle, and knew himself privileged to take some part in it. It made bearable the squalor and pain and death that he saw daily. It didn't matter to him what house sheltered a new child. Except that he charged double for his presence on Highland Avenue and nothing for his help on Division Street. The miracle was always the same to him.

"My wife?" Richard asked. "Is she all right?"

"That's a courageous girl, Mr. Cavendish. Not a whimper out of her. As you must know. Since, no doubt, you were listening." He waited. Then: "And it's a fine eight-pound son for you. The first of many, I trust."

John threw his head back and gave vent to an Indian war whoop.

But Richard silently savored the joy of the moment. Vicki was all right. And they had a son. They were a family now. Finally he rang for Nettie, and when she came, he asked for brandy.

"We're all so happy for you, Mr. Richard," she cried.

He thanked her, and when she returned with the tray, he served Dr. Stilton and John. They drank a toast to the new Cavendish, but Richard's mind wasn't on it. He wanted to go to Vicki, to be sure all was well with her. As soon as Dr. Stilton put down his snifter, Richard retied his cravat, smoothed his hair. "I'd like to see my wife."

"Your mother will tell you when Mrs. Cavendish is ready," the doctor answered. "Remember you mustn't stay long. I've never produced a son from my own body, but I assure you that it's tiring work. She needs to sleep and regain her strength."

The doctor was leaving when Matilda came into the hallway, smiling a signal at Richard.

He knew John's eyes followed him as he mounted the stairs. But John could wait a little longer to begin being a doting uncle. Richard wanted these first few minutes alone with Vicki.

At the head of the stairs, Maria Sandora, the nursemaid he had engaged earlier, stood beaming at him.

Her thick black hair was wrapped around her head in a tight braid, but small curls frizzed over her ears. Her black eyes were set deep in her plump face. Her silk uniform clung to her luscious curves. Matilda had objected to his choice of Maria, saying, "Try to find a Yankee. I don't like having a Portugee living in the house." But Richard had ignored her. He felt it wrong to pamper such old-fashioned prejudices.

Now Maria turned toward the nursery, saying, "You have a fine son."

But Richard said only, "Later."

He eased open the door to the bedroom. It was shadowed within. The bloodied sheets and buckets, the blankets and bandages, had been cleared away. Vicki lay beneath the big canopy looking hardly more than a child herself. Her body was slim and flat again under the light satin cover. Her hair was spread on the pillow. As he bent over her, she opened her eyes. "Have you seen him, Richard?"

"Not yet."

"The doctor says he's perfect, but I forgot to look. You look for me, will you?" she asked drowsily.

"He *will* be perfect, Vicki."

"I hope so." Then: "Shall we name him Charles?"

Charles, Richard thought. Another king. Richard, John, and now Charles. Revulsion rose up to fill him. The Cavendishes were too prone to royal names, and at least one of them, himself, was too prone to royal arrogance, too. He said quietly, "I had thought of Alban, Vicki."

"Alban. For my father."

"But only if it pleases you."

"It does," she said. After a moment, she asked, "But why, Richard?"

"Because he gave you to me," Richard answered.

As she closed her eyes tears glinted heavily on her lashes, and spilled slowly over the curve of her cheeks.

Disappointment was a blow deep in his belly. All through the long hours of waiting he had imagined that the baby's birth would mend the rift between them. Now he knew it wasn't to be. But he leaned to touch her shoulder gently. "Vicki, we must forget the past and begin anew."

She turned her head away, refusing to look at him, to answer.

He knew nothing more to say. He looked at her one last time, then left the room.

Maria Sandora was waiting. "Now, Mr. Cavendish?"

He had to clear his throat before he could speak. "Yes. Now I want to see my son."

The lamplight fell on the infant's tiny pink face. Its eyes were closed, a minute fist curled at a minute mouth. "Alban," Richard whispered. "Allie?"

"Such a perfect little boy," Maria breathed.

Richard said nothing. There was a crest of dark curly hair on the small head, the faint line of dark brows. But the bones were already visible in the little face. A dimple was pressed close to rosebud lips. Vicki. He was a small Vicki made into his own flesh. Richard smiled. Pain became elation. He didn't have Vicki. Not yet. But he had his son.

The next day Richard gave cigars to the men, candy to the women. When Gus Markeson received his, he grinned. "Congratulations, Mr. Cavendish. I know what a day this is for you."

But later Gus thought about the new baby with sullen bitterness. The crown prince is born. He'll have all he wants in this life. And Jamie will have nothing but struggle, the same as me.

That afternoon, when Richard had returned home, Carter, the loomfixer, collapsed, coughing great gouts of blood. Gus took him to City Hospital in a hansom Ezra paid for, although Carter gasped, "Home, man. I've no money. They won't let me in."

Gus feared he was right, but tried. Within the hour in which he argued, and finally pleaded, with no success, Carter worsened. By the time Gus got him back into the hansom, and then onto the cot in his tenement, with his wife weeping, and children surrounding him, Carter could no longer speak.

Gus went for Ezra, who stopped for a doctor. When

the three men reached Carter's quarters, he was dead.

The next day Richard gave Ezra a check for $1000 to be delivered to Mrs. Carter to help her in her widowhood. He wasn't obliged to do so since Carter's lung ailment wasn't an on-the-job accident. The operatives at the mill agreed that the gesture was generous, but that night Gus rejoined the loomfixers' union.

Chapter 15

"CAVENDISH COVE," RICHARD SAID, SMILING FAINTLY. "That's what I've named it, though I'm not sure why I did. We'll move there on the first of June. And I'll commute by the Old Colony line."

"Only a few weeks in which to ready ourselves," Matilda put in. "So much to do. But we'll manage it, I suppose."

Cavendish Cove, Vicki repeated silently. She saw the big house in her mind, the restless sea below it, the meadows of wildflowers, the outcroppings of wet black rock along Cliff Walk. She slid a quick look at Richard. If he remembered what had happened there, he showed no sign of it. She was confounded to think that what had scarred her so deeply had left no single mark on him.

"You must be pleased," Rosamund was saying, her eyes on Vicki. "Newport is lovely, and certainly the most fashionable summering place on the New England coast."

"Of course I am," Vicki said, but only because that was what was expected of her. She felt nothing but dread at the thought of returning to Cavendish Cove.

Matilda said, with a soft laugh, "It'll be lovely for our Allie."

Rosamund's smile was thin, her dark eyes alert. "We *will* see the baby, won't we?"

"Oh, indeed you will," Vicki answered. "As soon as he's awake." She got to her feet, the ruffled hem of her new pink gown flaring gracefully around her. "I'll just go and see."

Richard waved her back to her seat. "Maria will bring him down when he's dressed for company."

"You find the nursemaid satisfactory?" Elise asked.

"Yes," Vicki answered. "She seems to like babies very much."

But Matilda grumbled, "Well enough, though there's room for improvement."

"How long do you expect to remain in Newport?" Leslie asked.

"Until fall," Richard told him. "Or until the weather goes bad."

"It's quite a distance for you to travel twice a day," Leslie remarked thoughtfully. "Especially with the new building going up. I'd have imagined that you'd stay in town."

"It takes just ninety minutes, and I wouldn't like being separated from my family six days of the week," Richard told him.

Elise and Rosamund exchanged glances. They had, on the drive over, counted off the months of Richard's mid-September marriage to Vicki, and calculated on their fingers, until Leslie had laughed, saying, "Vicki and Richard are married. And that's the fact. The age of the infant hardly matters."

Still, the two women had wondered. The boy was born in mid-April. A newborn infant was hard to judge. But by this time it was a month old. It would be easier to decide if it had come after full term or if it had been premature as claimed.

Richard was aware of their interest, and didn't care. Vicki was, too, but the opinion of the two women didn't concern her. It was only Leslie that mattered. She resolutely kept her eyes away from him.

She had first seen him in February of 1902, just

four months after she met Richard. Now it was mid-May of 1903. In the year and some that had passed she had been a bride and become a mother. All was different except her feeling for Leslie. Only that remained.

Nettie entered, hurriedly serving refreshments. She hoped to slip out afterwards for a few moments with Mitch Ryan, who leaned against Rosamund's carriage under the porte cochere.

When Nettie left, Maria Sandora brought Allie and put him into Vicki's arms. He gazed at her sleepily, small fists settling under his tiny chin.

Elise and Rosamund fluttered around him, cooed and stroked his cheek, and at last returned to their chairs.

"He's a big baby," Matilda said. "For which I am grateful. I feared he would be undersized, since he came early."

Rosamund nodded, smiling. The boy looked as if he had been carried full term. But Leslie was right. It didn't matter. She wondered how soon she could respectably write to Davis Peabody again.

The talk continued, centering around Newport, around the regatta and the casinos, and the new mansions going up along the coast. Vicki no longer listened. She held the baby against her, feeling his soft warmth as if he were melting into her body, part of her again. She forgot then that there were times when she looked down at him as if he were some stranger, wondering how her flesh had once held him, how her blood had produced him, while she recalled the time he was conceived. Richard's mouth covering hers so that she was suffocating . . . his weight holding her so she couldn't move . . . the sense of being degraded and defiled, her very humanity torn from her . . .

As he watched her, Leslie's mouth went dry. There was a glow in her eyes, and her body looked slim and supple. He could almost feel its sinuous warmth writhing in his arms. If it hadn't been for Elise, Vicki could have been his. But she was lost to him forever. In that instant, she looked up. For the first time that day, their eyes met, held. It was he who broke the moment, conscious of Elise's brisk voice in the background. He got up, went to look out the window, fondling his pipe.

When Allie began to cry, Vicki took him to the nursery, relieved to be able to leave the room. She sat in the spoolback chair near the window, and bared her breast. Allie's tiny mouth fastened on her nipple, sucked and gulped in a frenzy. His small hands clutched her flesh. She watched Harry weed the borders near the carriage house while Mitch stood over him, smoking a cigarette.

She had never known how Richard had come to find her in Mrs. Wood's shop. Now, looking at Mitch, she believed she knew. Mitch had seen her by accident, and when she had curtly sent him away, he had taken his revenge. She smiled down at Allie, and shrugged. It no longer mattered. When the baby had sated himself, she continued to hold him, until Maria came and took him away. Vicki delayed as long as she could but finally returned to the morning room.

Elise had her auburn head thrust forward, was saying eagerly, "You must give thought to enrolling your Allie at the school, Richard."

He laughed. "There's time for that, I'd imagine."

"But it goes quickly." Elise laughed, too. "And who knows? By then we may have so little room that we'd be forced to refuse him. Why, Mr. Peabody has actually recommended two more boys. And I don't doubt that there'll be more."

"You'll have expanded by then," Richard told her. "If I know you."

"Perhaps," she agreed. "At least I've every reason to hope so. And I believe we're alike in trying to make the most of what we can."

Listening, Vicki tried to think ahead. Allie at five . . . Allie at seven . . . Was seven old enough to be sent away from home? That was how it was done in England. It was what Elise believed in. It was what Vicki herself ought to believe in, she supposed. But the thought was unpleasant. No, she couldn't imagine sending Allie so far away from her at such an age.

When Vicki listened again, Elise was saying, "Yes, we're doing better than we had hoped when we undertook the project."

Rosamund said, "I always knew it would be a good thing for you and Leslie." She looked directly at Richard, went on, "And I don't see why you don't buy it for them, Richard. You can surely afford it. Think of what a nice thing it would be for your son. The Alban Cavendish Athletic Field . . ."

"I will think of it," Richard told her. He didn't mention that he had already considered it at some length before, and had almost decided that he would provide funds for the school. He was waiting only for the new plant to be somewhat further under way. Turning to Vicki, he asked, "Is the baby sleeping now?"

"Maria took him to his cradle," she answered.

"I look forward to when he becomes a real person," Richard said. "Just now he's still like a doll. But one day he'll talk and walk, and then we can mean something to each other."

"Don't hurry time," Matilda said, smiling. "You don't realize how quickly it goes."

Don't hurry time, Vicki thought. It seemed to her that she did nothing but look ahead. And looking ahead brought her no relief from the past. She remembered wondering how she could live with Richard. How she could live without love. But live she did. She wouldn't allow herself to look at Leslie again, fearful that her eyes, her face, might give her thoughts away. But she could see him in her mind. The blond beard . . . the smiling lips . . . She still wanted him. When she lay in Richard's arms, it was of Leslie that she thought.

She was glad when Rosamund rose to leave, taking Elise and Leslie with her. It was difficult to maintain the mask of a young bride and mother, when her thoughts were in constant rebellion.

That night, as she rose to give Allie his feeding, Richard said, "It won't be too long, I suppose, and you'll be able to sleep through the night."

"I'm sorry I disturbed you," she whispered.

"I wasn't sleeping anyway."

She didn't answer that. She tiptoed into the nursery. Allie was just awakening, his lips puckered. His eyes began to open. As she took him up, he let out a scream of anger.

Maria mumbled apologetically, "I'm sorry, Mrs. Cavendish."

But Vicki murmured, "Hush, Allie. I'm here. What do you want?" When she felt his lips close at her nipple, she smiled. She sat in the rocking chair near the cradle, humming softly after she sent Maria back to her room next door. Long past the time that the baby had suckled his fill, and then fallen asleep, she sat holding him.

The silver moon sank lower. The mourning doves cooed in the hemlock grove. She held Allie's small warmth against her, enwrapped in contentment. She didn't hear Richard's step in the hall, didn't know when he opened the door. It was only when a ribbon of light fell across the carpet, with his shadow large inside it, that she knew he was there, and hastily covered her bared breast.

"Put him down and come back to bed," Richard said.

She laid the baby in his cradle, drew a light sheet over him, then bent to press a butterfly kiss on his round cheek.

When she returned to the bedroom, Richard was waiting.

The draperies were open. A warm breeze, scented with spring, filled the room. Bellbuoys clanged faintly in the harbor below. Moonlight filtered palely under the canopy where Richard sat.

"You needn't stay in the nursery to avoid me," he told her. "You must have your rest. And Maria can do for the baby everything that's necessary, except for the feeding of him."

"But I simply lost track of the time," Vicki protested. How to explain that when holding Allie she felt complete again? She felt the sense of love astir in her.

"Dreaming," Richard said.

She shrugged, hearing the contempt in his voice.

"There's something I ought to have spoken of to you before. I could never quite bring myself to it, I suppose. Now it's necessary."

She said nothing, but waited.

"We have Allie now," Richard said, his voice deep. "That part is done with. Do you understand me?"

"No, I don't. You say Allie is born, and so?"

"So I don't propose that you be a prisoner, Vicki."

She thought of how she had become his bride. If she wasn't his prisoner, then what was she? What, indeed, was any woman who wasn't free to follow her heart's desire?

He was saying, "My dear Vicki, do you think I'm blind?"

She said nothing, but she was frightened without knowing what she feared. It was, it seemed to her, a condition to which only Richard could reduce her.

He went on, "I know that you're still possessed of a childish infatuation, even though there's no hope in it for you, and no future either."

She said hotly, "Richard, I have in no way . . ."

"I'm accusing you of nothing. I only want you to know I realize it."

"I didn't come to you," she said. "It was your choice, your decision, that we marry. So what do you expect me to say to you now?"

He smiled faintly. "Why, nothing, my dear. I don't want you to deny it, or to defend yourself, or to blame me. I only want you to know that I'll not keep you as a prisoner. The child is safely born. You are free to do exactly as you please."

"You mean that," she whispered. "It was only that you wanted Allie. I was your brood mare, and now I have done my duty by you."

"That's not exactly true," he answered. "But I do mean you may be free, if you like." He waited for a moment, then went on, "Of course, if you decide to leave me, that will be entirely your affair. You have no grounds for divorce. And I would never permit it

161

in any event. I would also make certain that you never saw Allie again."

She stared at him, disbelief warring with certainty. His eyes were somber, shadowed; his mouth a firm line; his jaw set. He would do just as he said. Still, she stammered, "Richard, you . . . you would really take Allie from me?"

"I would have to, Vicki. I want my son. I must have my son." His voice dropped to a heavy whisper. "I want you, too, Vicki. But it will be your decision."

"But you permit me no decision. You know I could never leave Allie."

"I suppose you couldn't. I hope you couldn't. But it will be up to you."

"Then I'm your prisoner without being your prisoner," she whispered painfully.

"You can describe it that way, if you want to."

She said softly, "With all that's happened, and now this, I don't know . . . I just don't know if I can live this way."

"You can," he said quietly. Now he rose, stood over her. He put out his hand. "It will be much easier than you believe."

She closed her eyes briefly, felt his hand on her shoulders. When she opened them, he was smiling. "I won't ask too much of you, I promise."

Later, turning away from her, he said, with an edge of mockery in his voice, "I have decided to give the school its athletic field. Won't Elise and Leslie be pleased?"

Vicki clenched her hands into fists, but didn't reply.

Still later, Richard rose. She heard him pace about the room, then heard his footsteps in the hall. When there was silence, she knew that he leaned over Allie and watched while the baby slept.

The move to Cavendish Cove at the first of June was accomplished easily.

Nettie and Mrs. Beamis packed under Matilda's watchful eye. Harry, with John helping, loaded the carriage and made four trips to Newport.

They left very early on an already hot morning, with mists rising like steam over the river. The surrey and carriage were full to brimming as they rolled down the driveway to Highland Avenue, with Richard waving them off.

He would come later, by railway, he had said. It was a day when he wanted to be in town to watch while the footings for the new plant went in.

The drive was long, but pleasant. Vicki found herself remembering the last time she had gone that way. Then Richard had been beside her. Now it was John who pointed out the sights along the way.

They reached Newport some time after midday. The sun was high and bright. The sky a sharp and cloudless blue. Broadway was crowded with broughams and surreys and carriages. A few motor cars, carrying fashionable ladies with ruffled parasols over their heavily veiled heads, dodged dangerously through the slow-moving traffic. As they turned into Touro Street, John pointed out the old synagogue to Vicki, and when she looked back through the window she saw the white-tipped spire of Trinity Church on Spring Street towering over the other buildings.

"There's a lot of history here," John said. "We'll do some exploring together, Vicki. If you think you'd like to."

"Of course I would," she answered. She was glad of the suggestion. The summer months spread out before her, endless and empty, and she looked ahead to her first sight of the Newport house with dread.

Yet, when they arrived, she felt nothing. There was the veranda she had remembered, but it was different now. The outdoor furniture was fresh and new. Small wrought-iron tables and charis set with heavy striped orange and green cushions. A swing suspended by chains from the ceiling. A shaded electric light fixture hanging on each side of the front door.

It was nearly a week before all was disposed as Matilda felt it should be, and by then Vicki had come to take Cavendish Cove for granted.

Richard left very early each morning for Fall River

and returned late, in time for a delayed dinner hour. He spent only Sundays at Newport, and even then, he was hours working over bills of lading for the materials and machinery being delivered for the new plant.

Maria took car of Allie, soon berry brown and thriving. His eyes had turned dark. The black fuzz on his head became silky. When Vicki held him, he crooned and patted her cheek. But when Maria reached for him, his small hands clawed at Vicki and he screamed his displeasure, refusing to be comforted until she had gone.

Mostly she was free to do as she pleased. She and John rode together, walked together exploring Newport, Middletown and Portsmouth. The days passed, long, quiet, sun-filled. She spent hours on the widow's walk, watching the tiny white sails skim over the blue of the ocean, and the gulls wheel and swoop in the blue of the sky.

She never forgot, even for an instant, those moments when Allie had been conceived. But she learned with time's passage that Richard had been right when he said she could live as his dutiful wife. When, sometimes, she thought of leaving, her heart nearly stopped within her. Because there was Allie. Once she would have imagined that she could pack a few things, ride away, and never come back. She would work as she had before. But always, always, there was Allie. Since his birth his tiny body, silken in her arms, was the strongest of chains. She knew Richard would keep his word. If she left him, she would never see Allie again.

Yet, bound to him as she was, there were brief startling moments when she stared at him, wondering why that was so. He had been born of anger, not of the loving blend of two bodies. He was the issue of her own defilement. It was because of him that she had had to marry Richard. It was because of him that she dreaded those nights when Richard reached for her, made love to her, while she, with her eyes squeezed shut, only endured his touch and longed for another man's arms and lips.

At the end of June Eustacia and Albert Cosgrove came for a Sunday afternoon, having settled not far away in their Newport house.

"It surprises me how quickly your plant is going up," Albert said. "How many operatives will you be adding to your payroll?"

"I don't know yet," Richard answered.

"When do you expect to be running?"

Richard grinned. "As soon as I can be, of course. But probably not before next May."

Eustacia sighed loudly. "I didn't come to call to listen to talk of the mills."

"My dear," Albert murmured.

Eustacia glared at him, then turned to Vicki. "Do you enjoy it here? Have you yet been asked out?"

"My dear," Albert murmured again.

But Vicki laughed. "I find it pleasant."

"You haven't been to the casino?" Eustacia demanded.

"I plan to take her next Saturday night," Richard said.

"I've never gambled, nor thought much of it," Vicki answered.

"You'll enjoy it when you try," Richard told her.

But, when they went to the casino the following Saturday, Vicki found the spinning wheels and falling dice and fluttering cards not much to her liking, though she did enjoy the music, and the muted chandelier light on plush and velvet and glittering diamonds.

Richard played the wheel, and won and won and won. He played at cards and won there, too. When she congratulated him, he gave her a sober look. "I'm lucky at gambling. But not so lucky at love."

"It's your own doing," she said tartly.

That night he didn't reach for her. Instead, she lay listening, while he paced the room for hours. She was asleep when he left for Fall River the next morning.

In late July Rosamund and Elise drove out with

Leslie for a weekend consisting of Saturday and Sunday.

Vicki was on the veranda, playing with Allie when they arrived. He cried as usual as she relinquished him to Maria, who carried him quickly indoors.

Rising, smoothing her skirts, Vicki could still hear his screams as she greeted her guests, led them inside, and showed them to their rooms.

In the bustle of welcome she had hardly had time to think. But as she waited for them to come down she recalled how Leslie had smiled at her, how soft his voice had been when he said, "It's so good to see you, Vicki."

Now he appeared at the door, crossed the room to her. He took her hand, pressed it to his lips. "I've missed you." Then, "We must talk, Vicki."

She said, smiling, "There'll be plenty of time." And then, "Richard will be home about seven. He plans that we go to the casino after dinner. And tomorrow we'll have a small garden party."

"I wasn't speaking of the program for the weekend," Leslie told her.

"Oh?" She lowered her long dark lashes until they lay on her cheeks, and she could see only the tips of her shoes, and his, too, standing close.

"I meant talk to you alone, Vicki." It was all that he could do to keep from sweeping her into his arms. But he heard Rosamund's voice, and then Elise's. He went to the window as the two women, followed by Matilda, came into the room.

"It's a lovely house," Rosamund said. "I'm glad I came." She gave Vicki a narrow smile. "I almost didn't, for Davis asked me to visit him in Boston." She shrugged prettily. "But I can do that another time."

Elise beamed at Vicki, "My dear, we want to thank you. We know you helped Richard decide to donate the land for the athletic field."

"It was his own decision," Vicki said.

"That's what you tell us, of course," Leslie answered. "But we're very grateful to you."

"Richard will be glad," Vicki answered.

But when they expressed their appreciation later that evening, Richard simply shrugged their words aside, and changed the subject. He had gratified a whim by making Leslie a gift, and leaving the man in his debt.

They spent several hours at the casino. The others gambled, while Vicki watched. Richard won again. Leslie lost, but not a great deal. That time Richard didn't remark upon his fortune in either gambling or love.

They danced afterwards. Richard, a dutiful host, took a turn first with Elise, then with Rosamund, before drawing Vicki into his arms. He was silent, his face expressionless, but his fingers bit into the shoulder he held, and her hand was numb with the pressure of his grip. When she had danced with Leslie, she felt as if sparks were exploding all through her. As Richard held her, she seemed to feel those embers die into ashes.

That night she pretended to sleep when he came to bed. But he knew better, and took her into his arms, though she murmured, thinking of Leslie down the hall, "Not now, Richard. I'm so tired."

He ignored the words. He pressed brandy-tasting lips to her mouth, and took her quickly but without passion. When he let her go, she whispered against clenched teeth, "I'll make you sorry for that, Richard."

She rose early the next morning. The house was still when she slipped out. She wore a big white hat of straw, with veiling wrapped at its brim. Her dress was white, too, and soft, clinging against her body as she climbed down to Cliff Walk.

There was no one about, and she sat quietly, her arms wrapped around her drawn-up knees, looking at the slow undulations of the ocean. Soon, though, a shadow fell over her.

"You're up early," Leslie said. "I'm glad." He dropped down beside her. "I'd been hoping for a chance to talk."

"We've had time," she answered.

"But not alone." His mouth curled into a smile

within his blond beard. "Don't you know what I feel, Vicki?"

Her mouth was suddenly dry; her lips burning. A quick thrill of excitement rose up in her. She said slowly, "I know how I once *wanted* you to feel."

He leaned close, his voice hoarse. "And I did, Vicki. But I could do nothing about it."

When he didn't go on, she climbed down the rocks to the water's edge, hearing him follow but not looking back. She drew off her slippers and stockings and dangled her bare feet in the cool froth of the tide.

He settled next to her. "You have nothing to say?"

"I don't know, Leslie."

He turned, looked up to Cliff Walk and beyond, to where the house stood partly obscured by trees. He turned back to her, laughed softly. Then he took her into his arms, held her tightly against him, his mouth enfolding hers in a breath-stealing kiss. Even then, with the world spinning around her, and the gulls suddenly shrieking overhead, she thought of Richard, and knew what he would feel to find her thus in Leslie's arms.

Twice more in that summer Leslie met her on Cliff Walk, then returned to Fall River with none of the Cavendishes the wiser.

He would meet her for an early morning hour or even two. He courted her assiduously, and she enjoyed his flattery and kisses, but never made a commitment to him, though he pressed her for it in every way he knew, not realizing that when he was gone from her, she longed for him with every aching fiber of her heart.

Chapter 16

IT WAS MID-SEPTEMBER, WITH THE SUN STILL BRIGHT, but a coolness at morning and evening that presaged summer's end.

Matilda supervised Mrs. Beamis and Nettie at the packing. Harry and John had begun loading the carriage for its first trip back to the Fall River house.

Vicki stood on the widow's walk. The breeze folded her gown tightly against her body, so that it seemed to caress her breasts. They were smaller now, the milk drying from them, and however hard Allie suckled, she was no longer able to satisfy him. He would within days be on the bottle, and the last connection between their two bodies would be broken. The thought was an echo of the mood which had pursued her ever since the preparations to leave had begun. The freedom of the blossoming months was coming to an end. There would be no more solitary strolls on Cliff Walk, and no more meetings with Leslie, which for all her caution in responding to him, had become more and more important to her. A few stolen kisses were no longer enough, nor were the quick fevered embraces. Her body yearned for, demanded more. Only pride held her back. She remembered that his conquest of her had been immediate and total, and she had allowed him to know it. Her innocence had made her vulnerable. She knew now that he would risk nothing for her, but always put his safety before his need for her.

He had said once again that he was grateful for her help in getting the athletic field for the school, and she had denied any role in Richard's decision. But she hadn't told him that when Richard made the purchase it had been a devious mockery of Leslie himself, one from which Richard obtained an unspoken satisfaction. He proved to her that Leslie was the lesser man by accepting a favor to which he had no right. Such evidence was meaningless to Vicki. It made no difference in her feelings.

Now, with a last long look at the far horizon where a tanker seemed to hang motionless between ocean and sky, she went indoors.

She and Nettie packed together. The girl worked with the energy of enthusiasm as they folded gowns into a trunk. Her eyes shone, and she laughed as she chattered. "Oh, it'll be good to be home again. There'll be vaudeville at the Bijou, and ice skating later." Her voice trailed off. It wasn't the vaudeville or ice skating that was on her mind. She was thinking of Mitch Ryan, and only him, but she didn't want to say his name.

Vicki wished that she looked forward to the return to Fall River with Nettie's eagerness. But just as she had dreaded coming to Cavendish Cove, now she dreaded going back to Fall River. Here she had found a semblance of freedom. Richard left early for the mill, returned late. He had spent only Sunday at home. In Fall River he would be moments away from the mill and would return for the midday meal. The evenings would be longer, the mornings, too. And his presence only deepened her helpless anger. His generosity, his consideration, yes, even his love, was a burden to her.

The room was still in some disorder. A trunk remained to be unpacked, the hat boxes put away. Vicki decided that she and Nettie must complete the settling in that morning. They had been home for two days, but Allie had been fretful at the change, and Vicki had spent her time with him.

She supposed that Richard had had his breakfast and left, since he had gone down half an hour earlier.

She smoothed her gown before looking into the nursery. Allie, contentedly playing with Maria's fingers, let out a yell when he saw Vicki.

She bent to kiss him, while Maria glowered at her. All the way down the steps she heard his angry wails.

Richard was still at the table. He half-rose when she came in. "Good morning."

"Good morning," she answered, aware that he was watching her expectantly, but not knowing why.

She poured coffee for herself, noting by his place that John had already eaten and gone out, and by hers, that Matilda had not yet come down. The room was so quiet that Vicki could hear Mrs. Beamis murmuring in the kitchen, and the deep growl of Harry's response. She heard Richard sigh, and looked up.

He passed the newspaper to her. "You might have a look at this."

The headline concerned the discussions between the United States and Canada over the boundaries of the Alaska district. She raised her eyes questioningly.

"The date, Vicki."

She looked at it. September 23, 1903. For an instant it meant nothing to her. But then she understood. It was a year to the day since Richard had come for her at Mrs. Wood's. Their first wedding anniversary. She would rather have ignored it, to have allowed it to pass without comment. She remained Richard's wife only for Allie. But Richard was determined to pretend otherwise.

Her voice shook when she said, "Ah, yes, I see."

"I have something for you." He rose and came around the table, holding a long box wrapped in silver paper. When she didn't move to take it, he put it into her hands.

She slowly removed the white ribbon, the seals, and stripped the paper away. Nestled into the white satin of the box there was a necklace of garnets, with tiny drop earrings and a narrow bracelet to match. She raised her eyes to his. "They're lovely, Richard. Thank you very much."

"Let me see how they look," he said. When she

171

fumbled the catch of the necklace, he took it from her and placed it about her throat, his fingers warm against the sudden chill of her flesh. He put the bracelet on her wrist, while she sat motionless. "Yes," he said finally. "They *are* right for you."

She thanked him again, her voice cool. He kissed her, and left to go to the mill. To him she seemed a stubborn child, refusing to see that they were man and and woman, married and together, sharing the love of their son, sharing the same bed. If that bed brought her little satisfaction, he wasn't glad, but such was true of most women. They could dream of love, but the dream wasn't reality.

Still, when he reached for her that night, his hands were rough rather .than gentle; his body was heavy against hers. When, finally, he released her, she lay staring at the canopy, knowing that he was as wakeful as she, but not knowing what to say.

They had Thanksgiving dinner with Elise and Leslie at the school that year. Rosamund attended, too, escorted by Davis Peabody. The talk was largely of the recently signed Hays treaty, which gave the United States promise of perpetual use of a canal to be built, plus use of ten miles on each side of it, and promised an American guarantee of the neutrality of the canal when it was in operation, and payment of $10,000,-000 in addition to a still undetermined annual rental.

Most of the men agreed that this was a satisfactory arrangement, but Richard felt the government should annex the area called Panama and be done with it.

After dinner, Elise insisted that they walk around the ground soon to be the new athletic field. She took Richard's arm, describing to him what she would do there.

Leslie walked with Vicki, but Matilda joined them, so they could exchange only commonplaces.

Vicki was relieved when the day was over, and they returned home.

The house was gay at Christmas. There was a wreath of pine cones and holly on the front door, and mistletoe hung in the hall. The tree was brilliantly

172

ecorated with silver and blue baubles imported from
Germany and strings of popcorn and cranberries, and
short fat white candles set in silver holders along the
fragrant boughs. For a week Mrs. Beamis and Nettie
were busy in the kitchen, and delicious odors of roasting turkeys and baking hams drifted through the
rooms. One day Vicki went with Matilda to deliver
baskets of food to the City Almshouse on President
Avenue, and having spent an hour there among the
bewildered old and hopeless young, she remembered
her charity errands among her father's parishioners,
and returned to Highland Avenue in tears.

That night Matilda told Richard privately that she
wouldn't take Vicki again on such trips, explaining,
without criticism, that the younger girl cared too much.
He nodded his agreement. But when Matilda set out
again in the loaded carriage, this time to deliver gifts
to the mill operatives, Vicki insisted on going, too.

They made so many stops that last Sunday before
the holiday that the names and faces and addresses
and overcrowded, underheated rooms soon became a
single large blur to Vicki. Only two among that misty
group stood out afterwards in her mind. They were
Gus Markeson and his son Jamie. Jamie was thirteen
then, slim, straight in posture, with dark eyes and a
cap of curly dark hair. When Gus growled a surly
thanks for the plum pudding, Jamie ran to a back
room, and brought a small ship's model that he had
carved himself. "For Alban," he said, thrusting it toward her. "I'm sorry I don't have wrappings."

She hesitated, thinking she mustn't take away the
little he had.

"Please," he begged. "I want your son to have it.
And Ezra Saunders will help me make another."

She thanked him while Gus impatiently opened the
door.

"I don't like that man," Matilda said as they were
leaving.

"But Jamie's a nice little boy," Vicki answered.
Later, at home, she wrapped the ship's model and tied
it with a red bow and put it under the glistening tree.

On Christmas Eve the house was thrown open to the carolers who stopped outside to sing. There were bowls of punch and cider, and sugar cookies and towers of oranges and apples to pass around.

In the morning Allie crawled excitedly on the floor while the gifts were distributed, and talked incessantly saying no words except "Mama" and "Papa" that could be understood. He admired the ship's model that Jamie had given him, caressed the rocking horse that Richard had found in Boston, hugged the teddy bear that John had had made.

Mrs. Beamis had a new coat, Nettie a new gown and Harry a suit of matching trousers and jacket.

"It was a good holiday," Richard said that night, and kissed her under the mistletoe.

"Yes," she agreed, secretly glad that the festivities were over.

Rosamund gave a New Year's Eve ball to welcome in 1904. It was a gay affair, the buffet elaborate, the music rollicking. Vicki spun from one partner to another, her cheeks flushed, her eyes sparkling, the garnets agleam at her white throat over the purple velvet of her gown. She knew that Leslie's eyes followed her as she danced in Richard's arms, stood with him drinking punch, and laughing at Albert Cosgrove's sallies. Later Leslie led her to the floor with him, bent his head to say, "Richard is a fortunate man."

"Men make their fortune," she said lightly, wondering what Richard would think of the conversation.

"I want to see you, Vicki." Leslie's voice was deep. "We can arrange it, can't we?"

"I don't know," she said, with a glance toward Richard. He stood with Davis Peabody, but his eyes were on her. She tipped back her head, widened her smile. "But we might, Leslie."

At the end of January Richard decided to go to New York City for a few days of business. He asked if Vicki would accompany him.

She said, "I don't like to go so far from Allie."

"Maria can take care of him, you know. And my mother will supervise."

"I'd be uneasy about it. He's just nine months old."

"Do as you like," Richard told her, covering his disappointment with a shrug. "You can go another time, I suppose."

"When Allie's a little older."

Richard didn't tell her that he had hoped the journey, the change, going away togther, would mend what was torn between them. More and more he had come to see that while he had his son, he had only the outward show of a wife. Vicki ran his home with Matilda's help, entertained his guests, cared for Allie, and lay in his arms when he demanded it, but he grew more aware each day of a certain emptiness. She never turned to him. She was never his in the way he needed her to be.

She was relieved that he would be away for a few days. But there was no single pressing reason for that. It was only that when he was about she felt the weight of his ownership. She expected the same lightness she had known in Newport after he rode away on the electric streetcar.

She expected nothing beyond that. It snowed the day he left, and kept snowing late into the night. The next morning the roads were covered with fluffy white blankets, the lawns and trees enwrapped in a glistening ermine.

Harry brought the mail late. There was a letter from Leslie, asking Vicki to meet him that afternoon at the corner near Mrs. Wood's food shop. She had only a little while to prepare.

She recombed her hair, put on a snug cloche rimmed with veils and bows. She pulled on boots and wrapped herself in her fur-trimmed coat.

Matilda protested that she oughtn't to go out, saying there might be a blizzard. But Vicki answered that it was beautiful, and she wanted to take the air.

The wind seemed to hurry her along, white snow swirling around her. She was breathless when she reached the appointed meeting place. Leslie was there, waiting.

He helped her into the surrey, brushed flakes of

melting snow from her shoulder. "I wasn't sure you'
be able to come."

"Richard went to New York yesterday morning."

Leslie grinned. "I knew. I heard it through Rosa
mund."

"And I'm out taking a long walk in the snow."

His grin widened. "I'm seeing the bank manager
among other errands."

"And will you have accomplished all you told Elis
you would?"

"You worry too much," he answered. "I'll hav
done some. The rest had to be delayed. The weather
you know. It'll mean another trip to town soon."

"I wonder if it's snowing in New York."

"Probably. But Richard will manage. He alway
does."

"Yes," she agreed.

"You've not asked where we're going."

"I suppose we might ride, Leslie. What else is there
for us to do?"

"I've arranged something better. You've probably
never heard of it, but the Cosgroves have a summer
ing cottage at Fair Haven. They've not used it since
they took up their place in Newport."

She stared at him. "Is it all right, Leslie?"

"Of course. No one uses it now, nor has done so fo
more than three years. They'll never even know we've
been there."

"But how did you arrange for the key?"

"Who said I have one?" He took up the reins,
started the horses. "You'll see that I manage, too."

She wished that he hadn't indirectly referred to
Richard, but it happened now and again. She had her
self mentioned him only moments ago.

The road was hardly visible through blinding white
sheets, the meadows spread endlessly on both sides.
When the surrey turned into the path to the cottage,
Vicki almost demanded to be taken back to town. She
was suddenly uneasy. The wind-driven snow seemed
to whisper a warning at her. The surrey rolled to a
stop. Leslie took her hand from the muff in which it

176

was burried, and kissed her fingertips. She gave him a long still look, full of a doubt she had never known before. Then, with a shrug, she smiled at him. People who live by fear have nothing, she told herself. She wouldn't allow it to stop her.

Inside, she found that Leslie had been there before, had already prepared for their tryst. There was wine and cheese and bread. There were fresh sheets thrown over the Osnaburg covers on the divan.

As he drew her down beside him, slowly removing her coat, and opening her gown that he could slip his hands within to her breasts, she decided that she didn't like the place and would never go there again.

Mitch Ryan was cold. His hands burned with it as he rolled a cigarette. His eyes watered with it as he stared at the light in the carriage house. He'd had his cards with Harry, and his coffee, which no longer warmed him. Now he waited for the light to go out. Then he would wait a little longer. His toes were numb in his boots. His teeth ached when he dragged on his smoke. He heard the horses snorting and stamping in the stable close by, and more distant the hoot of tugs in the harbor. The wind had died with nightfall, and the snow, too, and nothing remained now but the bone-chilling cold.

He grinned, told himself that the warmth of Nettie's body was worth the chill. He hugged himself hard. When he looked up again, the light was gone from the window. He rolled another cigarette, lit it, and dragged deep. He turned to look at the dark windows of the big house. Richard Cavendish was in New York. His English wife slept under a velvet canopy, and so did his son. By the Virgin, Mitch thought, if only he had that kind of money. He'd not waste it on fripperies. He'd know what to do with it. Men couldn't be free without fighting for it. And to fight, men needed guns. He was in the midst of a conversation with his Uncle Shamus, the older man's face a study in joy and surprise, when Nettie clutched at his arm, and whispered, "Mitch, is that you?"

He silenced her with a kiss, and pulled her into the stable. It was cold there, the hay sweet-smelling but damp. He didn't notice. He pulled her down beside him, buried his face in her breasts. Soon he loosened her bodice. There was no struggle there. He'd done that many times before. But Nettie struggled when he lay full length on her, thrusting his hand between them, and between her thighs, pushing and pressing and rubbing until with a gasp, she opened her knees to him. He had her skirt up and his pants down while she was still saying "no," and reaching for his hand, and he was whispering, "Now, don't be afraid of me, Nettie. You know there's nothing to fear. I only want to hold you, Nettie. That's all I want." Murmuring at her, and pressing down against her, he heard only her gasps of pleasure and denial. Then the stable door slammed back, and the horses whinnied in sudden fright, and the darkness exploded with lantern light.

Nettie cried out, and Mitch rose up on his knees, and it was like living through a nightmare for a second time. But now it was Nettie beside him, weeping, and not his cousin Mary, and now it was Harry reaching for him, and not his Uncle Shamus.

Mitch hardly had time to get his pants up over his hips before Harry seized him, shook him as if he were a rat in the jaws of a dog, and flung him through the open stable door. He landed on hands and knees in the snow and struggled to his feet. Harry was on him again, picking him up and throwing him into the driveway. Nettie was screaming and crying, but she sounded like a mewling kitten in the face of Harry's roaring oaths. Stumbling, Mitch tried to flee, but Harry followed, caught him, whipped his chin with a big fist and threw him down again.

Some time, Mitch never knew when, John was there, saying, "Harry, stop. Let the man go," and limping between Mitch and the tall raging shadow that lunged at him. At three of them went down together. Harry, back in his senses at last, helped John to his feet, muttering wordlessly, while Mitch managed to crawl away into the dark.

The next day he had a black eye, one tooth lost from his grin, and three loosened, a cut on his chin, and a knot on his temple. He explained his wounds at Rosamund's house by saying he'd been set upon in Corky Row by some rowdies from out of town.

The next time he drove Rosamund to the Cavendish house, he stayed in the carriage under the porte cochere, and never ventured from it.

Chapter 17

To Richard the noise of New York was one loud unending bray that seemed to rise from the brink of hell. The hooting of tugs, the shrill of steam whistles, the whir and crack of spinning winches, the clatter of dock carts, the staccato backfires of sundry motor cars, all combined in a steady and palpable assault.

The stench of the city was compounded of the gases released by burning coal and damp lumber and sodden paper, of the decaying flesh and scales of dead fish, of rotting orange skins and green-molded bread, and the sweet-sour tang of hot and cooling horse droppings. Steaming through that stench, hanging heavy on the cold misty air of the pale morning, and stronger than any other, there was the odor of the mingled sweat and breath of close-packed, impatient, anxious humanity.

Richard's nose wrinkled and his lips thinned as he forced his way through the mobs near Pier 14 and looked for a hansom cab. He waved at one and it passed him by. He jerked his head at another. It stopped. He climbed in, gave the name of his hotel. It was too early for his appointment. He could drop his belongings off and take a short walk before he went to Thirty-fifth Street and the New York Clothing Company. He hadn't met Denton Paley, but they'd corresponded, and Richard was interested in the proposition Paley had offered him. If he were to guarantee delivery of twenty thousand yards of cotton by an agreed-on date, Paley would pay him a set price. If Richard failed of delivery, Paley would have the option of refusal, or acceptance at a lower price. The advantage to Richard was that he'd have a substantial predelivery payment to use for the purchase of raw cotton at a time when his assets were directed to the construction of his Plant No. 2. The arrangement profited Paley in that he'd be certain of what he'd have to pay for the fabric, and could make his sales before starting production. The eliminating of the jobber as middleman was an additional bonus to both of them. There were some few other mill owners who operated without commission agents, but not many. For Richard it was one more challenge.

His hansom rolled two short blocks and was immobilized in a traffic jam. Richard swore to himself. It was always like that. Whenever he came to New York City, he promised himself he'd never come again. Though he did return, it wasn't often. He wished that Vicki had come with him this time. It would have been pleasant to show her the biggest city in the country.

At last the hansom moved on. He finally reached the hotel. He was on time at Thirty-fifth Street, and spent two hours with Denton Paley. At the conclusion of their interview, they shook hands over their agreement. The papers would be prepared for signatures by the following afternoon.

Richard passed the rest of the day visiting various salons where motor cars were displayed. He saw Reos, Oldsmobiles, Mercedes and Packards. The Packard had had a good deal of publicity since the previous summer, when it had made the first transcontinental journey, taking fifty-two days to go from San Francisco

New York City. He was amused to notice in his wanderings that the motor car salesmen were much interested in the Wright brothers' feat of the past December. It seemed they felt that soon they would be selling flying machines on Fifth Avenue. He still hadn't made up his mind when he returned to the hotel, and decided to look further before committing himself to an automobile.

He had dinner at Delmonico's that night and spent long hours at the Men's Café in the Waldorf Hotel. There the talk was of Wall Street and the stock market, of Theodore Roosevelt and his reform politics, of the recent Supreme Court decision ruling Puerto Ricans not citizens of the United States but also not aliens, thereby permitting them free entry to the country.

In the morning, he rose late, and hurrying, scraped his chin with his straightedge razor. The hansom cab he had ordered before going to bed was delayed, making him later still. It wasn't far to Tiffany's, but it seemed to take hours, again because of the traffic. He tried for patience against the physical discomforts he knew he deserved for drinking an excess of whiskey. But patience eluded him and he spoke sharply to the driver. "Hurry it up, can't you?"

The man turned to give him a wide toothless grin. "Aye, sor. I could if only the others would give way." He pointed his whip at the barrel-laden cart ahead, slowed down by a motor car that belched smoke and flame at the shying horses behind it, then at the crowding hansoms at the right. "With wings, sor, we might fly over, I suppose. And since you're afire," here the toothless grin spread even wider, "we'll give it a try on wheels."

Richard leaned back as the driver cracked his whip and cried out. Beyond the window the slick grimy sidewalk was as thick with hurrying people as a garbage pile with black flies. They huddled within their heavy wrappings, rushing toward destinations Richard couldn't imagine. The hansom shivered and jerked, wheels creaking over uneven cobblestones. From all sides there were hot streams of the grossest obscenities.

The driver joyfully returned them in kind and in quantity.

It amused Richard to think how he improved his vocabulary when he had believed he already knew all the words, but now he was hearing new ones. His temper was restored by the time he reached the jewelry store. He spent an hour there before choosing a golden pendant for Vicki. Waiting, he imagined it nestled against the white flesh of her bosom, and a tightness surged through him. He hardly managed a civil "thank you" when the clerk handed him the wrapped package. He stepped into the street and a thin young boy shoved an elbow into his back. Richard swung around, the tightness exploding into singeing anger. He wanted to tear and smash and kick, to open the door to his bitterness and allow it to pour out. He growled, "Watch it, will you?"

The boy jerked back, sensing a danger he didn't understand. "I didn't mean . . . excuse it, please . . ." The words were heavily accented with a foreign flavor.

Ashamed, Richard murmured an apology. He wished the afternoon over, the night done. He wished he were back in Fall River. He mustn't take out his longing on some poor fellow who inadvertently touched him, when there was only one touch that he wanted. Even if that touch, too, never managed to satisfy. Ah, Vicki, he thought, sighing.

A faint sift of white drifted down from the gray of the skies, and suddenly the street lamps came on. Each one cast a yellow puddle along the shiny pavement. Each flickered into odd designs as shadows danced across it and darted away. Men of the Salvation Army, wearing blue uniforms, and women with blue bonnets and long blue skirts, marched by together, playing a familiar hymn on trumpets and drums. Richard pulled a few bills from his pockets, dropped them into the open kettle they carried for whatever donations people might want to make to the needs of humanity. As he turned away, he felt the package he carried in his pocket. He wondered if Vicki would understand that it was only one more peace offering. All he wanted was to forget what couldn't be changed. But how to accomplish that? For a long time he had asked himself if it were ever to be possible. But possible or not, they would go on together. Because of Allie. If nothing else would bind her to him, then their small beautiful son would.

He closed his mind to that as he turned into Thirty-fifth Street. He found Denton Paley had been delayed, and waited, growing impatient again. At last the man came. They smoked a cigar together, signed the agreements. Richard was well pleased when he left.

He had two drinks at the Men's Café in the Waldorf again, had dinner at Sherry's, then returned to his hotel. The lobby was golden with light from the huge chandeliers. The crimson carpet was soft as down underfoot. His own room was equally luxurious, but as he stared at the big bed, he knew that he wouldn't sleep. The restlessness that had come upon him as he bought the pendant for Vicki had grown stronger. He felt it burn in his loins, as he paced the room like an animal caged, until, with an oath, he put on his hat and coat and went downstairs.

He knew by *The New York Times* that there were a number of vaudeville shows he could see, a variety of plays on Broadway, and several nickelodeons where he could take his choice of new-made motion pictures. But none of these would satisfy.

The doorman, resplendent in livery that didn't quite fit, whistled up a hansom, and as Richard climbed in, the driver said, "Why, sor, it's you again, is it? And where shall I take you this time?"

With an effort, Richard explained his need through the usual circumlocution.

"Aye, sor. I can help you there," the driver assured him.

"Then get on with it." Richard leaned back, closed his eyes as the hansom rolled off, and at once he saw the image of Vicki's face, her small stubborn chin, her blazing dark blue eyes.

The hansom stopped, and the driver turned to grin.

"Here you are, sor. Just what you asked for. The finest bordello in all New York City. And that's saying a great deal, since there are so many of them. Speak to Madame Rose, and you'll come to no harm here."

Richard stepped out, thrust a coin into the man's hand.

The driver bowed in his seat. "A very good evening to you, sor!"

The hansom rattled away down the dark narrow street, wheels slipping on the thin layer of frozen snow. Richard climbed the black wrought-iron steps and seized the door knocker. It dropped from his gloved fingers with a thump that seemed to echo inside him.

The door opened only a few inches, caught by a brass chain. An impassive black face regarded him.

"I'm here to see Madame Rose," Richard said.

"Madame Rose?" Black eyes stared at him, showing neither welcome nor refusal. They moved slowly from the crown of Richard's hat, set aslant on his head, to the broad furred lapels of his coat. Then the chain rattled and fell away. The door opened.

Richard crossed the threshold into perfumed warmth. The door closed behind him. The brass chain hung in its slot again.

"I'll tell Madame Rose you've asked for her." The tall black man moved silently along the narrow foyer under the chandelier. The shining drops that hung from it like unshed tears set up a whisper that was not quite music.

Richard waited impatiently. If this Madame Rose didn't present herself soon, he'd go up those stairs without an invitation, and put his shoulder to whatever door stood closed in his way.

Even as he thought it Madame Rose was before him, a stout woman in black satin, with a décolletage that exposed too much powdered white flesh. "Good evening, sir," she said, smiling. "How may I help you?"

"You know how. Just tell me how long I'm to be kept waiting here."

"A friend sent you?" she asked, while from behind her the butler watched in silence.

"Apparently not so good a friend as I thought," Richard retorted. "But you'll no doubt find him at the back door, right now collecting whatever you pay him for the delivery."

"Ah," Madame Rose murmured. Now it was she who eyed him up and down. "May I ask where you're from?"

Impatience stung him. He hadn't expected that he would have to present his credentials to a whore mistress. He said stiffly, "From out of town."

"Ah," she repeated. But now he saw something left of a charm that must once have been remarkable. Dimples appeared in her raddled cheeks. An ember of amusement sparkled in her dark eyes. Warmth spilled from the powdered flesh of her hardly covered breasts. "Now then, my friend from out of town, you mustn't take my caution amiss. It's for your own protection as well as mine. And for your satisfaction, too."

Even as she spoke, the butler was taking Richard's hat, deftly removing his coat, drawing away his gloves.

"And if you'll follow me, sir . . ." She went ahead to the stairs. With each step, the round hips and neat bustle overlaid with a huge black satin bow swung saucily at him.

He was so surprised by the elegance of the room to which she led him that he gave the three girls clustered around the tinkling piano only the briefest of glances, and looked first at his surroundings. The windows were wide and high, curtained in thin white lace as clean as freshly fallen country snow, and draped in a heavy red damask shot through with gold threads. The manufacture of those, he knew, had cost a pretty penny. The mantel of the fireplace, in which a log burned discreetly, was of white marble, veined with gray, and probably Italian, he thought. The rug was soft and thick, so that every step was muffled, every sound muted. Love seats were set artfully about, and at each one, a small table held a vase of flowers, one roses, one violets, one lilacs, one daisies. He realized

185

that they were cleverly made of a cotton fabric that might even have rolled off the looms of the Cavendish mills. But they had been cunningly dyed, and after that, no doubt, cut and formed in the sweat-shop lofts by women and children squinting by gaslight.

"And now, my friend," Madame Rose was saying gaily, "I should like you to meet my three nieces. Charming girls all, of course. And in honor of your visit, and your stay in our beautiful city, we shall have champagne together." Her brows arched questioningly, and he nodded. The wine would appear on his bill, but that was to be expected.

The tiny black girl at the piano continued to pick out a tune Richard could not identify. He heard it even as the three smiling girls turned to him.

"Daisy," Madame Rose said.

The plump blonde girl, young and juicy as a peach, giggled while curtseying, the yellow flounces of her ruffled gown shifting around her.

"Violet," Madame Rose went on.

The petite girl bowed, and a black curl slipped along her cheek. "Good evening," she smiled. "And welcome."

"And Lilac," Madame Rose continued.

The girl introduced as Lilac neither bowed, nor curtseyed, nor smiled, nor even spoke. She was dressed in pale lavender lace that fit tightly at small high breasts. Her long and slender neck seemed not strong enough to hold the thick crown of her chestnut hair. She regarded Richard indifferently, while the piano's tinkling suddenly seemed louder.

Richard's amused glance rested briefly on the colored cotton flowers at each of the small tables, and he knew which of the women he would have that night.

Madame Rose saw his look, and said brightly, "I see, my dear sir, that you've penetrated my little jest."

"I'm not here for jesting," he answered.

At that moment the door opened. The butler came in carrying a huge silver tray that sparkled with glasses of pale wine. A maid dressed in black silk, with a frill of organza on her head, followed him. While the butler served Richard, then the others, the maid passed salvers of small spicy meatballs spiked by gold picks.

Richard had one, and saw that the gold pick was molded in the shape of a lusty nude woman. He grinned at Madame Rose. "I'll have this, if you please." That would also appear on his bill, he knew.

She nodded. "And what else will you have?"

He jerked his head at Lilac.

The cool, self-possessed expression on her face didn't change as she emptied her glass, languidly got to her feet.

Richard went with her down a long dim hall, past a series of closed doors, from behind each of which he heard the whisper of voices and subdued music. "A regular Tin Pan Alley," he said.

"People like it," she answered.

"And there are many parlors in your house."

She glanced at him over her white shoulder. "It's not my house," she said, and added, "More's the pity."

"I understand what you mean."

"I doubt that. And why should you? You visit and settle your accounts and leave. I remain."

"I know it's better to be owner than worker."

"On that we agree. Were the place mine, it would be different, believe me."

"You don't approve of so many parlors?"

"How does that matter? Madame prefers it so."

"But you?"

She shrugged. "One parlor is much like another."

"And the men in them?"

"The same," she answered. "Which is why I think the fripperies unnecessary and a waste of good profit."

He made no response, supposing that it must seem that way to her, but knowing that at least in him, she was wrong. He wasn't the same as other men. And while he, too, thought the fripperies superfluous, he guessed that other men might not.

The room to which she led him was as elegantly decorated as the parlor they had left. But here there was a great four-poster bed draped in lavender velvet, and on the ceiling above there was a mirror of equal dimensions.

Lilac looked at him, waiting. At last she said, "Do you think Madame's taste good enough? Or shall I go and tell her you've decided on something else?"

He didn't answer directly. But he shrugged out of his jacket, removed his cravat. With fingers at the fastenings of his waistcoat, he motioned her to the bed.

He closed his eyes as he lowered his body to hers. Later, while she writhed under him, he heard the soft chimes of a clock. It was midnight. He wondered if Vicki slept, and how she lay against the pillows, and whether her hair was braided that night or curled on her shoulders. The slim silken limbs beneath him rolled and rose and clasped him tighter. There was an instant when he heard thunder in his ears, felt a red mist burning in his mind. Then he rolled away from Lilac. The heat in his loins was grown cold, leaving his body drained, yet he knew the dissatisfaction of his heart.

A flicker of brightness caught Vicki's eyes. She knelt, her skirts puffing up around her, to reach for it.

Richard, seeing, said, "Let me."

But she had the gold pick in her fingers. By her face he knew that she saw what it represented.

She relinquished it disdainfully, as he said, "It's a small novelty I found in New York City."

He was glad that she didn't ask where he had found it, but piqued at her open lack of interest.

"It was a successful trip," he said. "I'll probably have to go back again however."

"Soon?"

"I'll be able to choose my own time," he answered. He didn't suggest that she consider making the trip with him. She had refused him once. He'd give her no opportunity to refuse him again. But he hoped she would think of it herself.

Instead she said, "I suppose New York City *is* the center of all business."

"It is." He waited, but she said nothing more. So he

asked, "And what of you? How did you spend your days while I was gone?"

She thought of Leslie, his arms holding her, the fresh sheets on the divan, the peculiar disappointment she had known in his embrace. She gave Richard a level look. "How do you think I spent my days?"

He was taken aback at her words, her ironic tone, but he made certain that he sounded no more than matter-of-fact when he asked, "Are you bored, Vicki? Haven't you anything to do that pleases you?"

"There's always something," she answered, and went to the door. "I'll say goodnight to Allie."

She knew that by lifting the boy out of his crib she disturbed him. He had been sound asleep until she touched him. Now he opened his eyes, and crowed, "Mama, how do?" and curled his arms around her neck. She would have to pay for this self-indulgence, she told herself. He would scream and cling to her when she put him down. But she had had so strong a need to feel his breathing warmth against her.

The gold pick that she had plucked from the floor covering seemed to glimmer at her from the shadows. She had noted the voluptuous breasts and twined limbs, and known instantly how Richard must have come by it. He had tasted one of the many delights offered by New York City. She had read of such places in exposés written up in the *Police Gazette,* in copies surreptitiously borrowed from John. That Richard had had such need, and satisfied it, didn't surprise her. But she had been nearly overwhelmed by a sense of something irrevocably lost and of threat beyond measure. The single word for the feeling was jealousy. Confounded by that recognition, she had escaped from Richard's presence as soon as she could.

Holding Allie close, she wondered why she cared what Richard did. Why this sick sensation at her heart. He had taken her by force, destroyed what had been the unviolated selfhood of a young girl. In the time since, she had tried to rebuild it whole, and had finally known triumph in Leslie's arms. She had at last shared her body with the man she had chosen, it had chosen. And triumph, she acknowledged ruefully, was indeed the only emotion she had felt. She was avenged against Richard, and nothing more. Leslie's gentleness, and then his passion, had left her empty. Was that why she had nearly drowned in a current of fierce jealousy when she knew that Richard had turned to another woman?

She had no answer to her bewilderments. To avoid them, she rose, leaned to put Allie into his crib. "No, Mama," he screamed. "Stay! Stay!"

Maria come quickly. "Why, Allie? Why . . ." Her sleepy black eyes gave Vicki a resentful look as she swept to the crib. "There, Allie. Night, night, it's sleep time."

Vicki backed helplessly from the room, closing the door behind her.

Richard lay under the canopy, unmoving, breathing deeply. She stared at him for a moment before she crept beneath the quilt, careful to leave him undisturbed.

But he was awake. He felt her small movements that avoided touching him. The inches between them seemed to grow to miles. He shut his eyes tightly, and thought of New York City and Lilac.

Chapter 18

THERE WAS A BIG WEEK IN APRIL. RICHARD'S LONG-planned-for Plant No. 2 was completed, a large, still-raw building adjacent to the older mill, and connected to it with an uncovered walkway at the third floor.

It was Allie's first birthday as well. He had progressed from a frustrated crawl to an uncertain walk. In spite of Maria Sandora's efforts he fell often, always sporting a bruise on his small nose, or a healing cut on his chin. He was tall for his age, but with shoulders already wide, reminding Vicki of Richard. His vocabulary had grown quickly. He said, "Grandma" and "Unky John" and "Maria," as well as "Mama" and "Papa." But his favorite word was becoming "no," spoken in varying tones of defiance, anger, or yearning. Matilda assured Vicki that such was normal for Cavendish men at that age, though precocious when compared to other one-year-olds.

Richard combined the celebration of the two important events. At ten o'clock in the morning, the power in Plant No. 1, as it was coming to be called, was cut. The shuttles went quiet, the looms and carding and slashing machines still.

The operatives gathered in the delivery yard, where planked tables had been set up, serving hot coffee and small cakes. The Germania band sat on a low platform, playing loudly against the cold wind that blew off the river.

Mayor John Abbott, two members of the Board of Aldermen, Albert and Eustacia Cosgrove, along with five other members of the Fall River Manufacturers' Association, had special seats. John and Matilda sat with them. Vicki, wearing a costume of blue velvet under a blue velvet cape, stood at Richard's side, while Allie rode his shoulders, shouting gleefully.

Maria, with Mrs. Beamis and Nettie and Harry, watched dolefully from a short distance away, and nodded when Mrs. Beamis said it was a great day. Nettie, equally doleful, didn't agree quickly enough, so Mrs. Beamis went on to say, "You need a spring tonic, my girl. And I'm going to stop at Adams' and get you one on the way home."

Nettie sighed, didn't answer. She looked anxiously to see if Rosamund Dean's carriage was tied up with the others, hoping to spy Mitch Ryan. Her brother's stern eye had been too much to contend with. She'd never been able even to slip out and say a word to

Mitch while he waited under the porte cochere during his mistress's increasingly rare visits to the Cavendish home.

Close by, George Thompson and Rex Taylor, both union weavers, stood with Gus Markeson and Jamie.

"It's all very well," Rex Taylor said. "Music and coffee and cakes. Only what about us?"

Gus Markeson slanted a yellow look at him. "Us? Whose concern is that? Except our own." He looked down at Jamie. The boy was fourteen now, growing out of his clothes, with thin wrists hanging from his sweater and bony ankles inches below the bottoms of his pants. "King Richard is preparing a treasury of his heir."

Jamie paid no attention to his father. He was fascinated by Vicki, her amber hair under her blue hat, the smile that came and went as she greeted new arrivals. He strained to watch Allie, still riding Richard's shoulders.

George Thompson stared admiringly at Nettie's ankles, and wondered how he could manage a word with her, so, while he, too, heard Gus, he didn't answer.

But Rex Taylor repeated, "A treasury for his heir? That remains to be seen. There's already too many mills on short time, running only three or four days a week. Borden City, Chace, King Phillips, Flint, Sagamore. Cavendish could be next."

"It's better than outright closing," Gus growled. "We can't live without pay for two or three weeks at a time. And that's what they're angling for." The scar tissue under his eyes reddened. "The profit margin's falling. What's that got to do with us? We don't get it anyway."

"Tell Albert Cosgrove," Rex Taylor grinned. "He'll explain it to you. You ought to hear him with the Textile Council."

"You know what you can do with your Textile Council."

At a signal from Richard, the band stopped playing. He reached to lift Allie from his shoulders, and the boy clutched his hair and screamed. Richard grinned as he set the small writhing child on the ground, while Maria hurried to take him. Allie flung himself onto his feet, bounced away from her reaching hands, and threw himself into the crowd. Nettie, spreading her arms wide for him, stumbled into George Thompson, who grinned happily and steadied her by the shoulder, while Allie dodged around the two of them and tumbled at Jamie's feet, screaming still. Jamie picked him up, carried him to Maria, but the boy refused a transfer, so Jamie put him on the ground. He clenched a small fist in Jamie's pants, leaned against him, and beamed into his face.

The dignitaries in their special seats were laughing, the band on its platform, too. Those of the workers who could see whistled and cheered him. Ezra, standing now beside Gus, said quietly, "Looks as if he's chosen sides, doesn't it?" Gus answered, "Let's see where he stands when it matters."

Richard stepped to the platform. He thanked his distinguished guests for their attendance, his operatives for joining in. He told the company that he hoped his two contributions of that day, his son Allie, and Plant No. 2, would both make Fall River proud of them. Then, turning to Vicki, he said, "My wife, who presided over the advent of the first of these, will now preside over the opening of the second."

She sat frozen, staring at him. She had known nothing of this part of his plans. He went to her, drew her to her feet, led her to the wide double doors of the building. A red satin ribbon closed them, a huge bow lacing their brass handles. On the wall nearby, a thin gauze cloth covered a brass plaque.

He said softly, "The plaque first, Vicki."

She drew the covering away, and read the words cut into the shining brass. *Cavendish and Sons. Plant No. 2. April 15, 1904*

"And now the ribbon," Richard went on.

She cut the bow with the gold scissors he put in her hand. The ribbon parted, fell.

Richard pulled the doors ajar, yelled, "There it is!" and the band burst into "Happy Birthday!" while

Richard filled Vicki's arms with a bouquet of yellow roses.

Before George Thompson returned to his loom he had managed an introduction to Nettie and Mrs. Beamis through Ezra, and secured the housekeeper's invitation to call.

The next day *The Daily Globe* and *The Fall River Herald* both had front-page headlines announcing the sinking at Port Arthur by the Japanese of the Russian battleship *Petropavlovsk,* with Admiral Makayoff on board. On their inner pages both newspapers mentioned the dual celebration. *The Fall River Herald,* in "Personal Mention," said, *Cavendish and Sons, Plant No. 2, opened with an unusual ceremony at which Mayor Abbott, Mr. Albert Cosgrove, of the Manufacturers' Association, and Mrs. Cosgrove, and the whole Cavendish family, including small son Alban, were present. The Daily Globe* in "Globe Gossip" wrote, *The opening of Plant No. 2 of Cavendish and Sons was celebrated yesterday when operatives from floor sweepers to weavers to loomfixer joined in a two-hour ceremony at which there were also present Mayor Abbott, Mr. Albert Cosgrove of the Manufacturers Association and other dignitaries. We wish the second plant of this company well.*

In the third week of May, with the winter cold forgotten, both newspapers again mentioned the Cavendish name. This time "Personal Mention" and "Globe Gossip" merely announced that Mr. Richard Cavendish had departed for New York City on the Fall River Line in connection with his business, and that on his return the Cavendish family would leave for the summer at Cavendish Cove in Newport.

By this time Richard was a familiar figure at Madame Rose's establishment, having visited there three times overnight since his first arrival in January. He was well known to the butler, called Henry, who greeted him with a warm smile, and immediately released the brass chain across the door. He was known to Madame Rose, who no longer studied him before leading him to the flower parlor, as he had learned it was named. He was known to Lilac, too.

This time, before embarking on the *Puritan* for his journey, he had withdrawn some five thousand dollars in cash to take with him. He had also located a small house on a side street off Eastern Avenue within bell-hearing distance of Notre Dame Church.

He checked in at the St. Regis, had a drink in the restaurant there and a second breakfast and then went for a walk on Fifth Avenue. He bought a game for Allie, a copy of Jack London's *Sea Wolf,* just published, for Vicki, and returned to the hotel to rid himself of his parcels. That done, he took a hansom to Madame Rose's.

She greeted him, concealing her surprise that he was so much earlier than usual, and went on to tell him regretfully that Lilac wasn't in, though she was expected soon.

"I'll wait," Richard told her. "But meanwhile I'd like to speak to you."

Her painted brows arched. She led him along the corridor to a small room behind the stairs and waved him to a seat.

While she poured brandy for the two of them, he looked about. The place was decorated all in white, with floor-to-ceiling bookcases filled with novels. From where he sat he could pick out the gold-embossed titles against the colorful bindings. There were representations from Winston Churchill, John Fox, Jack London, Edward Bellamy, Stephen Crane and Herman Melville. Her eclectic tastes amused him.

When she had passed him his snifter, she sat opposite him and he asked how she had come to collect her books.

"Is that the subject of our discussion?" she answered.

He grinned at her. "No." He savored a sip of the brandy. The house was still. There was no piano tinkle, no laughter. He was aware of the faint whisper of footsteps, but that was all.

He had planned it carefully. Now that he was here,

however, he was beset by sudden doubt. He took another sip of brandy, allowed it to spread warmth through his throat and dismissed his unease. At last he said, "I'd like to take Lilac away from you."

Madame Rose leaned back, the raddled skin of her throat tightening. "What am I supposed to say to that?"

"Whatever you like. Surely you've heard such a request before."

She waved that aside. "Lilac is an asset to me."

He took from his pocket the envelope of cash he had brought with him. He put it on the table at her elbow. "It's five thousand dollars. You may count it, if you like."

Her cold expression warmed. "That's neither here nor there. Lilac's not mine to sell, you know."

He said nothing. The money wasn't in the nature of payment. It was only to ease whatever pain Madame Rose might feel at Lilac's loss. He trusted she would see that, though she mightn't admit it.

She went on, "Lilac came here freely, and because she wanted to. She may leave any way or any time that she decides to."

"Of course," he agreed. "But she has a good opinion of your judgment. She's mentioned that many times. You could help her decide."

"What do you want of her?" Madame Rose asked curiously. At his laugh, she drew herself up. "You should know that many of my girls have married well. They've moved from here to a number of Fifth Avenue mansions. You can read their new names in the columns of any New York newspaper."

"You shan't read Lilac's name in the papers, I should hope. And what I want of her is my business."

"Have you discussed it with her yet?" Madame Rose asked.

"I'm speaking to you first. It seemed only right."

She refilled his snifter, but not her own. She looked consideringly at the money on the table. As she picked it up, she smiled. "I think you'll have your way. But I hope Lilac's not sorry for it."

"You'd allow her to return if she wanted to?"

"That would depend. I couldn't promise."

"If she were the same?"

"Oh, yes." Madame Rose got to her feet. "We understand each other. It's in your hands, and Lilac's, and I advise you to be persuasive, for she's been happy here these past two years and mightn't want to risk it."

He waited an hour. There were, he noted, flowers in the parlor. Roses, lilies, daisies, and lilacs. This time they were earth-and-sun-grown. The small black maid brought him coffee, refilled his cup. Slowly the hush of the house faded. There were giggles in the hall, footsteps on the stairs.

When Lilac came in, she said breathlessly, "Madame Rose told me you've been waiting. I'll go and change, and be with you in a minute."

"No, don't." He smiled at her, liking what he saw. She wore a dark blue walking suit and a high-collared white shirtwaist. Her hat was dark blue, too. "Sit down," he said.

Stripping white gloves from her hands, she did as he asked. But a frown began to gather between her brows. "What's wrong?"

"Madame Rose didn't say what I wanted?"

"Not her." Lilac grinned. "She doesn't give out the time of day when she's not paid for it." Lilac paused, then added, "I guess you could say the same of me."

"I've rented a house," he told her. "In Fall River. For you. It has some furniture, but you'll need more, for which I'll pay, when you've picked it out. I'd like you to come and live there. So I could see you more frequently."

Her indrawn breath was a hiss of surprise. "You want me to leave here?"

"Is that such a frightening idea for you?"

She sat motionless, plainly turning the suggestion over in her mind. At last she said, "No, it's not frightening. Only I owe Madame Rose a lot."

"She owes you a lot, too."

Lilac grinned again. "You bet your sweet life."

"What do you think?"

She pursed her lips. Then: "Why not? I've wanted to leave here since I first came."

He drew a ticket from his pocket. "I've made a reservation for you on the Fall River Line, at Pier 14. You'll have two weeks in which to prepare, and do whatever you feel you have to do."

"You're pretty sure of yourself, aren't you?"

"I am," he answered.

She rose, drew off her hat, letting it hang from her fingers. "What about it? One last time here for good luck?"

"That'll be fine," he told her, and followed her upstairs.

The whistle shrilled through the quiet morning. The gangplank went down. Sleepy-eyed passengers disembarked.

Lilac was one of the last. She had taken her time, hanging back, while the others hurried ahead. The dock was nearly cleared, the road outside quiet again, when she passed that way.

She hired a hansom, had her baggage loaded, and gave the driver the address. He admired her ankles as she stepped in. They were soon riding out Eastern Avenue. She was pleased with the shops she saw on the way, pleased when the hansom turned into a quiet side street. The house was surrounded by tall bushes, green now and thick, and set back from the street, with no close neighbors. She told herself that Richard had chosen the place well, as the bells of Notre Dame Church rang out. She found the key beneath the mat on the front stoop, where he had told her to look.

She was pleased, too, by what she found inside, but by the time Richard arrived at eleven o'clock, she had a long list of things that she wanted. She didn't mention them. She had prepared coffee and baked a pan of gingerbread. They ate it companionably over the butcher-block table in the kitchen.

"Do you think this will do for you?" he asked.

She smiled at him. "It's more like home than Madame Rose's was."

"But less luxurious."

"I can do without her luxuries." Lilac was silent for a moment. Then: "You've never asked me my real name."

"I thought it was Lilac," he grinned.

"You didn't! You understood perfectly well from the first that our names were Madame's little joke."

"It doesn't matter," he answered. "You can continue to call yourself Lilac, if you like. If not, then tell me your real name."

"Celeste," she said promptly. "Celeste Denver." It was no more her name than Lilac was. She chose it simply for what she thought to be a nice sound. "And it interests me that you've never asked about me. Where I come from, and why I was at Madame Rose's, and why I was so willing to leave for you."

"Those are things, I consider, that you'll tell me if you want to, and when you do."

"But you don't care," she accused him.

"Why should I?"

She shrugged. "No reason except that most men do."

"Most men aren't able to separate the past from the present, and either one from the future." He went on, "But now that you've brought it up, tell me how you came to be at Madame Rose's."

"You've probably heard the same thing a dozen times before."

"You're the only . . ." He paused. Then: "What I mean to say is that I've never spoken of such matters to anyone but you."

"What you mean to say is that I'm the only whore you've ever spoken to," she retorted.

"You misunderstand, but no matter."

She saw that bitterness wouldn't do, and immediately gave him a warm smile. "*My* little joke. You mustn't take me seriously." Before he could answer, she went on, "I'm from Missouri, from a town you haven't heard of. I always sang and danced and had a lot of dreams. I came to New York City, thinking to go into vaudeville. And I could have, would have, but for falling in love. The man promised to marry me, but he didn't. And when he knew I was pregnant, he disappeared. Madame Rose took me in. I stayed there afterwards because the baby died and I didn't care any more what happened to me." She sighed. "And I felt I owed Madame Rose whatever I could give her for all she did for me."

"I'm sure she was amply repaid for her kindness," Richard said.

"She was." Lilac, now calling herself Celeste, once again smiled warmly. She wondered if he believed her. It was impossible to tell from his face. The moment he had asked her to go to Fall River, where he could visit her regularly and often, she had begun to think ahead. She knew nothing of the town, his wife, family, life there. She imagined that he had his reasons for what he did, as all other men had their reasons. But if he wanted her closer, perhaps something could be made of it. Men had been known to leave wife and family. Divorce was frowned on, but so was keeping a mistress. She supposed the step from mistress to wife to be a huge one, but not impossible. So she had planned a biography that might explain what she was, yet lighten the stain of it.

She hadn't come from Missouri, had never sung and danced, nor thought to be in vaudeville. She had never been pregnant, either. Her name was Mary Cotten. She had come to New York City with a traveling salesman who had stopped in the Buffalo boardinghouse owned by her widowed and ailing mother. Mary had been kitchen drudge, scullery maid and unwilling nurse from the age of twelve. From that age, too, she had provided her body to those who would pay for the use of it. The salesman passed through when she was fifteen. She eagerly accepted his offer. She left her mother, then near death, and never heard of her again. He brought her to the city and deposited her at Madame Rose's when he tired of her. Now Mary was in Fall River, calling herself Celeste.

She determined to make the most of whatever opportunity presented itself. That was why she didn't mention to Richard the list of things she had decided that she would need in order to live in comfort. She didn't want him to think her greedy.

When he got to his feet, saying, "I must leave now. I'll see you tomorrow night," she smiled at him. "I'll be busy," and when he left fifty dollars on the table, she said, "Oh, I do have enough, but thank you."

"I'll see that payments are made regularly into your account at the bank as soon as you've made your own arrangements."

She nodded, liking the sound of that. It had the ring of permanency she hoped her.

He rode to the mill, satisfied with himself. It would be pleasant to have her close by. Vicki would feel only relief if he left her alone at Newport and spent an occasional night in town.

Ezra Saunders was waiting when he arrived, a neatly penned telephone message in hand. Denton Paley had received the shipment of yardage as per the January contract. Payment would be mailed on the tenth of June. Meanwhile, would Mr. Cavendish call to discuss another such delivery contract.

Richard grinned. "You see, Ezra?"

"It was to your advantage this time, I agree," Ezra answered, and then, worriedly, "But what about the next?"

Chapter 19

IN THE THIRD WEEK OF MAY, ON THE SAME AFTER-
noon that Richard made his arrangement with the girl
he had then called Lilac, Vicki had sat on the sheet-
covered divan in the Cosgroves' Fair Haven cottage
and had wondered what she was doing there. After
her first meeting with Leslie, she had decided she
didn't like the place and wouldn't go there again. She
had felt nothing but a vague emptiness she didn't
understand. Her long hunger to be part of Leslie
seemed meaningless to her then. Yet she had returned
to meet him, while wondering bleakly why she did.
That day, hardly able to conceal her impatience, she
listened while Leslie gossiped about Rosamund's engagement to Davis Peabody, and asked if Vicki had
seen her.

When Vicki had said that she hadn't, Leslie had
grinned. "You're sure too soon. She'll want you to
admire the ring he gave her."

Vicki had wished Leslie would be quiet. She had
no interest in Rosamund's affairs.

But he continued. "She's going to move to Boston,
of course. Let the servants go, close the house. Elise
will have a key, for looking after the place until
Rosamund decides what she wants to do with it." He
grinned. "It's a short walk from Highland Avenue."

"I begin to understand your interest in Rosamund's
arrangements," Vicki had said dryly. "But it's too
short a walk. And besides, I won't be there. We'll be
making the move to Newport within a few days."

"And what of after your return?" He sat beside her on the divan, put a hand under her chin and tipped her face up. "What is it? Ever since we arrived, you've been . . . what shall I call it? Abstracted? Yes. As if you aren't really here at all."

She had turned her face from his. "Yes. I know. And you speak of my return from Newport. You look so far ahead. I go on only from one day to the next. We're about ready to leave. The winter clothing has been stored in red cedar flakes. Our summer things are in the packing cases. Harry has driven out a load of linens and blankets, and many of Allie's toys. When Richard comes back from New York, we'll move. There's nothing beyond that."

"Nothing beyond that?" Leslie had echoed. "Why, I see a great deal. I can imagine meeting you again on Cliff Walk. And perhaps something more private can be arranged. And then, in the autumn . . ."

"It seems so useless," she had said, sighing. She had drawn on her hat, tied its green back ribbons, pulled on her elbow-length kid gloves.

"Vicki! What are you doing? You needn't leave so soon."

"I'd better go, Leslie." She had seen the instant alarm streak through him before he demanded, "You don't suspect Richard has any idea . . ."

Vicki had said with a level look, "No, I don't suspect Richard has any idea."

"Thank God for that!"

She had known that he heard the dryness of her tone, but that he had felt only relief. If Richard knew, then Leslie feared that Elise would soon know as well. She would never forgive him. She had her athletic field. Between that gift of Richard's, and Davis Peabody's generosity, the school was on a more solid footing than Elise and Leslie had dared hope for. But any scandal . . . how the *Herald* and *Globe* both enjoyed an adultery suit . . .

"Would it be awful for you," Vicki had said slowly, "if Elise were to discover our relationship?"

"I referred to Richard," Leslie had retorted.

"But you thought of Elise."

He hadn't replied to that.

As he had driven Vicki back to town, she consid ered why she scarcely looked ahead. It was, she de cided then, because she saw no future with Leslie Then why had she met with him before? Why con tinue to meet with him? The revenge she had onc thought would be so sweet had no savor. She remem bered how, in April, when they had celebrated Allie' birthday and the opening of the new plant, Richar had turned to her and made her a part of the cere mony so unexpectedly. And, only a few days late she had crept away to lie in Leslie's arms withou joy.

Riding beside Leslie, she hadn't feared that Rich ard might discover the truth. He was in New York The emptiness of the house testified to his absence. I hadn't been the first time she had noticed that whe he was gone a malaise afflicted her, so that she wan dered restlessly from room to room, hardly able t concentrate on what John or Matilda said to her bored by Nettie's chatter, impatient with Allie' never-ending demands. She was wakeful during th nights, and tired during the days. And these meet ings with Leslie did nothing to alter her mood.

She had sighed, and Leslie touched her hand "Vicki?"

Impatience had smitten her, hard and startling She snapped, "Yes! What is it!" and realized tha she had no pleasure with him. More than anythin then she wanted to be at home.

He had said softly, "You're angry with me."

"No, Leslie." It wasn't anger that she had felt. I was boredom. It had struck her suddenly that she n longer remembered what she had once found so en dearing in him.

"If you're not angry, then tell me when we ca meet again," he had asked.

"I don't know, Leslie." But even as she had an swered, she knew that she wouldn't meet with hin alone anymore. This affair, begun, she had thought, i love, was become only shameful to her. She had intended to avenge Richard's treatment. But what had it gained her?

Leslie had stopped at the corner near Mrs. Wood's shop. He helped her down and drove away. He always made his departure quickly to avoid watching eyes.

As she turned to leave, Vicki had seen a black bow on the shop door. Mr. Wood, she had thought.

Vicki had gone to the shop. It was empty. Dust had hidden the counters. As she had opened the door the familiar bell tinkled.

Vicki hesitated, remembering her ignominious departure from here with Richard and John so long before. She had never come back, but how much she wished she had done so. She went to the flowered curtain, thrust it aside.

Mrs. Wood had sat alone at the wooden table, smaller than ever, her blue eyes faded. The faintest of smiles glimmered on her face. "I'm glad to see you, my dear."

"What's happened?" Vicki had asked softly.

"He's gone, Vicki. It happened yesterday."

"I'm so sorry. You were so good to him, Mrs. Wood."

"Good to him? Oh, no, my dear, I took care of him because I loved him, and so I was good to myself. I was trying to keep him with me. He's at rest now, and I'm alone."

"And what will you do?" Vicki had asked.

"I don't know." Mrs. Wood raised bewildered eyes. "We've always had the shop, but the rent goes up next month. I can't manage that." She had shaken her head. "But never mind, tell me of you."

"I'm well, as you can see. I have a son named Allie. Alban, that is, for my father." Heat had suddenly burned in Vicki's cheeks. "I should have come to visit. You were always so kind to me. I thought of it, believe me. But I . . . oh, Mrs. Wood, do you understand? I was ashamed."

"Ashamed of love?" Mrs. Wood had asked. "You

needn't have been. *I* know. *I* can tell. Don't be ashamed."

The heat had become unbearable. It burned into Vicki's bones. Her shame hadn't been for love.

"And we knew of you," Mrs. Wood had said. "I read it in the papers, you see. And we were glad."

"Thank you," Vicki had whispered. When she rose to go, she had said, "I'll come again to see you, but in the autumn."

"If I'm not here, the neighbors will know," Mrs. Wood had answered.

Later, walking up Highland Avenue, Vicki had wondered what she could do to help the old woman. She had decided she would speak to Richard about it and see what he said. As she approached the house, her step had quickened. The sun was high, although it was nearly five o'clock. There would be an hour for playing with Allie before his early supper.

When Richard returned from New York Vicki had told him about Mrs. Wood's predicament. He made no comment beyond, "I must think about it, Vicki."

Two days later they had left for Newport. She rode alone with him in the surrey. The others had gone ahead in the carriage.

It was early afternoon, the sun hot and high, the meadows agleam with flowers. She remembered the first time she and Richard had passed that way together.

He said suddenly, "I almost forgot, Vicki. About Mrs. Wood, I mean."

"Perhaps I oughtn't to have troubled you, but she was so afraid. And I understand." She stopped herself suddenly, her mind racing backward in time, across the ocean to Rye, to those days when a halfpenny went into the rent box. It all seemed so long ago now.

"Your Mrs. Wood needn't be afraid anymore." Richard smiled at Vicki. He took from his coat pocket a wrinkled parchment stuck over with red and gold seals, and put it into Vicki's hands. "She has a new owner now."

Vicki read a few words, turned the dry old sheets

carefully, then saw her name, Victoria Davelle Cavendish. Suddenly there was a hush come upon the world. She no longer heard the creaking of the surrey wheels, nor the clip-clop of the horses. She raised her eyes to Richard. "But this says that *I* own the building."

"I've put it in your name. You'll decide the rent from now on."

"But Richard, why?" she gasped.

"The gentleman who used to control the property was adamant that Mrs. Wood should go, and he didn't care if it was to the almshouse. I did. Unfortunately for him, he had a mortgage on the building at one of the banks where Albert is a director. It made it easy for me to effect a purchase."

"But Richard," she said again. "Why? Why in my name?"

"I didn't want that good woman in the almshouse, and I wanted you to own the building."

"I must let her know at once."

"Yes. Do write to her. But she does know by now that she has a new owner to deal with, and that the increase has been wiped out, and her rent reduced." He grinned. "I had Ezra take care of that."

"I don't know how to thank you for being so kind," she said quietly.

His brows arched. "For making a property owner of you?"

"Oh, that, too, of course. But you needn't have. I shan't know what to do with it." She thrust the documents at him. "You must keep them. As long as Mrs. Wood is safe, I don't need them."

He tucked the papers away, saying, "Just ask when you want them." It was, he thought, the first time she had shown real enthusiasm for any gift he had given her. He was glad that he had done it. There was too little he could do to bring her pleasure.

The sun was near to setting when they had reached Cavendish Cove. The sky was layered with carmine and gold. As they stopped in the driveway the windows of the house caught the fiery light and suddenly flashed aglow, like rows of glittering jewels. The two shaded bulbs at the door shone in welcoming signal.

As Richard helped Vicki from the carriage, Allie flung himself from the steps, and fell and got up to come racing toward them, with Maria in protesting pursuit. Richard swung Allie over his head, and laughed and handed him to the nursemaid, but the boy screamed, reaching for Vicki.

She had taken him into her arms, and carrying him, she went inside, crossing the veranda without once thinking of what it had meant to her before.

She had remembered it only later, when she learned that Richard, without discussing it with her, had arranged with Mrs. Beamis that a separate bedroom be prepared for him. Vicki had made no comment on that, and neither did he. They had settled down to live out the summer, side by side, but not together.

Now, two weeks later, Vicki sat at the dressing table in the room that was her own. John and Matilda would be waiting, but she lingered there.

The family was well settled, the routine of life established. Richard, in the past two weeks, had spent only seven scattered nights in Newport. The other seven he had stayed in Fall River, pleading the demands of the two plants. Allie had discovered that he liked the small ripples of the quiet summer sea, and learned hide and seek in the tall grasses of the meadows. Matilda went calling every day, and John rode along the shore, solitary as always. Vicki herself read, took long ambling strolls on Cliff Walk and explored the town of Newport by herself. She supposed the whole of the summer would be the same.

Sighing, she went downstairs. John and Matilda were already at the dinner table. The silver gleamed by the light of two tall white tapers. The big silver bowl of roses filled the room with a heady scent.

When Nettie had served them, Matilda said that Rosamund and Leslie would visit the next day.

"Has she closed the house?" Vicki asked.

"I think so. I suppose she'll tell us all about it tomorrow."

Rosamund did indeed tell them all about her plans the following day. She went into great detail, and at some length, while Leslie covertly eyed Vicki, and crossed and uncrossed his legs.

She sat with her right hand conspicuously displayed against the blue of her gown, so that her ring sparkled as brightly as the ocean beyond the lawn, and told how she had closed the house, let the servants go and moved to Elise and Leslie's. She and Davis would be married from there in the autumn.

The instant she paused for breath, Leslie suggested a walk, turning to look at Vicki.

But Nettie came to the door to say that lunch was being served. Sighing, Leslie followed the others. When the meal was finished, he renewed his suggestion, and that time all agreed.

Vicki made certain that John limped along beside her, and that they went slowly, so that Rosamund and Matilda were just at their heels. Leslie had no opportunity for a private word with Vicki. He and Rosamund left well before twilight, with Vicki relieved to see them gone.

Richard came for Sunday, arriving with Matilda, who had been to Fall River that week for an appointment with Dr. Stilton.

It was at dinner that evening that Vicki first heard of the industrial trouble brewing in Fall River.

"Eustacia Cosgrove tells me," Matilda said, "that the association has met several times recently."

Richard answered, "So I've heard."

"You haven't attended?"

"I had other things on my mind."

"Albert is concerned," Matilda said disapprovingly. "He believes there'll be trouble of one sort or another. There are too many mills on short weeks now. The Textile Council is complaining."

"I've been aware of that," Richard said dryly.

"Are we involved?"

"Not yet," Richard told her. "Though we may come to be. The profit margin's dropping."

"But with our additional looms . . ."

"Even so." Richard smiled at his mother. "Still, don't concern yourself. It's my worry, and I'll see to it."

Later, when Vicki asked him if the situation were serious, he brushed her question aside with a shrug and went to play with Allie.

She listened to the boy's laughter, the deep sound of Richard's voice, then settled down to read. The words seemed to blur on the page, the meaning to evade her.

Finally she went in to kiss Allie good night. She found him on his knees, crowing, "Make tiger, Papa," while Richard hunched behind the spoolback chair, peering through its spokes as if they were bars, and growled fiercely.

It was the middle of the following week, a quiet gray morning. Vicki sat on the veranda, a shawl around her shoulders. She was thinking of Richard, in Fall River, when Leslie arrived.

He came in a hack rented on Broadway, bearing flowers for her, a carved rabbit for Allie and books for both Matilda and John. He had, he explained, taken an early electric trolley. He had seen Richard the day before, and Richard was working hard and believed it unlikely that he could come to Newport before the weekend.

"I hope you don't mind my coming unannounced," he said. And as she turned to the door: "Vicki, don't tell the others yet. I want to see you alone. I must, Vicki!"

She was glad it was too late. Allie had heard the visitor's voice and come running. When finally he was dragged away by Maria, there was Matilda, offering iced lemonade and raisin cookies. Finally, in desperation, Leslie suggested that Vicki go into town with him to help him select a wedding gift for Rosamund. Vicki agreed, deciding that she must deal with the situation she had herself created. She excused herself and went to put on a white lace hat.

When she returned, Leslie was waiting impatiently at the hack. He helped her up, drove quickly away from the house. They turned into Bellevue Avenue, slowing for a long gleaming Reo that jolted importantly down the road.

Leslie cursed it as she looked back at Cavendish Cove.

They drove on, small glimpses of the ocean flickering at them from between the gardens of vast estates.

At last, Leslie asked, "Has something happened?"

"No. Nothing."

"Then I don't understand." His voice was rough with urgency. "Vicki, I want you. It's been so long. Yet you've avoided me. You've given me no opportunity to make any arrangements. Even today . . ."

"There'll be no need for that," she said quietly. "I'm sorry, Leslie. Whatever there was between us is over."

The horse danced as Leslie jerked the reins. "But what is it? Why? You know what I feel for you. You know I'd do anything . . ."

She looked at him briefly, then dropped her gaze to her gloved hands. *Anything*. That was the word he used. Now, when it didn't matter, he could say that. He was safe in his hunger. He knew she would never ask him to take her from Richard. Because of Allie. Leslie was his sister's possession as much as she, Vicki, was Richard's possession. They would neither of them be free. And now she was certain she didn't want to be free for Leslie.

She raised her eyes to him again. "There's nothing to be done," she said. "You must have guessed what I've been thinking for some time."

But now he laughed. "You're flirting with me, aren't you? It's a game you've decided to play for the summer, and when you return home . . ."

She shook her head decisively. "No, Leslie. No game. I won't meet you again. There's no reason for me to do so. When we see each other, it will be as friends. Friends, Leslie. And nothing more."

"I see," he said slowly. "You turn off your feeling for me as if it were a faucet, don't you?"

"Perhaps I didn't know what that feeling was."

211

"And perhaps there's someone else," he suggested.

"No one," she answered, and thought of Richard. "No one," she repeated firmly. "But that's how it must be."

He would have protested more, and couldn't. She refused to listen, saying only, "We must see to a present for Rosamund, and then you must take me home."

Hurt pride made him grim. They found a suitable silver platter and returned to Cavendish Cove in silence. He left soon after, refusing Matilda's suggestion that he stay and dine.

The following Sunday Richard arrived for the weekend. Allie greeted him with the usual exuberant cries, swung on his hands and climbed on his shoulders. Vicki, watching, felt a peculiar tug at her heart. They were, the big Cavendish and the small one, so very good together. She turned away, biting her lip.

When they were alone, Richard asked, "How was your week?"

"As always," she answered. "Leslie visited again, you know. We went into town and bought a wedding gift for him to give to Rosamund. I suppose I'll do the same for us in the next few days."

"It's nice that you had company."

She didn't answer.

He looked at her cool profile. It was hard to know what she was thinking. Lilac was different. In his mind Richard always thought of her by that name, although she preferred to be called Celeste. He could somehow see through her every pretense. She acted as if she cared nothing for money, but he saw her greed more and more frequently. He didn't object. She was right to feel she should be paid for her services, even though she pretended to have fallen in love with him. He wasn't fooled by her moans of passion, or the dreamy looks she gave him. Yet it didn't matter to him. She was there when he wanted her, when he needed the release of her body, even as he thought of Vicki and wished for her.

Much later, when the house was dark and still, a storm came up with a sudden rustling in the trees and thunder echoing in vast drumrolls through the heavens, and lightning flushing the walls with eerie purple brilliance before fading.

He heard her moving about in the next room. He got up and went to her, knocking gently at her door. At the murmur of her voice, he stepped inside. She stood at the window, the curtains drawn back.

"It's nothing, Vicki. It'll soon pass," he told her. "The storms are always spectacularly noisy here."

"Yes," she agreed, not looking at him as he came to stand beside her. "I know it'll do no harm. But it seems as if the house shakes with the thunder, as if the ground beneath it might wash away when the rains come."

"No fear," he laughed. "It's well built."

"I remember," she answered. "You pointed the foundations out to me when we first came here."

His body went still. The first time they had come here was when he had spoiled whatever there might have grown between them. For a moment, he stared hot-eyed, into the wind-lashed garden. Then, without a word, he left her.

When she awakened to morning sunlight and rain-washed stillness, and went downstairs, Matilda said, "Richard left on the seven-fifteen, and didn't say when he'd be back," and looked at Vicki with anxious eyes.

Chapter 20

Ezra saunders was at his desk a few minutes before the starting whistle blew. Outside it was hot; the usual end-of-June sun burning down on the waters of Mount Hope Bay and the Taunton River. Inside it was hotter still. Ezra's glasses were misted with his own breath and the humid air. His collar, put on only a little while before, was already wilted. His spirits were wilted, too. He hadn't been able to dissuade Gus Markeson from taking Jamie out of school and putting the boy to work, though he had tried as hard as he could.

He looked at the yardage production figures for the past month. He had just reread with much unease the terms of the Denton Paley contract. He didn't hear the squeal of the pulleys, the rhythmic slam of the shuttles, but he raised his head at the yell, "Bobbin boy!" and within seconds, "Fixer! Fixer!"

It was George Thompson at his loom, calling for Gus. But Gus was at Plant No. 2 now. He couldn't be in more than one place at a time. "Fixer!" George yelled again, glaring at Ezra through the glass panel that separated them. Ezra turned away. The man would have to wait. A pity it had to be George. He was union, though not as noisy about it as some.

The telephone shrilled and Ezra went to answer it. Listening to Albert Cosgrove ask that Richard return the call as soon as he arrived, Ezra heard George Thompson again shout for the loomfixer.

He had just hung up when Richard came in. The

younger man nodded, put his white straw hat on the clothes tree and took his place behind the big scarred desk that had been his father's.

"Where's Gus?" Richard asked.

Ezra answered, with a jerk of his bald head, "Over there. As is becoming usual." He went on querulously, "I knew eight looms was stretching the men too far. They're used to five or six, and that's what they can do."

"They can cover eight with these looms," Richard told him. "If they want to," he added grimly.

Ezra shrugged. "Albert Cosgrove asked you to call him at the bank." Speaking, he put the new yardage production figures before Richard and returned to his seat.

Richard studied the figures, frowning. His estimates had proven all too true. There was no margin to allow for this. He knew that he wasn't alone. The margins were shrinking for every mill. But he had a new plant to consider. He wondered if Albert's call had to do with what was happening. He paused to study the Denton Paley delivery agreement, and then telephoned to Albert, who said, "I'm glad to catch you early. We're meeting here at the bank, to discuss what to do. There are already too many mills working two or three days a week. There'll soon be more. Unless something's done."

"I'll be there," Richard said.

Later, he left the mill and walked to the bank. North Main Street was sun-scorched and crowded. An Oldsmobile trapped behind an overloaded coal wagon honked furiously, making the two scrawny horses bolt into a vegetable cart, so that carrots and cucumbers and celery rained upon angry passersby, and the resultant tangle prevented movement in any direction.

Richard skirted the pocket of confusion and stopped at Wilmot's across from the public library. He had remembered that along with toys and other goods, the shop carried both Edison and Columbia records. Celeste, whom he still thought of as Lilac, had brought with her from New York City a phonograph, and played it often. He wondered if it reminded her of the tinkly piano at Madame Rose's, as he bought *The Navajo Medley* and *Down on the Farm*. On the way out, he paused to buy a small sailboat for Allie.

Thus laden, Richard continued on to the bank. He found the boardroom crowded. This time most of the Fall River mills were represented, and this time there was no social conversation beyond the greetings courtesy demanded. Soon after his arrival, the doors were closed, and the meeting was under way.

Albert Cosgrove, looking grim, rose to his feet to outline the situation. The profit margins for every mill had dropped dangerously low. Stockholders were complaining to directors. The directors were caught between the rising costs of cotton and its transportation, and competition with southern mills, which had lower labor costs. Those mills that had gone on short time were finding that even with smaller payrolls their margins continued to fall because of the decrease in production.

Richard listened grimly. There was no joy in having company in this situation. He knew what would have to be done, only waited to hear who would propose it. The call came from the end of the table, offered at once by three directors, representing among them ten mills, who had obviously had an earlier discussion among themselves.

"We need . . ." one began.

"And without delay . . ." the second put in.

"An immediate wage cut of some twelve to fourteen cents."

A shout of agreement went up from around the long mahogany table.

"And the Textile Council?" Albert Cosgrove asked, when at last the room became still again.

"We'll have to fight them," Richard said.

From across the table, there came agreement. "Yes. We'll have to. And if they ask for arbitration, which they will, we'll have to refuse it."

"And if there's a strike?" Albert asked.

"We'll go on as long as we can. But if we have to,

216

we'll close down," Richard said unwillingly. He knew how the whole of the town could be affected by such an action, but he saw no alternative. Plant No. 2 must either run at a profit or not run at all. As for arbitration, he was in principle opposed to it. He would pay his workers what he believed he could, not a cent more. It was his mill, with everything that he owned invested in it. No one, not the Manufacturers' Association nor the governor of the state, could tell him what his payroll must be.

Again there was a shout of general agreement to his statement.

There was an hour devoted to discussing the actual size of the wage cut, and by consensus it was placed at twelve and a half cents. Half an hour was passed in setting the date on which the industry announcement would be made. It was decided that the announcement should come immediately after Independence Day and that the cut would take effect on July 20. The meeting broke up shortly thereafter.

Albert stopped Richard to ask if he and the family were free to visit with Albert and Eustacia for the Fourth of July celebration, and Richard promised that they would and then hurried out to avoid being detained any longer.

He returned to the mill just as the closing-time whistles went off, and stood watching as the men and women poured out through the tall gates. Some nodded at him, some smiled. They were his people, many of them known to him for more than ten years. George Thompson had begun as a sweeper; Rex Taylor in the shipping room. Both were weavers now, having learned their trade on Cavendish looms. The wage cut would hurt them all. But Richard saw no way out of it. The mill, his mill, had to come before anything, anyone.

He went inside, found Ezra still at his desk. The older man gave him a questioning look, but Richard said nothing about the meeting. There was time enough for that later. He didn't want to think of it now, talk of it now. He left the sailboat for Allie in the office, bade Ezra good evening and got into the buggy. He heard the chimes of Notre Dame Church as he rode up Eastern Avenue. There was the rattle of a fast-moving cart disappearing at the end of the street when he tied up before Celeste's house.

She opened the door to him, laughing. Her cheeks were pink, her eyes bright. "I was watching at the window, and just the one minute I looked away, you were suddenly there. As if you'd dropped from the sky."

"I came the usual way," he said, and handed her the records.

She wore a thin white lawn shirtwaist. Through the camisole beneath, he could see the shape of her breasts. Her skirt was a dark blue that reminded him suddenly of Vicki's eyes. Smiling, Celeste tore open the wrapper and hurried into the parlor, with Richard following. She wound the phonograph briskly and stood back to listen. But by the time *The Navajo Medley* was ended, she lay gasping in Richard's arms, and clawing his back, and thrusting her thighs against his pinioning weight.

Later, as they ate dinner together, she asked, "When will you be coming back, Richard?"

"Perhaps one night next week."

"After July Fourth? Because if that's so, and you don't mind, I'd go down to New York City for a few days. To visit Madame Rose and the girls. And to do some shopping."

"If you like," he said indifferently.

"But I won't go, if you'll be coming."

"You'll be back before I do."

"I was thinking about a summer cape, and perhaps a gown of China silk."

"Whatever you want," he said.

"And I *would* like to bring Madame a present," she added.

He grinned to indicate his understanding. She was hinting that he leave her a small something to spend on her trip. He didn't mind, but it surprised him. She had never done that before.

It was dark and late when he prepared to leave. She hugged him, whispered, "I wish you didn't have to go." She said it every time he left her. But he knew it was simply a form with her. She wasn't in love with him, although she pretended to be. He didn't care. She provided him with what he needed, which was all he asked of her.

He drove away, thinking of the empty house that awaited him, and of Vicki at Cavendish Cove in Newport.

When the buggy swung around the corner, Celeste, as she now called herself, whirled away from the door to hurry into the parlor. She wound the phonograph and hummed along with *Down on the Farm*, bending to smooth the divan cushions.

She heard the back door open and close softly. She continued to plump the cushions.

"Don't bother," Mitch Ryan said, pausing on the threshold. "We'll soon mess them up again." And before she could turn, "Did you get it then?"

She swung around, laughing, and threw herself on the divan, kicking her feet in the air. "What? No 'hello' and no 'good evening'?"

He put his ginger head down and stared hard at her. "Did you get it?" he repeated.

"On the mantel."

He took up the bills and counted them. "Fifty! You could have done better if you'd tried." He thrust the money into his shirt pocket.

"Hey," she cried. "Leave me some eating money."

"You don't need it."

Her dark eyes widened. "You listen, Mitch Ryan . . ."

He crossed the room quickly, shoved her back on the divan, and pulled her robe open. His pale eyes raked her nude body up and down. "I suppose it's worth something," he conceded. "But fifty's not all that much."

"I'd like to see you do better," she pouted.

"I will," he said softly. He dropped down beside her, closed his fingers around her shoulder. He swung

219

her to face him. "That is, *you'll* do better for me one of these days."

"Not if you don't leave me a penny to spend, I won't."

His fingers tightened into her shoulder. He thrust her back into the cushions and said through his teeth, "You'll do what I say, and if you think different, I know how to change your mind."

She forced a giggle, answered, "Aw, Mitch, you never can take a joke. There's enough for the two of us."

He put his face against her breast. His day-old whiskers cut a burn path where he touched her. She curled her fingers in his hair and pulled him closer still, while he said, "There's enough for the two of us, and more to come.'"

She was quiet, thinking of how they'd met just days after she had come to Fall River. There had been a hard rain, and she had walked down Pleasant Street after a three-hour shopping spree, cherishing her purchases and avoiding the puddles as she went. A cart had come banging and crashing down the road, its driver lashing the horse. As it flew past, its wheels churned up a sheet of mud, liquid horse droppings and greasy water. It covered her from her broad-brimmed green hat to the tips of her kid slippers. She gave out a shrill cry. The driver looked back at her. He gave her a funny turned-down grin. It was so full of triumphant joy that she forgot she was a lady going about her business on a public street. She shot at him a stream of vituperation in the choice words that she'd learned over the years. They had hardly quit burning her lips when, to her astonishment, he stopped, returned, pulled up at her side. He hopped down, smiling apologetically. "I'm sorry, darling," he said, and rubbed at the mud on her cheek with a thick calloused finger. "I thought you were a lady until you opened your mouth. Then I knew what you were." She had stared at him speechlessly, while he went on, looking her up and down. "It won't do at all. Come on, I'll take you home, and you can forgive me there for my mistake."

Later, he had told her that he had only recently lost his job, after four years, with a five-dollar tip and a "thank you, Mitch. I'm sure you'll get another one." He had moved to a room in Corky Row, an Irish neighborhood, where he felt at home.

By the time he had left her that evening, they had been to bed three times. The first was when he followed her in as she was about to change her soiled outfit. He had ignored her tart protest and tossed her down and thrown himself on her. The second time came after she had fed him a meal of short steak and boiled cabbage, and he had patted his belly and asked who paid for it. She had answered, "None of your business," and found herself flat on her back again, with him between her thighs, and her torn robe on the floor. The third time was as he prepared to go, saying, "I'll see you soon." She had answered, "What for?" and he'd snapped, "I'll show you!" and did.

She had been glad he returned until he asked again how she paid for the food she served him, and made the rent on the house and the spending money she left lying about. "How do you think?" she had asked irritably.

"I know by your hours that you're not a lady typewriter in an office, nor a clerk in a shop, nor a hand in a mill." She had agreed she was none of those, and he kept at her until she admitted that she had a friend, but not who the friend was. Mitch had only grinned, and suggested the signal. When the coast was clear, she was to tie the kitchen curtain back. When her friend was there, she was to make sure the curtain hung straight. She had been so relieved that she gave him a few dollars to buy himself a new suit of clothes. He had taken the money without thanks and continued to wear what he had before.

Thinking of that, she said now, "And what'll you do with that cash you're going to have off me?"

He sat up. "That's my affair." But he grinned. He couldn't help it. He was already planning the trip to

Boston. He'd have money in his pants for a day's drinking. Shamus would bend an elbow with him again. They'd laugh together, and sing the old songs, when Mitch told Shamus what he was going to do.

Celeste moved her hand along his thigh, and said tentatively, "Maybe, one of these days, I could move out of here, Mitch. And we'd get a little place together. Just the two of us . . . and . . ."

His pale eyes turned red. He grabbed her by both hands, crushing them in the vise of his fingers. "You dumb whore! You stick with Richard Cavendish until I tell you to quit him! And don't you even think of anything else."

Her eyes widened. She moaned. "Mitch, stop. All right. Sure. I only thought . . ."

He let her go. "Don't think. That's not what you're for."

But she said, "I never told you who my friend was."

Mitch grinned again. "I wanted to know. So I stayed around one night and watched him come in."

She nodded. It didn't matter to her.

"When's he coming back?" Mitch asked.

"He didn't say."

"When he does, you do what I tell you to." He put his face down to her breasts once more. "You will, won't you?"

"Sure," she said, holding him tightly. "As long as you think I should."

On July 5, as planned, Albert Cosgrove, speaking for the Manufacturers' Association, announced the industry-wide cut of twelve and a half cents, to be effective on July 20.

By the same evening the Textile Council had called a meeting of the five craft unions it represented in their dealings with the mill owners. Men from the Loom-fixers' Association, the Federation of Textile Operatives (who were weavers), the Union of Card Room Operatives, the Mule Spinners Association and the Union of Slashers sat down together to discuss what was to be done. The pay reduction was the most important grievance, but there were others, among them he increase in machine load at the Cavendish mills from six to eight looms in the new Plant No. 2, a practice which would quickly spread, if not stopped at its inception.

The Council prepared an agenda for discussion and presented it to the Manufacturers' Association within two weeks. It was ignored. The wage reduction went into effect. The Textile Council asked for outside arbitration of the dispute, and that, too, was rejected.

The Textile Council, with permission of the New England Federation of Textile Workers, the affiliate of the American Federation of Labor, called for a strike on July 25. On that day, all union members walked off their jobs. There were some five to six thousand of them, but they were all skilled. For a period of some three weeks, the mills continued in operation, some running only three out of the usual six days. Then, seeing that the major fall-off in production offset the pay cut, they closed down by mutual agreement. Richard Cavendish was the first of these.

He went daily to the silent plant, worked at his papers and took the Old Colony train back to Newport on some nights. On other nights he visited for a few hours with Celeste, before returning to the house on Highland Avenue.

On one of his visits, not long after the strike had begun, Celeste asked, "Did I tell you about my friend Tina?"

He shook his head, thinking of his contract with Denton Paley.

"I didn't? Goodness, I wonder why not. I was so upset when I got back from New York. And about her. She'd left Madame Rose, you know. Now she's ill, and has no one to take care of her."

Richard smiled faintly, waiting.

"I'd help her, if I could," Celeste sighed. She looked around the parlor. "But more fool me, I never put anything by. Not for myself, and not for her either. I don't know what'll happen to her." Celeste snuggled

223

under Richard's arm. "You're always so kind," she said softly.

He laughed, knowing what she was about, but when he left her that night, he gave her a hundred dollars which Mitch took away from her half an hour later.

In August Richard spent a long weekend in Newport. He and Vicki visited the Cosgroves for an evening, spent another at the casino. One day he took Allie and Vicki to the waterfront in town and sailed the small boat he had bought for Allie earlier that summer. He thought, seeing the wind tousle her hair and brighten her cheeks while Allie played at her feet, that she was the most beautiful sight he had ever seen in his life, barring one other, and that was the way she had looked to him when he first saw her, on the steps of the Rye house.

That night, when Matilda questioned him about the strike, and what he meant to do, he was impatient. He refused an after-dinner game of chess with John, went for a walk alone. When he returned the house was still, all the lights out.

He went to his room, but paced the floor. The strike had already affected the town. On every corner down street, idle men stood together, empty hands jammed into their empty pockets. Women were going from house to house, with children clinging to their skirts, to ask for a day's work at window washing. The docks were quiet, the steamships of the Fall River Line sailing empty of cargo. The freight cars stood silent in the yards. He had already notified Denton Paley that he would fail on delivery, and Paley had telegraphed an immediate cancellation. The yardage completed for him would be a loss. But that was as nothing to what the loss would have been had there been no pay reduction. Yet the mill was dead; Plant No. 1 and Plant No. 2 were like tombs to him. If they didn't produce, they were stone piles in which he had buried his dreams.

He punched one fist into the other, wishing he had remained in Fall River. At least there, with Celeste, he didn't find himself sinking in the mire of memory that sucked at him here.

He was startled when Vicki tapped at the door, and let her in quickly. "Is something wrong?" he asked, thinking of Allie. She shook her head, looked silently around the place she'd never before entered when he was there. She sat in the chair near the window, the moonlight on her face, and said, "I wanted to talk to you."

He leaned against the broad ledge of the sill. "Of course."

She glanced up, then away. "Richard, when will the strike end?"

"When the operatives are ready to go back to work, I suppose."

"Is it really so simple as that?"

"Yes."

"I've been reading in the papers. They make it sound somewhat more complicated, you know."

He laughed. "They tend to."

"There are some twenty-six thousand people out of work," she went on. "It's the owners that have locked them out."

"It was necessary, Vicki."

"Perhaps." She drew a deep breath. "But you know, Richard, I think of them, of their children. How do they manage? How will they live? If this goes on, how will they eat and survive?"

"When they're hungry enough they'll come to work for what we can pay," he answered.

"It doesn't seem right," she said softly. "There must be some other way."

He gave her an amused look. "There speaks the parson's daughter."

"Yes," she agreed, and then, with a bitterness that surprised him, "I never thought of myself as that, and when it was forced on me, I resented it. But the mark of it is on me all the same." She got to her feet. "I'm sorry I troubled you."

"But you didn't. I wish it could be different." He

was speaking of the strike, but he was thinking of the life they lived.

She understood, and stiffened, and turned toward the door. He went to open it for her, and of its own accord, his hand lifted, he brushed her cheek gently. He felt her wince away from him, and stepped back quickly.

"Good night," she whispered, and slipped out into the dark.

She lay awake through long hours, an undefinable ache gnawing at her body, so that she twisted and turned from one side of the bed to the other, seeking a spot in which she could rest with comfort. In moments of fitful sleep, she dreamed of sallow-faced netmakers, and hop pickers standing before the butcher shops with hungry eyes, but the streets she saw mistily were those of Fall River, and not of Rye.

She was tired in the morning, with a feeling of dread to which she could assign no real cause. She sat at her dressing table, putting up her hair, when the bedroom door opened, and Allie, on all fours, peered around its edge and shouted, "Peek-a-boo!"

"What is it?" she demanded. "What do you want, Allie?"

He rose, trotted to her, and flung himself against her skirts, beaming with good will. "Mama! Peek-a-boo!"

"Not now," she said. "Go to Maria. You must put on your clothes."

But he pressed to her, stroking her gown with one small hand, reaching for her face with the other.

"What do you want, Allie?" she asked tartly. "Are you ill? Why do you bother me?"

"Mama!" he yelled, all smiles gone, dark eyes abrim with tears.

"Now stop," she told him, rising while he clung to her. "Go to Maria and she'll dress you."

Maria came running then, breathless, apologetic. "I just turned my back to take out his suit, and he got out the door." She took Allie up, shushed him while he yelled louder, his face growing red as he reached for Vicki.

Maria went to the door, holding the twisting, writhing bundle as firmly as she could.

But Vicki called to her to wait. She took the boy into her arms, whispering to him. She sat in the chair and held him. Slowly, his sobs faded and his choked breathing slowed; the tears dried on his cheeks. With a sigh, he nestled his head into her shoulder and fell into exhausted sleep.

Some time later, Vicki looked up with a sudden start. Richard leaned at the door, staring at her expressionlessly across the length of the silent room.

Chapter 21

THE STRIKE, AND ENSUING SHUTDOWN, LASTED FOR something just over nineteen weeks, but by mid-September, when the Cavendish family returned from its summer in Newport, Vicki instantly recognized one sign of it. The sky over Fall River was a clear sharp blue, with small white clouds drifting over Mount Hope Bay. The mill smokestacks were looming black silhouettes against the horizon, the furnaces that had fed them long since grown cold.

That same week she and John went for a ride in the surrey. The air was beginning to carry the edge of winter chill, but the sun was still warm. Allie, well-bundled, poked his small head from his fur-trimmed hood and fingered the sable collar of Vicki's coat, and laughed happily as they drove down street, until suddenly, he straightened up in her arms, and let out a piercing yell, pointing with both mittened hands.

Vicki understood when she saw Jamie Markeson teetering on the curb. She asked John to pull over, and when he did, she leaned down. "Jamie, how are you?"

He nodded, smiled, while Allie cried, with his arms outthrust. "Come, come, boy."

"I can't," Jamie answered. He stroked Allie's hand, and the child was still, beaming an adoring grin at him.

"Not in school today?" Vicki asked.

"I'm finished, and looking for work."

"And it's not a good time for that," John said.

"No," Jamie agreed. "Nobody's hiring. And if they were, there are twenty men to take my place."

"But how do you manage? You, and your father?" Vicki asked.

"The way they all do," Jamie said with a shrug. He looked at Allie. "He's getting bigger. And he talks good."

As if in answer, Allie stuck his hand into Jamie's. "Boy, you come."

"Jamie . . . Jamie . . . can you say it?"

"Jamie," Allie announced, and chuckling, "Horse. Cow. Dog. Boy, you come, Jamie!"

"He *does* talk good."

"We'll drive you where you like," John offered.

Jamie shook his head, but smiled his thanks and turned away.

Allie yelled as the surrey rolled on. Vicki hushed him, saying, "Let me think." And to John: "Let's stop at Mrs. Wood's. I want to ask her something."

Twice in two short blocks they passed disconsolate families gathered around meager heaps of the belongings. "Evictions," Vicki murmured, remembering the rent-money box in the Rye house kitchen. Soon she noticed that wherever she looked, she saw men with bundles on their backs or under their arms, men with hunched shoulders, walking slowly on the roads that led away from town.

She mentioned them to John, and he nodded. "Yes,

they're beginning to move out, many of those that can. Going elsewhere to hunt jobs. The few who can are riding the trains. The rest do it on foot."

As they turned a corner, Vicki saw a huddle of men standing before a shop. Its door was open, its windows empty. She wondered what was going on in the place.

John jerked his head toward it, seeing her glance. "A relief station. For the nonunion workers. They distribute whatever food they can get hold of, and clothes."

"Who supports it, John?"

"The unions do what they can, but they've got their members to look after. Five dollars a week per man goes pretty fast. Something like ten thousand dollars has come in from other towns to help. There have been some benefit balls and there'll probably be more."

"You think it's going to go on," she said.

"I'm afraid so. But they'll find they can't win this one. The owners have less to lose than they have."

"That's us."

"Yes, Vicki."

"Us!" Allie crowed.

But neither John nor Vicki looked at him.

Mrs. Wood welcomed them with glad cries. She lost her worried expression while she played with Allie, but when Vicki asked how she fared, the worry came back to her face.

"My customers don't have much to spend for food these days," she sighed. "I don't know what they're going to do."

Vicki understood. The shop had been empty when she arrived. The doorbell had tinkled only once since. But she kept thinking of Jamie Markeson. He needed work. Mrs. Wood was alone. When Vicki broached the subject, Mrs. Wood shook her head. "I'd like to, and I need help, but I can't put out even a dollar a week. Not now."

Vicki reached into her reticule. "There's a way, Mrs. Wood. If you wouldn't object to a harmless deception." She drew out a ten-dollar bill. "This would pay the boy for some weeks."

"You don't know how long this may last," Mrs. Wood protested. "While I thank you, I can't let you do it."

"It's for Jamie," Vicki said. "Truly, he badly needs work. And if he'll be good for you, then I'll be glad."

John, seeing that Vicki had taken out the only bill she had with her, added another ten dollars to it. "Ten weeks, Mrs. Wood. Make sure Jamie earns it."

It was John who gave Ezra Saunders the message to take to Jamie. The next morning he was there when Mrs. Wood opened the shop. Less than ten minutes later, he was washing down the front window. While he worked, he whistled softly. Now he could give something to Ezra. He and his father wouldn't have to live altogether free off the older man any more. He thought of Vicki, and smiled radiantly at his own reflection in the newly bright window.

It rained steadily during the last week of the month. The roads were awash with mud when the Cavendish family drove to the school for Rosamund's marriage to Davis Peabody.

Peering out into the gray afternoon, Matilda sighed, "I hope it isn't an omen of things to come."

"Superstition," Richard grinned.

Matilda's jet-black eyes moved from Richard to Vicki. She said, "Just the same, I hope it clears for tomorrow."

The next day was the second anniversary of Vicki's marriage to Richard. Vicki hadn't needed the reminder. She had thought of it for days. She was a wife, but had no husband, it seemed to her. It was, she supposed, what she had wanted, and certainly her just due. But half alive was not at all alive to her. When she had returned from Newport with the family, she had found that, again without comment, Richard had continued their separation. Now, as in Cavendish Cove, she often heard him pace the next room in the night. She wondered, as they arrived at the school, whether Rosamund, taking her vows with Davis, would think of Richard, and whether, when she lay in his arms that night, she would think of Richard again.

If so, there was no sign of that in her face when Davis put his ring on her finger, held her close for a kiss. There was no sign of it, either, when Richard and Vicki wished her happiness later, and congratulated Davis. In spite of the dampening weather, the wedding party was gay. Vicki would have had a good time but for Leslie, who trailed after her, seeking, as she herself had once sought, to create a moment between them. She managed to avoid him, but was glad when the affair was over.

The following day was sunny, warm with Indian summer. The long sloping lawn before the house was mottled golden with maple leaves, its surrounding bushes sprinkled with glowing red berries.

Richard lingered at breakfast, having an extra cup of coffee. But when Maria brought Allie down to play out-of-doors, he rose, excusing himself, and went with them. Soon after, John followed them.

Matilda asked Vicki to have Nettie clear the table, and went upstairs.

Left alone, Vicki looked at the wedding ring she wore, touched the diamond that had been her engagement present. Only half alive, she thought. And once, hardly more than two years before, all that she had wanted was to go out to life, to love. To follow her heart's desire. But then, hearing Allie's shrill laugh, she raised her head, smiling.

Nettie came in, dragging her feet, to ask hoarsely if Vicki wanted anything else. The girl's face was drawn, her eyes puffy and red.

"What's the matter?" Vicki asked quickly.

"It's going to spoil everything!" Nettie cried. "Oh, I can't stand it, knowing what'll happen, and not being able to change it. Why can't I have any luck? It was different with Mitch! Harry was right then, but George . . ."

Vicki rose, went to the girl, and put an arm around her shoulder. "It can't be so bad," she said softly. She didn't know what Nettie was talking about. Mitch,

Harry, George . . . the confusion of names bewildered her, but her quick sympathy was aroused by Nettie's tears. She pressed the girl into a chair. "Now, stop weeping, and tell me. Perhaps I can help."

Nettie sank into a seat, buried her face in her hands. "No one can. If only they'd stop it. If only the men could go back to work . . ."

"The strike," Vicki whispered.

"And he's so good. He gives his five dollars away to the men who have families. He goes hungry."

Mrs. Beamis appeared in the doorway, her cheeks flushed. "Nettie, you stop that." Then, to Vicki: "Oh, I am sorry. What am I to do with the girl? Love, she says. Love. It's turned her head. Though George is a good man."

The mother was no more coherent than the daughter, Vicki thought. She could sort out nothing either of them had told her, except that it had something to do with the strike, with a man named George Thompson, and with love.

She said, "Mrs. Beamis, who is George Thompson?"

Nettie answered, "The most wonderful man! He's a weaver at the mill. I met him at the party for the new plant. We've been keeping company since, except when I had to go with you to Newport. We'd be married, I think. Only there's the strike. And if it doesn't end soon George will have to push on. And if he goes . . ."

He had looked gaunt when he visited the night before. Harry had noticed it, and Mrs. Beamis, too. She had gone back to the kitchen in the big house and made up a plate of meat and vegetables for him, and while he ate, Nettie's heart had quivered. He was hungry, and his shoulders were slumped in a new way. When he had finished, he'd sat with his hands hanging between his knees, and nothing left of his bright grin, and said to Harry, "It's bad, and it's going to get worse. There's talk that the owners'll be bringing in foreigners, maybe Greeks or something, to reopen the mills. And that means people like me will push on."

Nettie's heart had stopped quivering. She thought it had stopped beating. "But where to?" she'd asked quickly.

He'd only shaken his head. But she'd known that if he left she'd never see him again. And this time it was different, not like with Mitch, who had turned her head, but had truly meant nothing to her. This time she couldn't give up as she had before, and know it was right. She had to have George. She had cried through the night, and cried into the breakfast grapefruit, and now she was crying again.

Mrs. Beamis thrust a handkerchief at her and said gently, "All right, Nettie. There's nothing we can do about it, nor Miss Vicki either, so stop your weeping, there's a good girl, and get to work in the kitchen."

Sobbing, Nettie fled the room.

Mrs. Beamis sighed. "She's young."

"It isn't fair," Vicki answered. "Why should the strike hurt her? She has nothing to do with it."

"We all have," Mrs. Beamis answered heavily.

John looked into the dining room then. "Vicki? Can you come out? I want to show you something."

She rose, saying to Mrs. Beamis, "Perhaps there's something I can do."

John had gone ahead of her, and waited at the door. When he opened it for her, she stepped outside.

"Mama, look!" Allie shrilled.

The motor car was long, black, with glistening chrome. Allie hung from a window. Richard sat behind the wheel. Vicki stared at it until John laughed, "It's your anniversary, Vicki. Had you forgotten? We'll have you driving it in no time."

"And you'll need this," Matilda said, suddenly at her side.

This, Vicki found, was a driving coat of red wool, with black frog fastenings and a black velvet stand-up collar. *This* was also a pair of red driving gloves, and a small red hat that dripped black veilings.

"And," Matilda went on, "I hope the outfit is the

233

right size. I did have trouble with Richard over it. He feared everything would be too large, from the hat to the gloves."

"It's beautiful," Vicki told Matilda, and went down to the motor car. "It's beautiful," she told Richard. And: "Thank you."

"Get in," he said. "We'll go for a ride."

Vicki beckoned to John and Matilda, and when they were settled, Richard drove off.

They rolled along Highland Avenue, jogged around St. Patrick's Cemetery, with Allie shouting, "Car! Car!" at the carriages they passed, while Richard explained the mechanics of the Mercedes. Vicki felt the warm wind on her cheeks, and with it, a sudden lift of spirits. How smooth the ride was! What a speed they attained! But, when they rode down street, and passed the clusters of men standing at the corners, when they rolled by a relief station, her spirits flagged. She saw how all eyes followed their progress, how everyone, man and woman and child, turned to stare. They were out of work, and desperate, while she rode in flaunting luxury. She stared straight ahead now, all pleasure in the gift gone. Were she to try to explain how she felt to Richard she knew that he would say, "There speaks the parson's daughter again," and laugh at her. When Richard said, "Soon you'll be driving yourself about," she merely smiled, but she knew that she wouldn't.

Later that evening she told him about Nettie.

Richard listened gravely. "George Thompson? A good man. It's too bad."

"But couldn't you do something?"

He gave Vicki a level look. "What shall I do? Open the plants so that he can marry his Nettie?"

"But suppose he leaves?"

"Then she'll wait for him to come back, or she'll find herself another man, won't she?"

"That's unkind," Vicki flared. "She loves him, Richard."

"I know you think me that," he answered. "But

234

there's nothing I can do except have his place for him when we reopen."

"And when will that be?"

"I don't know," Richard said quietly. "I hope it'll be soon. Some of the owners are talking about bringing in outside labor."

"That's what George said, Nettie told me. And you? Will you do it, too?"

"Perhaps I should, but I think it would be bad for the town. I don't want to see my people fighting new workers for their jobs."

"And meanwhile Nettie must weep," Vicki murmured.

"I'm sorry."

"I'll tell Nettie how you feel," Vicki retorted.

"If you like. But please don't put George on your personal payroll. You can't hire every man on strike, you know."

Her eyes flew to his face. She saw that he was smiling. "How did you know about Jamie?"

"John. Then Erza, who told me that Jamie insists on adding his pay to the food money. They'd both like to suggest you for sainthood."

She drew a deep breath, preparing herself for anger, hoping for it even. Then: "You don't object, do you?"

His smile became a grin. "I don't think I'll be consulted about your status." Then, he sobered, went on. "As for your helping Jamie . . . Of course I don't. Nor would I object if you found something for George, though I don't think you will." ·

She tried, but to no avail. She spoke to Albert Cosgrove, who shrugged his regrets. She even telephoned to Elise to ask if there were work at the school George could do. There was nothing.

Nettie stopped crying. She grew quieter and thinner.

Then, on the evening of Vicki's twentieth birthday, Nettie was suddenly herself again.

Vicki had just come down the steps. She wore a white satin gown, and a string of pearls at her bare throat. She carried her cape and a chatelaine bag. She and Richard were going to the Academy that evening to see Florence Hamilton in a play called *White Slaves of Russia*. She had not felt very festive. As she had dressed the name of the show had suddenly come to mind, and she had found herself thinking about the workers of the Fall River mills. The strike had gone on for nearly eight weeks now. It was a very long time for people who had never earned enough to save.

Nettie had come bounding from the back of the house, crying, "Miss Vicki! It's going to be all right! And I'm so happy."

"What is? What's happened," Vicki demanded.

"My George. He'll have a job in Lowell. He'll be able to come and see me. He's just been here and told me and promised to come back on Sunday even if he has to walk the whole way."

"I'm so glad," Vicki said, laughing. "Oh, Nettie, isn't that wonderful?"

"But you're not surprised! You can't be. You're the one who did it," Nettie said. "You must have told Mr. Richard. And he found the job for George, and sent George over to see about it." Then she danced away, humming.

Later, as they rode in the Mercedes to the Academy, Richard spoke of the election coming up in November. He was certain that Theodore Roosevelt would be elected, but Vicki interrupted his comments to say, "You've made Netti happy."

"It was luck that I found something for George. But he's a fine weaver, and that helped."

The good feeling left her when, as they approached the theater, she saw an elderly woman standing on the curb, her chin sunk on her chest, her eyes cast down and averted from the tin cup she held out to passersby.

Vicki thought of that elderly woman often while she and Matilda prepared Thanksgiving baskets, when they begged food and clothing from the city merchants before Christmas time. Harry drove them about in the oaded carriage just a few days before both holidays, but what they could do seemed so little when the need was so great.

John bought ten tickets to a benefit dance held at Anawan Hall, and ten more to a show at the Bijou held under the auspices of the Textile Council. He gave them to Ezra Saunders, who passed them out on the street.

On December 20 the Textile Council recommended again that the craft unions accept arbitration of the dispute. The unions agreed to do so, but the manufacturers refused.

By then some of the mills had reopened, running a few days a week with nonunion operatives, and the people of Fall River knew they couldn't go on much longer.

There was little celebrating on New Year's Eve when the church bells rang to announce the arrival of 1905.

On January 18, a vat boiled over in the Stevens Mill, scalding four boys eating their lunches nearby. Two of them died soon after. The other two were badly burned but survived.

It was on that day, too, that the unions finally accepted the twelve-and-a-half-cent wage reduction that had been instituted the previous July, agreed to having future wages set by the governor of the state, who would base them on industry conditions as shown by mill profit margins, and voted to go back to work.

The strike was over. The manufacturers had won. There had been 26,000 operatives out of work for some nineteen weeks, affecting 2,300,000 spindles in seventy-one mills controlled by thirty-three corporations, with a combined capital of $25,000,000. The aggregate loss sustained by the industry was later calculated to be some $5,000,000.

In late February Richard took Vicki to the Bijou to see the vaudeville being performed there.

A three-day snow covered the roads and blew in thick drifts along the fences, but the sky was clear

and a quarter moon hung over the river. On the wa[y]
she told him of Nettie's joy that George Thompso[n]
was back in Fall River and working at Plant No. [2]
again. "I'd promised it to him," was all Richard sai[d.]

The place was crowded, but when he handed Vick[i]
into her seat, one out of the rows of women behin[d]
suddenly held his attention. Celeste, with a boa [of]
pink feathers at her throat, gave him a brilliant smile[.]
He stared at her blankly, then turned his back and sa[t]
beside Vicki.

He saw nothing of the performance. He heard noth[-]
ing of the music, nor the jokes. He was remember[-]
ing that he had mentioned the Bijou to Celeste th[e]
night she played "Yankee Doodle Dandy" on her pho[-]
nograph.

Her presence in the Bijou was a deliberate act.

The following evening he asked her about it. Sh[e]
answered, "I wanted to see the show, Richard."

"You knew I'd be there."

"I forgot. Really I did. I was ever so surprised whe[n]
I saw you." Then: "But what does it matter? I didn'[t]
speak to you. No one would guess we were ac[-]
quainted."

"Don't do that again." He didn't explain that it mat[-]
tered to him, though he didn't know why.

"Then you'll have to tell me every place you go wit[h]
your wife. Otherwise how can I avoid meeting you? [I]
shan't stay indoors always after dark. It makes for
such lonely nights."

His eyes narrowed. "What's bothering you?"

She came and sat on his lap, curling around him.
"I just said, I'm lonesome. Surely you understand
that."

He didn't move, nor hold her, nor answer.

She sighed, closed her eyes. It was good to lie
against him, to feel the strength of his body so close,
and good, too, to know that he would give her whatever money she asked for, without question and without complaint. But there was more that she'd wanted,
dreamed of. That was why she'd gone to the Bijou,
knowing he'd be there with his wife. She'd wanted to

238

e the woman who lived with him on Highland Avenue. Now that she had seen Vicki Cavendish her opes had withered while the worm of jealousy expanded in her. Still, as Madame Rose had always said, "Nobody knows what goes on between a man and a oman." There was one thing the pretty lady couldn't ive Richard that she herself could, and had; one thing e plainly wanted. That would do her nicely, thank ou. And there was Mitch. Richard had her for his urposes, and she had Mitch for her own. It was a ood arrangement. She decided she wouldn't go to the ijou again.

Richard put her away from him with a suddenness hat startled her. She stood wavering uncertainly as he ot to his feet. "You're not going?"

"Yes. I'll see you tomorrow evening."

"But why?" she wailed, pouting.

"There's something I must do."

As soon as she heard the surrey disappear down he icy road, she went to the kitchen to pull the curtain ack. Mitch would see the signal. In a little while he'd e there, demanding to know why Richard had left so arly, and if he'd given her a small present before going.

Chapter 22

DENTON PALEY TELEPHONED FROM NEW YORK City," Ezra said. The crack in his old voice indicated is unwillingness to pass on the message. Only the trike, and lockout, had saved Richard last time.

Richard grinned. "It's nice that he hasn't given up on me, but I'll pass any offer he makes this time."

Ezra sighed with relief. "Then you've noted th
margins?"

"Of course. And we may have to make anoth
wage reduction by summer."

"More trouble," Ezra said, thinking of what G
had told him with so much relish. The operatives we
restive and angry. The Manufacturers' Associatio
hadn't kept their promises. At some of the mills know
union men hadn't been rehired. At others, such
Cavendish No. 2, eight looms to a weaver had becom
standard. Many skilled hands talked of migrating
other towns.

"There won't be trouble," Richard was saying. "Th
Textile Council hasn't the treasury for it."

"Bobbin boy!" The yell came clearly through th
glass panels. The shuttles slammed back and forth
The pulleys hummed. "Loomfixer!"

Ezra watched Gus shamble across the loft. Tim
was when a man wanted his son to better himself, bu
Gus wanted Jamie to have no more schooling than h
himself had had. So Jamie continued to work at Mr
Wood's.

"I'll see you tomorrow," Richard said from th
doorway.

He drove to the bank through early twilight. Snov
clouds hung low over the city and the boulevard lamp
cast steady light on the icy pavements, where until jus
the year before, the flames fed by oil and gas ha
flickered fitfully.

His transaction took only a little while, but by th
time he returned to the surrey, dark had fallen. H
drove slowly out Eastern Avenue. The bells of Notr
Dame chimed six o'clock as the horse clip-clopped int
the familiar turn. He passed a dimly lit house. A lin
of laundry hung across its upper porch, a man's frozer
union suit hanging like a stiff body from it.

Richard stopped before Celeste's house, tethered th
horse and went up the steps.

Though he was much earlier than usual, she hac
plainly been awaiting his arrival. Her dark hair curlec
on her shoulders, freshly brushed and shining. He

face had been artfully touched with color, her blue gown carefully chosen to expose her small breasts near to their pink nipples.

She said gaily, "Oh, I'm so glad you're here," opening the door wide.

He went into the parlor. A fire burned on the hearth. The lamps glowed on the fringed velvet cushions. It had seemed a pleasant place to him once. Now he saw it with new eyes. It was dismal, even shoddy. The homelike atmosphere mocked him. He had thought of this house as a refuge. In this moment he saw it as a sinkhole to which he had brought lust and hurt pride for relief.

"Take off your coat," Celeste said, tugging at his arm.

He drew away from her touch. He pulled off his gloves, his coat, and dropped them on a straight chair near the door.

She curled on the divan, her head back, an inviting smile on her lips. He didn't go to her. Instead, he went to the window, looked into the dark street. Then he paced to the hearth, stared into the flames. "I want to talk to you," he said finally.

"Talk?" she purred. "Is that what you've come for? I *am* surprised. I thought you'd have something else in mind."

"No, Lilac."

"Lilac?" Her hand stopped patting the divan, and went still. Her eyes were fixed on his face. "But I told you my real name is Celeste. Celeste Denver. And you've called me that ever since."

"I've called you Lilac in my mind," he answered.

She shrugged. "You must do as you please."

But she looked around the room she had tried to make comfortable for him. The room that she had thought of as Celeste's place, as Madame Rose's had been Lilac's place. There had been no difference to him, but to her there had been.

He said, "I want you to go back to New York City, Lilac. It's over between us."

She stared at him first in shock, then rallied to

smile. "Is it? Are you quite sure, Richard?" She uncoiled her lithe body, and rose slowly.

He gave her a long level look. "Don't trouble yourself to try to change my mind." Then: "I'll give you something to get started on, of course."

"But what's wrong?" she asked. "What did I do? What's happened?"

"Nothing." He reached inside his coat for his wallet. "It's just time, that's all."

But she suddenly knew. It was because she had gone to the Bijou, and he had seen her staring at his wife.

"All right," she said slowly. "And I do thank you," she added, as she put out her hand.

Mitch's face frightened her. His pale eyes seemed to turn flaming red. His mouth turned down, but his teeth showed in a bared grin that put her in mind of a raging dog she had seen as a child. "What the hell did you do?" he demanded.

"Nothing," she cried. "He just came and told me to go back to New York City."

"Did he find out about me?"

"No, no, of course not."

"Then what?" He rolled a cigarette with shaking hands, glared at her. "You'd better tell me, Celeste. I'll find out if it's the last thing I do."

"Oh, Mitch," she said softly. "It's not the worst thing in the world. Now I can be with you all the time. And that's what I want."

"You dumb whore! That may be what you want, but I want more."

"And you've got it," she said triumphantly. "He left me a present."

Mitch grew quiet. He cocked his head. "A present?"

"One thousand dollars," she crowed. "What do you say to that?"

"A thousand dollars . . . You *are* a dumb whore."

"You've no right to call me that," she yelled. "You're just a damned ponce!"

242

His fists doubled. He took a step toward her, and she backed away. Catching her heel in her gown, she wavered off balance and then fell into the easy chair. He was on her before she could move, his hands tight at her throat. "You watch your lip! Whatever I took wasn't for me, and don't you forget it. It's guns I want. Guns, my girl. And I'm going to have them." He held her tightly a moment longer, just to be sure she was properly cowed. Then he made himself let her go. He needed her and he knew it. He forced a grin. "You're not the only one here who's got a hot temper. It's just I was thinking that you're satisfied with too little."

"I suppose you could do better?"

"I could, my girl. I haven't tried." He paced the room, hands linked behind him. "So your Richard's finished with you."

She didn't answer. She felt no triumph now. She thought of the time she'd given Richard. But then she remembered. What was that Mitch had said about guns? And besides, the thousand dollars was hers.

"All the time you've faithfully served him," Mitch said. He grinned suddenly. He wondered what the high-and-mighty Richard Cavendish would think if he knew poor Mitch Ryan had been sharing his piece with him.

"Faithful as far as he knew," Celeste answered.

Mitch took a half tumbler of whiskey, and stretched out on the divan. "And you're going to do as he told you, I suppose."

"I don't know. I was thinking of you. You and me, Mitch."

"If you go back to New York, it won't be you and me, my girl."

"I'd rather stay. If you asked me." But she was still wondering what he had said about the money and guns. Her eyes crept to the mantel where she had put the sheaf of bills.

He saw her glance, and laughed. "Don't worry about it. It's still there. But there'll be more, if you listen to me."

"Mitch . . . you don't know . . ." she said uneasily. "Richard Cavendish isn't soft. He's given what he's going to."

"It's not enough!" Mitch said harshly. "I want ten thousand dollars."

Her mouth hung open. "Ten thousand! You're crazy. He'd never . . . I wouldn't dare ask . . ."

"Dare or not, you'll do it." Mitch stared at her over the whiskey tumbler. "You'll go to the mill tomorrow. You'll have a little talk with him."

"I couldn't. He'd just stare me down and throw me out."

"And what about me?" Mitch demanded.

"You come with me to New York. There's nothing to keep you here." Her voice was soft now, purring. "Say you will."

He got up, went to the door. "I'll see you, Celeste."

"But what are you going to do?" she cried.

"Me? Nothing."

"You'll be back later?"

"Maybe. I don't know."

She went to him, put her arms around him. "Mitch, why're you acting like this?"

He pulled away roughly. "Bodies, Celeste . . . they're a dime a dozen."

"You don't have to tell me."

"The only thing that counts is money. If we had good hard cash, we'd be free."

"We have enough."

He laughed, opened the door.

"We could figure out something," she said.

"Maybe," he agreed.

"And you'll come back later?"

"Maybe," he repeated.

But he didn't return that day, nor the next. Instead he took a closed hack from the stable and drove into town. He had a few drinks in a saloon on a street in Corky Row, listening to the drunken maunderings of a man who looked like his Uncle Shamus. The next afternoon, after a few more drinks in the same place, he drove to Highland Avenue.

244

That night, well after dark, he went back to tell
Celeste a part of what he had decided. She was so
happy to see him that she didn't question him too
closely. She started packing at once, and by midnight
the house was empty.

"Criminal," Eustacia Cosgrove said, "the way that
woman rides about in her limousine. And her poor
sister, trying so hard all these years to hold up her
head. I suppose it's a sign of what the world's coming
to. The foreigners, you know. Even our cottage in
Fair Haven . . . broken into, used . . . I never dreamed
it could happen."

"My dear," Albert Cosgrove said, leaning against
her massive bulk. She moved only an inch or two.

But Richard took advantage of the small space. He
handed Vicki before him, murmured a quick farewell
and hastened out as Eustacia breathed deeply, preparing to continue even though her audience was fast
disappearing.

"I thought you'd never escape," Matilda said tartly.

Richard grinned, helped Vicki into the Mercedes,
closed the door and went around to start the motor.

As they left the Cosgroves' house, Matilda said,
"Albert's worried about the New York state bakers'
law. He says that if the Supreme Court rules it con-
stitutional, then every state and every industry will be
pressed mercilessly for a ten-hour day."

"Albert worries without need," Richard answered.
"We're already on a ten-hour day, as you know. My
operatives would only produce less if they worked
longer."

"He says it'll lead to demands for less. And if a
state can once require employers to limit to ten hours,
what's to keep it from requiring a limit to eight, as
some speak of now, or even six?"

Richard grinned. "Our legislature will require nothing of us that we don't agree to. It's not in the public
interest to drive industry out by making it impossible
to operate and expand." He looked sideways at Vicki.
"You're frowning. What is it?"

245

But she was still thinking about Eustacia. "I do[n]t understand why Eustacia has so morbid an intere[st] in that poor woman. Liz Borden, I mean. It was [so] long ago, and she *was* acquitted. Yet Eustacia seem[s] to brood on it."

"Yes," Matilda agreed. "Perhaps we all do. But silence. True, it's a long time since it happened. B[ut] she was one of us, and it's not been resolved. L[iz] Borden was acquitted. But then who murdered h[er] father and stepmother?"

Vicki was no longer listening. She leaned forwar[d] to stare through the bare limbs of the trees that line[d] the avenue at a glow of lights. Richard turned into th[e] driveway. The house was lit at every window, an[d] each one burned like a glittering eye through th[e] night-time dark.

They had hardly stopped under the porte coche[re] when Nettie came running. "Oh, I'm so glad you'r[e] back! Allie's not himself. Harry was about to start fo[r] the Cosgroves' to tell you, and Mother's sent m[y] George to Dr. Stilton's, for their telephone is out [of] order."

Vicki gave a small cry, turned toward the step[s.] But Richard was ahead of her, his long legs leapin[g] the stairs two at a time.

Following as quickly as she could, she fought th[e] weight of dread that seemed to slow her.

The nursery lamps were bright. Maria bent ove[r] the small bed, whispering, "Allie, what is it? Wher[e] does it hurt you?"

The boy coughed, moaned, his eyes wide an[d] glazed and unseeing.

Richard brushed Maria away, put a gentle han[d] on the boy's cheek. "He's burning with fever."

Vicki dropped to her knees beside the bed and too[k] Allie's limp hands in hers. The small velvety finger[s] didn't tighten in recognition. The glazed eyes didn['t] move to look at her. Her voice broke as she whis[-] pered, "Allie? Allie, what's wrong, darling?"

Chapter 23

OR WEEKS A STILLNESS WRAPPED THE HOUSE, AN IN-
sible winding sheet that bound the occupants within.
here was the occasional knock at the door, the rustle
f skirts on the stairs, the muted voices in despairing
xchanges. Dominating all these, resounding through
ie hush, with the heart-stopping clap of imminent
under, there came Allie's sudden spells of scream-
ig.

They had begun that first night, while Dr. Stilton
ood at his bedside. He had come in cheerfully, had
niled, "What's the trouble, Vicki?" And: "Why so
rim, Richard? There's measels about. It wouldn't sur-
rise me if your Allie broke out in red spots at any
me."

But even as he spoke, leaning over the boy, the
mall body stiffened and then arched in an awful con-
ulsion. Eyes wide, unseeing, bulging from beneath
elicate dark brows. Mouth agape to suck air. Arms,
gs, a part of the rigid upward arch. A moment
assed, another. All at once there was collapse. Allie
ielted down beneath the quilt. His hands became
mall fists that beat his temples with dreadful violence.
Ie screamed, and screamed again. When he became
till the silence was deafening.

Dr. Stilton's brisk cheerfulness disappeared. To as-
ist at a birth, which was creation, was his greatest
oy. He felt only sorrow now. For to assist at death,
vhich was destruction, meant defeat. And this was
ife-threatening, he knew. "No," he murmured. "We
lon't have measles here."

Vicki stared at him, her throat aching with t[h]
strain of Allie's screams, her breath gone in the effo[rt]
to breathe for him.

It was Richard who asked, "Then what is it?"

Dr. Stilton didn't reply. He rummaged in his ba[g]
took out two small bottles. One contained brom[o]
caffeine, the other tincture of laudanum. "These are [to]
relax him, make him comfortable. Directions a[re]
there." When, finally, he answered Richard's questio[n]
his usual jocularity had become a businesslike gru[f]
ness. "I'm not certain what we have here. I'll be bac[k]
in the morning. Call me if there's a change during t[he]
rest of the night."

Vicki sat with Allie through the long dark hour[s]
listening to the slow uneven sound of his breath. Whe[n]
he moaned, her heart stopped within her. She leane[d]
over him quickly, whispered wordless reassurance. Sh[e]
waited for his eyes to open, for his face to turn t[o]
ward her. But he remained unknowing and unreacha[-]
ble. She knew that people came, went, that there wa[s]
a stir in the room, the hall. But her attention remaine[d]
fixed on Allie, as if by the exercise of her will sh[e]
could break the mysterious spell upon him.

Once Richard came, put a shawl around her shou[l-]
ders. Other times he stood in the doorway, not movin[g]
not speaking. Matilda brought her a cup of tea. Joh[n]
limped in, looked at Allie, at Vicki, disappeared int[o]
the dimness of the corridor. Maria drifted in, moane[d]
wrung her hands, and crept away.

At dawn Allie's body rose up in its terrible arc[h]
again, and his hands beat his temples, and the awf[ul]
screams poured from his pale gaping lips.

Every breath in the house stopped, every move[-]
ment. Only the clocks ticked on, time passing heedles[s]
of pain.

Dr. Stilton arrived early, his eyes anxious. He lis[-]
tened to Vicki describe the night. He looked at Alli[e]
That same morning he telephoned to Boston. By lat[e]
afternoon, two Boston physicians, young men devote[d]
to the just barely developing specialty called pediatric[s]
arrived on Highland Avenue. They examined Alli[e]

248

consulted with Dr. Stilton in private. They agreed with his tentative diagnosis, that Allie was victim to a species of meningitis, but they had no course of treatment to suggest.

When they had gone, Dr. Stilton said, "I fear you must prepare for a long situation. I can only speculate about what might help the boy, and can only keep trying."

Vicki listened, hearing the sound of doom in his voice. He was saying surely that Allie might linger, but at the end he would die. She looked at Richard, standing rigid beside her, and whispered aloud, "No."

And silently, No, it couldn't be. She wouldn't allow it. She would fight for Allie, hold him, keep him. She would never let him go, not so long as life remained in her.

She moved through the following days as in a dream. She was aware of Richard, of John, of Matilda, but her consciousness was directed always to the small form on the bed.

She sat with him through the day, through the night. She fed him every two hours, slowly spooning thin gruels into his quiescent mouth, holding him in her arms, and watching to see that he swallowed each mouthful before giving him more. She poured warmed milk thickened with bread drop by drop between his lips. She fed him the egg puddings and jellies that he had once greeted with glee and now accepted without recognition. Every day, morning and evening, she carefully bathed him from head to toe, covering each part of him, lest a stray draft do harm. Maria stood by, handing her spoon and bowl for the feedings, towels, soaps and clothes for the bathing. Vicki allowed her to do little else. She and she alone must be with Allie.

She left his side rarely, hurrying through her bath and toilette, to return to him, absentmindedly greeting those who came, while her heart and soul left her to hover protectively near him while she was gone.

In midweek, Elise and Leslie called to ask if they could help. They sat in the parlor, discussing the

Roosevelt inauguration, with Matilda haggard an saying little. John told Vicki that they were waiting She went down, spoke a few words to them, accepte with thanks the picture book they had brought to Alli and returned to his room, her hands atremble, as sh wondered if Allie's suffering were the harvest of he sowing. Mrs. McVey would have said it was so Vicki's father would have only looked sad.

One evening, as she sat by the boy, he opened hi eyes. She screamed, "Richard!"

He came, breathing hard from his run up the steps But the boy's eyes had closed once more.

She said, "I didn't imagine it, Richard. Allie looked at me. He knew me. But then, as I reached fo: him . . ."

"It'll happen again," Richard told her gently.

On Sunday morning Jamie Markeson tapped at th: front door. He carried a bouquet of red roses in one hand, a small package in the other. When Nettie le him in, he gave over both to her, and turned to depart But she insisted that he wait and led him into the morning room, where Matilda sat alone, embroidery silks on her lap under her folded hands.

She thanked Jamie for the gifts, while Nettie wen to tell Vicki and Richard that he was there.

Richard spoke to him first, then sent for Vicki.

Jamie jumped to his feet when she entered the room, his boyish face alight, to stammer a greeting.

She thanked him for the flowers, which Nettie had put in a vase and brought to the morning room, and for the other gift that the girl gave to her unopened.

"That's for Allie," Jamie said. "I made it for him."

Vicki forced a smile, untied the carefully done bow. A clown's face looked up at her from the wrapping. It was cut of wood and painted with red circles on its cheeks, and huge smiling eyes, and red laughing lips. There were strings attached to its head, and when she lifted it up, she saw arms and legs with carved ruffs and buttons. "A puppet, Jamie! Thank you."

"Mr. Saunders helped me," Jamie said. "He makes

lots of them. Children and animals, too, mostly. The clown was my idea. I wanted one for Allie. So Mr. Saunders and I worked it out together." He spoke gravely, in his father's slow voice, almost a man at fifteen, but still very shy.

Vicki repeated her thanks, and started upstairs. Halfway to the upper floor, she stopped. She hadn't asked after Mrs. Wood. Even more, she had never sent additional money for the older woman to use to pay Jamie his weekly wage.

But the boy was already at the door, his cap on his head. It was too late to stop him, to ask how the shop fared, and whether he liked his work.

Vicki went up to Allie, sent Maria away. He was the same, his eyes closed, his body limp. She looped the clown's strings over one of the posts. If Allie opened his eyes, he could see the bright, smiling face.

Later, when John came in, she spoke to him about Jamie. That evening John went to the food shop. When he came back he told Vicki that Jamie no longer worked for Mrs. Wood, hadn't since the day the strike had been settled. Mrs. Wood had wanted him to stay on, but Gus Markeson had come there one afternoon and taken Jamie away with him, saying that he wanted Jamie to work in a mill, and not in a food shop, and that was the last she had seen of the boy.

"He's intelligent and should be in school," Vicki said distractedly.

"There's nothing we can do." John limped to the door, but stopped, turning as Allie screamed and screamed again, small fists beating his temples.

With all thoughts of Jamie gone, Vicki bent over her son, whispering to him as his body arched up in convulsion.

She was still in the rocker beside Allie's bed, late that night, when Richard drew her to her feet, saying, "You must come and rest."

She whispered, "I'm afraid to leave him."

"Maria will stay. And she won't sleep. Lie down for a little while."

He had said the words before, but always, when she demurred, he had not insisted. This time he felt that he must. As Allie's small body had shrunk in his bed so had Vicki's shrunk with him. Her face was become all eyes, their dark blue brilliance heightened by her pallor. Fear and fatigue had bowed her slim shoulders and stolen the lightness from her walk. He was nearly as frightened for her as he was for Allie. He couldn't imagine life without either of them.

Now when she said, "I'll rest here, Richard," he took her hand and led her from the room. Maria nodded at him and closed the door softly.

He said, "Lie down for a few hours only . . . even if you don't sleep . . ."

"You'll call me if . . . if there's anything?"

"You know I will."

He watched her go into the bedroom, then went downstairs. Ezra had brought him papers from the mill. He should go over them. In the past week, he had forgotten everything but Allie. He had gone in a few times, stayed an hour or so, then returned home, unable to remain away. Like Vicki, he felt that if he were to turn his back, close his eyes, the battle for Allie might be lost. Cavendish and Sons, once so important to him, seemed nothing now.

The papers Ezra had brought him were stacked neatly on the desk. He took them up, flipped through them slowly. Production was down, he noticed. At one time that would have caught his eye. It didn't matter now. There had been two accidents. He didn't even notice the names of those involved, or indeed what had happened. The price of coal was rising. He shrugged. Plant No. 2 showed unusual absenteeism. He flung the papers aside.

He prowled the house as snow fell softly out-of-doors. Harry was carrying hay to the horses. Mrs. Beamis and Nettie were busy in the kitchen. Matilda and John sat in the morning room before a cold hearth, both sunk in uncomfortable silence. He lit a fire for them, then went up to look in at Vicki. She sat on the edge of the bed, her head leaning against the curved poster, her hands limp in her lap.

He looked in on Allie, and Maria simply raised her eyes to him. He nodded and went back to Vicki. She hadn't moved.

He drew her to her feet. Slowly, with infinitely gentle hands, he loosened her gown. He took the pins from her hair and smoothed it free. She murmured a protest when he pressed her to the pillows, covered her. He hushed her, saying, "He's the same. Maria's there. Just rest a minute." But he saw, when he turned out the light, that her eyes were wide open.

He lay down beside her, and felt her stir and said, "Stay, Vicki." How long since he had been this close to her, he wondered. It seemed a lifetime to him.

She whispered, her face wet with tears, "Don't be kind to me now, Richard. I can't bear it if you are."

His arms enclosed her, held her as a loving father holds his child. He said, "Nothing matters but Allie."

On Sunday Elise and Leslie came again, and later on, Jamie visited, too. That time he brought a small lion puppet, and George Thompson was with him, carrying an armful of flowers. "From the mill," he said. "We're all praying for your boy."

Again Vicki came down for a few moments. She thanked George for the flowers, asked him to relay her appreciation to the other operatives. She held Jamie's lion puppet and told him how she had hung up the clown, and that she would do the same with the animal. When the boy asked if Allie liked the clown, she faltered, saying, "He sleeps, Jamie. He hasn't played with it yet."

That night Jamie looked into his father's face and said, "Allie's sicker than I thought. He's maybe dying."

Gus Markeson shrugged. "The rich die just like the poor, except more comfortably. And sometimes their money helps them last a little longer."

Jamie turned from his father's sullen yellow eyes, a seed of disgust expanding in his chest, and went to Ezra for help in making a dog puppet.

On the same Sunday night Eustacia and Albert Cosgrove came for another visit. Greeting them, Richard thought that the calls would soon diminish. As time passed, and hope waned, there would be less to say and fewer consolations to offer. He sent Nettie to tell Vicki, but she returned word that it was time for Maria to have her supper, that she herself must stay with Allie.

Eustacia, her square bottom filling the chair, leaned back, thrusting her bosom before her. "The child is no better?"

Matilda only shook her head, and braided her fingers.

"It's almost stopped snowing," Albert said, clearing his throat.

"Richard still stays home from the mill?" Eustacia went on. Matilda didn't answer, and she continued. "He shouldn't. It needs supervision."

"My dear," Albert murmured.

"Then John should go," Eustacia said firmly. "It's time he took an interest. Especially in the circumstances."

"My dear," Albert said loudly.

"And they don't know how to treat it? Dr. Stilton is truly at a loss?" After a silent moment, she spoke again. "It's the Portugee. She's brought something here, an awful European disease. When did she last go home?"

Maria, on her way to the kitchen, froze just beyond the door. Her black eyes flashed. Her pink mouth thinned.

"Yes, it's the Portugee. That's what happens when you bring them into your house. You ought never to have allowed it, Matilda."

With a gasp of rage, Maria went on to the kitchen. She didn't hear Matilda say, "We don't know what's wrong with Allie, Eustacia. That being the case, we can hardly blame Maria. And she's been most devoted. Vicki couldn't have managed without her."

Moments later, Allie's shrill scream brought a swift silence to the room. It seemed to go on and on. When it faded, Eustacia suddenly rose and went to the window. There, with her face turned from the others, she mopped her streaming eyes with a lace handkerchief.

She had just managed to regain her composure when Rosamund and Davis Peabody arrived. They had brought a large stuffed giraffe for Allie, a box of bonbons for Vicki, cigars for Richard.

"It's terrible," Rosamund said, sinking into a chair. "I'm so sorry, Matilda. We've wanted to come since we heard, but Davis had so many obligations. We've only just been able to get away." Her high sweet voice seemed softer than it used to, her dark eyes warmer.

Davis drew Richard aside when he came in, asked, "Is there something I can do? Perhaps someone in Boston to contact?"

Richard explained about the two consultants.

Davis nodded. "But if you think of anything, you'll let me know, won't you? I have a son myself, remember."

Richard thanked him, spoke a few words to Rosamund and went upstairs, carrying the stuffed giraffe under his arm.

While the conversation continued in the morning room below, he sat beside Vicki in shared silence, and looked longingly into Allie's face.

A sharp thin icicle broke from a tree limb beyond the window. It fell with a loud crackle. Vicki glanced sideways toward the sound, her eyes narrowing against the sun's brightness. When she turned back to Allie, she thought she saw his lips move. She leaned forward. Yes. His lips had moved. Now, as she watched, his chin quivered, and his almost translucent lids rose over his sunken eyes. Even as she reached for him, he said softly, "Maria, dear, run and call my husband."

"What's the matter?" the girl gasped.

"Quickly. I think . . . oh, dear God, I think Allie's awakening . . ." She had spoken without moving her eyes from the child's face, but she knew that Maria was transformed from a lost waif into a fleet messenger of joy as she flew from the room. Vicki leaned closer, took Allie's hands carefully into hers, feeling the tiny bones of his fingers, the narrowness of his wrists. "Allie?" Her voice was the barest of hoping whispers, but she knew that he heard. His shadowed eyes turned toward her. His lips moved soundlessly.

It seemed only an instant since the icicle's fall, but Allie had looked at her, and Richard was there, his long body bent over hers to the bed.

After a single disbelieving look, he said, "Maria, telephone to Dr. Stilton," and once again there was the patter of swift footsteps.

While Vicki and Richard waited, confusion exploded below. Matilda made the call to the doctor. He was out, Mrs. Stilton said, gone to visit two patients in Corky Row. Hearing Matilda repeat that information aloud, Mrs. Beamis sent Nettie to get Harry. Within minutes, he was in the surrey and away. He found Dr. Stilton, who promised to come as quickly as he could and returned to Highland Avenue with that information.

Matilda and John awaited the doctor's arrival, standing together at the window. An hour later he was there, red-faced, blowing on his cold hands, asking as he headed for the stairs, "What's happened?" and not stopping for a reply.

He found Allie propped high against his pillows, still and unmoving, except for his eyes, which shifted between Vicki and Richard, and then to the doctor himself as he crossed the threshold.

Silently, he examined the child, thinking that the word for what had happened was the simplest one, yet one with the most complicated idea the doctor could imagine. *Miracle.* Helpless these past weeks, he had watched Allie's small body go into convulsions, had heard the screams pour from him, had watched in horror as the tiny fists beat at the little dark head. In his heart, he had given the boy up to whatever fate was to befall him, and prepared to do what he could for Vicki and Richard.

But now he allowed himself a cautious but hopeful smile. "Yes. There's been a change for the better. We must wait and see."

It was nearly a week before Allie turned his head, raised his arms and fluttered his fingertips at the clown that grinned at him from the bedpost.

Vicki took it down, made it dance on its strings above the boy's chest, saying, "Jamie made it for you. Do you remember Jamie?"

There was no answer then, although Allie's lips moved. A few days later, he murmured, "Mama," and in minutes, "Papa!" The third word he spoke was, "Jamie!" in a voice of triumph. Within a few more days he was speaking as well as before his sudden illness had struck him mute. He played with the clown puppet and with the lion, murmuring, "Jamie, Jamie, come," in a happy singsong.

One morning Richard went to the mill. It was the first time in weeks he had been there. The once-familiar noise seemed strange to him. The air he had always breathed without a thought seemed fetid and thick.

As word of his arrival rippled through the lofts, he saw Jamie at work with a broom. Surprised, he went to him. "Jamie, I didn't know you were here."

"Mr. Saunders put me on," Jamie said. "It's all right, isn't it?"

"Of course," Richard answered. Later he heard from Ezra that Jamie had gone from mill to mill, seeking work, but with no luck. When a sweeper's job became available in Plant No. 1, Ezra had hired the boy.

But now Jamie was asking, "How's Allie, Mr. Cavendish?"

"Improving, Jamie. And he enjoys the puppets you made for him."

"Could I visit him sometime?"

"Whenever you want to."

"Tonight?" Jamie asked. "When the plant closes?"

Richard grinned. "Come back with me this afternoon. I'll let you know when I'm going."

Whistling, Jamie turned away, sweeping the strings and threads and fibers away from the machines.

"Bobbin boy!" was being shouted as Richard went

into his office. A few hours later, restless, he heard it again as he went to tell Jamie to get his coat and hat.

Allie's squeal of joy rang through the house. "Jamie, come!"

Soon those happy words became familiar. Jamie spemt an hour with Allie that day, returned on Sunday to spend two hours with him. Each time, when he left, Allie yelled after him, "Jamie, come!"

At midweek, Vicki heard the usual shout, and smiled. She went into the hall to speak to Jamie. She had hardly said his name when she heard Maria cry out.

She and Jamie both lunged for the nursery.

Allie, still shouting, "Jamie, come!" was on his knees beside the bed, beginning an awkward crawl for the door.

Vicki caught him up in her arms, kissed him, danced around the room with him, and then swooped on Jamie to hug him to her, at the same time crying, "Run tell my husband, Maria! Allie's starting to walk again!"

The long slope of the lawn was April green, and Harry worked at the lily pond, with Allie nearby and Maria hovering over him.

Vicki looked down from the window, recalling what Dr. Stilton had told her the previous week. "It's over," he had said. "You must forget that the boy was ill, or you'll make a permanent invalid out of him. He's fit enough to go outside to play, to do whatever he's been accustomed to."

It was easy, she thought, for the doctor to say that the weeks of terror must be forgotten. Allie's face and body had begun to fill out. He laughed and played as before. Yet when she looked at him, she remembered. She had to go to him, to reassure herself that all was well.

Richard had noticed, said, "Vicki, you must put an end to this cosseting. You'll spoil Allie, if you don't." She tried, but no matter where she was in the house, what chore occupied her attention, she was suddenly forced to find him, to touch his cheek, look into his eyes, hear his laughter.

Now, as she watched him run toward the house, she picked up her book again. She held it but the print blurred before her eyes. It would be his third birthday next week. How well she remembered the time. His first cry. Her yearning to hold him. And then the awful wave of bitterness that had swept her.

"Mama!" Allie came shouting. "Where Jamie?"

"He'll visit you soon," she answered.

Maria smoothed back his tousled curls and said, "I want to tell you . . . I'm going to go away tomorrow."

Vicki dropped her book. "What's this?"

"I'm leaving," Maria said. "Allie's well. I promised myself I'd stay to see that. And now I'm going."

"But why, Maria? What's happened?"

The girl's lip jutted. "It wasn't my fault," she said. "Allie didn't have a Portuguese disease. And I don't bring it home from my people's house."

Vicki rose slowly. "What *are* you talking about? Who ever said such a thing?"

Maria shrugged. "It's not so, and I don't like it. And now Allie's all right, I'm leaving."

Neither Vicki, nor Matilda, nor later, even Richard, could change her mind. By the end of that week, Maria had packed her belongings and gone.

Chapter 24

MITCH FINGERED THE NEAT BLUE CRAVAT, THEN PUT it away in the chest with the new shirt. He had had them both since early in the year and still hadn't worn them. The same was true of the new blue suit that hung on the hook behind the door under a wrapping of newspaper. He could see himself in that outfit, sitting with his Uncle Shamus and telling him about the guns all that money would buy. He could see Shamus' blue eyes widen with respect, hear him laugh, "Mitch, me boyo, who'd have thought you'd bring such honor to our name?"

Mitch was glad now that he hadn't told Celeste what he was going to do. It was better this way. He supposed that she imagined he had forgotten Richard Cavendish. He'd been careful not to mention the man's name. She had only spoken of him twice. One she had said, "Mitch, look here. There's something in the *Daily Globe* about Allie Cavendish. He's very sick."

Mitch had made certain that he sounded properly surprised, but he had already known about it. He had been watching the house on Highland Avenue for days when he saw Dr. Stilton drive in. At first he had thought the boy must have the measles or another baby disease. But soon Mitch knew it had to be something worse. Dr. Stilton came and went twice a day, and always looked worried. Mitch gave up then, deciding he would have to wait and see. If it weren't through the boy, then it would be another way. He had told himself to be patient.

The other time Celeste mentioned the Cavendish name was when the *Daily Globe* wrote of the child's recovery. Mitch had already known about that, too. He had driven past the house and seen Allie running on the lawn.

"Going out?" Celeste asked, as Mitch went to the door.

"I'll be back soon."

"Are you going to look for work?"

Mitch shrugged, slammed the door behind him. He had been fired two weeks before, partly for keeping such irregular hours that the owner never knew when he'd be at the stables or when he wouldn't, but mostly for using the cart and horses without permission.

Celeste had been upset, but he hadn't cared. He'd known by then that it wouldn't be long. He'd bought another cart at auction, an old nag of a horse, too. He kept them stabled within walking distance but used them rarely.

He stepped into the street. The sun of late April warmed him. His thoughts warmed him, too. Soon. Soon. A small black dog darted into his path, barked at his ankles, nipped at his pants. He aimed a kick at it, cursed and walked by, while behind him a small boy shouted, "Doggie, come here!" Turning, he watched the neighbor's child dodge around a fast moving carriage and leap into the road after the dog. A smile flickered at Mitch's lips as he went on.

The black puppy, freed from the hands that retrained it, gave a joyful bark and leaped from the shadows under the bushes into the damp twilight and frisked toward Allie.

"Dog," he shouted, laughing. "Doggie, come here!"

The puppy ran, tongue lolling out, then circled back, then stopped, barked, and began a game of chasing his tail.

"Doggie!" Allie cried. "How do, doggie! Come to me."

Mitch watched, his trolley conductor cap pulled low on his ginger head, his ill-fitting uniform nondescript. He had seen it hanging on a clothesline months before and stolen it. He had bought the cap from a second-hand shop in New Bedford. He was sure that no one, looking at him, would think of Mitch Ryan, the groom. He crouched low, his pale eyes intent, his big hands working. Mrs. Beamis stood close to the house, her head turned away. There was a light in one of the lower windows, another on the upper floor. Neither Nettie nor Harry was in sight. The avenue was empty and silent. Beyond the hemlock grove the cart waited, wheels creaking each time the old nag stamped away the big black flies that plagued it.

His patience had proven itself. Everything had fallen together. Every piece fit as he'd planned. Mitch took a deep breath. Now, me boyo, he told himself. He gave a short sharp whistle between his teeth.

Allie cocked his head, grinned. The black puppy raced into the bushes, and the boy came charging after.

Mitch's calloused hand went over the small mouth, his arms folded tightly around the narrow waist. Within the instant, it was done.

Mrs. Beamis still stood near the house. The avenue was still empty and silent.

Mitch tucked the bound and gagged child under a filthy gray tarpaulin and drove away, whistling soundlessly between his teeth, the black dog snuggled beside him.

He drove aimlessly for an hour, allowing darkness to fall, before he returned to the room he shared with Celeste.

He climbed down from the cart, peered up and down the road. It was empty. No one watched, from window or street, as he carried the bundled tarpaulin inside.

"It's about time," Celeste said. Then, staring, "What's that you've brought in?"

Mitch grinned, put the tarpaulin on the bed, and whipped it back. Allie's eyes were wide open, fearful. Tears ran down his cheeks into the rag that bound his mouth. His small body jerked and twitched at the ropes that bound his hands and ankles.

Celeste's mouth opened, closed. Her face went dead white. Finally she croaked, "Mitch, who . . . who is that?"

"You know." Mitch grinned at her. "I've done it. We're going to be rich. Richer than you ever imagined. We're going to have everything." That time he didn't mention the guns. Let her quarrel with him later. Right now he needed her. Let her think she'd wear diamonds and furs until she had to know different.

"You've gone mad," she whispered.

"It's done," he retorted. "It's as good as finished."

"No. No, it's impossible."

"Never mind." He leaned over the boy, gave him a smile meant to be reassuring. "It's okay," he said. "Nothing's going to happen to you. You're going to be all right. I'm going to give you some hot milk, and you'll go to sleep, and when you wake up tomorrow morning, you'll be home again." He didn't know if the boy understood. It didn't matter. "You'll be okay," he repeated. He went to the stove, heated milk in a saucepan, laced it with a strong dose of laudanum.

"What're you doing?" Celeste screamed.

"The boy needs his sleep," Mitch said, smiling crookedly. "I'm going to make sure he has it."

"No," she whispered. "No, Mitch, listen. It's all wrong. You can't do it. I don't want any part of this. Just take him away from here. Do whatever you want, I can't stop you. But don't do it here!"

"But here's where we are," Mitch retorted. "And here's where we stay. At least here's where you and the boy will be while I do my errands."

"No," she said. "I won't do it, Mitch."

"You will," he said softly. "Believe me, you will. I've got it all figured out, and you're not going to spoil it for me."

He turned his back on her, bent over the boy, said, "Now be quiet and I'm going to take this out of your mouth. Hear me? Be quiet, or I'll give you a clout on the head that'll shut you up quick enough." He slipped the gag from between the boy's lips, a hand at the ready to seal away any possible scream.

But Allie only whimpered, "Mama? Papa? Papa?"

"Drink," Mitch said, shoving the mug against his mouth.

Allie twisted his head away, but Mitch grabbed him by the chin, forced his head back and poured milk into his mouth. Some ran out, spreading stains on his shoulders and chest. But he gulped air and choked and swallowed enough of the bitter stuff. His whimpers soon faded. His writhing body was soon still. Mitch looked up, grinned at Celeste. "You see? There won't be any trouble with him."

She shook her head slowly from side to side. "I'm not afraid of trouble from him. It's Richard. The police. You'll never get away with it. The boy will know us . . . he'll say . . ."

"He'll know nothing but our faces, and he won't ever see them again." Mitch crossed the room to her, took her by the shoulders. "We'll have the money by midday tomorrow. Do you hear me? By midday tomorrow. We'll be all ready to go when I pick it up. And we'll be out and away before they even find the boy."

"I can't," she said. "I'll do whatever you want, but not this, Mitch. Whatever you want, Mitch, I promise. I'll get you money somehow. As much as you want, too. But not this . . . I'm scared, I tell you. I'm just too scared of this."

He held her close, put a hand behind her head as if about to kiss her. Instead he doubled his fist and thrust it against her mouth, knuckles pressing tightly. "It's done, and it can't be changed. In a little while I'm going to go and leave a note. They'll have it by morning most likely. I'll say how much I want, and where to leave it, and what'll happen to the boy if they don't follow through. By midday we'll have it, and turn the boy loose, and be gone."

She was locked in his grip, could only whisper against his knuckles, "Mitch, please . . . please . . ."

He pressed down hard, suddenly. He ground his fist into her mouth, her lip onto her lower teeth. "It's too late," he told her. "You've got to help me. I want that money, and I'll have it."

Tears slipped down her cheeks while she nodded. Her mouth was bloodied, already swelling when she said, "All right. Mitch. We'll do it then."

He let her go with a triumphant laugh. He tore the newspaper from his new suit, and sat down with his knife and paste to get the note prepared. Within the hour, satisfied with his work, he put on his trolley conductor's cap and set out to fulfill the next step in his plan.

Chapter 25

"ALLIE! ALLIE, COME HERE, BOY!"

The words hung gently on the soft springtime air, and lingered in small diminishing echoes through the stillness of late afternoon.

Hearing them, Vicki smiled. Since his recovery Allie was become a fount of inexhaustible energy. She worried sometimes that he overreached himself. But she knew that she mustn't allow the residue of her fear to mark him. Richard was right in that.

"Allie?" Mrs. Beamis called again.

Vicki drew the brush through her hair one last stroke. It was several hours before dinner, but she was nearly ready. She would see Allie through his supper and bath, while Mrs. Beamis was in the kitchen preparing the company meal. Eustacia and Albert would be coming, and Elise and Leslie, too.

It would be the first entertainment in the house since Allie's illness. Richard had insisted on it, saying, "We must begin to live normally again, Vicki." He was right in that, too, she knew. Yet she didn't look forward to the evening.

"Allie! No more hide and seek. Come to me now!"

Vicki frowned, put the brush on the dresser and turned from the glass. There had been a note of concern in Mrs. Beamis' voice. It was too bad of Allie to behave so. Mrs. Beamis was no longer a young woman. She couldn't chase after him as Maria had done. It was proving difficult to find another nurse as devoted as the girl had been.

"Allie? Allie, where are you?" The note of concern was become outright fear.

Vicki heard, and felt the blood drain from her head. She caught up her skirts and raced for the stairs. John met her on the landing, and Matilda came after.

Not speaking, they hurried outside.

Mrs. Beamis trotted toward them panting. "I can't find him," she gasped. "He was there one minute and gone the next, and he won't answer me."

Vicki saw for an instant a picture in her mind. Allie lying somewhere in the trees, his body convulsing . . . It took an effort of will to banish it, to say in a level tone, "He's surely somewhere nearby, Mrs. Beamis. But perhaps you'd better have Harry and Nettie come out. We'll give the whole property a good search."

Mrs. Beamis hurried away.

John asked, "Richard?"

"I'll telephone him," Matilda said.

As she disappeared inside, Mrs. Beamis came around the side of the house, with Harry and Nettie hurrying ahead of her.

"Where did you see Allie last?" John asked.

Mrs. Beamis pointed a plump, trembling hand at the hemlock grove. "Over there. Close to the bushes. And I was here, just where we are, but I could see him quite clearly. He was just trotting around, stretching his legs, you know, and laughing . . . and then . . ." Her eyes widened. "Oh, I almost forgot. It must have been the puppy. A small black one. It came running out suddenly."

Vicki mopped quickly at a sudden gush of blinding tears. Nothing could have happened. Allie had simply wandered off. He was somewhere among the trees. By the time Richard could get back to the house, he would be found. She would roundly scold him for running off, and Richard would scold him again. It would be all right. Nothing had happened. But terror chilled her bare arms as she followed John down the lawn.

Harry and Nettie had gone toward the back of the grounds.

"Allie!" the hard bellow of Harry's voice . . .

Shrill, but carrying, "Allie?" Nettie . . .

"Wait here," John said, as he limped into the trees.

"I called him," Mrs. Beamis said softly. "As soon as e went after the puppy, I called to him."

"Yes," Vicki murmured. "Yes, I heard you."

"And then I called again. I thought he must be hiding, you see. That game he always loved to play with Maria. So I . . ."

"Yes," Vicki murmured again. "It's all right, Mrs. Beamis. We'll find him. Go in now and catch your breath. We must think of dinner, you know."

Mrs. Beamis took an irresolute step toward the house, then stopped and turned back. "I can't. Not until we find him."

"Allie! It's Uncle John. Come to Uncle, Allie!"

And then, far off in the distance . . . "Allie. Allie!"

Nettie, red-faced and breathless, came running. "I don't see him!"

"Oh, what will we do?" Mrs. Beamis moaned.

The rattle of the racing surrey echoed along the avenue. It turned in, jerked to a stop in the driveway.

Richard jumped down, came on the run. "You've not found him yet?"

Vicki shook her head, not trusting herself to speak.

John came slowly from the shadow of the trees through gathering twilight. His eyes avoided Vicki's. He said, "I doubt he's on the grounds, Richard. Harry's done a careful search at the rear, and Nettie, too. He isn't in the grove. I'm afraid we'd better telephone to the marshal's office and have some men begin to look through the neighborhood."

Vicki, listening, shuddered. All those streets, yards, lawns, bushes and trees, stables and outbuildings of all kinds . . . all those places where a small boy could creep away, frightened and hiding . . . or simply lost, and not knowing where he was or where to turn to find what was familiar to him. She bit her lip to keep from crying out.

Richard put a hand on her shoulder. "We'll find him, Vicki. Go into the house and wait."

She shook her head. "I'll go with you."

267

"No," he said firmly. "Wait indoors."

He couldn't bear to see the fear in her face. It w[as] a mirror to what he felt himself. The instant he h[ad] heard Matilda's voice on the telephone, he had knov[n] there was trouble. He had thought Allie stricken agai[n]. When she explained, he had said only, "I'll be hon[e] at once," and put down the telephone.

"What's wrong?" Ezra had asked, seeing him sta[rt] for the door.

Over his shoulder, Richard had answered, "Allie['s] lost."

He remembered nothing of the drive home. H[e] heard Harry shout, "Allie, where are you?"

Vicki turned wearily toward the house. When sl[e] reached the steps, she paused. Her legs refused to tal[e] her indoors. The light was fading. The sun lowerin[g]. Soon dark would fall. Allie would be somewhere alor[e] in the night. She sank down on the steps. From wher[e] she crouched she could see the full stretch of the lawr[n], the grove of hemlocks, the avenue beyond the bushe[s].

John moved around her, and went in. Soon sl[e] heard the murmur of his voice.

In a few minutes he came outside and went to stan[d] at the foot of the driveway with Richard.

Matilda stood in the doorway. "Vicki, please d[o] come in."

She was unable to answer, but simply shook he[r] head. Matilda came out, sank down beside her. Ther[e] was the sound of horses running at the gallop along th[e] quiet avenue. It came closer and closer. The two wag[-] ons pulled up, and four uniformed policemen jumpe[d] down. Matilda clutched Vicki's hand, as they sur[-] rounded Richard and John, and then turned to wher[e] Mrs. Beamis stood, anxious and shaking.

"Just a few questions," the chief marshal aske[d] quietly. "Your name, if you please?"

Mrs. Beamis answered. And added: "But that won'[t] help you find him. He was there, and then the pupp[y] ran out, and he was just gone. You have to look fo[r] him, I tell you!"

"We need a search party," John said softly.

"And the boy's name?" the marshal asked.

"Alban," Richard told him. "Allie . . . that's what he's used to."

"He's how old?"

"Just three," Richard said hoarsely.

"And wearing what?"

Mrs. Beamis answered. "He was wearing blue. A blue shirt. Blue trousers." She drew a deep breath. "He's so tall." She made a gesture. "And has dark hair and dark eyes, and . . . and the smile of an angel." Her hands went up over her face, and she went stumbling toward the house.

Matilda rose to meet her, whispering, "There, Mrs. Beamis. Sit down and rest with us. No one blames you. They'll find him soon. You'll see it's all right."

The marshal pulled his thick brown mustache, looked at his men. "You all heard the description. Spread out and go over the grounds one more time. If he's not here, we'll go into the roads around."

He went up to where Vicki sat, smiled at her. "Don't worry, Mrs. Cavendish. Little boys are always adventurous. We'll find him somewhere close by."

Much later, she was to remember those words. But long hours lay ahead of her before then.

The men spread out through the grounds, their voices calling, slowly fading into echoes, as Harry's had earlier.

It was dark by the time the police had withdrawn and had begun to move along the avenue. By then the road was no longer empty. It was crowded with carts and carriages and wagons. Men and women stood shoulder to shoulder, staring at the house, their faces grim in the pale riding lights. There was such a crush that Elise and Leslie were unable to make their way through. They abandoned their carriage a block away and walked to the house, learning what had happened from the people they passed.

When Vicki saw them turn into the driveway, she whispered, "I forgot. What shall we do?"

Matilda gave her a grim smile. "I did, too. We'll explain."

But Elise cried, "Oh, I'm sorry. We've just heard."

"I'm going to join the search," Leslie said, and hurried away.

Elise went into the house and returned to drape a shawl around Vicki's shoulder.

Vicki nodded acknowledgment.

There was a breaking of the crowd at the end of the driveway. A group of men pushed through. Ezra, Jamie, Gus Markeson. They made their way to the house.

"The men from the plants," Ezra said.

Vicki murmured her thanks.

Jamie smiled at her. "We'll find him. Don't worry."

"Thank you, Jamie." Her voice broke. She looked down at her hands.

He came closer to whisper, "Don't be scared."

He had heard about it half an hour after Richard left the mill. Word spread from loom to loom, through the big lofts. He had put his broom aside, prepared to set out for Highland Avenue at once. His father had stopped him, saying, "What do you think you're doing?"

"I want to go help," Jamie had answered.

"What for? You don't owe them anything."

"Because I want to," Jamie had said.

By then Ezra had had twenty offers. The men went together, Jamie with them. Gus trailed after.

Now Vicki looked up at Jamie and managed to smile back at him. "If Allie hears your voice, he'll come to you, Jamie. You, of all people, will hear him answer."

"That's why I said, Don't be scared," he told her.

The men from the mill went together down to the avenue, disappearing into the crowd, then moving beyond them.

"Allie . . ."

"Allie . . ."

At each bush, they stopped, looked. They studied every shadow. They plunged off the road and into the gardens along the way. They knocked at each door, asked if anyone within had seen or heard a small lost boy. Block by block, house by house, they covered

Highland Avenue and well beyond St. Patrick's Cemetery, and every bypath and lane that fed into it, until at last Ezra said, "We'd better go back and see what's happening at the house."

"I'm for going home," Gus growled.

Jamie only shook his head.

Vicki was still on the steps with Matilda and Elise. Now Eustacia had joined them. Albert had gone off to find the police.

Ezra said nothing as he turned away, taking his men with him back into the avenue. There Gus said, "I'll come again tomorrow" and started off. But Jamie remained behind.

Soon Richard and John returned. Richard leaned over Vicki and said softly, "Go inside now. Have Mrs. Beamis make a pot of tea. The police are sending for more men. We'll search through the night if need be."

She looked deep into his eyes. She didn't know what to say to him. At last she whispered, "Please, Richard, please . . ."

He drew her to her feet. "Just wait. You must be here when we bring him back to you."

She watched as he disappeared into the dark at the end of the driveway, then, along with the others, she went indoors. Moments later, reporters from the *Herald* and the *Daily Globe* came to ask questions. Eustacia sent them away with a few tart words. But they didn't go far.

Hours passed. The moon rose over the hemlock trees. The avenue grew more and more quiet as the search spread further afield, yet out of that very quietness there came a constant whisper and shuffle. The whole of the long block was filled with staring people. Silent, motionless, their faces grim in the light of the boulevard lamps and the flickering torches, they watched the house.

Observing them from the window, Vicki shuddered. She remembered hearing that thirteen years before on a hot August day a large part of the town had converged on Second Street to stare at the Borden house. On the day that she had first met Richard, Vicki recalled, Mrs. McVey had spoken of those silent watching crowds.

Vicki pressed her fingertips into her eyelids until she saw a flash of exploding suns. She mustn't let herself weep. Were she to cry she feared she would melt away flesh and bone, in a current of unending acid tears.

Behind her in the parlor there was the murmur of voices. Elsie, saying, "It's nearly nine. I wonder if there's news." "Richard will come home the moment he hears." That was Matilda. Eustacia sighed, whispered as if to herself, "But it's taking so long . . . if he were only lost . . ." One of the women hushed her quickly, but Vicki had heard.

It was true. An adventurous small boy might have become lost in the neighborhood chasing after a black puppy, just as the chief marshal had suggested. It was now over four hours since Allie had disappeared, and with the number of men looking for him, he'd surely have been found if he were close by.

She raised her head, listening. The dark night no longer resounded with echoes. She didn't hear now, from the distance, "Allie . . . Allie . . . Allie . . ."

There was only the soft murmur from the crowd below as it shifted and swayed, and then broke open.

Richard appeared in the driveway, his tall square-shouldered body a black silhouette against the deeper blackness of the night.

There was no news. She could tell by the way he moved, by his arms, hanging emptily at his side. Still, she went hurrying to meet him, while the women behind her murmured soft protests.

He was near the porte cochere. Behind him, there was a commotion. A small dark-clad woman broke through the press of bodies, crying, "Mr. Cavendish, Mr. Cavendish, I must speak to you."

Vicki said, "It's Mrs. Wood, Richard."

He nodded, turned.

Vicki clung to his arm. "But tell me . . ."

"Nothing," he said. "Except that . . ." He stopped, stonyfaced. "Let me go to see what Mrs. Wood wants."

But Vicki still held him. "Except what?" she demanded. "Tell me, Richard. You must tell me."

"They've found the black dog. It means nothing, of course. But they have found him."

"But where? And what of Allie?"

"The dog was in some bushes off President Avenue."

"So far," she whispered. Then: "What haven't you told me, Richard?"

"The dog is dead."

She gasped, swayed on her feet, as if, suddenly, the world had slipped on a slant.

"Mr. Cavendish, I must . . . Oh, Vicki, my dear . . . I'm so sorry . . ."

She heard the words but couldn't respond.

Mrs. Wood said, "I'd not bother you at this time, but see here what I've found just a little while ago in my shop." She thrust an envelope at Richard. "With your name on it."

Richard took the envelope into his hands. For a moment, he held it, and then, with a brisk settling of his shoulders, he opened it carefully.

"It was under the dusting cloth on the counter, you understand, and I'd not touched that cloth, not since perhaps seven this evening. There was a rush in the shop." Mrs. Wood's worried voice paused. She peered into Richard's pale face, but said, "You recall, Vicki. I so often have a seven-o'clock rush. And . . . and well, just a little while ago, there it was, so I set out to deliver it . . ." Again her voice paused.

Vicki was saying, "Richard? Richard, what is it? Does it have to do with Allie?"

He nodded his dark head, unable to speak. He read again the words formed of letters cut from a newspaper and pasted on a sheet of paper. *If you want your son back leave twenty thousand dollars in the confessional at St. Mary's Church by nine o'clock tomorrow morning. You won't see him again if the police are there.*

It was what he had feared ever since he had learned that the black dog had been found dead, and no sign of Allie nearby. The moment he had begun to think of

273

that he had also thought of Celeste. Before returnin
to the avenue, he had gone to the house off Easter
Avenue. It had been bleak, empty. The neighbors ha
told him she had moved away months before. He ha
wasted no further time but had come home.

"Richard, please. . . ."

"Mr. Cavendish, what can I . . . ?"

Vicki.

Mrs. Wood.

They looked at him pleadingly.

He said, "Mrs. Wood, thank you. This is importan
Will you go inside with Vicki?" He put his hands o
Vicki's shoulders then, held her tightly, but briefly
"I must go to find the chief marshal at once. Just wai
for me to come back."

"What is that?" she demanded hoarsely. "What doe
it say?"

He closed his eyes to shut away the sight of he
agonized face. But she had to know. She had to b
forewarned. He opened them, met her gaze full on
and said gently, "It's a . . . a demand for money. Ir
exchange for Allie. I'll find the marshal, and then ge
Albert. We must move quickly." He turned away,
hurried into the dark.

"They'll not find him now," George Thompson said
"Not until dawn at least."

Ezra agreed sadly.

Jamie said nothing. He shifted his weight from
foot to foot, considering. They had gone out Highland
Avenue as far as the cemetery and passed its tall
locked gates by another half a mile or so before turning back. Allie wasn't along the way. Not in the fields,
nor the yards, nor the lanes. The search teams were
moving slowly through all the surrounding roads. But
Allie was so little . . . small feet, short legs . . . how far
could he have gone?

He said nothing to the others, but he allowed himself to be moved, slowly, hardly noticeably, with the
shift and sway of the crowd, until he was at its outer
fringes, well into the shadows. From there, he stepped

a pace back and then another, and merged into the dark.

He pulled his cap firmly down on his head, jammed his hands in his pockets. The others could give up, could stand and watch under the scatter of torches and riding lights. But he couldn't. He had to go on. He pictured the tall gates of St. Patrick's. They were closed now. But had they been closed before? Weren't they always open until sundown?

At the end of the block, he broke into a full trot.

The bells of Notre Dame Church rang the hour of nine. Mitch paused to listen, to count. Only twelve more hours. He had had it all worked out for so long, had been so patient, that the twelve hours ahead seemed nothing to him.

He must make sure that Celeste was packed and ready, and then tell her what she was to do next, and exactly when.

He would mingle with the crowds going into St. Mary's for seven-o'clock Mass. He would be there when Richard Cavendish delivered the money. The man would take no chances with his son's life, so there would be no police about. Still, by being early, Mitch knew he could make doubly certain of that. He would get the money and go directly to the North Main Street railway depot, where she would already be waiting for him, the tickets in her hand. When she saw him, she would carry Allie outside. Mitch would take him. Within moments the sleeping boy would be left somewhere, on the steps of the public library or wherever else along the street that seemed safe enough. Within another few minutes he would rejoin Celeste and be boarding the train for Boston. He'd be wearing the new suit, the shirt with its collar, the cravat. He'd have on his head a derby from Lamson and Hubbard. Just Let Uncle Shamus laughed at him then . . .

The door latch creaked as it closed behind him.

Celeste sat crouched in the straight-backed chair. The room was in darkness, but silver light from the

rising moon poured through the uncurtained window
She raised her haggard face and looked at him.

"What the hell!" he swore. "Can't you light the
lamp?"

She didn't answer him. Her tongue flicked out to
moisten her lips. Her eyes slipped away from his.

Alarm hit him quick, and hard, and fast. He felt it
inside his chest, exploding into a huge heat that burned
through his blood.

He grabbed for a lamp, knocked it over, swearing
He managed to get it lit, and came close to knocking it
over again.

The gray tarpaulin lay where he had left it on the
bed. But Allie was gone.

A strangling sound came from Mitch's throat. He
turned to Celeste, and asked in a soft pleading whisper, "Where is he?"

"I told you," she said. "I told you I couldn't do it."
"Where is he?"

"You won't find him," she said. And, "Oh, Mitch
listen, it was a dumb thing to do! Believe me, it was
We don't need all that money. You and me, we can
get along. We don't need it, I tell you."

It was what she had said to herself as she sat on
the edge of the bed, looking down at Allie. He whimpered in his drugged sleep, and his small body
twitched, and she found herself shivering and saying
softly in her mind, "We don't need the money. And
what was that Mitch was saying about guns anyway?"
It was wrong, and something terrible would happen
And they didn't need the money. She'd make what they
had to have. She'd go back on the street, or into a
house, or whatever Mitch wanted.

Allie whimpered, twitched. She eased the tarpaulin
over his chest. Richard's son . . .

She was supposed to be packing. That was what
Mitch had told her to do. She got to her feet and began
to fold her gowns into a trunk. Silk and lace soft on
her fingers . . . a cart rattling by in the street . . . Allie
coughed. She jumped at the sound of it. Suddenly, without thinking of it, she found a large white bath sheet.

276

She pulled the tarpaulin off and wrapped Allie snugly into its white folds. She held him tight against her and felt his heart beat against her breast. Still without thinking, she went quickly into the road. It was dark but for the boulevard lights on Eastern Avenue. She walked slowly, steadily, always uphill. A police wagon rolled by. Carriages and carts passed her. She didn't turn to look at them. No one challenged her. Suddenly the quiet roads were busy. A tide of people rolled swiftly in one direction. Highland Avenue. She turned away from it, took a side lane, then another. She didn't dare go too close to the house. She went on and on, sheltered by the night, by springtime shadow. She had left the tide of people behind and gone on into emptiness, but from somewhere behind her she heard voices.

Allie stirred within her arms, and panic stirred within her breast. She must leave him now. Somehow, somewhere, she must leave him where he could be found. The iron gates of St. Patrick's loomed open ahead. She hesitated, then skimmed through them, stumbling in the ruts of the dirt road. A white marble angel rose out of the dark. She dropped the boy at its feet, and fled.

Mitch stood frozen, staring. A night wind rattled the window. The lamp hissed. "What did you do?" he asked finally. "You whore! What did you do?"

"I took him where he'll be found," she cried. "And one day you'll thank me for it!"

He lurched across the small space between them, his hands fastening on her throat. He jerked her up, out of the chair, and shook her. "You've wrecked it," he yelled. "Oh, damn you, damn you! You've wrecked what I wanted to do."

She squealed and squirmed and struggled, fighting him with all her strength. But he shook her and flung her away and was on her again. He punched and kicked and tore at her. She was become fate to him, his future that would never be, forgiveness and love that were lost forever.

Sobbing, cursing, threatening, he exhausted himself

long after she had given up. When, finally, he fell t
his knees beside her, he realized that she was dead.

As the bells of Notre Dame chimed ten o'clock, h
carried a trunk to the cart and drove away.

"Albert is seeing to the money," Richard said.

His face was gray, Vicki saw. Stony. His dark eye
were narrowed, veiled.

"You spoke to the chief marshal?" she asked dully

"I have his oath that he'll not interfere. The mone
will be at St. Mary's in good time. But he'll do nothin
to endanger Allie."

"Then they'll stop searching," she murmured. "The
must do that."

"It's done." He drew a deep ragged breath. "Nov
we can only wait."

From where she stood beside him at the window
she heard the murmur of voices behind her in the parlor.

Only Matilda and Eustacia remained, Leslie having
picked up Elise some time before.

"A terrible thing," Eustacia was saying.

Matilda answered, "We must hope." But there was
only hopelessness in her voice. She had aged by ten
years in the past seven hours.

A door latch clicked. Mrs. Beamis said, her voice
aquaver, "Is there news?"

"Not yet," Richard answered. "It'll be a long while
before we . . . we know anything."

"I keep thinking, trying to understand. I keep wondering. Was there something I could do? Ought I to
have guessed when I saw the puppy? Ought I to have
screamed when Allie ran into the bushes?"

"No," Vicki told her. "Don't reproach yourself, Mrs.
Beamis." Then, leaning close to the window to look
into the silvery dark, she went on, "Richard, I must
go out for a walk in the air, or else go mad."

He took her arm, led her out-of-doors. Once there,
though, she paused, looking down the long slope of the
lawn.

The crowd on the avenue had thinned. It was no

longer a black hulking mass, silent and unmoving. It had become individual groups of twos and threes, silhouettes against the night. There were whispers, murmurs. As she watched, one small figure standing alone stepped back two paces, and bent a shawl-wrapped head.

It was Maria Sandora. She looked at Vicki, at Richard, their faces ghost-white in the rays of the moon, and said to herself that they would have blamed her. She would have been at fault if little Allic had wandered away while she looked after him. She wondered bitterly who they blamed now. Who they called a Portugee. But, even as her mouth twisted in anger, she clutched a crucifix in her hand, and prayed the boy would soon be found, and found safely.

Vicki couldn't see her. To her searching eyes, there were only figures, ominous, waiting, faceless and heartless. She whispered, in sudden panic, "Richard, they don't *know*, do they?"

He shook his head.

Sighing, she took a single slow step, then another. Rainbow-streaked mists had gathered in long trailing ribbons over the river. The trees were still, shadow-black sentinels against the night. Far off a train whistle wailed thinly, a tug hooted, horses' hoofs drummed on cobblestone.

Richard went with her across the lawn, realizing that she was drifting in that silent walk to the place where Allie had last been seen. "I must go to Albert now," he said. "Come back to the house."

She looked into his face as if she didn't understand him, then turned her head siffly to stare down the avenue. "I want to go along the road," she whispered.

"Vicki, no."

But she moved away from him, a sleepwalker with fixed eyes. Slowly she made her way to the street.

When she reached it, there was a shifting and stirring among the groups waiting there. The rainbow-streaked mists drifted before the moon and dimmed its light, so that alien darkness blanketed the place. With

Richard following her, she continued on. Gatherin
her gown in her hands, and holding it high, as sh
stepped down from the curbing, she turned away int
the thickest of shadows.

Far ahead a light gleamed in a window, reflected o
a painted gate in pale streaks. Beyond that ther
was nothing.

"Vicki . . ." Richard said her name, then paused.

The light in that distant window had been momen
tarily hidden as something passed rapidly before i
Now there was a voice calling, a shout. Sounds tha
were not quite words came closer.

And Vicki suddenly gasped. She knew! Her mother'
heart told her before she could see or hear. She knew
With a muted cry, she began to run. She seemec
hardly to touch the ground as she flew down the road
her gown billowing out behind her, her hair streaming
free and whipping back from her face. Tears streamec
down her cheeks, but she was smiling.

"He's coming," she screamed. "He's coming." And
then, from out of the shadows, there came the breathless call.

"I have him. He's all right!"

It was then that the ribbons of rainbow mist were
shredded, and through their fading streamers, the
silver light of the moon poured through, bleaching the
sky and casting an eerie glow ahead.

Jamie, moving at a fast trot, with his face shining
with sweat, and his breath a deep hard pull, was
caught within it. In his arms, cradled gently, he carried
mud-streaked, bedraggled Allie.

They raced toward each other, Vicki making soft
wordless sounds, Allie crying "Mama! Papa!" while
Jamie yelled, "He's all right," and Richard whispered
hoarsely, "Thank God!"

They met in one great swirling hug, clinging, kissing,
weeping, all swept into Richard's wide enclosing embrace, while beyond them, closer to the house, the
silent watchers suddenly were silent no longer, but
burst into wild yells under the flickering torches.

Chapter 26

"Puppy," Allie said. "He went all gone." And:
"The old man was there." A shadow seemed to drift
over his face. But then he turned to look at Jamie, and
grinned. "How do?"

Dr. Stilton sat back, and smiled. "He's all right as
far as I can see. His pupils are enlarged, from lauda-
num, would be my guess. I suspect he slept a lot.
Maybe most of the time he was gone. Some cuts and
bruises from stumbling about in the cemetery."

"I want eats," Allie announced. He slipped away
from the doctor, went to Vicki, tugged her gown.
"Mama, we need to eats. Jamie and me." She reached
down to pick him up, to hug him, but he dodged her
yearning arms. "We go for Mrs. Beamis now." Vicki
arched a brown at the doctor.

"It's a good idea."

"Come on," she said, laughing. "Let's go see what
Mrs. Beamis has for us." With her hand smoothing
Allie's unruly hair, another on Jamie's shoulder, she
led them from the room.

"We didn't get much from him," Richard said
quietly.

"I don't think he remembers. A child that age . . .
Or if he does, he doesn't know how to tell us. I
wouldn't ask him too much about it, Richard. It'll only
make it stick more firmly in his mind. Eventually,
whatever comes back to him will come out."

"If we only knew . . ."

"It's over. That's what counts." The doctor got to
his feet. "Extraordinary, how young Jamie found him."

"Yes," Richard agreed.

They had questioned the boy once the excitement of reunion was over. He had been exhausted, sweat-streaked, still breathless. He had rubbed his dark curly hair, and shrugged, and said, "I don't know why I went there. I just remembered that we'd gone by, and the gates had been closed. And I got to thinking . . . well, what if before, those gates had been open, and Allie had somehow wandered in . . ."

He was bewildered by the way it had happened. Ezra, his father, all the others had given up and gone. But he had lingered in the avenue, unable to tear himself away from the waiting house. He knew nothing of the note that Mrs. Wood had brought to Richard. He had just been unable to accept what had happened. So he'd gone back to St. Patrick's, to the tall iron gates. They had been unlocked, and he swung them open, grateful for the moonlight. He went in, gazing into the shadows in quick fearful glances, determination overcoming the uneasy feelings that pressed him back. A yard or two down the dirt road a tall white angel had loomed before him, and he found himself jerking into frozen stillness. There was a sudden scuttling nearby, the whisper of leaves, and then a plaintive, "Mama!" Sleepy. "Mama!" Irate. Then: "Mama!" a frightened wail.

From almost beneath his feet, a small bedraggled form rose up, something thick and white trailing from it shoulders.

"Allie!" Hardly knowing his own voice, Jamie shouted again. "Allie!"

The boy looked up at him, and grinned, "How do, Jamie?" and held out his arms.

Jamie had caught him, lifted him, hugged him and begun to run.

"A fine boy," Dr. Stilton was saying. "Well, I'll be on my way, but I'll stop in and see how Mrs. Beamis is doing before I go. I fear she has more ill effects than Allie from his misadventure."

No sooner had Vicki and Richard brought Allie into the house than Mrs. Beamis collapsed. Until then, through the long hours, she had twisted her hands and murmured incoherent explanations to the others, questions to herself. But when she saw the boy, she broke into tears. After she had squeezed him, kissed him to assure herself that he was really home, Nettie had had to take her to the carriage house with George Thompson's help, to put her to bed. Richard had telephoned to Dr. Stilton, who came at once, and gave her a quieting medication before having his look at Allie. Harry had taken a message to the chief marshal on Center Street, and then to Albert Cosgrove, still at the bank.

Having seen Dr. Stilton out, Richard went into the morning room, led there by laughter.

Allie sat on the floor, a big bowl on the rug between his knees. "Iced cream," he said, grinning, waving his spoon. He wore a small mustache of white that melted as Richard watched. There were stains on his shirt front, and small bits of leaves and twigs in his hair. Jamie sat next to him, handling his spoon with much greater neatness but otherwise equally disheveled.

Vicki looked up at Richard, and smiled. "Aren't they beautiful?" And then, softly, "I'll never forget this night, not as long as I live."

"Nor will I," he answered, thinking of the crude note Mrs. Wood had brought him.

She heard him move about the room next door. Five steps one way, five steps another.

He was alone, with the fear now become relief, and she was alone, too, struggling to understand what had happened. Allie's illness and recovery . . . his having been taken, and then found. What did it mean? What more would she, both she and Richard, learn of terror? And still the wall between them remained unchanged, plaster, lathing, paper embossed with flowers, and strongest of all, memory. She gasped and went hurrying into the hallway, and to his door. She raised her hand to knock. A quick searing weakness rose up to overwhelm her. She lost breath and courage at the same time. Trembling, she crept away.

He heard the whisper of her approach, the rustle of her retreat. His mouth opened to call out, but he was silent. He stood in the middle of the dark room, his hands on his hips, frowning. The old hunger for her stung him deep in his belly. He went to the window, leaned big fists on the sill, staring into the street. He was afraid as he had never been before. He had never supposed he could know such a blind unreasoning horror of what might come. Allie's illness had taught Richard his first vulnerability. What had taken place this evening had taught him the second. He saw the possibilities now as limitless. Life was become as dark and shadowed and empty as the avenue below, a place where sudden loss could strike without warning or pity.

How was he to protect Allie and Vicki?

What did the note mean? Who had witten it? Where was the threatener now?

Richard remained at the window until dawn turned the sky pink, the clouds over the Taunton River golden, but nothing had stirred on the road below. No one had come that way.

Mrs. Beamis served him an early breakfast, her eyes still swollen and red, but her smile summer-sun-bright. "It's a glorious day," she said, and lingered until he looked up questioningly.

"I've someone in the kitchen," Mrs. Beamis said. "I don't know if you . . . but I think you should." She stopped, twisted her hands in her apron. "Maria Sandora."

"What does she want?"

"She'd better tell you."

The girl had been there early, waiting when Mrs. Beamis and Nettie came down from the carriage house. She'd been pale. She slipped her red shawl off her dark head and whispered, "Did they blame you, Mrs. Beamis?"

"It wasn't Mama's fault," Nettie cried. "Nobody thinks so."

Mrs. Beamis hushed her before she could say more. No one beyond the family knew what had really hap-

-pened. That was as it should be. She said, "Maria, you were wrong to go as you did. We need you. Allie needs you."

"That's why I'm here," Maria said.

When Mrs. Beamis brought her in to Richard, she stood silent, her head down, her mouth twisting.

"You wanted to talk to me?" he asked. He had his watch in his hand. There wasn't much time.

"Please . . . if you'll have me, I could come back."

He smiled at her. "You're not angry anymore."

"Allie need me," she answered.

"Have Harry drive you down to your parents' to get your things," Richard told her. He got to his feet. It was time to go. He paused in the hall, heard Allie's laughter, and then went on.

When the bells rang for the seven-o'clock Mass at St. Mary's, there were plainclothes detectives among the worshippers who poured through the big doors of the church. There were others on the corner of Second Street. Men, women, children came and went. The package on the floor of the confessional remained undisturbed.

At noon, the observers withdrew.

An hour later, the chief marshal said, "Well, we don't know, and maybe we won't ever know. But it was worth a try. Just in case."

"I hoped you'd learn something," Richard said.

When the chief marshal had first seen the ransom note he had mentioned a kidnapping he'd heard of several years before. A child named Edward Cudahy had been taken from his Kansas City home and held for ransom. He had asked Richard if Richard had any enemies. Richard had thought of Celeste, then told himself she was gone. She could have nothing to do with this.

Now the marshal asked, "The boy could tell you nothing?"

"No. He spoke of the puppy. And an old man. The doctor felt he might have been drugged."

"I don't know what we can do," the marshal said.

"It could be that the boy was taken for money, as the note indicates, and that whoever did it became frightened and left him in the cemetery. But it could also be that someone heard he was lost from home and took advantage of that to perpetrate a hoax."

"Meanwhile we don't know."

"It's all I can say. If we learn more, I'll tell you."

Richard heard nothing further from the marshal.

Two weeks later a broken trunk drifted ashore at Tiverton. A few days after, the swollen, nearly unrecognizable body of a woman was found at the mouth of Sin and Flesh Brook where it entered Nannaquaket Pond. At the end of the month Mitch Ryan collapsed in a New Orleans gutter. He lay where he fell, ignored as a falling-down drunk, and died the same night of yellow fever.

When Richard left the chief marshal's office in the Center Street Station, he went to the mill.

There was the usual hum, hiss, bang, the crack of the flying shuttles. But added to that backdrop of noise, there were shouts. "It's a great day," George Thompson yelled, grinning from behind his loom. And his cry was taken up, passed through the huge busy room in quick resounding echoes.

Richard paused, waved his thanks, then went into his office.

Ezra peered at him cautiously over his spectacles. "Everything all right?"

"Perfect," Richard said. And then: "Isn't Jamie here?"

"I sent him down to supplies. His broom was coming to shreds."

"I should have told him to sleep in. It was late before Harry got him home last night."

"Yes. But he wouldn't have. He'd have thought it was taking advantage."

"As if he doesn't deserve to," Richard returned. "I want to do something for him, Ezra. I want to do everything for him."

"It won't be easy." Ezra polished his bald head,

thinking of Gus. The big man had paced the room, a caged animal, with yellow eyes burning like sullen flame. "What's Jamie doing?" he growled. "Why didn't he come with us? What's it matter to him?"

Gus had been at the window when Harry drew up outside and leaned down, laughing with Jamie, before the boy came inside. "So you finally remembered where you belong," Gus had sneered. "And come home like an aristocrat, too. Riding in a fine surrey, with a groom to take you."

"I found Allie," Jamie said. He had stretched and yawned, as if he were a small boy.

But Ezra had suddenly realized how he had grown. He was more man now than boy. Only Gus didn't seem to know that.

"You found him?" Gus sneered. "I can imagine. And how did you accomplish that?"

Jamie stared at his father.

"It was a miracle, I guess. I don't know how I did it."

"Hooray for Jamie Markeson!" Gus grinned. "And did you get a tip for it?"

The brightness had faded out of Jamie's face. He said, "I wouldn't have one if it was offered," and turned his back on his father.

"It won't be easy?" Richard was repeating. But Ezra shrugged, bent his head over the ledgers.

When Richard saw Jamie come into the loft, pushing a new sweeper, he went out to the boy, greeted him, then said, smiling, "I don't think I thanked you last night. And my wife is sure she didn't. Come home with me when I leave this afternoon. We'll see you get back in time for a night's rest." When Jamie answered he'd like to, if he was wanted, Richard said he'd let the boy know when it was time to leave. Soon after, Richard found Gus in Plant No. 2 and broached the subject of school for Jamie. The scar tissue under Gus's eyes turned red. He growled, "Jamie can read and write and figure. He knows the first ten amendments to the Constitution. And that's all he needs of books. He'll start now being what he's going to be." With that off his chest, Gus shambled away.

Richard decided to wait, then raise the subject again. Back at his desk, he stared sightlessly at the straps and loops and wires that criss-crossed the ceiling. The bushes around the house and property were no protection, and even with Harry watching and John, too, anyone could enter and leave without being known. What had happened once, could happen again. He was designing a fence when Albert Cosgrove came in.

"I need a few words with you, Richard," he said, adding, "Things all right at home? No ill effects in Allie?"

"He seems to be fine," Richard answered. "Sit down, why don't you?"

"It's a nice day," Albert replied. "Let's take a turn around the block."

Richard saw that Albert's eyes were on Ezra's bent head. Shrugging, he rose, followed Albert into the street.

"I don't like to bring this up now," Albert said, trotting to keep up with Richard's long stride. "So soon, I mean, after last night. But there's little time. We've been discussing the possibility of another wage reduction. Where do you stand?"

"I'm against it. It's only five months since the last one."

"Everybody is hurting, Richard. The others won't like your position."

"That's nothing to me. I won't reduce now, and it's my decision. I run the mill, Albert. No one, not the unions, nor the Manufacturers' Association, can tell me what I must do."

"Very well," Albert answered. "I'll explain. But there's something else. Did you know that Gus Markeson's an organizer for the Knights of Labor? Or used to be?"

"The Knights of Labor? Albert, what are you talking about? You know as well as I do that they're no longer a factor to be considered."

"We can't be certain of that. Just a couple of years ago there was that trouble between the Knights sympathizers and the immigrant boot and shoe workers. It could happen again."

Richard grinned. "You're straining for worry."

"I'm telling you that your Gus Markeson is a known rabblerouser from way back."

"How do you know that?" Richard demanded.

"We have our means, Richard."

"I suppose you do. Well, what of it? Are you saying I ought to lay him off? If you are, I'll tell you that I won't. He's the best loomfixer in Fall River. And besides . . . there's his boy, his Jamie. After what he did for me last night, can you suppose I'd turn on the father?"

"I'm only passing on to you information I believe you should have," Albert said.

"Thank you," Richard answered dryly.

They parted company at the mill, and Richard went inside. But he was too restless to settle down at his desk.

He got Jamie, and they walked together to a nearby foundry, where Richard placed an order for the fence he had designed. Then, they drove in the surrey to the house on Highland Avenue.

Harry met them at the porte cochere and said, "No one's been about, Mr. Cavendish."

Inside, Allie came at a full trot from the morning room. "Papa! Jamie! I want to go out!"

Vicki hushed the boy, went to Jamie. She touched his cheek gently. "I don't think that I said thank you. It was so good of you, Jamie . . . not giving up. We'll never forget it."

The boy's face flamed. He looked at her, then quickly looked away. "Only luck," he mumbled. "Really, that's all." And then, with a glance at Allie, "Would you like me to take him outside for a little while?"

"Yes," Allie cried. "We'll play."

"Near the house," Richard said.

Jamie nodded, and he and Allie went out together, trailing laughter.

Vicki said quietly, "Allie's home, but it's not over, is it?"

"I believe that it is, but I want to make sure."

"Just that? There's nothing else?"

"No, Vicki. If there were I'd tell you. You'd have to know." Richard went into the morning room, Vicki following him. Instead of taking a chair, he stood at the window, watching Allie and Jamie race down the slope of the lawn. After a moment, he turned, looked at her. "Would you mind very much if we went to Cavendish Cove somewhat earlier this year?"

"I wouldn't mind. And actually your mother mentioned that same thing to me earlier today. She thinks the change would be good for Allie."

"I do, too. Let's prepare as quicky as we can."

Just ten days later, the family made the move. That time, by Richard's request, there had been no announcement in the *Herald*'s "Personal Mention" column, no mention in the *Globe*'s "Globe Gossip."

It had been a hurried time. Mrs. Beamis and Nettie worked long hours packing, while Matilda supervised. Harry had gone out to Newport and opened the house there and stocked it, and then began the chore of ferrying the trunks.

They were all of them, Vicki thought, glad to be leaving Fall River behind for the summer months. It was as if they were leaving behind forever the pain and terror of the winter months, Allie's illness, and then the horror of his being taken away.

Now, driving through the fields as they approached Newport, she saw the fields of blue cornflowers under the brilliance of the May sun. Memory touched her briefly . . . the candlelight flickering on the veranda . . . Richard's hard bruising hands . . . his demanding lips . . . her helplessness before his strength . . . her sense that his will to have her was a mindless lust applied to an object, not a love grown from a knowing need of her.

290

She slid a sideways glance at him at the same time that he took his eyes off the road ahead to glance at her. The two gazes held for a moment. Neither of them spoke. His hands moved on the wheel of the Mercedes, and he looked ahead again.

It was a year since he had made any physical demands on her. She wondered if he, too, was remembering that.

Not long after, they drove into Newport and rolled along sun-hot Bellevue Avenue.

Allie was waiting on the veranda to greet them. He kissed Vicki, clung to his father's legs and then peered hopefully at the Mercedes. "Where's Jamie?"

"He'll come to visit you one day soon," Richard told the boy.

"I want my friend Jamie," Allie retorted, his lower lip coming out, small dark brows angled in a lowering frown, a replica of Richard's, Vicki thought.

All through the weekend that followed, it was a refrain on Allie's lips. "Jamie," he cried when he awakened in the morning. "Jamie coming soon?" he asked as he wandered through the house. "Jamie?" he whispered when he fell asleep at night.

"I'll bring him with me next Saturday," Richard finally told Vicki. "If it's all right with his father. And with him."

Jamie was thankful for the invitation, but Gus gave only grudging agreement.

In spite of that, however, Jamie's weekend at Cavendish Cove was the first of many. He spent all but two of them that summer with the Cavendish family. On the two exceptions he told Richard that he had to go fishing with his father.

In mid-July, Gus greeted Jamie one Monday morning, by saying, "And did you have a fine time with your rich friends?"

"I did," Jamie said shortly. He and Richard and Allie had gone sailing on Sunday morning. The family had had a big picnic above Cliff Walk the same afternoon. There had been callers in the evening.

"I notice you've brought home a new suit for yourself," Gus said.

"Mr. Cavendish wanted me to have it."

"Mind you milk them well," Gus sneered.

Jamie pushed the broom a few feet, looked back at his father, and said, "Papa, you know it's not that."

"You don't belong with them," Gus snarled.

The cry of "Loomfixer!" ended that conversation. Jamie watched Gus shamble away. It didn't matter whether he belonged with the Cavendishes. They were good to him and cared about him. And that was what counted.

Another time Gus said, "They've got themselves a good unpaid bodyguard. That's what it is. What else would they want of you?"

Jamie didn't answer. He knew that Vicki rested more easily when he was about to keep an eye on Allie. But why not? What was wrong with that? She trusted him. It made him happy that she did.

For Vicki, the weekdays, when neither Richard nor Jamie was there, were slow and quiet. She and Maria and Matilda all spent a good deal of time with Allie. Harry was never away, and John had given up his hours of solitary riding. He bought a well-trained pony and began to teach Allie how to sit in the saddle. He built a play shanty within view of the front windows of the house.

Three times that summer, Elise and Leslie came to call. They were both grown heavier, Elise's face full and florid, Leslie's thickening over his beard. They bickered between them like a long-married couple instead of brother and sister. Listening, Vicki wondered that she had ever thought Elise worldly or Leslie handsome. The single-minded passion she had once felt for him seemed a dream now, and not a very good one at that. She couldn't understand how she had once supposed him her heart's desire.

Rosamund and Davis Peabody stopped by for tea one Sunday afternoon, and Albert and Eustacia Cosgrove came that evening.

Albert took Richard aside to say that since the May

wage cut had gone into effect, some of the mill owners were reporting a loss of their most skilled personnel. He wanted to know if Richard was noting the same situation. Richard had not, and said so without further comment. "We calculate a migration of some thirteen thousand workers since the strike, Richard. It can be catastrophic if we push for full production soon."

"Tell the Association to raise wages," Richard said shortly.

"I should like you to come to the next meeting, Richard. Then you can tell them yourself. You're an owner, as I am not, so that what you say has more force."

Richard agreed, and the following week he sat in the smoke-filled boardroom at the bank, listening to the complaints. Eventually he spoke his piece. The others didn't take his argument well. He, they grumbled, didn't have boards of directors to answer to, and investors demanding a high return. He was free to do as he pleased, but they themselves weren't.

Restless, he left the meeting before it was adjourned. He drove to the empty house on Highland Avenue, remembering how so many of his nights the summer before had been spent with the girl he had called Lilac, but who claimed to be named Celeste. He didn't regret having sent her away. He didn't miss her. Long after the moon had set, he stood at the window, thinking of Vicki and looking down at the half-finished fence.

Chapter 27

BY THE FIRST WEEK IN SEPTEMBER, WHEN THE FAMily moved back to the Highland Avenue house, the whole property was fenced. It was a raw-looking, ugly thing, a reminder of hours of terror. At Vicki's suggestion, Harry immediately began to plant ornamental bushes that would eventually grow tall enough to hide the black iron bars.

The first Saturday night after their return, Vicki and Richard went to the Academy for a performance of *H.M.S. Pinafore*. It had been a pleasant evening, and as she slipped into her blue lace peignoir, she found herself humming a melody from the show. Beyond the wall that separated her room from Richard's, she heard the deep sound of his voice, and realized that he was humming, too.

She was smiling as she fell asleep.

An hour later, she awakened with a start. Something, some unidentifiable sound, had disturbed her. She turned on the pillow, listened, but heard nothing. She was drowsing, only half awake, when the sound came again. That time she rose, drew on her peignoir. She listened at Richard's door for a moment. All was quiet within.

She went into the nursery. Just as she crossed the threshold, she heard the sound again, and knew it was Allie. He made that soft moaning cry once more, and even as she turned on the lamp, reached for him, his small body stiffened and arched. His fists beat at his temples. He screamed.

Maria came on the instant, and Richard just after. Matilda hovered at the door, while John limped away to telephone to the doctor.

The warmth of the autumn night was suddenly chill. Allie screamed, screamed again, and then went silent.

Vicki held him, rocked him, pressed his face to her breast. When Richard murmured, "Let me put the boy to bed," and reached for him, Vicki fended Richard off. "No," she cried. "No, I must hold him. I must! I must!"

When he reached again, saying gently, "Vicki, let me see. Please, my love, you must let me see," she backed away, her eyes blazing. "No, no, I tell you. I shall hold him."

She knew even then what had happened. She knew but refused to acknowledge it. The black iron fence could hold one danger at bay, but not the other, and while she had held her son so tightly, he had somehow been stolen away.

Richard saw, understood. She wept and screamed, but he took Allie's limp body from her. He laid the boy on the bed, and Matilda closed the now dull eyes, and then drew the coverlet over his emptied face.

Watching, Vicki screamed, "No, no, no. I shan't let him go!"

Chapter 28

LEANING ON RICHARD'S ARM, SHE STOOD IN LAUDA-num calm while Allie was buried in Oak Grove Cemetery. The small white coffin was lowered into its final resting place beside the gave of the grandfather, Ed-

ward Cavendish, born in mid-Atlantic, whom Allie
had never known. It was filled in, then covered over
with wreaths of white flowers. When Richard drew her
away, she followed, aware only of her loss. Except
when Jamie came and touched her hand, and she murmured behind the heavy black veiling, "You're a good
friend, Jamie," she spoke to no one.

In the days after, she continued the same. She rose
when Nettie brought a breakfast tray, and dressed
when Nettie handed her a gown. She nodded at the
girl's small attempts at conversation, listened when
Matilda discussed household affairs with her, but she
made no attempt at response. When Maria Sandora
came tearfully to bid her goodbye, Vicki only pressed
her hands tightly, then closed her eyes.

Dr. Stilton called it a crisis of nerves and said it
would pass. Time would heal her. The strength of her
youth would have its way. But the days became
weeks, and the weeks months.

There were no celebrations in the Cavendish house
that winter. The wedding anniversary that Richard
had always before insisted upon noting went by unre-
marked. Her birthday was ignored. Thanksgiving,
Christmas, even the New Year, accompanied by the
ringing of church bells and the shrill of mill whistles
all over the city, were commonplace days.

Hour after hour, gowned, perfumed, her hair
brushed and pinned high, Vicki lay in the easy chair
near the window, her thin hands idle in her lap or
plucking at the rings on her fingers. The infant she
had sheltered in her womb was torn from her. He,
whose conception she had cursed, and then borne, was
no more. Bright-eyed Allie, the chain that had held
her to Richard, was gone. Having fled the house in
Rye in search of love, she found that she had come
full circle. Mrs. McVey would say tartly, "As you
sow, so shall you reap."

Once it had seemed to her that Richard's sin against
her was the blackest of any. Now she remembered it,
but it was meaningless next to her own. She had resented the seed of her body, the flesh of her flesh, and

he had sensed it, and clung to her, until even she, in her preoccupation with the beginning, knew that he was the end. But he was taken from her. She would lie in the chair, watching the snowflakes drift in white curtains around the boulevard lamps, and whisper softly, "Allie, Allie," as if there were comfort in the sound of his name. She would gaze at the sepia-toned picture of her mother, still saying, "Allie, Allie . . ." and hold the heart-shaped pin in her cold hands.

In September the Russo-Japanese war was ended by the treaty of Portsmouth, mediated through the interest of President Theodore Roosevelt.

In October the yellow fever of which Mitch Ryan had died in New Orleans months before grew to epidemic proportions there. In that same month, Anthony Comstock instituted the closing by the New York police of a play called *Mrs. Warren's Profession*, written by George Bernard Shaw.

In November there was a long discussion of the Supreme Court's April decision that had rendered unconstitutional the New York State law limiting bakers' working hours to a ten-hour day.

In December there was a blizzard in Chicago.

John read these events to her from the newspapers, but she made no comment. He noted, too, casually, that the *Daily Globe*'s "Globe Gossip" wished "for Mrs. Richard Cavendish a quick recovery from her illness." She didn't seem to hear.

Once a week, though, for a brief moment or two, there showed in her face the spark of her true self. It was when Jamie Markeson came to call.

Always at the same time, on Saturday afternoon, the newly declared half-day, he trudged up Highland Avenue and passed through the open iron gates built to protect Allie. In the fall he scraped the mud from his boots; in the winter he stamped off snow.

Nettie would answer his knock, ask, "How's it going, Jamie?" and lead him into the morning room.

He was almost as tall as his father now, with big knobby hands and a face growing squarer by the day.

His dark hair was unruly, though he water-brushed it carefully, with Ezra worriedly looking on, before he left home. Gus growled about these regular visits, but Jamie neither answered nor argued, until the day Gus said, "All right, you tell me. Why do you do it? They don't need you anymore for a guard for their boy. He's dead. So why do you go now?"

"She needs me," Jamie had said then.

"Needs you?" Gus had sneered. "And what for? The woman's got everything in the world."

"No. She hasn't," Jamie had told him. "So she needs me."

Jamie couldn't explain what he felt for Vicki. He had adored her since he first saw her at the opening of Plant 2, when Allie had run into his arms. Jamie had adored her because she was a woman, and he was trying to fill in his life that emptiness he had never been able even to define to himself. She was a woman, and beautiful, and he had had no mother, and precious little beauty, to cherish.

But Gus took his words with another meaning. Victoria Cavendish had everything, to his mind, everything but a son. It was all she lacked.

When Jamie had gone that day, Gus said to Ezra, "They're trying to steal my son from me."

For every visit to Vicki, Jamie brought a gift. Once it was a puppet of a fairy princess. When he saw how she turned it in her hands, then set it aside, he wished that he hadn't. Another time he brougt her a pine cone painted gold and decorated with a narrow red ribbon. He found a sprig of mistletoe. He bought a copy of *Leslie's Weekly*.

Nettie would show him into the morning room, and she'd look at Vicki and sigh. But Jamie would grin. "Good afternoon, Mrs. Cavendish," and sit on the velvet hassock near the chair in which she lay. Then he would present her with his gift.

She would smile, gamin dimples showing briefly at the corners of her mouth. Sometimes she wouldn't speak at all. Sometimes she would thank him. He would stay an hour, and tell her before leaving, "I'll see you next Saturday for sure."

In mid-January the snows were heavy, and Jamie was delayed. Vicki lay in her chair, staring into the garden. The clock chimed one o'clock, then chimed two. She moved restlessly. She leaned forward at the sound of sleigh bells singing in the road. She leaned forward again when the carriage, bringing Richard home from the mill, turned into the driveway. The clock chimed the quarter as he came in, stripping his fur-lined gloves from his hands.

Always, as soon as he entered the house, he went to say a few words to her. Sometimes she answered, sometimes not. He didn't try to force her attention. He believed that he had no right to make any demands on her. It was his love that had brought her to this state. He, determined to have her, had led her from her Rye home to the marriage she had never wanted, to the death of their son. Not for an instant, not for the space of a breath, did he allow himself to forget that.

"It's snowing heavily," he told her now, noting the fixed stare with which she regarded the road below. "The traffic is hardly moving down street."

"Yes," she said. "I see. It's beautiful to watch."

"Is there something I can bring you?"

"Nothing," she answered.

Heartened by the few words of the exchange, he went to put his coat away. When he turned from the halltree, he saw her going slowly toward the front door. He couldn't remember the last time she had moved from the chair in the morning room without having it suggested to her. He said, "Vicki, what is it?"

"It's Jamie," she answered. "He's coming now."

Moments later, Richard heard the stamp of boots, the scrape of ice. He opened the door. Jamie grinned, red-cheeked, wind-blown. "I'm sorry I'm so late. It's the snow."

Vicki smiled faintly. "You've had a fall."

"Two of them coming up the hill."

"Richard," she said, "you must brush him off well."

But when Jamie joined her a little while later in the

morning room, she stared into the flames. She didn't even speak when he gave her the small silver button he had fashioned into a pin. She only smiled, and held it tightly in her clenched fist.

Later, Matilda and John and Richard joined them, and Nettie served hot chocolate and gingerbread covered with thick cream. The fire burned high on the hearth, and the room was a warm sanctuary against the storm that whipped the draped windows.

There was conversation, but Vicki took no part in it, yet when Jamie rose to go, and bent to take her hand and say, "I'll see you next week, Mrs. Cavendish," she turned to look at Richard. "He mustn't walk to Bogle Hill in this weather," she said.

During the next few days, Richard considered, and at midweek he sent for Gus, and waved him to a chair near his desk. "It's Jamie I want to talk about."

Gus nodded, waited, pulling his straggling mustache.

"I've spoken of it before, you'll remember. You weren't for it. So I let it go. But I can't anymore. The boy should have his chance. He needs his schooling."

Gus shrugged. "I've said my piece on that."

"He's too smart to push a broom all his life, Gus."

"He can learn my trade."

"Wouldn't you want him to do more?"

"No. And I know he can't. I'll be a poor man in hell, just as I've been in this life. It'll be the same for him. So why give him different ideas? You'll only weaken him to survive what's ahead."

"There's the new Textile School the Durfee family built . . ."

"Loomfixer!" The cry resounded over the snap and pop and hiss of the cables and wheels on the ceiling. "Loomfixer!" It echoed over the crack of the flying shuttles.

Gus got to his feet. "It sounds as if somebody needs me."

"But what if Jamie wanted it? Would you deny him?" Richard demanded.

"Let him decide," Gus retorted. "I'll take my chances on that."

At noon Richard had lunch with Albert Cosgrove, who was on the board of the Bradford Durfee Textile School. He answered Richard's questions and promised to do whatever he could.

That evening, not long after Nettie had led Vicki to her bedroom and seen her settled in the canopied bed for the night, Richard went in to sit with her for a little while. She lay like a sleeping princess, her amber hair spread on the white satin pillow, her dark blue eyes tightly closed. He wondered if she even knew of his presence. But finally he leaned forward and said, "I spoke to Gus Markeson again about more schooling for Jamie. He's against it, but he grudgingly agreed to let Jamie decide. I don't understand the man, and I never will."

"I do," she answered softly. "And so do you. He's afraid of losing his son."

"Yes," Richard said. "Yes. That's his fear. But it needn't happen. And if he holds Jamie back . . ."

"You must show him, Richard."

Richard kept his voice steady, though he felt a pressure in his throat that signaled the rise of tears. "You're wise, Vicki. That's just what we must do. But there is a problem. I spoke to Albert today about the Textile School. Jamie needs more background before he can be admitted. He must have tutoring in mathematics and history and grammar."

"You could surely find some teacher for him."

"I think that would embarrass him. But if some good friend were to work with him . . ."

She turned her head, a sudden warm smile lighting her face. "Richard, you mean me to be the friend, don't you?"

"It would be best. If you felt that you could do it."

"I can't do the mathematics. I never learned it properly myself." A small laugh touched her words as she went on. "And Papa never had a head for figures so there was no one to help me. But John could teach mathematics to Jamie. The rest I could do myself. We'd need books, of course."

"I'd see to that for you, if you were to give me a

301

list." He marveled at how casual he managed t
sound. He had just heard her speak more words to
gether than he had since Allie's death.

"You must persuade Jamie," she went on slowly. "
will make up the list in the morning."

Jamie listened doubtfully to Richard's proposal. H
wanted the schooling more than anything he had eve
wanted in his life. But he knew his father's feelings
He wavered one way, then the other. At last he said
"I could try for a little while, I guess. And if Pap;
wasn't too upset . . ."

That was when Richard said, "My wife has promised to help you, Jamie."

All doubt disappeared from Jamie's face. H
grinned. "I'll do it, of course." Then: "You knew
would."

They began the following week. Jamie worked unti
noon at the mill. From there he went to the Highlan
Avenue house to study with Vicki and to spend two
hours each day with John.

In the beginning, she spoke little. She gave him
books to read, questioned him later. Gradually,
though, she became more outgoing, too interested in
what she was doing to be aware of the change in herself. Often, when the weather was bad, she would in-
sist that Jamie remain for dinner with the family, and
though she spoke little then, she would listen and
smile. Afterward Harry would drive him down to
Bogle Hill.

On one such night Gus was up and waiting. "Ah,
here's the fine gentleman, driven down street in his
fancy carriage."

Jamie said nothing to that.

"And what did you have for dinner at the elegant
house? Roast beef, was it?"

Ezra put in, "Why, Gus, what does it matter? As
long as the boy had his supper?"

"And along with the numbers, are they teaching
you good manners?" Gus sneered at Ezra, crooked his
little finger beneath Jamie's nose. "Can you curl your
pinkie nicely by now?"

302

"I'm going to bed," Jamie said wearily, and put his books on the table.

Gus snatched them up, tore out the pages of one, flung the other against the wall.

"You didn't have to do that, Papa," was all Jamie said.

He slept little that night. He had thought that if his father really objected, he would give up his learning and go back to the mill full time. But it was turning out less easy to do than he had expected. Now he was drawn to his time with Vicki, as much in seeing the continuing improvement in her, as in his learning. He no longer felt he could stop because of his father.

He went on through February and March, ignoring his father's comments, studying only after his father had gone to sleep. He rarely accepted an invitation to dinner, excusing himself by saying that he had to get home.

Ezra watched, listening uneasily as Gus grumbled that his boy had no time for him, but only for the fine folk that lived on Highland Avenue.

It was a warm April day. The forsythia had begun to glow along the fences like feathery signal fires. The river was running high with melted snow. A new softness began to touch the air, and the days grew longer.

Gus walked out of Plant No. 2 an hour before closing time. He made his shambling way to Highland Avenue, a long-simmering anger filling his chest. He went up the narrow driveway under the porte cochere and around the back. He pounded hard on the door.

Mrs. Beamis opened it, asked what he wanted.

"I want my son." At her blank stare, he added, "I'm Gus Markeson."

"Oh, you're Jamie's father, are you? Then come in."

"No," Gus answered, "you tell him to come down to me."

She sent Nettie to the morning room, where Vicki and Jamie were working on spelling.

Jamie frowned when he heard, but said, "I'll be

right back," and went to see what his father wanted.

"Come home," Gus told him.

"I'm not through, Papa."

"You're through. For good. I don't want you here anymore. You come home where you belong."

Jamie saw how his father's big gnarled hand worked, and his twisting mouth, and the flame in his yellow eyes. He said, "I'll just say I'm going. And get my books."

But Gus grabbed his arm, pulled him into the yard. "You'll say nothing. You don't need those books any more. I mean it. I don't want you here."

Jamie cast a beseeching look at Mrs. Beamis, saw her understanding nod and went with his father.

Mrs. Beamis watched the two trudge away together, the big man, tall, fierce, with shoulders bent, the boy tall, too, but thin, dragging his feet. Sighing, she went to tell Vicki that Jamie had gone.

Vicki nodded, closed the book she held, closed her eyes at the same time and whispered, "Perhaps he'll come back tomorrow."

But Jamie didn't return the next day, and the following morning Richard saw him once again at work in the mill, and asked what had happened.

"I can't go ahead," the boy said softly. "He doesn't want me to."

"I see," Richard answered. "But what happened just now to make you give in when you haven't before?"

The boy looked at his boots, and shifted his weight from one to the other, and finally shrugged.

He and Gus had argued it out all through the night and day before. Gus had yelled, "Tell me what you see in them. What do they see in you? Tell me why you have to be better than me."

"I don't," Jamie cried. "It's not that. They need me, Papa! Don't you see that? They just need me."

Gus stared at him for a long moment, and then answered softly, "Well, I need you, too."

So Jamie decided to give up his lessons, to return to work full time at the mill.

"You won't change your mind?" Richard was asking.

"I can't. But I thank you."

In the days that followed, Vicki spoke when spoken to. She moved occasionally from her chair near the window in the morning room to go into the parlor. But she did little else. She had closed the books, and set them aside. She had carefully put away Jamie's papers. She withdrew into her own empty thoughts and lost herself within them.

One night Elise and Leslie came to visit. Elise said briskly, "You must get out more, Vicki. Have John drive you to the school for a visit. It will do you good."

Vicki nodded, smiled faintly, said nothing. But she got to her feet.

"My dear, truly, you've given way for too long," Leslie told her. He reached for her hand, but she drew away to cling to Richard's arm.

Matilda asked, "Are you tired, Vicki? Would you like to go up now?"

Vicki nodded, and Matilda drew her into the hall, and then up the steps, mumbling, "I'd not have thought them such fools. Visit the school indeed! People make me sick!"

Again Vicki nodded, but then she whispered, "Thank you, Matilda." For Matilda understood. At the school was the athletic field named for Allie. At the school there would be small boys running and laughing.

It was a relief to sink at last into the bed, to turn her head into the pillow and weep.

The trellis roses drooped in a scarlet fall beyond the window. The end-of-May sun glistened on the lily pond.

Quick footsteps and voices filled the house. Mrs. Beamis was packing the last of the sheets and towels. Matilda busily folded Vicki's gowns into trunks. Nettie had polished the silver that was to remain at home and stored it, and was now wrapping the silver that would go. It was time for the move to Cavendish Cove.

Vicki listened indifferently to the bustle of activity, but took no part in it. When the time came, she supposed, she would ride in the Mercedes with Richard along the river, and cross on the ferry, and then go on amid the fields to Newport. The sun would glisten on the ocean, and pink parasols would bob along Cliff Walk, and it would all be the same to her.

She frowned faintly when the surrey pulled into the driveway and stopped, and Richard threw the reins to Harry and climbed down. It was well before noon, an odd time for him to leave the mill. He walked slowly, with his head bent, and for the first time, she saw that there was a fine webbing of silver in his dark hair.

A pulse began a quick tattoo in her temple. She half rose, then let herself fall back. She waited, plucking nervously at the lace at her throat.

He came in, and looked at her, and saw how she braced herself. He went to her quickly, said, "Vicki, I must tell you . . ."

Her dark blue eyes widened. She whispered, "Jamie?"

"There's been an accident. Do you think you can come with me?"

She rose, though she trembled. She went with him into the hallway, where he wrapped a shawl around her. As they drove to the City Hospital, he told her.

Jamie had been working near one of the vats. It had suddenly boiled over, sending a sheet of scalding sizing and cloth over him. George Thompson had shouted a warning, but Jamie didn't seem to have heard it, and only the weaver's quickness had kept the boy from worse harm. As it was, he was badly burned on both legs.

"Poor Jamie," she whispered. "Poor boy. We must do what we can, Richard."

"We will," Richard said.

"We shan't go to Cavendish Cove yet," she told him. "We must move him as soon as it's possible to ur house here." She drew a deep breath. "I want to nd him, Richard. And have Dr. Stilton in."

"Yes," he agreed. "If Gus Markeson allows it."

"For Jamie's sake, he will."

But when they arrived at the hospital, Gus was just aving. He gave Richard a hard stare, raked Vicki ith a sightless yellow gaze and walked away even as ey tried to talk to him.

Jamie smiled when he saw Vicki.

She bent over him. "I never thanked you for all you d for me."

"I didn't do all I wanted to," he answered.

They stayed with him until a starchy nurse in white pron and spread-wing cap murmured disapprovingly. e didn't mention his father in all that time.

The next day, just before the Saturday noon closing, us shambled into Richard's office.

He planted himself in front of Richard's desk like ative Fall River granite. "You stay away from my n Jamie."

"Now Gus," Ezra protested, "Mr. Cavendish wants) do what's right for Jamie."

"You stay away from my boy," Gus repeated, ig- oring the older man's reproof. "If it wasn't for you, it ouldn't have happened. You did it. You and your ool ideas. You made him of two minds, and that's hat makes for trouble. You made him, as is nothing ut a working stiff who couldn't be anything else, alfway into a gentleman. That's why he got burned."

"If it hadn't been for you, he'd not have been in the lant at all," Richard said coldly. "I'll do for him what can, and you'll not stop me. Now get out and go to im, and act like a father should."

The big man stood there a moment, silent and un- moving. Then he left the mill. He walked the long locks to Bogle Hill through hot sunlight, mumbling to imself, "It's because they made him of two minds. It's heir fault. It's their mill."

If Jamie hadn't been in the mill, but at his books in- tead, he'd not have been injured. Those raw and gly legs of his would be whole. Gus knew it. He

couldn't face it, think it, accept it. All through
long hours of the day he wandered through the roo
telling himself that the Cavendishes had stolen his b
from him. They'd taken all that he had. It was th
fault that he had no son.

Ezra argued a little and finally crept to bed. He w
sound asleep when Gus left the tenement and return
to Cavendish and Sons.

The telephone shrilled through midnight stillne
Richard swore, stumbling through the dark to pick
up before it awakened everyone in the house.

He listened, then put the instrument down. I
dressed in a hurry, raced outside. In the distance,
heard the clanging of the fire bells, the first shrill wh
tles. Harry came down as he harnessed the horses.
took them only a moment working together. Then th
went at a gallop into Highland Avenue.

Mrs. Beamis heard the clatter of the hoofs a
awakened Nettie. They went out into the moonlit da
and heard the clanging bells and the shrilling whistle
They looked at each other, shivering, and hurried i
to the big house.

Fire was a terror in the old mill town. The ravag
of the last big one were well remembered, even thou
that had been in 1843. Only the year before, the A
Borden building had just barely been saved.

John and Matilda had heard, too, and they can
down. They all stood at the windows, speaking quiet
and looking at the sky over the down-street area, n
realizing then that it was Cavendish and Sons aflam

It was Albert Cosgrove, pausing on his way dov
street, that told them. Vicki, halfway down the ste
heard him and ran out to his surrey. In her thin gow
with only a light robe over her shoulders and h
hair flying loose, she climbed to the seat. She whipp
the horse into a run. Not hearing the shouts behir
her, she plunged wildly down the drive and careen
into the dark of the empty avenue. Within block
though, the roads were filled with jostling vehicle
Word of the blaze had spread even as the flam

emselves spread. The clanging of the fire bells, the
ailing of mill whistles, became background to the
eak and rattle of wheels and axles, the thud of hoofs,
e crack of anxiously wielded whips. Questions, curses
d speculations added a human counterpoint to the
ar. The clear midnight blue of the summer sky was
ayed with a billowing pall of smoke, so that one by
e the stars winked out, and the silver face of the
oon dimmed. Slowly, the warm night air grew hot,
d the winds off Mount Hope Bay sent wave after
ave of ember and ash over the town.

The grit stung Vicki's cheeks and eyes and streaked
e pale green of her gown and robe. Ash and dead
mber drifting on the wind settled on her hair. She
ressed on, guiding the rocketing surrey, until at the
lymouth Street Bridge a wheel hit a stone abutment
d snapped in two. The surrey tipped; the horse
eared. She was flung into the road. She got to her
et, brushed dirt and dung from herself and pressed
n. Here the way was thick with shoving people. Here
e sky held an awful red. The air was heavy with
moke. Fiercely, she thrust her way through. She had
nly one thought in mind. She must get to Richard.
he must be with him now.

The loose threads on which she had brooded for
months came together in a single strand. Richard. He
ad asked if she would come to him, and with those
words he'd asked even more. She had promised that
he would, that she'd remember him. But she had forgotten. It was the promise not kept that had led to her
ebasement. And for that she had hated him.

The fear she had felt when he first touched her had
een the flinching away from a commitment to the demanding passion of love; a turning from it to the softer
equirements of an empty infatuation. Without know-
ng it, she had refused her heart's desire.

Through the din of bells and neighing horses, she
heard the hiss of water on fire, and the sudden explosive roar of rising steam, and closer to her, as she
fought her way with elbow and shoulder, she heard,

"They've given it up, and are trying to save the others!"

Now, at the foot of the block, she saw what looked
like the end of the world. The sky seemed aflame
above billowing white clouds. Plant No. 1 was an island of fire, and gaping windows spilled rivers of light
down its granite walls. Plant No. 2 was half gone, with
two blackened walls still burning.

There, in the glare of the holocaust, she finally saw
Richard. He stood on a cart in the middle of the road
before the broken gates. He was motionless amid the
turmoil of running, pushing and shoving bodies. He was
silent amid the mingled roar of shouting voices. His
dark head was tilted back, and he stared without
blinking at the walkway that connected Plant No. 1
and Plant No. 2 of Cavendish and Sons.

Richard. She had to get to him. Sobbing, she
bounded on the broad back of a stranger who blocked
her path. "Let me through," she cried. "Let me
through. I must go to him."

She passed the one obstacle and two others con-
fronted her. She broke her way beyond those, and
there were more. Finally, though, there were sudden
murmurs of recognition. A swift hushed whisper arose
around her. "It's Mrs. Cavendish. It's Mrs. Cavendish,
you see?" and with that the crowds eased back and
away from her, and she could run again. She found
herself clinging to side of the cart on which Richard
stood and calling up to him, "Richard, Richard, come
down from there, Richard, can you hear me?"

But he remained statue-still, red light flickering on
pale face. She set her slippered foot into the spoke
of a wheel, and though it turned beneath her weight,
she managed to clamber into the cart.

"Richard!" She caught his hand and felt his fingers
tighten around hers. He neither looked at her nor
spoke. And now, finally, she saw what held his stricken
attention. On the walkway that connected the two
plants, there stood a hulking figure outlined in leaping
flame. Gus Markeson. Below him were spread nets
criss-crossing ladders. Below him men shouted.

ut he stood still, yelling wordlessly into the din. Even she watched, the walkway began to crumble. A aming brace fell free, a charred beam splintered. hen, with a quick explosive roar, the whole of the ing collapsed. Gus Markeson dropped into the self-eated pyre beneath him.

It was then that Richard spoke in a hard dry voice. It's gone. Everything. Everything. I have nothing ow."

She tried to remember what she had once felt, her age at him, her sense of having been degraded and espoiled. None of that remained in her. It was gone ito the unreal past. All that she knew was anguish or him, for what he had lost. All that she knew was ove.

She held tightly to his hand, and whispered, "Rich-rd, you have me."

He turned and stared at her for a long still moment. Then the grimness fell away from his face. He smiled, nd took her into his arms.